THE
LOST GIRLS
OF ROME

DONATO CARRISI

Translation by Howard Curtis

ABACUS

First published in Italy in 2011 as *Il Tribunale delle Anime* by Longanesi & C.
First published in Great Britain in 2012 by Abacus

A CIP catalogue record for this book
is available from the British Library.

ISBN 978-0-349-00030-5

Typeset in Horley by M Rules
Printed and bound in Great Britain by
Clays Ltd, St Ives plc

Papers used by Abacus are from well-managed forests
and other responsible sources.

MIX
Paper from
responsible sources
FSC® C104740

Abacus
An imprint of
Little, Brown Book Group
100 Victoria Embankment
London EC4Y 0DY

An Hachette UK Company
www.hachette.co.uk

www.littlebrown.co.uk

There is no witness so dreadful, no accuser so terrible,
as the conscience that dwells in the heart of every man.

POLYBIUS

Donato Carrisi was born in 1973 and studied law and criminology. He lives in Rome, where he works as a TV screenwriter. His first novel, *The Whisperer*, was an international bestseller and winner of three Italian and two French literary awards.

7.37 a.m.

The corpse opened his eyes.

He was lying on his back in bed. The room was white with day-light. On the wall facing him was a wooden crucifix.

He looked at his own hands, lying at his sides on the snow-white sheets. It was as if they didn't belong to him, as if they were some-one else's. He lifted one – the right – and held it in front of his eyes to get a better look at it. It was then that he felt the bandages cover-ing his head. He had clearly sustained an injury, but the strange thing was, he didn't feel any pain.

He turned towards the window and saw a dim reflection of his face in the glass. That was when he started to feel afraid. A question hit him, a painful question. But what was even more painful was the awareness that he did not know the answer.

Who am I?

FIVE DAYS AGO

12.03 a.m.

The address was outside the city. Because of the bad weather and the satnav's inability to find the house, it had taken them more than half an hour to reach this isolated spot. If it had not been for the little street lamp at the entrance to the drive, they might have thought the whole area uninhabited.

The ambulance proceeded slowly through the untended garden. The flashing light awoke statues from the darkness, moss-covered nymphs and mutilated Venuses, who greeted their passage with lopsided smiles and elegant, uncompleted gestures, dancing motionlessly for them alone.

An old villa welcomed them like a port in a storm. There were no lights on inside, but the front door was open.

The house was waiting for them.

There were three of them: Monica, a young intern who was on duty in Emergency that night, Tony, a paramedic with years of experience, and the driver, who stayed in the ambulance while the other two defied the storm and set off towards the house. Before crossing the threshold, they called out to see if they could attract anyone's attention.

There was no reply. They went in.

A stale odour, dark walls, a corridor dimly lit by a row of yellowish bulbs. To the right, a staircase leading to the first floor.

At the end of the corridor, through the open doorway of the living room, they caught sight of a body lying on the floor.

They rushed to him. All the furniture in the room was covered with white sheets, apart from a worn armchair in the middle, positioned to face an old-fashioned TV set. Everything smelled of age.

Monica knelt beside the man on the floor. He seemed to be unconscious, and was breathing with difficulty.

'He's cyanotic,' she observed.

Tony made sure the respiratory tract was clear, then placed the Ambu bag over his mouth, while Monica checked his irises with a torch.

The man could not have been more than fifty. He was wearing striped pyjamas, leather slippers and a dressing gown. With several days' growth of beard and his sparse, dishevelled hair, he looked like someone who didn't take care of himself. In one hand, he was still clutching the mobile phone he had used to call Emergency, complaining of terrible chest pains.

The nearest hospital was the Gemelli. In a serious emergency, whichever doctor was on duty joined the paramedics in the first available ambulance.

That was why Monica was there.

A small table had been overturned, a bowl broken. Spilt milk and biscuits lay everywhere, mixed with urine. The man must have been taken ill while watching TV and knocked everything over as he fell. It appeared to be a classic case, Monica thought. A middle-aged man, living alone, has a heart attack and, if he can't manage to call for help, is usually discovered, long dead, only when the neighbours start to notice the stench. In an isolated villa such as this, of course, that wouldn't have happened. If he didn't have close relatives, years might have passed before someone noticed what had happened. In either case, it was a familiar scene, and she felt sorry for him. At least until they opened his pyjama jacket to massage his heart and saw the words on his chest.

Kill me.

They both pretended they hadn't seen it. Their task was to save a life. But from that moment on, they moved with especial care.

'The saturation's dropping,' Tony said, checking the oximeter. That meant that no air was getting into the man's lungs.

'We have to intubate him or we'll lose him.' Monica took out the laryngoscope and moved to position herself behind the patient's head.

In doing so, she cleared Tony's field of vision. She saw a strange look suddenly come into his eyes. Tony was a professional, trained

6

to deal with any kind of situation, and yet something had startled him. Something that was right behind her.

Everyone in the hospital knew the story of the young doctor and her sister. No one ever talked about it, but she was aware of them looking at her with compassion and concern, wondering in their hearts how she could live with such a burden.

Now there was the same kind of expression on Tony's face, combined with a kind of fear. So Monica turned, and saw what Tony had seen.

A roller skate, abandoned in a corner of the room. A roller skate that unleashed hell.

It was red, with gold buckles. Identical to its twin, which wasn't here, but belonged to another life. Monica had always found them rather kitsch, but Teresa had preferred to call them 'vintage'. The two girls were twins, too, so Monica had had the feeling she was seeing herself when her sister's body had been found in a clearing near the river on a cold December morning.

She was only twenty-one years old, and her throat had been cut.

They say that twins feel things simultaneously, even when they are miles away from each other. But Monica did not believe that. She hadn't had any feelings of fear or danger when Teresa was abducted one Sunday afternoon on her way back from roller skating with her friends. Her body had been found a month later, wearing the same clothes she had had on when she had disappeared.

And that red roller skate, like a grotesque prosthesis on one foot.

For six years Monica had kept it, wondering what had happened to the other one and if it would ever be found. The number of times she had tried to imagine the face of the person who had taken it. The number of times she had peered into the faces of strangers in the street, thinking one of them might be him. Over time, it had become a kind of game.

Now, perhaps, Monica had found what she was looking for.

She looked down at the man on the floor. With his cracked, pudgy hands, the hair sprouting from his nostrils, the urine stain on the crotch of his trousers, he didn't look like the monster she had

7

always imagined. He was a creature of flesh and blood, an ordinary human being – and one with a weak heart, to boot.

Tony's voice jolted her from her thoughts. 'I know what's going through your mind,' he said. 'We can stop whenever you want, and wait for the inevitable to happen. You only have to say the word. Nobody will ever know.'

He had already seen her hesitate with the laryngoscope poised over the man's mouth. Once more, Monica looked at his chest.

Kill me.

That might well have been the last thing her sister had seen while he was cutting her throat as if she were an animal in a slaughter-house. No words of comfort, the kind that any human being who is about to leave this life forever deserves. Instead, her killer had mocked her with those words. It had probably amused him. Perhaps Teresa, too, had begged for death, wanting it all to end quickly. Angrily, Monica gripped the handle of the laryngoscope until her knuckles turned white.

Kill me.

The coward had carved the words on his chest but, when he had felt ill, he had called Emergency. He was just like anyone else. He was scared of dying.

Monica died inside herself. Those who had known Teresa saw her as a kind of copy, like a statue in a wax museum. To her family, she represented what her sister might have been and would never be. They watched her grow and saw Teresa. Now Monica had an opportunity to distinguish herself and exorcise the ghost of the twin who dwelt within her. I'm a doctor, she reminded herself. She would have liked to find a glimmer of pity for the human being lying in front of her, or the fear of a superior justice, or else something that resembled a sign. Instead she realised that she felt nothing. So she tried desperately to think of something that might convince her this man had nothing to do with Teresa's death. But, however hard she thought about it, there was only one reason that red skate was there.

Kill me.

At that moment, Monica realised she had already made her decision.

8

The rain covered Rome like a funeral pall. The silent, weeping facades of the buildings in the historic centre were draped in long shadows. The alleys that wound like intestines around the Piazza Navona were deserted. But a stone's throw from the Bramante cloister, light spilled through the windows of the long-established Caffè della Pace on to the wet street.

Inside, red velvet chairs, grey-veined marble tables, neo-Renaissance statues, and the usual customers: artists, especially painters and musicians, greeting the uneasy dawn, shopkeepers and antique dealers waiting to open, and a few actors who dropped in for a cappuccino after an all-night rehearsal before going home to sleep. They were all in search of a little relief from the terrible weather, and all deep in conversation. Nobody paid any attention to the two black-clad strangers sitting at a table facing the entrance.

'How are the migraines?' the younger of the two men asked.

The older man stopped gathering grains of sugar around his empty cup and instinctively stroked the scar on his left temple. 'They keep me awake sometimes, but generally I feel better.'

'Do you still have that dream?'

'Every night,' the man replied, raising his deep-set, melancholy blue eyes.

'It'll pass.'

'Yes, it'll pass.'

The silence that followed was interrupted by a long hiss of steam from the espresso machine.

'Marcus,' the younger man said, 'the moment has come.'

'I'm not ready yet.'

'We can't wait any longer. They're asking me about you. They're anxious to know how you're getting on.'

'I'm making progress, aren't I?'

'Yes, it's true: you're better every day, and I'm pleased, believe me. But expectations are high. There's a lot depending on you.'

'But who are these people who take such an interest in me? I'd

9

like to meet them, talk to them. The only one I know is you, Clemente.'

'We've discussed that before. It's not possible.'

'Why?'

'Because that's the way things have always been.'

Marcus touched his scar again, as he did whenever he was nervous.

Clemente leaned forward, forcing Marcus to look at him. 'It's for your own safety.'

'Theirs, you mean.'

'Theirs, too, if you want to see it that way.'

'I could turn out to be a source of embarrassment. And that mustn't be allowed to happen, must it?'

Marcus's sarcasm did not faze Clemente. 'What's your problem?'

'I don't exist,' Marcus said, his voice painfully constricted.

'The fact that I'm the only one who knows your face leaves you free. Don't you see that? All they know is your name. For everything else, they trust me. So there are no limits to your remit. If they don't know who you are, they can't hinder you.'

'Why?' Marcus retorted.

'Because what we are chasing can corrupt even them. If all the other measures were to fail, if the barriers they've put up turned out to be useless, there'd still be someone keeping alert. You are their last defence.'

'Answer me one question,' Marcus said, a gleam of defiance in his eyes. 'Are there others like me?'

After a brief silence, Clemente said, 'I don't know. There's no way I could know.'

'You should have left me in that hospital . . .'

'Don't say that, Marcus. Don't disappoint me.'

Marcus looked outside, at the few passers-by taking advantage of a lull in the storm to emerge from their makeshift shelters and continue on their way. He still had many questions for Clemente. Things that did not directly concern him, things he no longer knew. Clemente was his one contact with the world. In fact, Clemente *was* his world. Marcus never spoke to anyone, had no friends. Yet he knew things he would have preferred not to know. Things about men and the evil they do. Things so terrible as to make anyone's confidence waver, and contaminate anyone's heart for ever. He looked at the people around him, people who lived without that burden of knowledge, and envied them. Clemente had saved him. But his salvation had coincided with his entrance into a world of shadows.

'Why me?' he asked, continuing to look away.

Clemente smiled. *'Dogs are colour blind.'* That was the phrase he always used. 'So, are you with me?'

Marcus turned away from the window and looked at his one friend. 'Yes, I'm with you.'

Without a word, Clemente slipped his hand into the pocket of the raincoat draped over the back of his chair. He took out an envelope, placed it on the table and pushed it towards Marcus. Marcus took it and, with the care that distinguished every one of his gestures, opened it.

Inside, there were three photographs.

The first was of a group of young people at a beach party. Closest to the camera were two girls in bathing costumes toasting with bottles of beer in front of a bonfire. One of the girls reappeared in the second photograph, wearing glasses and with her hair pulled back: she was smiling, pointing behind her at the Palazzo della Civiltà Italiana in the EUR area of Rome. In the third photograph, the same girl was seen embracing a man and a woman, presumably her parents.

'Who is she?' Marcus asked.

'Her name is Lara. She's twenty-three years old. She's from the south, and has been in Rome for a year, studying at the faculty of architecture.'

'What happened to her?'

'That's the problem: nobody knows. She disappeared nearly a month ago.'

Blocking out his surroundings, Marcus concentrated on Lara's face. She seemed a typical provincial girl transplanted to a big city. Pretty, with delicate features, and no make-up. He assumed she usually wore her hair in a ponytail because she couldn't afford to go to the hairdresser's. Maybe, in order to save money, she only had her hair done when she went home to see her parents. Her clothes were a compromise. She was wearing jeans and a T-shirt, which absolved her of the need to keep up with the latest fashions. Her face showed traces of nights spent poring over her books and dinners consisting of a tin of tuna, the last resource of students living away from home for the first time, when they have exhausted their monthly budget and are waiting for another transfer from Mum and Dad. He imagined her daily struggle with homesickness, kept at bay by her dream of becoming an architect.

'Tell me what happened.'

Clemente took out a notebook, moved the coffee cup aside, and began consulting his notes. 'The day she disappeared, Lara spent part of the evening with a few friends in a club. Her friends say she seemed perfectly normal. They chatted about the usual things, then about nine she said she felt tired and wanted to go home. Two of her friends gave her a lift in their car and waited as she went in through the front door.'

'Where does she live?'

'In an old apartment block in the centre.'

'Are there other tenants?'

'About twenty of them. The building belongs to a university agency that rents the apartments to students. Lara's is on the ground floor. Until August she'd been sharing it with a friend. She was looking for a new flatmate.'

'What's the last trace we have of her?'

'We know she was in the apartment over the next hour, because she made two calls from her mobile: one at eight twenty-seven p.m. and the other at ten twelve. The first one, which lasted ten minutes, was to her mother, the second to her best friend. At ten nineteen her phone was switched off, and wasn't switched on again.'

A young waitress approached the table to take away the cups. She lingered to give them time to order something else. But neither of them did so. They simply remained silent until she had gone away again.

'When was her disappearance reported?' Marcus asked.

'The following evening. When she didn't turn up at the faculty next day, her friends called her several times, but all they got was a recorded message. About eight o'clock, they went and knocked at her door, but there was no reply.'

'What do the police think?'

'The day before she disappeared, Lara withdrew four hundred euros from her bank account to pay her rent. But the agency never received the money. According to her mother, there are some clothes and a rucksack missing from the wardrobe. And there's no trace of her mobile phone either. That's why the police decided she ran away of her own free will.'

'Very convenient for them.'

'You know how it is. If there's nothing to make them fear the worst, after a while they just stop looking and wait.'

Maybe for a corpse to show up, Marcus thought.

'Lara lived quite a regular life, spent much of her time at the university, and always kept within the same small circle of acquaintances.'

'What do her friends think?'

'That Lara wasn't the kind of person to do anything on a whim. Although she had changed a bit lately. They say she seemed tired and distracted.'

'Any boyfriends?'

'From her mobile phone records, she doesn't seem to have called anyone outside her circle, and nobody mentioned a boyfriend.'

'Did she use the internet?'

'Mostly from the library in her department or from an internet point near the station. There were no suspicious messages in her inbox.'

At that moment the glass door of the café was flung open to allow a new customer to come in, and a gust of wind blew through the room. Everyone turned in annoyance, except Marcus, who was lost in his own thoughts. 'Lara returns home, just as she does every evening. She's tired, as she's quite often been lately. Her last contact with the world is at ten nineteen, when she switches off her phone, which then disappears with her and isn't switched on again. That's the last anyone hears from her. Some of her clothes are missing, along with money and a rucksack, which is why the police think she left home voluntarily. She may have gone alone, or with someone else, but nobody saw her go.' Marcus stared at Clemente. 'Why should we think that something bad happened to her? I mean why us?'

The look Clemente gave him spoke for itself. They had reached the crucial point. *Anomalies*: that was what they always looked for. Tiny tears in the thread of normality. Little departures from the logical sequence of a straightforward criminal investigation. It was in those insignificant details that something else often lay concealed, something that pointed to a different, unimaginable truth. That was where their task began.

'Lara never left home, Marcus. Her door was locked on the inside.'

Clemente and Marcus went straight to the scene of Lara's disappearance. The building was in the Via dei Coronari, not far from the Piazza San Salvatore in Lauro with its little sixteenth-century church. It took them only a few seconds to get into the ground-floor apartment. Nobody noticed them.

As soon as he set foot in Lara's apartment, Marcus began looking around. First of all, he noted the broken door chain. In order to get into the apartment, the police had had to smash the door down, and they had not noticed the chain that had come loose and was now dangling from the doorpost.

The apartment covered no more than a hundred and fifty square feet, divided between two levels. The first was a single room with a kitchen area. There was a wall cabinet and an electric hotplate with cupboards above it. Next to it, a refrigerator with coloured magnets on the door. On top of the refrigerator was a vase containing a now dry cyclamen plant. There was a table with four chairs and, in the centre, a tray with a tea service. In the corner, two sofas arranged around a television set. On the green walls, not the usual pictures or posters, but plans of famous buildings around the world. There was a window that, like all those in the apartment, looked out on the inner courtyard. It was protected by iron bars. Nobody could get in or out that way.

Marcus registered every detail with his eyes. Without saying a word, he made the sign of the cross, and Clemente immediately did the same. Then he started moving around the room. He did not limit himself to looking. He touched the objects, brushing them lightly with the palm of his hand, almost as if he was trying to perceive a residue of energy, a radio signal, as if they could communicate with him, reveal to him what they knew or had seen. Like a water diviner who listens for the call of strata hidden underground, Marcus was probing the deep, inanimate silence of things.

Clemente watched him, keeping well back in order not to distract him. Marcus did not seem to hesitate: he was totally concentrated on the task in hand. This was an important test for both of them. Marcus would demonstrate to himself that he was again able to do the work for which he had been trained, and Clemente would know whether or not he had been right about Marcus's ability to recover.

He watched as Marcus moved towards the far end of the apartment, where a door led to a small bathroom. It was covered in white tiles, illumined by a fluorescent light. The shower was an unpartitioned area between the wash basin and the toilet. There was a washing machine and a broom cupboard. On the back of the door hung a calendar.

Marcus turned back and walked along the left-hand side of the living room: here, a staircase led to the upper floor. He went up three steps at a time, and found himself on a narrow landing, faced with the doors to two bedrooms.

The first was the one vacated by Lara's flatmate. Inside it was only a bare mattress, a small armchair and a chest of drawers.

The other was Lara's bedroom.

The shutters on the window were open. In a corner was a table with a computer and shelves filled with books. Marcus approached and ran his fingers along the spines of books, mostly on architecture, and over a sheet of paper containing an uncompleted plan for a bridge. There was a glass filled with pencils. He took one out and sniffed it, then did the same with a piece of rubber, savouring the secret pleasure that only articles of stationery can instil.

That smell was part of Lara's world. This was the place where she had felt happy. Her little kingdom.

He opened the wardrobe doors and looked through the clothes. Some of the hangers were empty. Three pairs of shoes stood in a row on the lower shelf. Two pairs of trainers and one of court shoes, for special occasions. But there was space for a fourth pair, which was missing.

The bed was a large single. A teddy bear sat between the pillows. It had probably been a witness to Lara's life ever since she was a child. But now it was alone.

On the bedside table stood a framed photograph of Lara with her parents and a tin box containing a small sapphire ring, a coral bracelet and a bit of costume jewellery. Marcus took a closer look at the photograph. He recognised it: it was one of those that Clemente had shown him at the Caffè della Pace. In it, Lara was wearing a crucifix with a gold chain, but there was no sign of that in the jewellery box.

Clemente was waiting for him at the foot of the stairs. 'Well?'

'She may have been abducted.' As he said it, he became certain that it was true.

'What makes you say that?'

'It's too tidy. As if the missing clothes and mobile phone were all a set-up. Whoever was responsible, though, missed one detail: the chain on the door.'

'But how did he—'

'We'll get to that,' Marcus interrupted him. He moved around the room, trying to focus on the exact sequence of events. His head was whirling. The pieces of the mosaic were starting to come together before his eyes. 'Lara had a visitor.'

Clemente knew what was happening. Marcus was beginning a process of identification. That was his talent.

He was seeing what the intruder had seen.

'He was here when Lara was out. He sat down on her sofa, he lay on her bed, he searched among her things. He looked at her photographs, he made her memories his own. He touched her toothbrush, sniffed her clothes, tried to find her smell. He drank from the same glass she'd left in the sink to be washed.'

'I don't follow you . . .'

'He knew where everything was. He knew everything about Lara, her timetable, her habits.'

'But there's nothing here to suggest an abduction. There are no signs of struggle, nobody in the building heard screams or cries for help. How can you be so sure?'

'Because she was asleep when he took her.'

Clemente was about to speak, but Marcus got in first. 'Help me find the sugar.'

Even though Clemente didn't quite grasp what was going through Marcus's head, he decided to humour him. In a cupboard over the oven he found a box with the word SUGAR on it. In the meantime, Marcus examined the sugar bowl in the middle of the table, next to the tea things.

They were both empty.

The two men looked at each other with these objects in their hands, a charge of energy vibrating between them. It wasn't mere coincidence, and Marcus hadn't made a random supposition. He had had an intuition that might confirm his theory.

'Sugar is the best place to hide a drug. It conceals the taste and guarantees that the victim will absorb it easily.'

And Lara had been feeling tired lately, her friends said. This clinched it for Clemente, although he couldn't tell Marcus.

'It happened gradually, there was no hurry,' Marcus continued. 'That proves that the person who took her had been here before that night. Along with her clothes and mobile phone, he also got rid of the sugar containing the drug.'

'But you're forgetting the chain on the door,' Clemente said. That was the one detail that blew any theory to pieces. 'How did he get in? And above all, how did they both get out?'

Marcus looked around again. 'Where are we?' Rome was the

greatest inhabited archaeological site in the world. The city had developed in layers; you only had to dig a few feet down to find traces of earlier periods, earlier civilisations. Marcus knew very well that even on the surface life had become stratified over the course of time. Every place contained many histories, many lives, within it. 'What is this place? I don't mean now, but before. You told me the building dates from the eighteenth century.'

'It was one of the residences of the Costaldi family.'

'Of course. The nobles occupied the upper floors, and down here were the storerooms and the stables.' Marcus touched the scar on his left temple. He had no idea where that memory came from. How did he know that? Much had vanished for ever from his memory. But odd fragments of information surfaced unexpectedly from time to time, provoking the awkward question as to where they came from. There was a place within him where certain things existed but remained hidden, a place of mist and darkness that he was afraid he would never find.

'You're right,' Clemente said. 'That's how the building used to be. The university authorities received it as a bequest about ten years ago and converted it into apartments.'

Marcus looked down. The parquet floor was of solid, untreated wood, with narrow floorboards. 'No, not here,' he muttered to himself. Undaunted, he headed for the bathroom, followed by Clemente.

He took a bucket from the broom cupboard, placed it under the shower and half filled it. Then he took a step back. Clemente, who was standing behind him, still did not understand.

Marcus tilted the bucket so that the water spilled on to the tiled floor. A puddle spread beneath their feet. They stood looking at it, expectantly.

After a few seconds, the water began to disappear.

It looked like a conjuring trick – just like a girl disappearing from an apartment locked on the inside. Except that this time there was an explanation.

The water had filtered through the floor.

Along the sides of some of the tiles, little bubbles of air appeared, eventually forming a perfect square, each side approximately three feet.

Marcus crouched down and felt the tiles with his fingertips, trying to discover a crack. When he thought he had located one, he stood up again and searched for something to use as a crowbar. He found a pair of scissors that did the trick. He put his fingers into the opening and lifted the square, revealing a stone trapdoor.

'Wait, I'll give you a hand,' Clemente said.

They slid the lid to one side, uncovering a flight of time-worn travertine steps that went down six feet until it met what appeared to be a passage.

'This is the way the intruder came,' Marcus announced. 'At least twice: when he came in and when he went away with Lara.' He took out the little torch he always carried with him, lit it, and aimed it at the opening.

'You want to go down there?'

He turned towards Clemente. 'Do I have any choice?'

Holding the torch in one hand, Marcus descended the stone steps. Reaching the bottom, he realised he was in a tunnel that ran under the building in two directions. It was not clear where it led.

'Are you all right?' Clemente called down to him.

'Yes,' Marcus replied distractedly. In the eighteenth century, the gallery had probably been an escape route in case of danger. All he had to do was venture in one of the two directions. He chose the one from which he seemed to hear the distant noise of pouring rain. He went at least fifty yards, slipping a couple of times because of the wet ground. A few rats brushed against his calves with their hot smooth bodies before scurrying away into the darkness. He recognised the roar of the Tiber, swollen by days of persistent rain, and the sickly odour of the river, reminiscent of an animal in a headlong race. He followed it and soon came to a solid grille through which the grey light of day filtered. Impossible to go any further this way. So he turned back, went past the steps, and set off in the other direction. Almost immediately, he spotted something shining on the ground.

He bent down and picked it up: it was a crucifix on a gold chain.

The crucifix Lara had been wearing around her neck in the photograph of her and her parents that she kept on the chest of drawers. It was the final proof that his theory had been correct.

Clemente was right. This was his talent.

Electrified by his discovery, Marcus did not notice that Clemente had come down to join him until he was right on top of him.

He showed him the chain. 'Look . . .'

Clemente took it in his hands and examined it.

'Lara might still be alive,' Marcus said, excited by his discovery. 'Now that we have a lead, we can find out who took her.' But he realised that his friend did not share his enthusiasm. On the contrary, he seemed troubled.

'We already know. We just needed confirmation. Unfortunately, we now have it.'

'What are you talking about?'

'The drug in the sugar.'

Marcus still did not understand. 'So what's the problem?'

Clemente gave him a solemn look. 'I think it's time you met Jeremiah Smith.'

8:40 a.m.

The first lesson Sandra Vega had learned was that houses and apartments never lie.

People, when they talk about themselves, are capable of creating all kinds of trappings around themselves that they actually end up believing. But the place where they choose to live inevitably reveals all.

In the course of her work, Sandra had visited many houses and apartments. Every time she was about to cross a threshold, she felt as if she ought to ask permission, even though, for what she had come to do, she didn't even need to ring the doorbell.

Years before taking up her profession, whenever she travelled by train at night, she would look at the lighted windows in the buildings and wonder what was going on behind them, what stories were being played out. Every now and again she'd caught a glimpse of one of these stories. A woman ironing while watching television. A man in an armchair sending up smoke rings from his cigarette. A child standing on a chair rummaging through a cupboard. Still images from a film, each captured in its little window. Then the train would pass. And those lives would continue on their way, unaware of her.

She had always tried to imagine what it would be like to prolong that exploration. To walk unseen among those people's most precious possessions, to watch them as they went about their everyday lives, as if they were fish in an aquarium.

And in all the places she had lived, Sandra had asked herself what had happened within those walls before she entered them. What joys, quarrels and sorrows had flared then faded without leaving an echo.

She would wonder about the tragedies and horrors preserved like secrets in those places. Luckily, houses and apartments forget quickly. The occupants change, and everything starts all over again from the beginning.

Once in a while, those who go away leave traces of their passing. A lipstick forgotten in a bathroom cabinet. An old magazine on a shelf. A sheet of paper with the telephone number of a rape crisis centre hidden at the back of a drawer.

Through these little clues, it is sometimes possible to trace someone's story.

She had never imagined that the search for such details would actually become her profession. But there was a difference: by the time she arrived in these places, they had lost their innocence for ever.

Sandra had joined the police through a competitive examination. The training had been standard. She carried a service gun, and knew how to use it. But her uniform was the white coat of the forensics team. After a specialisation course, she had chosen to become a forensic photographer.

She would arrive at a scene with her cameras, her sole purpose that of stopping time. Once everything was frozen by her lens, it would never change again.

The second lesson Sandra Vega had learned was that, like people, houses and apartments die.

And her destiny was to be there just before they died, when their inhabitants would never again set foot in them. The signs of that slow death agony were unmade beds, dishes in the sink, a sock abandoned on the floor. As if the inhabitants had fled, leaving everything in disorder, to escape the sudden end of the world. When in reality the end of the world had actually happened within those walls.

And so, as soon as Sandra crossed the threshold of an apartment on the fifth floor of a tower block on the outskirts of Milan, she realised that what was awaiting her would be a particularly unforgettable crime scene. The first thing she saw was the decorated tree, even though it was a long time since Christmas. Instinctively she understood why it was there. Her sister, too, at the age of five, had stopped her parents from taking down the decorations once the holiday was over. She had cried and screamed one whole afternoon, and in the end her parents had given up, hoping that sooner or later it would pass. Instead of which, the plastic fir tree with its little lights and coloured balls had stayed in its corner for the whole summer and the following winter. That was why Sandra suddenly felt her stomach gripped in a vice.

The tree told her there was a child in this apartment.

She could feel the child's presence in the air. Because the third lesson she had learned was that houses and apartments have a smell. It belongs to those who live in them, and it is always different and unique. When tenants change, the smell disappears, to give way to a new one. It forms over time, mixing in other odours, natural and artificial – fabric softeners and coffee, schoolbooks and indoor plants, floor polish and cabbage soup – and it becomes the smell of that family, of the people who comprise it. They carry it on them and don't even smell it.

The smell was the one thing that distinguished the apartment she saw now from the dwellings of other single-income families. Three rooms and a kitchen. The furniture acquired at different times, depending on financial circumstances. The framed photographs, mostly of summer holidays: the only ones they could afford. The tartan cover on the sofa in front of the TV: it was here that they took refuge every evening, sitting crammed together watching the programmes until sleep overcame them.

Sandra mentally catalogued these images. There was no warning in them of what was going to happen. No one could have predicted that.

The police officers were moving through the rooms like uninvited guests, violating the family's privacy with their mere presence. But she had long since got past the feeling that she was an intruder.

Hardly anyone spoke at crime scenes like this one. Even horror had its code. In this silent choreography, words were superfluous, because everyone knew exactly what to do.

But there were always exceptions. One of these was Fabio Sergi. She heard him cursing from somewhere in the apartment.

'Fuck, I don't believe it!'

All Sandra had to do was follow his voice: it came from a narrow windowless bathroom.

'What's happening?' she asked, putting the two bags with her equipment down on the floor of the corridor and slipping on plastic overshoes.

'It's been a great day so far,' he replied sarcastically, without looking at her. He was busy giving energetic taps to a portable gas fire. 'This damn thing doesn't work!'

'I hope you're not going to blow us all up.'

Sergi glared at her. Sandra didn't say anything else, her colleague was too nervous. Instead she looked down at the corpse of the man occupying the space between the bathroom door and the toilet bowl. He was lying face down, stark naked. Forty years old, she estimated. Weight approximately fourteen stone, height six feet. The head was twisted at an unnatural angle, and there was an oblique gash across his skull. Blood had formed a dark pool on the black-and-white tiles.

He was clutching a gun in his hand.

Next to the body lay a chunk of porcelain that corresponded to the left-hand corner of the wash basin. It had presumably broken off when the man had fallen on it.

'What do you need a gas fire for?' Sandra asked.

'I need to recreate the scene,' he replied curtly. 'The guy was having his shower and he brought this thing in to heat the bathroom. In a while I'll also turn the water on, so you'd better get your stuff sorted as soon as possible.'

Sandra knew what Sergi had in mind: the steam would bring out the footprints on the floor. That way they would be able to reconstruct the victim's movements within the room.

'I need a screwdriver,' Sergi said angrily. 'I'll be right back. Try to stay as close to the walls as you can.'

Sandra didn't reply, she was used to that kind of instruction: fingerprint experts always thought they were the only ones capable of preserving a crime scene. And there was also the fact that she was a twenty-nine-year-old woman operating in a predominantly masculine environment. She was accustomed to being patronised by her colleagues. Sergi was the worst of the lot; they had never bonded and she didn't enjoy working with him.

While he was out of the room, Sandra took the opportunity to take the camera and tripod from her bags. She placed sponges on the feet of the tripod, to avoid leaving marks. Then she mounted the camera with the lens pointing upwards. After wiping it with a piece of gauze impregnated with ammonia, to stop it steaming up, she attached a single-shot panoramic optic, which would allow her to take 360-degree photographs of the room.

From the general to the particular, that was the rule.

The camera would focus on the entire scenario of the event through a series of automatic shots, then she would complete the reconstruction of events by manually taking ever more detailed photographs, marking her discoveries with numbered stickers to indicate the chronology.

Sandra had just finished positioning the camera in the middle of the room when she noticed a little tank on a shelf. In it were two small turtles. She felt a pang in her heart, thinking of the person in that family who had looked after them, feeding them from the feed box next to the tank, periodically changing the inch or two of water in which they were immersed and embellishing their habitat with pebbles and a plastic palm.

Not an adult, she told herself.

At that moment, Sergei returned with the screwdriver and again started fiddling with the gas fire. Within a few seconds, he had managed to get it working.

'I knew I'd do it in the end,' he said smugly.

The room was narrow and the body occupied almost all the space. It was barely large enough for the three of them. It wouldn't be easy to work in these conditions, Sandra thought. 'How are we going to move?'

'Let me get the sauna working first,' Sergi said, turning the hot water tap in the shower to full. It was obvious he wanted to get rid of her. 'In the meantime, you could start in the kitchen. We've got a twin in there . . . '

Crime scenes are divided into primary and secondary, to distinguish the location where the crime has actually been committed from those which are merely linked to it, such as the place where a body has been hidden or the murder weapon found.

When Sandra heard that there was a 'twin' in this apartment, she immediately understood that Sergi was referring to a second primary scene. And that could only mean one thing. More victims. She recalled the turtles and the Christmas tree.

Sandra stood motionless in the doorway of the kitchen. To maintain her self-control in such situations, it was important to follow the manual to the letter. Its dictates brought order to chaos. At least, that was the illusion she clung to, and she had to believe it was true.

Simba the lion winked at her from the TV, then started singing with the other denizens of the jungle. She would have liked to switch it off, but she couldn't.

Resolving to ignore it, she clipped the recorder to her belt, ready to make a verbal record of the whole procedure. She pulled back her long brown hair and tied it with an elastic band she always kept on her wrist, then arranged the microphone over her head, to keep her hands free to manoeuvre the second camera she had taken from her bag. She aimed the camera at the scene, glad that it allowed her to place a safe distance between herself and what she had in front of her.

Conventionally, the photographic survey of a crime scene went from right to left, from bottom to top.

She glanced at her watch, then started the recording. First, she stated her name and rank. Then the place, date and time when the procedure started. She began shooting, simultaneously describing what she saw.

'The table is in the middle of the room. It's laid for breakfast. One of the chairs has been overturned. Lying next to it on the floor is the first body: a woman, aged between thirty and forty.'

The woman was wearing a light nightdress that had ridden up her thighs, leaving her legs and pubis blatantly exposed. Her hair was gathered with a clip in the shape of a flower. She had lost one of her slippers.

'Numerous gunshot wounds. In one hand she is clutching a piece of paper.'

She had been making a shopping list. The pen was still on the table.

'The corpse is turned towards the door. She must have seen the killer come in and tried to stop him. She rose from the table, but only took one step.'

The clicking of the camera was the sole measure of time. Sandra concentrated on that sound, like a musician letting himself be guided by a metronome. In reality, she was assimilating every detail of the scene as it imprinted itself into the digital memory of the camera and into her own memory.

'Second body: male, approximately ten to twelve years old. Sitting with his back to the door.'

He hadn't even realised what was happening. But, as far as Sandra was concerned, the idea of an unconscious death was a relief only for the living.

'He's wearing blue pyjamas. He's lying prone on the table, his face buried in a bowl of cornflakes. There's a deep gunshot wound on the back of his neck.'

For Sandra, death was not in the two bullet-riddled bodies, or in the blood that had spattered everywhere and was slowly drying at their feet. It wasn't in their glassy eyes that continued to look without seeing, or in the unfinished gestures with which they had taken their leave of the world. It was elsewhere. Sandra had learned that death's greatest talent was being able to hide in details, and it was in those details that she would reveal it with her camera. In the coffee stains on the oven, where it had spilled from the old coffee maker that had continued to boil until someone switched it off after discovering the scene. In the hum of the refrigerator, which continued impassively to keep the food fresh in its belly. In the TV, which was still broadcasting cheerful cartoons. After the massacre, this artificial life had continued, unheeding and pointless. It was in that deception that death lay hidden.

'Nice way to start the day, eh?'

Sandra switched off the recorder and turned.

Inspector De Michelis stood in the doorway with his arms folded, an unlit cigarette drooping from his lips. 'The man you saw in the bathroom worked as a guard for a security company. The gun was licensed. They lived on his salary. What with the rent and the car insurance, they probably found it hard to make ends meet. But who doesn't?'

'Why did he do it?'

'We're interviewing the neighbours. The husband and wife quarrelled frequently, but not violently enough for anyone to call the police.'

'So there were problems in the marriage?'

'Apparently, yes. He was into Thai boxing, he was even provincial champion for a while, but he gave it up after being disqualified for using anabolic steroids.'

'Did he beat her?'

'The pathologist should be able to tell us that. What we do know is that he was very jealous.'

Sandra looked at the woman lying on the floor, half-naked from the waist down. You can't be jealous of a corpse, she thought. Not any more.

'Think she had a lover?'

'Maybe. Who can say?' De Michelis shrugged. 'How are you getting on in the bathroom?'

'I set up the first camera, it's already taking the panoramic shots. I'm waiting either for it to finish or for Sergi to call me.'

'It didn't happen the way it looks ...'

Sandra looked at De Michelis. 'What do you mean?'

'The man didn't shoot himself. We've counted the cartridge cases: they're all in the kitchen.'

'So what happened?'

De Michelis took the cigarette from his lips and stepped inside the room. 'He was having a shower. He left the bathroom naked, took the gun, which he kept in the hall in a holster next to his uniform, came into the kitchen, and, more or less where you are now, shot his son. One shot in the back of the neck, at point-blank range.' He mimed the gesture with his hand. 'Then he turned the gun on his wife. The whole thing only lasted a few seconds. He went back to the bathroom. The floor was still wet. He slipped and as he fell he hit his head really hard on the wash basin, so hard he broke a piece off. Death was instantaneous.' The inspector paused, then added sarcastically, 'God is great sometimes.'

God had nothing to do with it, Sandra thought, her eyes on the little boy. This morning, He was looking the other way.

'By seven twenty it was all over.'

She went back to the bathroom, feeling distinctly uneasy. De Michelis's last words had shaken her more than they should have done. Opening the door, she was overcome by the steam that filled the room. Sergi had already turned off the tap and was leaning over his small case of reagents.

'The cranberries, the problem's always the cranberries ...'

Sandra had no idea what he was talking about. He seemed completely absorbed, so she decided not to say anything, for fear of provoking a reaction. She checked that the camera had completed all the panoramic photographs and then took it off the tripod.

Before leaving the room, she turned back to Sergi. 'I'm just replacing the memory card and then I'll start in on the detailed shots.' She looked around. 'There are no windows and the light isn't very bright, so we'll need a couple of low-energy lamps. What do you think?'

Sergi looked up. 'I think I'd rather be beaten like a whore by one of those big bikers. Yes, that'd really be good.'

Sergi's words took her aback. If it was a joke, she didn't get it. But from the way he was staring at her, he didn't seem to be expecting her to laugh. Then, as if nothing had happened, he started fiddling with his reagents and Sandra went out into the corridor.

Trying to dismiss her colleague's ravings from her mind, she started checking the photographs on the screen of the camera. The 360-degree panoramic shots of the bathroom had come out quite well. The camera had taken six of them, at three-minute intervals. The steam had brought out the killer's bare footprints, but they were quite hard to decipher. At first, she had thought that there had been a quarrel between him and his wife in the bathroom, which had then led to the murder. But if that had been the case, the woman's slippers would also have left prints on the floor.

She was betraying one of the rules of the manual. She was looking for an explanation. However absurd this slaughter seemed, she had to report the facts in an objective manner. It didn't matter that she couldn't figure out a reason, her duty was to remain impartial.

In the past five months, though, that had become increasingly difficult.

From the general to the particular. Sandra began to focus on the details, looking for meaning.

On the screen, she saw the razor on the shelf under the mirror. The Winnie the Pooh shower gel. The stockings hanging up to dry. The daily gestures and habits of an ordinary family. Innocent objects that had witnessed a terrible act.

They're not mute, she thought. Objects talk to us from the silence, you just have to know how to listen to them.

As the images ran past her, Sandra kept wondering what could have unleashed such violence. Her sense of unease had increased, and she also felt a migraine coming on. Her eyes clouded over for a moment. All she wanted was to understand.

How had this little domestic apocalypse come into being?

The family wakes up shortly before seven. The woman gets out of bed and goes to make breakfast for her son. The man is the first to use the bathroom, he has to take the boy to school and then go to work. It's cold, so he takes a little gas fire in with him.

What happened while he was taking his shower?

The water pours down, and his anger mounts. Maybe he's been awake all night. Something is disturbing him. An idea, an obsession. Jealousy? Has he found out his wife had a lover? They often quarrelled, De Michelis had said.

But there was no quarrel this morning. Why?

The man comes out of the shower, takes the gun and goes to the kitchen. No words exchanged before he opens fire. What broke inside his head? An unbearable sense of anxiety, panic: the usual symptoms that precede a fit.

On the screen, three dressing gowns hanging next to each other. From the largest to the smallest. Side by side. In a glass, the family of three toothbrushes. Sandra was looking for the little crack in the idyllic picture. The hairline fracture that had sent the whole thing tumbling down.

By 7.20 it was all over, the inspector had said. That was when the neighbours heard the shots and called the police. A shower lasts a quarter of an hour at most. A quarter of an hour that decides everything.

On the screen, the small tank with the two turtles. The box with feed. The plastic palm. The pebbles.

The turtles, she told herself.

Sandra checked all the panoramic shots, zooming each time into that one detail. One photograph every three minutes. Six in all. Sergi had turned the hot water tap full on, the room was filled with steam . . . And yet the turtles hadn't moved.

Objects speak. Death is in the details.

Sandra's eyes clouded over again, and for a moment she was afraid she was going to faint.

De Michelis came in. 'Aren't you feeling well?'

At that moment, Sandra understood everything. 'The gas fire!'

'What?' De Michelis didn't understand. But she had no time to explain.

'Sergi! We have to get him out of there right now!'

A fire engine and an ambulance were parked outside the building. The ambulance was there for Sergi.

He was already unconscious when they entered the bathroom. Luckily for him, they had been in time. On the pavement in front of the building, Sandra showed De Michelis the image of the little tank with the dead turtles, trying to reconstruct the sequence of events.

'When we arrived, Sergi was trying to start the gas fire.'

'That imbecile could have snuffed it at any moment. There were no windows: the firemen said the bathroom was saturated with carbon monoxide.'

'Sergi was trying to reconstruct the condition of the room. But think about it: it happened only this morning, while the man was having his shower.'

De Michelis frowned. 'I'm sorry, I don't understand.'

'Carbon monoxide is a product of combustion. It's odourless, colourless and tasteless.'

'I know what it is,' the inspector said ironically. 'But can it also fire a gun?'

'You know the symptoms of carbon monoxide poisoning? Headache, dizziness, and in some cases hallucinations and paranoia . . . After being exposed to the gas while shut in the bathroom, Sergi was raving. He was talking about cranberries, saying things that didn't make any sense.'

De Michelis grimaced: he didn't like it. 'Listen, Sandra, I know where you're going with this, but it won't stand up.'

'The father was also shut in that bathroom before he started shooting.'

'It can't be proved.'

'But it's an explanation! At least admit the possibility that it happened like this: the man breathed in the monoxide, he's confused, hallucinating, paranoid. He doesn't faint straight away, the way Sergi did. Instead, he comes out of the bathroom naked, grabs the gun and shoots his wife and son. Afterwards he goes back in the bathroom, and it's only then that the lack of oxygen makes him lose consciousness and he falls, hitting his head.'

De Michelis folded his arms. His attitude exasperated her. But she was well aware that the inspector could never support such a far-fetched theory. She had known him for years, and she was sure he'd be only too pleased if the responsibility for these absurd deaths was down to something other than human volition. But he was right: there was no proof.

'I'll tell the pathologist. They can do a toxicological test on the man's body.'

Better than nothing, Sandra thought. De Michelis was a scrupulous man, a good policeman, she liked working with him. He was crazy about art, which for her was an indication of sensitivity. As far as she knew, he had no children and when he went on holiday with his wife they always tried to visit as many museums as possible. He maintained that every work of art contained many meanings and that discovering these meanings was the task of those who admired them. That was why he was not the kind of policeman who would be content with a first impression.

'Sometimes we'd prefer reality to be different. And if we can't change things, then we try to explain it to ourselves in our own way. But we don't always succeed.'

'No, we don't,' Sandra said, and immediately regretted it. What he had said certainly applied to her, but she wouldn't admit it.

She turned to leave.

'Listen, I wanted to say . . . ' De Michelis ran his hand through his grey hair, looking for the most appropriate words. 'I'm sorry about what happened to you. I know it's been six months . . . '

'Five,' she corrected him.

'Yes, but I should have said this earlier . . . '

'Don't worry,' she replied, forcing a smile. 'Thank you, anyway.'

Sandra turned to go back to her car. She walked quickly, with that strange sensation in her chest that never left her and that the others did not even suspect. It was like a ball inside her, a ball made up of anxiety, anger and grief. She called it *the thing*.

She wouldn't admit it, but for the past five months *the thing* had replaced her heart.

The rain had started falling again with dogged persistence. Unlike those around them, Marcus and Clemente were in no hurry as they made their way along one of the paths leading to the city's major hospital, the Gemelli.

'The police are guarding the main entrance,' Clemente said. 'And we have to avoid the security cameras.'

He turned left, leaving the path, and led Marcus towards a small white building. There was a platform roof, beneath which stood drums of detergent and trolleys filled with dirty sheets. An iron staircase led to a service entrance, which was open. They entered and found themselves in the storage area of the hospital's laundry. From here they took a lift to the lower floor and walked along a narrow corridor until they came to a security door. They put on white coats, masks and overshoes, which they found on a trolley, then Clemente handed Marcus a magnetic card. With that around his neck, nobody would ask any questions. They used it to open the electronic lock. At last, they were inside.

Ahead of them was a long corridor with blue walls. It smelled of alcohol and floor polish.

Unlike the other departments, intensive care was enveloped in silence. The constant rush of doctors and nurses was absent here; staff moved through the corridors unhurriedly and without making any noise. There was no sound beyond the hum of the machines keeping patients alive.

And yet it was in this silent realm that the most desperate life-and-death struggles took place. Whenever one of the combatants fell, it happened without any clamour. Nobody screamed, no alarms sounded, the sole announcement was a red light that went on in the nurses' station, indicating as simply as possible the cessation of vital functions.

In other departments, the fight to save lives meant a race against time. In IC, time passed differently, expanding to such an extent as to seem absent.

Among those who worked here, this place was known as *the border*.

'Some choose to cross that border,' Clemente said, 'while others turn back.'

They were standing in front of the glass partition separating the corridor from one of the recovery rooms. There were six beds in the room.

Only one was occupied.

In it lay a man of around fifty, connected to a respirator. Looking at him, Marcus thought again about himself and about the time Clemente had found him in a similar bed, fighting his own battle, hovering between life and death.

He had chosen to remain on this side of the border.

Clemente pointed beyond the glass. 'Last night an ambulance was called to a villa outside the city. A man had phoned Emergency, saying that he was having a heart attack. In his house they found a number of objects – a hair ribbon, a coral bracelet, a pink scarf and a roller skate – that belonged to the victims of a previously uniden-tified serial killer. The man's name is Jeremiah Smith.'

Jeremiah: a pious name, was Marcus's first thought. Not really suited to a serial killer.

Clemente took a folder from the inside pocket of his raincoat. It was unmarked apart from a code number: *c.g. 97-95-6.*

'Four victims in the space of six years. All with their throats cut. All female, aged between seventeen and twenty-eight.'

As Clemente went through these sterile, impersonal facts, Marcus concentrated on the man's face. He mustn't let himself be deceived. The body was merely a disguise, a way to pass unobserved.

'The doctors say he's in a coma,' Clemente said, almost guessing his thoughts. 'And yet he was immediately intubated by the ambu-lance team that came to his rescue. As it happens . . . '

'What?'

'By a twist of fate, one of the team was the sister of Jeremiah

Smith's first victim. She's twenty-seven years old and she's a doctor.'

Marcus looked surprised. 'Does she know whose life she saved?'

'She was the one who reported finding in the house a roller skate that had belonged to her twin sister, who was killed six years ago. There's another thing that made this more than just a routine intervention.'

Clemente took a photograph from the folder. It showed the man's chest, with the words *Kill me*. 'He was walking around with that on his body.'

'It's the symbol of his divided nature,' Marcus said. 'It's as if he's telling us that we have to look beyond appearances. We usually stop at the first level, the level of clothes, to judge a person, when the real truth is written on the skin. It's within everyone's reach, hidden and yet close. But nobody sees it. In the case of Jeremiah Smith, people brushed against him in the street without imagining the danger, nobody saw him for what he really was.'

'There was a challenge in those words: Kill me, if you can.'

Marcus turned towards Clemente. 'And what's the challenge now?'

'Lara.'

'What makes you think she's still alive?'

'He kept the others alive for at least a month before killing them and dumping their bodies.'

'How do we know he was the one who took her?'

'The sugar. The other girls had also been drugged. He took them all in the same way: approaching them in broad daylight under some pretext and offering them a drink. In each case he dosed the drinks with GHB, better known as the date rape drug. It's a narcotic with hypnotic effects that inhibits the ability to reason and choose. It seems to be his signature.'

'A rape drug,' Marcus said. 'So the motive is sexual?'

Clemente shook his head. 'There were no signs of sexual violence on the victims. He tied them up, kept them alive for a month, then cut their throats.'

'But he took Lara from her own home,' Marcus said. 'How do we explain that?'

'Some serial killers perfect their modus operandi as their sadistic fantasies evolve. Every now and again, they add a new detail, something that increases their pleasure. Over time, killing becomes a job, and they try to get better at it.'

Clemente's explanation was plausible, but didn't totally convince Marcus. He decided to let that go for the moment. 'Tell me about Jeremiah Smith's villa.'

'The police are still searching it, so we can't go there yet. But apparently he didn't take his victims there. He has another place somewhere. If we find it, we'll find Lara.'

'But the police aren't looking for her.'

'Maybe there's something in that house that'll connect him to her.'

'Shouldn't we put them on the right track?'

'No.'

'Why not?' Marcus asked, incredulous.

'That's not the way we operate.'

'Lara would have more chance of being saved.'

'The police might get in your way. You need complete freedom of action.'

'Freedom of action? What does that mean? I don't even know where to begin!'

Clemente looked him straight in the eye. 'I understand you find it daunting, because it all seems new to you. But this isn't your first time. You used to be good at what you did, and you can be good again. I assure you that if there's anyone who can locate that girl, it's you. The sooner you realise that, the better. Because I get the feeling Lara doesn't have much time left.'

Marcus looked over Clemente's shoulder at the patient – attached to a respirator, hovering over the final border – then at the reflection of his own face in the glass pane, superimposed over that image, as if in an optical illusion. He quickly took his eyes away. It wasn't the view of the monster that had disturbed him. It was the fact that he couldn't stand mirrors, because he still didn't recognise himself. 'What will happen to me if I fail?'

'So that's it: you're worried about yourself.'

'I don't know who I am any more, Clemente.'

'You'll find out soon, my friend.' He handed him the case file. 'We trust you. But from now on, you're on your own.'

8:56 p.m.

The third lesson that Sandra Vega had learned is that houses and apartments have a smell. It belongs to those who live in them, and it's always different and unique. When the occupants leave, the smell vanishes. That was why every time Sandra got back to her apartment on the Navigli, she immediately looked for David's smell.

Aftershave and aniseed-flavoured cigarettes.

She knew that one day she would come home, sniff the air and not smell it. Once the smell had gone, David really wouldn't be there any more.

That thought made her despair. And she tried to be out as much as possible. In order not to contaminate the apartment with her presence, not to fill it with her own smell.

At first, she had hated the cheap supermarket aftershave David insisted on buying. It seemed to her aggressive and all-pervading. In the three years they had lived together, she had tried many times to find him a replacement. Every birthday, Christmas or anniversary, in addition to the official gift there was a new scent. He would use it for a week, then put it away together with the others on a shelf in the bathroom. Each time he would attempt to justify himself with the words: 'Sorry, Ginger, but it's just not me.' The way he would wink as he said this was intensely irritating.

Sandra could never have imagined that a time would come when she would buy twenty bottles of that aftershave and sprinkle it around the apartment. She had bought so many out of the senseless fear that one day they would take it off the market. And she had even purchased those terrible aniseed-flavoured cigarettes. She would leave them, alight, in ashtrays around the rooms. But the alchemy hadn't worked. It was David's physical presence that had linked those smells indissolubly. It was his skin, his breath, his mood that made that union special.

After a long day's work, Sandra closed the apartment door behind her and waited a few seconds, motionless in the darkness. Then, at last, her husband's smell came to greet her.

She put the bags down on the armchair in the hall: she would have to clean the equipment, but for now she was putting everything off. She would see to it after dinner. In the meantime she ran herself a hot bath and lay in the water until her fingers became wrinkled. She put on a blue T-shirt and opened a bottle of wine. It was her way of escaping. She couldn't bear to switch on the television any more, and she didn't have the concentration necessary to read a book. So she spent her evenings on the sofa, with a bottle of Negroamaro in her hands and her vision gradually blurring.

She was only twenty-nine, and found it hard to think of herself as a widow.

The second lesson Sandra Vega had learned was that, like people, houses and apartments die.

Since David had died, she had never felt his presence in objects. Perhaps because most of the things here belonged to her.

Her husband had been a freelance photojournalist, and he had travelled the world in his work. Before meeting her he had never needed a home, making do with hotel rooms and other temporary accommodation. He had told her that in Bosnia once he had slept in a graveyard, inside a walled niche.

Everything that David owned was packed into two large green canvas bags. There was his wardrobe: some things for summer, others for winter, because he never knew where he might be sent for a story. There was the dented laptop that he never let out of his sight, and there were utensils of every kind: multi-use knives, batteries for his mobile phones, even a kit for purifying urine in case he ended up in a place without drinking water.

He had pared everything down to essentials. For example, he had never owned a book. He read a lot, but every time he finished one, he gave it away. He had only stopped since he had come to live with her. Sandra had created a space for him in the bookcase and he had started to warm to the idea of having a collection. It had been his way of putting down roots. After the funeral, his friends had come up to Sandra and each one had brought her a book that David had given to them. The books were full of his annotations, corners turned down to mark the page, little burns or oil stains. She imagined him calmly reading Calvino, smoking a cigarette in the burning heat of some desert, next to a broken-down off-road vehicle, waiting for someone to come and rescue him.

I'll continue to see him everywhere, they all said to her, it'll be difficult to shake off his presence. And yet it wasn't like that. She had never had the feeling she could hear his voice calling her name, nor had she ever unthinkingly put an extra plate on the table.

What she did miss, desperately, was the daily routine, those little, unimportant moments that had made up their lives.

On Sundays, she would usually get up after him and find him sitting in the kitchen, drinking his third pot of coffee and leafing through the newspaper in a cloud of aniseed-scented smoke, with his elbow placed on the table and the cigarette held between his fingers, the ash on the verge of falling, so absorbed in his reading as to forget everything else. As soon as she appeared in the doorway with her usual disapproving expression, he would lift his head with its mop of curly hair and smile at her. She would try to ignore him while she made breakfast for herself, but David would continue to stare at her with that goofy smile on his face until she couldn't hold out any longer. It was that crooked smile, the result of a broken incisor, a memento of falling from his bicycle when he was seven. It was his glasses, with their fake tortoiseshell frames held together with scotch tape, that made him look like an old English lady. It was David, who within a few moments would draw her on to his knees and place a damp kiss on her neck.

At that memory, Sandra put down the glass of wine on the table next to the sofa. She reached out an arm to pick up her mobile phone, then dialled voicemail.

The electronic voice informed her as always of the presence of one message, which she had already listened to. It was dated five months earlier.

'Hi, I called a couple of times but I always get the recorded message ... I don't have much time, so I just want to make a list of what I

39

miss . . . I miss your cold feet searching for me under the blankets when you come to bed. I miss you making me taste things from the fridge to make sure they haven't gone off. Or when you wake me up screaming at three in the morning because you've got a cramp. And I know you won't believe this, but I even miss you using my razor to shave your legs and then not telling me . . . Anyway, it's freezing cold here in Oslo and I can't wait to get back. I love you, Ginger!'

David's last words seemed to sum up a perfect harmony. The kind possessed by butterflies, snowflakes and a very small number of tap dancers.

Sandra switched off the phone. 'I love you too, Fred.'

Every time she listened to the message, she felt the same sensation. Nostalgia, grief, tenderness, but also anguish. A question was hidden in those last words, a question Sandra could not and would not answer.

It's freezing cold here in Oslo and I can't wait to get back.

She had been used to David's travelling. It was his work, his life. She had always known that. However much she might harbour the desire to hold him back, she had realised that she had to let him go.

It was the only way to make sure he came back to her.

His profession often took him to the most hostile places in the world. God alone knew how many times he had risked his life. But that was how David was, it was his nature. He had to see everything with his own eyes, touch it with his own hands. To describe a war, he needed to smell the smoke of burning buildings, to know that the sound of bullets is different depending on which objects they hit. He had never wanted to be exclusively tied to any of the great newspapers, although they would certainly have fought to get him. He couldn't bear the idea of anyone controlling him. And Sandra had learned to dismiss her worst fears, confining her anxiety to a place buried deep in her mind. Trying to live in a normal manner, pretending she was married to a clerk or a factory worker.

There had been a kind of unwritten pact between her and David. It entailed a series of strange courtship rituals, which were their way of communicating. So he might stay in Milan for long periods and they would start to have a stable married life. Then, one evening, she would return home and find him preparing his famous shellfish soup, the one with at least five varieties of vegetable, accompanied by salted sponge cake. It was his speciality. But in their code, it was also his way of telling her that he would be leaving the next day. They would have dinner as usual, talking of this and that, he would make her laugh and then they would make love. And the next morning she would wake up alone in bed. He might be away for weeks, sometimes months. Then one day he would open the door, and everything would start again from where they had left off.

David never told her where he was going. Except that last time.

Sandra emptied the glass of the remaining wine. She drank everything in one gulp. She had always avoided the thought that anything bad could happen to David. He ran risks. If he had to die, then it had to happen in a war or at the hands of one of those criminals he often investigated. It all seemed equally stupid to her, but she could accept it somehow. Instead, it had happened in the most banal way.

She was starting to doze off when her mobile phone rang. She looked at the screen, but did not recognise the number. It was nearly eleven o'clock.

'Could I speak to David Leoni's wife?'

It was a man's voice, speaking in a foreign accent, possibly German.

'Who is that?'

'My name's Schalber, I work for Interpol. We're colleagues.'

Sandra sat up, rubbing her eyes.

'I'm sorry to phone you so late, but I only just got your number.'

'Couldn't it have waited until tomorrow?'

There was a cheerful laugh at the other end. Schalber, whoever he was, had a curiously boyish voice. 'I'm sorry, I can't help it, whenever there's a question that's nagging at me, I have to ask it. Otherwise I might not sleep tonight. Doesn't that ever happen to you?'

Sandra didn't know what to make of the man's tone; she couldn't figure out if he was hostile or simply flippant. She decided to be businesslike. 'How can I help you?'

'We've opened a file on your husband's death and I need to clarify a few things.'

Sandra's face darkened. 'It was an accident.'

Schalber had probably been expecting this reaction. 'Yes, I read the police report,' he said calmly. 'One moment . . .'

Sandra heard the sound of pages being turned.

'It says here that your husband fell from the fifth floor of a building but survived the fall, dying many hours later from the fractures sustained and from internal bleeding . . .' He stopped reading. 'It must be hard for you, I imagine. It can't be easy to accept something like that.'

'You have no idea.' The words came out sounding cold, and Sandra hated herself as she said them.

'According to the police, Signor Leoni was on that construction site because it offered an excellent vantage point for a photograph.'

'Yes, that's right.'

'Have you been there?'

'No,' she replied irritably.

'I have.'

'What are you trying to tell me?'

Schalber's pause lasted a moment too long. 'Your husband's camera was destroyed in the fall. A pity we'll never see that photograph.' His tone was sarcastic.

'Since when has Interpol bothered with accidental deaths?'

'True, it's an exception. What I'm curious about is not so much the circumstances in which your husband died.'

'What, then?'

'There are some obscure aspects to the case. I found out that Signor Leoni's luggage was returned to you.'

'Yes, two bags.' She was starting to get annoyed, which she suspected was actually Schalber's intention.

'I put in a request to see them, but apparently I was too late.'

'Why would you want to see them? What possible interest could they have for you?'

There was a brief silence at the other end. 'I've never been married, but I came close to it a couple of times.'

'And how does that concern me?'

'I don't know if it concerns you, but I do think that when you trust your life to someone – I mean someone really special like a spouse ... well, you stop asking yourself certain questions. For example, what that person is doing every moment you're not together. Some people call it trust. The truth is that sometimes it's fear ... Fear of the answers.'

'And what kind of questions should I have asked myself about David, in your opinion?' But Sandra already knew the answer.

Schalber's tone turned solemn. 'We all have secrets, Officer Vega.'

'I didn't know every detail of David's life, but I knew the kind of person he was, and that's enough for me.'

'Yes, but did it ever occur to you that he might not always have told you the whole truth?'

Sandra was furious. 'Listen, it's pointless for you to try and make me doubt my husband.'

'Indeed it is. Because you already doubt him.'

'You don't know anything about me,' she protested.

'The bags that were sent back to you five months ago are being kept in a storeroom at Headquarters. Why haven't you collected them yet?'

Sandra smiled bitterly. 'I don't have to explain to anyone how painful it might be to see those things again. Because, when that happens, I'll have to admit that it really is all over, that David will never come back and that nobody can do anything about it.'

'That's bullshit and you know it.'

The man's lack of tact left her stunned. For a moment she couldn't say anything. When at last she was able to react, she did so angrily. 'Go fuck yourself, Schalber.'

She slammed the phone down, then grabbed the empty glass, which was the first thing to hand, and flung it at the wall. The man had no right! She'd been wrong to let him go on talking, she should have hung up sooner. She stood up and began pacing nervously about the room. Up until that moment she hadn't wanted to admit it, but Schalber was right: she was afraid. The phone call hadn't surprised her. It was as if part of her had expected it.

This is crazy, she thought. It was an accident. An accident.

Then she started to calm down. She looked around her. The corner of the bookcase with David's volumes. The boxes of aniseed-flavoured cigarettes piled up on the desk. The aftershave, now past its use-by date, on the shelf in the bathroom. The place in the kitchen where he read the newspaper on Sunday mornings.

The first lesson that Sandra Vega had learned was that houses and apartments never lie.

But people do.

It's freezing cold here in Oslo and I can't wait to get back.

That had been a lie, because David had died in Rome.

11:36 p.m.

The corpse woke up.

Around him, darkness. He felt cold, disorientated and scared. And this mixture of emotions was strangely familiar to him.

He remembered the gunshot, the smell of it, then the smell of burning flesh. The muscles yielding simultaneously, sending him crashing to the floor. He realised that he could reach out his hand, and he did so. He should have found himself in a pool of blood, but there wasn't one. He should have been dead, but he wasn't.

First of all, the name.

'My name is Marcus,' he told himself.

At that moment, reality attacked him, reminding him of the reasons why he was still alive. And of the fact that he was in Rome, in the place where he lived, lying on his own bed and that, until a few moments earlier, he had been asleep. His heartbeat had accelerated and refused to slow down. He was bathed in sweat and was breathing with difficulty.

But once again he had survived the dream.

To avoid the sense of panic, he usually kept the light on. But this time he had forgotten. Sleep must have taken him by surprise: he was still fully dressed. He switched on the light and checked the time. He had slept barely twenty-five minutes.

They had been sufficient.

He picked up the felt-tip pen he kept next to the pillow, and wrote on the wall: *Shattered windows.*

The white wall next to the camp bed was his diary. Around him, a bare room. This attic in the Via dei Serpenti was the place without memory in which he had chosen to live in order to be able to remember. Two rooms. No furniture, apart from the bed and a lamp. His clothes in a suitcase on the floor.

Every time he re-emerged from sleep he brought something with him. An image, a word, a sound. This time it was the noise of a window smashing.

But what window?

Still images of a scene, always the same one. He wrote everything on the wall. Over the past year he had put together a few details, but they still weren't enough for him to reconstruct what had happened in that hotel room.

He knew for certain that he had been there and that Devok, his best friend, the person who would have done anything for him, had been there, too. Devok had struck him as afraid and confused. He could not have said why, but it must have been something pretty dire. He remembered a sense of danger. Perhaps Devok had been trying to warn him.

But they had not been alone. There was a third person with them.

He was still an indistinct shadow. The threat came from him. It was a man, of that he was certain. But Marcus did not know who he was. Why was he there? He had a gun with him, and at a certain point he had taken it out and opened fire.

Devok had been hit. He had fallen, in slow motion. The eyes that had stared at him during the fall were already empty. His hands pressed to his chest, at the level of his heart. Gouts of black blood between his fingers.

There had been a second shot. And almost simultaneously, he had seen a flash. The bullet had hit him. He had distinctly felt the crack, the bone shattering, that foreign body penetrating his brain like a finger, the blood oozing, hot and oily, from the wound.

That black hole in his head had sucked everything out. His past, his identity, his best friend. But above all, his enemy's face.

Because what really tormented Marcus was his inability to remember the appearance of the person who had shot him.

Paradoxically, if he wanted to find him he had to avoid looking for him, because in order to see that justice was done it was necessary for him to go back to being the Marcus he once was. And, to succeed in that, he couldn't allow himself to think of what had happened to Devok. He had to start over from the beginning, and find himself again.

And the only way was to find Lara.

Shattered windows. He set aside the information and thought again about Clemente's last words. 'From now on, you're on your own.' There were occasions when he doubted that there was anyone else apart from the two of them. When Clemente had found him in that hospital bed – half dead and deprived of memory – and had revealed to him who he was, he hadn't believed him. It had taken time to get used to the idea.

'Dogs are colour blind,' he repeated, to convince himself that it was all true. Then he picked up the file on Jeremiah Smith – *c.g.* 97-95-6 – sat down on the bed and started studying the contents in search of anything that might lead him to the missing student.

He started with the potted biography of the killer. Jeremiah was fifty years old and unmarried. He came from a well-to-do middle-class family. His mother was Italian and his father English, both of them now dead. They had owned five draper's shops in the city, but had given up their commercial activities some time in the 1980s. Jeremiah was an only child, and had no close relatives. Having been provided with a respectable income, he had never worked. At this point, information about him petered out. The last two lines of the profile reported laconically that he lived in complete isolation in his villa in the hills outside Rome.

Jeremiah Smith struck Marcus as a fairly unremarkable person. Nevertheless, all the conditions were there for him to become what he was. His solitude, his emotional immaturity, and his inability to relate to his fellow men all worked against any desire he might harbour to have someone near him.

You knew that the only way to get a woman's attention was to kidnap her and keep her tied up, didn't you? Of course you did. What were you trying to gain, what was your purpose? You didn't take them to have sex with them. You didn't rape them, and you didn't torture them.

What you wanted from them was a sense of family.

These were attempts at forced cohabitation. You tried to make things work, to love them like a good little husband, but they were too scared to give you anything in return. You kept trying to be with them, but after a month you realised it wasn't possible. You realised that it was a sick, twisted kind of relationship, and that it existed entirely in your mind. And then – let's admit it   you were eager to put a knife to their throats. So in the end you killed them. But all the same, what you were searching for was love.

However coherent the idea might be, most people would have found it intolerable. Marcus, on the other hand, had not only grasped it but had even managed to accept it. He asked himself why, but couldn't give himself an answer. Was that also part of his talent? Sometimes, it scared him.

He went on to analyse Jeremiah's modus operandi. He had worked undisturbed for six years, killing four victims. Each had been followed by a lull, during which the memory of the violence perpetrated was sufficient for the murderer to keep the urge to kill again under control. When this beneficial effect faded, he started to hatch a new fantasy that led to a new kidnapping. It wasn't a plan, it was a genuine physiological process.

Jeremiah's victims were young women, aged between seventeen and twenty-eight. He sought them out in broad daylight. He approached them on some pretext or other, offered to buy them a drink, then put a drug in it: GHB, the date-rape drug. Once they were in a dazed state, it was easy to persuade them to follow him.

But why did the girls agree to have a drink with him?

That was what Marcus found strange. Someone like Jeremiah – a middle-aged man, far from handsome – should have made his victims suspicious of his real intentions. And yet the girls let him approach them.

47

They trusted him.

Perhaps he had offered them money or an opportunity of some kind. One of the techniques of luring women – much favoured by perverts and their kind – was to promise them a chance to earn some easy money, or to take part in a beauty contest, or to audition for a part in a film or a television programme. But such stratagems required a definite ability to socialise. That didn't tally with what was known of Jeremiah, who was antisocial, a hermit.

How did you trick them?

And why had nobody noticed him as he was approaching them? Before Lara, four young women had been abducted in public places and there had not been a single witness. And yet his courting of these women must have taken time. But maybe the question already contained the answer: Jeremiah Smith was so insignificant in other people's eyes as to be invisible.

You moved among them undisturbed. But you felt strong, because nobody could see you.

He thought again of the words on Jeremiah's chest. *Kill me.* 'It's as if he's telling us to look beyond appearances,' he had said to Clemente. 'The truth is written on the skin, it's within everyone's reach, hidden and yet close.'

You were like a cockroach scuttling across the floor during a party: nobody notices it, nobody's interested. All it has to do is take care not to be crushed. And you became good at that. But with Lara you decided to change. You took her from her own apartment, from her own bed.

Just thinking again about Lara, Marcus was assailed by a series of painful questions. Where was she now? Was she still alive? And if she was, what was she feeling? Was there water or food in her prison? How much longer could she hold out? Was she conscious or drugged? Was she injured? Had her captor tied her up?

Marcus cleared his head of these emotional distractions. He needed to remain lucid, detached. Because there had to be a reason why Jeremiah Smith had radically modified his own modus operandi when it came to Lara. Referring to Jeremiah, Clemente had expounded the theory that some serial killers change their methods as they go along, adding elements that increase their pleasure. So the abduction of the student could be considered a kind of variation on a theme. But Marcus didn't believe that: the change had been too drastic, too sudden.

Maybe Jeremiah had tired of resorting to that complex chain of deceptions to reach his goal. Or perhaps he knew that little game wouldn't work for much longer. One of the girls might have heard about the previous victims and could have unmasked him. He was becoming famous. The risk was increasing exponentially.

No. That's not why you modified your tactics. What makes Lara different from the others?

What complicated things was the fact that the four girls who had preceded her had nothing in common: neither their ages nor their looks. Jeremiah didn't seem to have a specific taste in women. The word that came to Marcus's mind was random. He had trusted to fate in choosing them, otherwise they would all have resembled one another. The more he looked at the photographs of the murdered women, the more convinced he was that the killer had chosen them simply because they were in an exposed position, which made them easier to approach. That was why he had taken them in broad daylight from public places. But he didn't know them.

Lara, though, was *special*. Jeremiah couldn't risk losing her. That was why he had taken her from her own home and, above all, why he had acted at night.

For a moment Marcus put down the file, got up from the camp bed, and went to the window. When evening fell, the uneven roofs of Rome were a turbulent sea of shadows. It was the time of day he preferred. A strange calm took possession of him, and he felt at peace. Thanks to this calm, Marcus realised where he was going wrong. He had visited Lara's apartment in daylight. But he ought to do it in the dark, because that was how her abductor had worked.

If he wanted to understand the man's mental processes, he had to reproduce the exact conditions in which Jeremiah had acted.

Marcus picked up his raincoat and rushed out of the attic. He had to go back to the building in the Via dei Coronari.

ONE YEAR EARLIER
PARIS

The hunter knew the value of time. His prime gift was patience. He knew how to wait, and in the meantime he prepared for the moment, savouring the anticipation of victory.

A sudden breeze lifted the tablecloth, making the glasses tinkle on the next table. The hunter lifted his pastis to his lips, enjoying the late afternoon sunshine. He watched the cars pass in front of the bistro. The hurrying pedestrians paid no attention to him.

He was wearing a blue suit with a blue shirt and tie, loosened in such a way as to make him look like an office worker stopping off for a drink on the way home. Knowing that solitary people attract attention, he had a small paper shopping bag on the seat next to him. A baguette, a clump of parsley and a tube of coloured sweets stuck out from the top of it. He would be taken for a family man. He was even wearing a wedding ring.

But he didn't have anyone.

Over the years he had reduced his needs to a minimum, and led a frugal life. He thought of himself as an ascetic. He had quashed every aspiration that was not useful to his one purpose, avoiding the distraction of desire. He needed only one thing.

His prey.

After all that time spent following him in vain, he had received information that suggested he was in Paris. Without waiting for confirmation, he had moved here himself. He needed to know his prey's new territory. He had to see what his prey saw, walk the same streets, experience the curious sensation that he might meet him at any moment, even if he didn't recognise him. He needed to know that they were both under the same sky. This excited him, made him think that sooner or later he would manage to flush him out.

To keep a low profile, he had changed accommodation every three weeks, always choosing smaller hotels or rented rooms, covering an ever broader area of the city.

For a while now he had been staying at the Hôtel des Saints-Pères, in the sixth arrondissement. In his room he had piles of newspapers that he had accumulated during that long period, all underlined feverishly in search of a clue – however remote – that might open a breach in that terrible wall of darkness and silence.

He had been in Paris for almost nine months, but had not made any progress. His confidence had wavered. But then, unexpectedly, the event he had been waiting for occurred. A sign. A clue that he alone could decipher. He had never given up, he had kept to the rules he had set himself, and now he was rewarded.

Twenty-four hours earlier, workers digging on a building site in the Rue Malmaison in Bagnolet had uncovered a body.

Male, aged around thirty, no clothes or personal objects. Death was believed to have occurred over a year earlier. While waiting for the results of the autopsy, nobody had asked too many questions. Given the amount of time that had elapsed, the police regarded it as a cold case. Any evidence – if there had ever been any – was now faded or compromised.

The fact that the discovery had been made on the outskirts of the city suggested a settling of accounts between drug gangs. In order not to draw the attention of the police, the perpetrators had taken the precaution of getting rid of the body.

The police were so used to that kind of thing, it didn't get them too excited. Even the one truly macabre aspect of the case, which should have set alarm bells ringing, hadn't aroused any suspicions.

The body didn't have a face.

It had not been an act of pure cruelty, or the final outrage visited on an enemy. All the muscles and bones of the face had been meticulously broken. Anyone taking so much care must have had a reason.

That was the kind of detail the hunter was always on the lookout for.

Since the day he had arrived in Paris, he had kept an eye on the bodies arriving at the morgues of the large hospitals. That was how he had learned of this discovery. An hour later, he had stolen a white coat and broken into the cold room of the Saint-Antoine hospital.

With a pad, he had taken the corpse's fingerprints. Back at the hotel he had scanned them and then hacked into the government databases. The hunter knew that every time a piece of information is put on the internet, it can't be removed. It's like the human mind: all it takes is one detail to reawaken the synapses and bring back things we thought we had forgotten.

The web never forgets.

The hunter had sat in the dark, waiting for the response, praying and thinking again about how he had got here. Seven years had passed since the first disfigured corpse in Memphis. That had been followed by Buenos Aires, Toronto and Panama. Then Europe: Turin, Vienna, Budapest. And finally, Paris.

These at least were the cases he had managed to identify. There might have been many more, which would never be discovered. These murders had taken place in such widely flung places and at such long intervals that nobody, apart from him, had linked them to a single perpetrator.

His prey was also a predator.

At first the hunter had assumed he was dealing with a 'pilgrim': a serial killer who travelled in order to conceal his crimes. If that were the case, he would only have needed to locate his base. Clearly, he was dealing with a Westerner, someone who lived in a large city. Pilgrims were socially integrated individuals, with families, children and enough money to afford frequent travel. They were clever, cautious, able to camouflage their movements as business trips.

But then he had noticed something about that chain of crimes, something that had escaped him at first but now threw a new light on everything.

The age of the victims was increasing.

That was when he had realised that the criminal mind he was dealing with was much more complex and terrifying than he had thought.

He was not killing and then leaving. He was killing and then staying.

That was why, here in Paris, this could finally be it, or it could turn out to be yet another failure.

After a couple of hours, a response had arrived from the government files. The faceless corpse found in Bagnolet had a criminal record.

He was not a drug dealer, but a normal man who had committed a youthful sin: at the age of sixteen he had stolen a model car, a Bugatti, from a shop for collectors. At that time, the police even took the fingerprints of minors. The charge had been withdrawn and the case had been closed, but although his file had been deleted from police records it had ended up in the archives of a government body that was carrying out a statistical investigation at the time into crimes committed by adolescents.

This time, his prey had made a mistake. The corpse without a face now had a name.

Jean Duez.

After this, it had been easy to discover the rest. Jean Duez was thirty-three years old and unmarried. He had lost both his parents in a road accident, and had no close relatives except for an elderly aunt in Avignon who suffered from Alzheimer's. He had set up a small business on the internet, working from home, selling model cars to collectors. Human relationships reduced to the minimum, no companion in his life, no friends. A passion for miniature racing cars.

Jean Duez was perfect. Nobody would notice his absence. Nobody would bother to look for him.

The hunter assumed that the previous victims had had similar profiles. Nondescript people, with no distinguishing features. Jobs that required no special gifts or abilities. A solitary life verging on the misanthropic, with no acquaintances and few human contacts. No close relatives, no family.

The hunter was impressed with his prey's cleverness. He might be committing the sin of pride, but he was pleased when the challenge was of such a high level.

He looked at his watch: it was almost seven. Regulars were starting to come into the bistro, having made reservations for early dinner. He signalled to a waitress that he wanted to pay. A boy was walking between the tables, selling the latest edition of the evening newspaper. The hunter bought one, although he knew that the news of the discovery of Jean Duez's body would not appear until the next day, which was why he still had an advantage over his prey. He was excited, the wait was finally over. The best part of the chase was about to begin. He only needed one thing to confirm it. That was why he was here, sitting in this bistro.

Again the breeze blew along the street, carrying with it a cloud of coloured pollen from the florist's stall on the corner. He didn't know spring in Paris could be so beautiful.

Then he felt a shudder. He had just seen his prey in the middle of the crowds emerging from the Metro. The man was wearing a blue anorak, grey velvet trousers, trainers and a small peaked cap. The hunter's eyes tracked him as he walked along the pavement on the other side of the street. The man was looking down, hands in his pockets; it hadn't occurred to him that there was someone pursuing him, so he wasn't taking any precautions. Excellent, the hunter said to himself as the prey walked calmly towards a green door in the Rue Lamarck.

The waitress approached with his bill. 'How was the pastis?'

'Very good,' he replied with a smile.

And as the hunter put his hand in his pocket to find his wallet, Jean Duez, unaware of his presence, entered the building.

The age of the victims is increasing, he kept telling himself. The hunter had cottoned on to his prey almost by chance: linking these faceless bodies spread around the world, he had realised that over the course of the years someone had taken over their lives. As the killer grew older, the age of the victims changed accordingly, as if he was changing his outfit.

His prey was a transformist.

He still did not know the reason why the man acted as he did, but he would soon – very soon – find out. The hunter took up a position a few yards from the green door, holding the paper shopping bag, waiting to take advantage of someone coming out in order to get inside the building.

At last he was rewarded. An elderly man in a heavy overcoat, a wide-brimmed hat and thick glasses appeared in the doorway. He had a brown cocker spaniel with him, and the dog was tugging at its leash, anxious to get to the little park nearby. The hunter put his hand out to stop the door from closing without the old man even noticing him.

The stairwell was dark and narrow. He stood there listening. The voices and other noises coming from the apartments mingled together in a single echo. He looked at the letter boxes: Jean Duez lived in Apartment 3Q.

He put the shopping bag down on the first step, took out the baguette and the clump of parsley, and recovered from the bottom of the bag the Barretta M92F, adapted as a tranquilliser gun by the American army, which he had bought from a mercenary in Jerusalem. In order for the tranquilliser to work immediately, you had to aim at the head, heart or groin. It took five seconds to expel the cartridge and recharge. It wasn't a long time, which meant that the first shot had to be accurate. It was quite likely that his prey also had a weapon, but with real bullets. The hunter did not care: the tranquilliser gun would be enough for him.

He wanted him alive.

He had not had time to study his prey's habits. But over the years, he had realised that his guiding principle was continuity. He would not stray far from the life he had assigned himself. If you scrupulously repeat your actions in a pre-established order, it's easier to remain inconspicuous and to control the situation: that, too, was something the hunter had learned from him. When you came down to it, his prey had become a kind of example to him. He had taught him the value of discipline and self-denial. He adapted to circumstances, even the most hostile. Like those organisms that live in the depths of the ocean, where no light penetrates and the cold and pressure would kill a man instantly. That was what the prey reminded him of. It was the only way of life he knew. The hunter actually admired him a little. Basically, his was a struggle for survival.

Clutching the tranquilliser gun, he ascended the stairs to the third floor. He came to a halt outside the door of Jean Duez's apartment and easily picked the lock. There was no sound but the ticking of a grandfather clock. The apartment was not very large, no more than eight hundred and fifty square feet, divided into three rooms plus bathroom. In front of him was a short corridor.

A light filtered from under the one closed door.

The hunter advanced, stepping carefully in order not to make a noise. He reached the first room. Rapidly, he moved to the doorway and aimed the gun inside. It was a kitchen, and it was empty. Everything was clean and tidy. The china on the dresser, the toaster, the dishcloth hanging from the oven handle. He felt a strange emotion, finding himself in the prey's lair, in contact with his world. He proceeded to the bathroom. There was nobody here either. White and green tiles in a chessboard pattern. A single toothbrush. A fake tortoiseshell comb. In the next room there was a large double bed with a brown satin quilt. A glass of water on the bedside table. Leather slippers. A wall of shelves filled with model cars: Jean Duez's passion.

The hunter left the bathroom and at last came to the closed door. He listened. There was no sound coming from the other side. He looked down at the floor. He could see the line of light below the door. But no shadows passed across it to show that there was someone there. What he did see on the floor was something he had never seen before.

A ring of small brown stains.

Blood, he thought. But now was not the time to become distracted. His prey was a ruthless, complex man, he could not forget that. However fascinated he might be by him, he knew there was a total lack of pity in the man's soul, and he had no desire to stand up to him in equal combat.

The only way was to act first, take him by surprise. The moment had come. The hunt was nearing its end. Only then would all this have a meaning.

He took a step back and kicked the door open. He aimed the tranquilliser gun, hoping to locate his target immediately. But he couldn't see him. The door bounced back on its hinges, and he had to put out his hand to stop it. He entered and looked rapidly around.

There was nobody in the room.

An ironing board. A cabinet with an old radio and a lighted lamp. A coat rack with some clothes hanging on it.

The hunter approached the rack. How was it possible? These were the clothes his prey had been wearing when he had seen him enter the building. The blue anorak, the grey velvet trousers, the trainers, the peaked cap. The hunter looked down and noticed the bowl in a corner.

The name *Fyodor* was written around the edge of it. He recalled the old man taking his cocker spaniel out for a walk.

Damn, he said to himself, but then, realising how cleverly he had been tricked, he burst into laughter. He had to admire the method the transformist had devised to trick anyone who might be after him. Every day he returned home, put on that disguise, and took his dog to the park. From there, he could keep an eye on the building.

That meant that Jean Duez – or, more precisely, the foul creature who had taken his place – now knew about him.

FOUR DAYS AGO

1.40 a.m.

After the storm, stray dogs had taken possession of the side streets in the historic centre. They moved about in silent packs, keeping close to the walls. Marcus saw a pack coming towards him as he walked along the Via Coronari. It was led by a red mongrel with one eye missing. For a moment their eyes met, and they recognised each other. Then they turned away again, each continuing on his way.

A few moments later, he again entered Lara's apartment.

In the dark, just like Jeremiah Smith.

He reached out a hand towards the light switch, but thought better of it. Lara's kidnapper had probably had a torch with him. So he took out the one he had in his pocket and began searching the apartment. In the beam of light, the furniture and fittings loomed up out of the shadows.

He didn't know exactly what he was looking for, but he was con-vinced that there was a connection between the young student and Jeremiah. Lara was much more than a mere victim, she was an object of desire. Marcus had to find out what linked them: that was the only way he could hope to discover where the girl was being kept prisoner. This was all speculation, but at the moment he couldn't rule anything out.

From the distance there came the barking of the stray dogs.

With that melancholy sound in the background, he began his exploration of the lower level, starting with the small bathroom that concealed the trapdoor beneath its floor. On the shelf next to the shower stood bottles of shower gel, shampoo and balm, all neatly lined up according to height. The same care was noticeable in the arrangement of the detergents next to the washing machine. Behind the mirror above the wash basin was a small cabinet containing cosmetics and toiletries. The calendar on the door was open at the page corresponding to last month.

The dogs outside started barking and growling, as if they had got into a fight.

Marcus returned to the small living room and kitchen. Before heading to the upper level, Jeremiah Smith had taken care to empty the sugar bowl on the table and the box on the shelf with the word SUGAR on it, in order to get rid of all traces of the drug. He had done everything calmly and unhurriedly. He wasn't taking any risks. With Lara asleep, he had all the time in the world.

You're good, you didn't make any mistakes, but there must be something. Marcus knew that the idea that serial killers were dying to reveal their work to the world and deliberately challenged their pursuers was just a fairy story, one circulated by the media to keep the public's attention alive. But serial killers did enjoy what they did. Which meant they wanted to continue doing it as long as possible. They weren't interested in fame – that would only be a hindrance – but they did sometimes leave signs. Not to communicate, but to share.

What did you leave for me? Marcus wondered.

He aimed his torch at the kitchen shelves. On one of them stood a line of cookery books. He imagined that Lara had never had to cook when she lived with her parents. As soon as she had moved to Rome, though, she had had to start looking after herself, which included learning to cook. But in among these volumes with their coloured spines, one stood out because it was black. Marcus went closer and bent his head to read the title. It was a Bible.

Anomalies, he thought.

He took it out and opened it at the page marked by a red satin bookmark. It was Paul's first epistle to the Thessalonians.

The day of the Lord will come like a thief in the night.

A macabre irony, and definitely not a coincidence. Had someone put the book there? The words referred to the day of judgement, but could also describe what had happened to Lara. Someone had carried her off. The thief, this time, had stolen a person. The young student had not been aware of the presence of Jeremiah Smith, moving around her like a shadow. Marcus surveyed his surround-ings: the sofa, the TV set, the magazines on the table, the refrigerator with the magnets, the worn parquet floor. This little apartment was the place where Lara had felt most secure. But that had not been enough to protect her. How could she have known that? Nature leads human beings to be optimists, he told himself. It's fundamental to the survival of the species to neglect potential dangers, apart from the most obvious.

We can't live in fear.

A positive vision is what keeps us going despite the setbacks and misfortunes that fill our lives. The sole disadvantage is that it tends to stop us seeing evil.

At that moment the stray dogs stopped barking, and he felt an icy tingle at the back of his neck: he had heard a new sound. An almost imperceptible creaking of the floorboards.

The day of the Lord will come like a thief in the night, he told himself, realising that it had been a mistake not to check the upper level first.

'Turn it off.'

The voice came from the stairs behind him and clearly referred to the torch he was holding. Without turning round, he did as he was told. Whoever it was had been here when he arrived. Marcus con-centrated on the silence around him. The man was no more than five or six feet from him. God alone knew how long he had been watching him.

'Turn around,' the voice ordered.

Marcus did so, slowly. The light from the courtyard filtered dimly through the bars over the window, projecting a cage-like pattern on the wall. Within it, enclosed like a wild beast, was a dark, threatening silhouette. The man was about eight inches taller than him, and solidly built. They both stood there motionless for a time, without speaking. Then the voice emerged again from the darkness.

'Is it you?'

From the timbre, he sounded little more than a boy. Marcus recognised anger in the tone, but also fear.

'It is you, you son of a bitch.'

He had no idea if this man was armed. He kept silent, letting him speak.

'I saw you come here with that other man yesterday morning.' Marcus guessed that he was referring to his first visit with Clemente. 'I've had an eye on this place for two days. What do you people want with me?'

Marcus tried to make sense of these words, but in vain. And there was no way to predict what would happen.

'Are you trying to rip me off?'

The shadow took a step towards him, and Marcus saw his hands: he wasn't carrying a weapon. 'I don't know what you're talking about.'

'You're fucking with me.'

'Maybe we should go somewhere else and discuss this calmly.'

'Let's talk about it now.'

Marcus decided to come out into the open. 'Are you here because of the missing girl?'

'I don't know anything about the girl, I had nothing to do with that. Are you trying to frame me, you bastard?'

Marcus sensed that he was genuine. If he was an accomplice of Jeremiah Smith, why run the risk of coming back?

Before Marcus could think of an answer, the stranger rushed at him, grabbed him by the collar and pushed him up against the wall. Pinning him there with one hand, he took out an envelope with the other and waved it under Marcus's nose. 'Are you the one who wrote me this fucking letter?'

'That wasn't me.'

'Then what are you doing here?'

First, Marcus needed to understand how this situation might be connected with Lara's disappearance. 'Let's talk about that letter if you like.'

But the young man had no intention of yielding control of the conversation. 'Did Ranieri send you? You can tell that bastard I'm through with him.'

'I don't know anybody called Ranieri, you have to believe me.'

He tried to get away, but the man was still holding him firmly. He hadn't finished with him yet.

'Are you a policeman?'

'No.'

'What about the symbol, then? Nobody knew about the symbol.'

'What symbol?'

'The one in the letter, you arsehole.'

The letter and the symbol: Marcus stored away this information. It wasn't much, but it might help him to understand the young man's intentions. Unless, quite simply, he was mad. He had to take charge of the situation. 'Forget about the letter. I don't know anything.'

'Who the fuck are you?'

Marcus did not reply, hoping he would calm down. Instead of which, he was thrown to the floor and found himself crushed beneath the other man's weight. He tried to defend himself, but the young man was pressing down on his chest and hitting him. He lifted his arms to protect his head, but the blows stunned him, and the taste of blood filled his mouth. He had the feeling he was about to lose consciousness, until he realised it was all over. From where he lay, he saw the young man opening the door of the apartment. For a moment he saw him from behind, framed in the light from the courtyard. Then the door closed, and he heard his steps quickly move away.

Marcus waited a while before trying to stand. He felt dizzy and his ears were whistling. He did not feel any pain. Not yet. It would come all at once, he knew, but it would take time. That was always how it happened. He would feel bad all over his body, even where he had not been hit. He did not remember what past experience that memory came from, but he knew that was how it was.

He lifted himself into a sitting position and tried to put his thoughts back into some kind of order. He had let the young man escape when he should have found a way to detain him. He tried to be lenient with himself, telling himself he wouldn't have been able to make him see reason anyway. And he had achieved one result, at least.

In the fight, he had got hold of the letter.

He groped on the floor for the torch, which had slipped from his hand earlier. He found it, gave it a couple of knocks to switch it on and aimed it at the envelope.

There was no sender indicated, but it was addressed to someone called Raffaele Altieri. The date on the postmark was three days earlier. Inside was a sheet of paper containing only the address of Lara's apartment in the Via dei Coronari. But what struck him was the symbol that seemed to serve as a signature.

Three small red dots forming a triangle.

6 a.m.

She hadn't slept. After Schalber's phone call, she had tossed and turned in bed for hours. Finally the alarm clock had told her that it was five o'clock and Sandra had got up.

She got ready in a hurry and called a taxi to take her to Headquarters: she didn't want any of her colleagues to spot her car. They certainly wouldn't have asked for an explanation, but for some time now she had been irritated by the way they looked at her. The widow. Was that what they called her? It was certainly the way they thought of her. Their compassion hit her like a nasty slap whenever they passed her. The worst of it was that some of them felt obliged to say something. She'd built up quite a collection of platitudes. The most popular was: 'Be brave, David would have wanted you to be strong.' She would have liked to record all of these phrases so that she could then demonstrate to the world that if there is anything worse than indifference to other people's grief it's the trite way most of us try to deal with it.

But maybe that was just her being over-sensitive. All the same, she wanted to get to the storeroom a fraction before the night shift ended.

It took her twenty minutes to reach her destination. En route, she dropped into the canteen for a takeaway croissant and cappuccino.

Her colleague was getting ready to leave. 'Hello, Vega,' he said, seeing her come in. 'What are you doing here at this hour?'

Sandra put on her sweetest smile. 'I brought you breakfast.'

His eyes lit up. 'You're a friend. It's been a busy night: they arrested a gang of Colombians who were dealing outside the Lambrate station.'

Sandra didn't want to get involved in a pointless conversation, so she came straight to the point. 'I'd like to pick up the bags I left here five months ago.'

Her colleague looked at her in surprise, but didn't hesitate. 'I'll fetch them.'

He disappeared into the depths of the storeroom. Sandra heard him muttering to himself as he searched. She was impatient, but tried to control herself. She had been extremely irritable lately. Her sister said that she was going through one of the four phases that follow the death of a loved one. She had seen that in a book, though she couldn't remember the sequence, which meant she couldn't tell Sandra which phase she was in now and if she'd soon have got through all of them. Sandra doubted she would, but she had let her talk. The same went for the rest of the family, none of whom really wanted to deal with what had happened to her. Not out of insensitivity, but because there wasn't really any advice you could give a twenty-nine-year-old widow. So they simply told her things they had read in magazines or cited the experience of a distant acquaintance. This was sufficient for them to feel they were doing the right thing, and that was fine with Sandra.

After five minutes, her colleague returned with David's two large bags.

He was carrying them by the handles, unlike David who always put them over his shoulders. One on the right, one on the left, which always made him sway as he walked.

'You look like a pack mule, Fred.'

'But you still love me, Ginger.'

As she had feared, the sight of those bags hit her like a punch in the chest. Her David was in those bags, they contained his whole world. If it had been up to her, they would have stayed in the

69

storeroom until someone had unthinkingly sent them to be pulped along with all the other things that had outlived their usefulness. But last night Schalber had given substance to the questions that had been clinging to her heart ever since she had discovered that David had lied to her. She could not allow anyone to harbour suspicions about her man – and that included her.

'Here they are,' her colleague said, placing the bags on the counter.

There was no need to sign a receipt. After all, they had been doing her a favour by keeping the bags there. They had arrived from Rome police headquarters after the accident, and she simply hadn't collected them.

'Do you want to check if anything's missing?'

'No, thanks. I'm sure everything's fine.'

But her colleague continued to stare at her, his expression suddenly sad.

Don't say it, she thought.

But he did. 'Be brave, Vega, Daniel would have wanted you to be strong.'

Who the hell was Daniel? she wondered, forcing herself to smile. Then she thanked him and walked out with David's bags.

Half an hour later, she was back home. She put the bags down on the floor by the door and left them there. For a while she stood at a certain distance from them, looking at them like a stray dog inspecting its food, trying to figure out whether it was suspect. What she was actually looking for was courage to confront the test. She walked towards the bags and then moved away again. She made herself some tea and sat on the sofa, cradling her cup and looking at the bags. For the first time, she realised what she had done.

She had brought David home.

In all those months, part of her may have hoped, imagined, believed that sooner or later he would come back. The thought that they would never again make love drove her crazy. There were times when she forgot that he was dead, something would come into her mind and she would say to herself, 'I have to tell David.' A moment later the truth would hit her, in all its bitterness.

David would never come back. Full stop.

Sandra remembered the day she had first been confronted with that reality. It had happened here, at the door of her apartment, on a quiet morning like this one. She had left the two policemen standing at the door, convinced that, as long as they remained there, as long as they did not cross that border, then the news of David's death would not materialise. And she would not have to face what was about to come into her house. A hurricane that would devastate everything, even though it left everything intact. She didn't think she could do it.

And yet here I am, she told herself. And if Schalber is interested in this luggage, there has to be a reason.

She put the cup of tea down on the floor and resolutely walked towards the bags. First she picked up the less heavy of the two: the one containing only clothes. She emptied it on to the floor. The shirts, trousers and sweaters tumbled out. The smell of David's skin overcame her, but she tried to ignore it.

God, how I miss you, Fred.

She held back her tears as she rummaged among the clothes in a desperate frenzy. Images came back to her of David wearing them, brief moments of their life together. She felt a mixture of nostalgia and anger.

There was nothing among these things. She even checked the pockets. Nothing.

She was exhausted. But the worst part was over. Now it was the turn of his work things. They represented the reason David was no longer here, but they weren't part of her memories. So looking through them ought to be easier.

First of all, she took out David's second camera. The other one had been broken in the fall. It was a Canon, whereas Sandra favoured a Nikon. They had had many lively discussions on the subject.

She activated it. The memory was empty.

She crossed the camera off the list and continued. She connected the various electronic devices to the mains, because the batteries had worn out in those months of inactivity. Then she checked through them. On the satellite phone the last call went back a very long way and was of no interest to her. The mobile phone she had already checked when she had gone to Rome to identify the body. David had used it only to book taxis and for the last telephone call he had made to her answering service: *It's freezing cold here in Oslo.* Otherwise, it was as if he had isolated himself from the world.

She switched on the laptop, hoping that here at least she would find something. But all the files seemed to be old and of no great consequence. Even the emails yielded nothing interesting or new. In none of his documents or messages did David make any reference to the reason he was in Rome.

Why maintain such a level of secrecy? she wondered. She was again assailed by the question that had kept her awake all night.

She could have sworn her husband was as honest as the day was long, but what on earth was he up to in Rome?

Go fuck yourself, Schalber, she repeated to herself. It was his fault she had all these doubts.

She went back to the bag and, putting aside whatever didn't seem to be of any interest for the moment, like the multi-use knife or the telefoto lenses, came across a leather-bound diary. It was worn at the edges and very old. Every year, David replaced only the central part of it. It was one of those objects he never let out of his sight. Like the brown sandals with the worn soles or that felt cardigan he wore whenever he wrote at the computer. Sandra had tried endlessly to get rid of them. For a few days he would pretend not to notice, but then would always somehow discover where she had hidden them.

She smiled at that memory. That was the way David was. Another man would have protested vociferously, but he never challenged her little abuses of power, just quietly went back to doing what he wanted.

Sandra opened the diary. On some of the pages corresponding to the period when David was in Rome, he had noted down one or two addresses. He had also marked the same addresses on a map of the city. In all, there were about twenty of them.

As she was pondering the meaning of these addresses, she noticed there was a new object in the bag, one not on the list. A two-way radio. She instinctively checked the frequency. Channel 81. It didn't mean anything to her.

What was David doing with a radio like that?

Searching through the remaining objects, she realised that something was missing: the little voice recorder David always carried with him. He called it his spare memory. Yet he hadn't had it with him when he had fallen. There were many ways it might have got lost, of course, but Sandra decided to make a note of it.

Before continuing, she quickly went over what she had discovered so far.

She had found some addresses in a diary, addresses that were also marked on a map of Rome. A two-way radio tuned to a mysterious frequency. And finally, the recorder that David used to make notes was missing.

As she turned these things over in her mind, looking for a logical connection between them, she was overcome with a sense of unease. After the accident, she had asked Reuters and the Associated Press – the agencies her husband usually worked for – if by any chance he was doing a job for them in Rome. Both had said no. Whatever he had been doing, he was doing it alone. Of course, it wouldn't have been the first time he had worked on a story then placed it afterwards with the highest bidder. But Sandra had the terrible feeling that this time there had been more to it. And she was not sure she wanted to discover what.

Dismissing these unpleasant thoughts, she again devoted herself to the contents of the bag.

From the bottom she extracted the Leica. This was an original camera from 1925, made by Oskar Barnack and developed by Ernst Leitz. It was the first truly portable camera. Given its extreme flexibility, it had made a revolutionary impact on war photography in particular.

It was a beautiful camera. A focal plane shutter, with a range from 1/20 to 1/500 of a second, and a fixed 50 mm lens. A real collector's item.

Sandra had given it to David for their first anniversary. She still remembered his surprise when he had unwrapped the package. With what they earned, they would never have been able to afford it. But Sandra had inherited it from her grandfather, who had passed his passion for photography on to her.

It was a family heirloom, and David never let it out of his sight. He called it his lucky charm.

But it didn't help to save your life, Sandra thought.

It was in its original leather case, on which she had had his initials – DL – inscribed. She opened it and sat looking at it, trying to recall the way David's eyes had shone like a child's whenever he handled it. She was about to put it away when she noticed that the screw that activated the shutter mechanism was in place. There was film in the camera.

David had used it to take photographs.

7.10 a.m.

They called them safe houses: apartments spread around the city, used for logistical support, as a temporary refuge or simply as places to have a bite to eat and relax a little. Next to the bell at the front door, there was usually the name of a non-existent business.

The apartment Marcus entered now was one he knew from having been there once with Clemente. It was Clemente who had revealed to him that they owned numerous properties in Rome. The key was hidden in a crack next to the door.

As Marcus had foreseen, the pain had started up at dawn. The attack he had suffered had certainly left its mark. Apart from a couple of bruises on his ribs that reminded him of what had happened last night with every breath he took, he had a broken lip and a swollen cheek. All of which, added to the scar on his temple, must have made him look very strange.

In a safe house you could usually find food, a bed, hot water, a first-aid kit, false documents, and a secure computer with which to connect to the internet. But the one Marcus had chosen was empty.

There was no furniture and the blinds were down. In one of the rooms there was a telephone on the floor.

The sole purpose of the place was to house that apparatus.

It was Clemente who had first pointed out to him that it wasn't advisable for them to own mobile phones. Marcus never left any traces behind.

I don't exist, he thought before calling an information service.

A few minutes later, a polite operator gave him the address and telephone number of Raffaele Altieri, the attacker who had surprised him in Lara's apartment. Marcus hung up and called the number. He let the phone at the other end ring for quite a while to make sure there was nobody at home. He decided it was safe to pay the young man a return visit.

Within a short time, he was standing in the pouring rain at the corner of the Via Rubens, in the posh Parioli neighbourhood, looking at a four-storey building.

He got in through the garage. The apartment that interested him was on the third floor. Marcus put his ear to the door, to make doubly sure it was temporarily uninhabited. There were no noises. He decided to risk it: he had to know who his attacker was.

He forced the lock and entered.

The apartment that greeted him was a large one. The furniture suggested both good taste and ready availability of money. There were antique pieces and valuable paintings. The floors were of clear marble, the doors lacquered in white. The most interesting thing about the place was that it did not seem like the home of a street tough.

Marcus started his search. He had to be quick, someone could come back at any moment.

One of the rooms had been fitted out as a gym. There was a bodybuilding bench with barbells, Swedish wall bars, a treadmill and various other kinds of gymnastic equipment. Raffaele Altieri obviously kept himself in shape. Marcus had felt the results of that passion on his own body.

The kitchen indicated that he lived alone. In the refrigerator, there was nothing but skimmed milk and energy drinks. On the shelves, tins of vitamins and boxes of vitamin supplements.

The third room was just as revealing of the kind of life the young man led. There was a single bed, neatly made. The sheets had images from *Star Wars* on them. On the wall behind the bed was a Bruce Lee poster. There were posters on the other walls, too, of rock groups and racing bikes. A stereo stood on a shelf and there was an electric guitar in a corner.

It was a teenager's room.

How old was Raffaele? Marcus wondered. He got his answer when he went into the fourth room.

A chair and a desk stood against one wall. They were the only furniture. On the opposite wall, a collage of newspaper articles. The paper was yellow with age, but they had been well preserved.

They went back nineteen years.

Marcus went closer to read them. They were arranged in chronological order from left to right.

There had been a double murder. The victims were Valeria Altieri, Raffaele's mother, and her lover.

Marcus lingered over the photographs accompanying the articles, photographs that had appeared not only in newspapers but also in gossip magazines.

The ingredients for gossip were certainly not lacking.

Valeria Altieri was beautiful, elegant, pampered, accustomed to luxury. Her husband was Guido Altieri, a well-known commercial lawyer, who was often abroad: rich, open-minded and very powerful. Marcus saw him in a photograph taken at his wife's funeral, looking serious and self-composed despite the scandal that had overwhelmed him, watching the coffin and holding the hand of his son Raffaele, who was three years old at the time. Valeria's erstwhile lover was a well-known yachtsman, the winner of numerous regattas. A kind of gigolo, some years younger than her.

The murders had created quite a stir, given the fame of those involved and also the manner in which they had been carried out. The lovers had been surprised as they lay in bed together. The police had established that there had been at least two people involved. But there had been no arrests, nor were there any suspects. The identity of the killers was never discovered.

Then Marcus spotted a detail that had escaped him at first reading. The murders had happened right here, in this apartment where Raffaele still lived at the age of twenty-two.

While his mother was being slaughtered, he had been asleep in his bed.

The killers had either been unaware of him or had decided to spare him. But the next morning, the child had woken up, gone into the other bedroom and seen the two bodies, which bore more than seventy stab wounds between them. Marcus could imagine him bursting into tears at the sight of horrors he could make no sense of at that age.

Valeria had sent the servants away in order to receive her lover, so the murders went undiscovered until her husband returned from a business trip to London.

The little boy had been alone with the bodies for two whole days.

However hard he tried, Marcus found it hard to imagine a worse nightmare. Yet something emerged now from the depths of his memory: a feeling of solitude and abandonment.

He did not know when he had experienced it, but it was present in him. His parents were no longer alive to tell him where the memory came from. He had even forgotten the pain of losing them. But maybe that was one of the few positive sides of his amnesia.

He concentrated again on his work, shifting his attention to the surface of the desk.

There were mountains of files. Marcus would have liked to sit down and go through them carefully. But there was no time. It would be risky to stay here much longer. So he made do with a superficial examination, leafing through them rapidly.

There were photographs, copies of police reports, evidence lists. These documents should not have been here. Together with notes of various kinds and personal reflections written by Raffaele Altieri himself, there were also reports from a private investigator. He noticed a business card from a detective agency.

The name on it was Ranieri.

It was a name Raffaele had mentioned last night: 'Did Ranieri send you? You can tell that bastard I'm through with him.'

Marcus slipped it into his pocket, then looked up again at the wall covered with articles and tried to take it all in at a single glance. It was obvious that a shrewd investigator could screw a lot of money out of a young man obsessed with a single, overriding idea.

Finding his mother's killers.

The cuttings, the reports, the papers were all evidence of an obsession. Raffaele wanted to give a face to the monsters who had defiled his childhood. Children have enemies made of air, dust and shadow, Marcus thought, the Bogeyman, the Big Bad Wolf. These monsters live in stories and come out only when they throw tantrums and their parents want to scare them. But then they always disappear, going back to the darkness that generated them.

Raffaele's monsters, though, had remained.

There was one last detail that Marcus had to check. He started looking for anything that might throw light on the symbol: the three little red dots at the bottom of the letter summoning Raffaele to Lara's apartment.

'What about the symbol, then?' Raffaele had said. 'Nobody knew about the symbol.'

In the files, Marcus managed to find a document from the prosecutor's department that mentioned it specifically, although there seemed to be some omissions. There was an explanation for that: the police often concealed certain details of a case from the press and the public. That helped to prevent false testimonies from the kinds of cranks who confessed to every crime, but also to make the guilty parties believe they were in the clear. In the case of the murder of Valeria Altieri, something important had been discovered at the scene of the crime. An element that the police, for some reason, had decided not to reveal.

Marcus still didn't know what any of this had to do with Jeremiah Smith or Lara's disappearance. The crime was nineteen years old and, even if there had been clues not picked up by the police at the time, they would be impossible to recover now.

The crime scene was gone for ever.

He looked at his watch: twenty minutes had already passed, and the last thing he wanted was another close encounter with Raffaele.

But he decided it was worth taking at least a quick look at the bedroom in which Valeria Altieri had been killed.

When he opened the door, he realised immediately that he had been wrong about the crime scene being gone.

The first thing he saw was the blood.

The double bed with the blue sheets was drenched in it. There was so much of it, you could see exactly how the victims had been positioned during the murder. The mattress and pillows still bore the shapes of their bodies. Lying side by side, locked in a desperate embrace, unable to resist the homicidal rage unleashed on them.

From the bed, the blood had overflowed like lava on to the white carpet, soaking the fibres, colouring them a red so glossy, so sumptuous, as to clash with the very idea of death.

The blood had hit the walls, too, but what was most striking was how neatly and coherently the stains seemed to be arranged, as if that frenzied attack had produced a strange harmony.

And some of the blood had also been used to write on the wall over the bed. A single word, in English.

EVIL

Everything now was fixed, motionless. But it was also startlingly vivid and real, as if the murders had just taken place. Marcus felt as though, merely by opening that door, he had taken a journey back in time.

It isn't possible, he said to himself.

There was no way the room could have been preserved exactly as it had been on that tragic day nineteen years earlier.

There was only one explanation, and he found confirmation for it in the paint pots and brushes in a corner of the room, as well as in the forensic photographs Raffaele had somehow got his hands on, showing the actual scene: the scene as encountered by Guido Altieri, returning home on a quiet March morning.

Subsequently, everything had been altered. By the intervention of the police, but also by whoever had immediately afterwards cleaned

79

everything, trying to wipe out all memory of the horror and restore the place to its original state.

That always happens when there has been a violent death, Marcus told himself. The bodies are taken away, the blood dries, and life returns to normal.

Nobody wants to preserve those memories. Not even me, he thought.

Raffaele Altieri, though, had decided to faithfully reproduce the scene of the crime. Pursuing his own obsession, he had built a shrine to the atrocity. And in trying to enclose the evil within that shrine, he himself had been imprisoned by it.

But at least this faithful reproduction gave Marcus the opportunity to examine it and look for the anomalies he needed. So he made a belated sign of the cross and went in.

As he approached what looked like a sacrificial altar, he understood why the slaughter must have been carried out by at least two people.

The victims were to be allowed no escape.

He tried to imagine Valeria Altieri and her lover, surprised by that inhuman violence. Had she screamed, or had she held back in order not to wake her little son, who was asleep in the next room, and stop him running in to see what was happening?

At the foot of the bed, on the right, a pool of blood had formed, while to the left Marcus noted three small circular marks.

He bent down to get a better look. They formed a perfect equilateral triangle. Each side measuring roughly twenty inches.

The symbol.

He was considering the possible meanings of that sign, when, looking up for a moment, he saw something he had not noticed at first glance.

There on the carpet were the prints of small bare feet.

He imagined the three-year-old Raffaele putting his head in at the door of that room the morning after the massacre, seeing that horror and being unable to understand the meaning of it. He saw him running to the bed, dipping his feet in the pool of blood as he did so, and desperately shaking his mother, trying to wake her.

Marcus could also imagine his little body on the blood-soaked sheets: after crying for hours, he must have huddled by his mother's body and, exhausted, have fallen asleep.

He had spent two days in this apartment before his father had found him and taken him away. Two days and two very long nights, confronting alone whatever lurked in the darkness.

Children don't need memories, they learn by forgetting.

Those forty-eight hours, on the other hand, had been sufficient to mark the existence of Raffaele Altieri for ever.

Marcus could not move. He started taking deep breaths, fearing a panic attack. Was this his talent, then? To understand the obscure messages that evil left in objects? To listen to the silent voices of the dead? To witness the spectacle of human wickedness, powerless to intervene?

Dogs are colour blind.

That was why only he had understood something the world did not know about Raffaele. That three-year-old boy was still asking to be saved.

9.04 a.m.

'There are things you have to see with your own eyes, Ginger.'

Those were the words David always used whenever a discussion arose about the risks of his work. For Sandra, the camera was a necessary refuge, to lessen the impact of the violence she documented every day. For him, it was merely an instrument.

That distinction had occurred to her as she put together a makeshift darkroom in the bathroom of her apartment, as she had seen David do many times.

She had sealed the door and window, replacing the small light over the mirror with one that emitted a non-actinic red light. She had recovered the enlarger from the attic and the tank for developing and fixing negatives. For the rest, she had improvised. The three small basins she would use for the processing were those she washed her underwear in. From the kitchen she had taken pliers, scissors and a ladle. The photographic paper and chemical products, which she put to one side, had not yet reached their expiry date and were still usable.

The Leica I used 35 mm film. Sandra rewound the roll and took it out of its compartment.

The operation she was about to carry out required absolute darkness. After putting on gloves, she opened the spool and extracted the film. Relying on her memory, she cut the initial part with the scissors, rounding the corners, then slipped it into the spiral of the tank. She poured the developing liquid, which she had previously prepared, and started calculating the times. She repeated the operation with the fixing liquid, then rinsed everything under the running water, put a few drops of colourless shampoo in the tank, because she did not have absorbent, and finally placed the roll to dry on the bath.

She started the timer on her watch and leaned back against the tiled wall. She sighed. This wait in the darkness was nerve-wracking. She wondered why David had used that old camera. Part of her hoped that there was no particular significance to it, that the sole reason she was placing so much importance on it was because she couldn't resign herself to his senseless death.

David only used the Leica to try it out, she told herself.

Even though photography was their passion and their work, there were no photographs of the two of them together. Every now and again, she reflected on this. It hadn't seemed so strange when her husband was alive. They hadn't felt the necessity. When the present is so intense, you don't need a past. She had never thought she ought to be hoarding memories because she would need them one day to survive. But now, as time went on, her stock of memories was dwindling. The time they had spent together had been too short compared to the time that, statistically, she still had to live. What would she do with all those days? Would she ever again be capable of feelings as strong as those she had felt for him?

The sound of the timer roused her. At last she could switch on the red light. First she took the roll that she had hung and viewed it against the light.

Five photographs had been taken with the Leica.

At the moment, she couldn't make out their contents. She made haste to print them. She filled the three containers. The first with the developer, the second with water and acetic acid for the stop bath, the third with the fixer, also diluted in water.

Next she used the enlarger to project the negatives on to photographic paper until they were imprinted. Then she immersed the first sheet in the basin with the developer. She gave it a gentle shake and, gradually, the image began to appear in the liquid.

But it was too dark to see anything in it.

Maybe David had made a mistake while taking the shot. She bathed it in the other two containers anyway, then hung it over the bath with a clothes peg. She did the same with the other negatives.

The second photograph showed David bare-chested, reflected in a mirror. With one hand he was holding the camera in front of his face and with the other he was waving. But he wasn't smiling. On the contrary, his expression was serious. Behind him there was a calendar, and the month displayed was the one in which he had died. This might well be the last image of David when he was still alive, Sandra thought.

The grim farewell of a ghost.

The third photograph was of a building site. She could see the bare pillars of a building under construction. The walls were missing and the area around it was empty. This might have been taken in the building from which David had fallen, she thought, although obviously before his death.

Why had he gone there with the Leica?

David's accident had happened at night. This picture, on the other hand, had been taken by day. Perhaps he had been reconnoitring the place.

The fourth photograph was very strange. It was of a painting — seventeenth century, she thought. But she was sure it was only part of a larger canvas. It showed a child, moving his body as if on the verge of running, but with his head still turned, incapable of averting his gaze from something that both terrified and attracted him. He had a stunned expression, his mouth wide open in astonishment.

Sandra was convinced she had seen this image before. But she could not remember what the painting was. She recalled Inspector de Michelis's passion for art: she would ask him.

Of one thing she was certain: the painting was in Rome. And it was there that she had to go.

Her shift was due to begin at two in the afternoon, but she would ask for a few days off. After David's death, she hadn't taken the compassionate leave she was entitled to. If she took an express train, she would be there in less than three hours. She wanted to see with her own eyes, as David used to say. She felt the need to understand, because now she was certain that there was an explanation.

She planned the journey in her head as she printed the final photograph in the roll. The first four had provided nothing but questions, to be added to all the unanswered questions she had accumulated up until now.

Maybe there was some kind of answer in the fifth photograph.

She treated it with particular delicacy as the image emerged on the paper. A dark stain on a clear background. It became clearer, one detail at a time. Like a wreck gradually re-emerging from the bottom of the sea after having spent decades in absolute darkness.

It was a face, in profile.

The person had clearly not realised that someone was photographing him. Did he have anything to do with what David was doing in Rome? Might he even be involved in his death? Sandra knew she would have to find this person.

Hair as black as the clothes he wore. Sad, evasive eyes.

And a scar on his temple.

9.56 a.m.

Marcus let his gaze wander over the view of Rome from the terrace of the castle. Behind him rose the Archangel Michael, his wings unfolded and his sword unsheathed, watching over human beings and their infinite miseries. To the left of the bronze statue, the bell

84

of mercy, whose tolling had announced executions during the dark days when the Castel Sant'Angelo was the papal prison.

This place of torture and despair had become a magnet for tourists. Here they all were now, happily snapping away, taking advantage of the sliver of sun that had peeped out from behind the clouds and was shining down on the rain-washed city.

Clemente joined Marcus and stood by his side without taking his eyes from the view. 'What's happening?' he asked.

They used voicemail to make appointments. When one of the two wanted to see the other, all they needed to do was leave a message with the time and place indicated. Neither had ever missed any of these appointments.

'The murder of Valeria Altieri,' Marcus said.

Before replying, Clemente looked at his swollen face. 'Who did that to you?'

'I met her son Raffaele last night.'

Clemente shook his head. 'A nasty business. The crime was never solved.'

He said it as if he knew the case well, which seemed somewhat odd to Marcus, given that at the time of the events his friend must have been little more than ten years old. There could only be one explanation: *they* had dealt with it.

'Is there anything in the archive?'

Clemente didn't like it being mentioned in public. 'Careful,' he said.

'This is important. What do you know?'

'There were two lines of inquiry the police followed. Both involved Guido Altieri. When an adulterous wife is murdered, the first suspect is always the husband. Guido had the contacts and the resources. If he'd wanted someone to kill her for him, he could have done so and got away with it.'

But if Guido Altieri was guilty, he had knowingly left his son with the corpses for two days merely to strengthen his own alibi. Marcus found that hard to believe.

'And the second line of inquiry?'

'Altieri is a big wheel in finance. At the time he was in London, finalising an important merger. In fact, there were some pretty dubious elements to the business – something to do with oil, and also something to do with arms. There were important interests involved. The English word "Evil", written over the bed, could be interpreted as a message for Altieri.'

'A warning.'

'Well, the killers did spare his son.'

Some children ran past Marcus, and he followed them with his eyes, envying their ease and self-confidence.

'How come the two lines of inquiry didn't lead anywhere?'

'As far as the former is concerned, Guido and Valeria Altieri were on the verge of divorcing anyway. She was too free with her favours: the yachtsman was only the latest in a long line. The lawyer can't have been too grief-stricken, given that he remarried a few months after the murders. He has another family now, other children. And besides, let's admit it, if someone like Altieri had wanted to get rid of his wife, he would have chosen a less cruel method.'

'And Raffaele?'

'He hasn't spoken to his father in years. From what I understand, the boy is mentally disturbed, forever in and out of psychiatric clinics. He blames his father for what happened.'

'And the second line of inquiry, that it was a warning from someone who knew about his shady dealings?'

'They pursued it for a while, but there was no evidence.'

'Weren't there any prints, any clues at the scene of the crime?'

'It may have looked like a frenzied attack, but the killers did a clean job.'

Even if they hadn't, Marcus thought, the murders had happened at a time when forensics still used outdated methods and DNA analysis was not in general use. In addition, the crime scene had been contaminated by the presence of the child for forty-eight hours, and then wiped out forever. He thought again of the replica that Raffaele Altieri had constructed in the hope of finding an answer.

'There was a third line of inquiry, wasn't there?'

Marcus was guessing: why else would *they* have shown an interest in the case? He didn't understand why his friend had not mentioned it. And in fact, Clemente immediately tried to change the subject. 'What has this got to do with Jeremiah Smith and Lara's disappearance?'

'I don't know yet. Raffaele Altieri was in Lara's apartment last night. Someone sent him a letter telling him to go there.'

'Who?'

'I have no idea, but in the apartment I found a Bible among the cookery books. It was an anomaly I hadn't spotted during the first inspection. Sometimes you need darkness to see things better: that's why I went back to the apartment last night. I wanted to reproduce the same conditions in which Jeremiah had acted.'

'A Bible?' Clemente echoed, uncomprehending.

'There was a bookmark indicating St Paul's Epistle to the Thessalonians: "The day of the Lord will come like a thief in the night ..." If it wasn't absurd, I'd say someone put that message there for us, specifically so that we should meet Raffaele Altieri.'

Clemente stiffened. 'Nobody knows about us.'

'Of course not,' Marcus said. Nobody, he repeated to himself bitterly.

'We don't have much time to save Lara, you know that.'

'You told me I'm the only person who can find her, and that I should follow my instincts. That's what I'm doing.' Marcus had no intention of letting go. 'Now tell me about that other line of inquiry. At the crime scene, apart from the word "Evil", there were also three circular marks in the pool of blood, arranged in the shape of a triangle.'

Clemente turned towards the bronze archangel, almost as if to invoke its protection. 'It's an occult symbol.'

It was hardly surprising that the police had decided to omit that detail from the files, Marcus thought. The police were practical people, they didn't like cases that touched on the world of the occult. It wasn't an easy subject to bring up in a court of law, and could easily give a defendant the chance to claim mental illness. Not to mention the fact that it could make the police look bad.

But Clemente clearly took the matter seriously. 'According to some,' he said, 'a ritual was celebrated in that bedroom.'

Crimes linked to the occult were precisely the kind of anomalies *they* dealt with. While waiting for Clemente to procure the file on the Altieri case from the archive, Marcus was anxious to understand the meaning of the triangular symbol, so he had gone to the one place where he might find the answer.

The Biblioteca Angelica was located in a former Augustine monastery in the Piazza Sant'Agostino. The monks had been collecting, cataloguing and preserving since the seventeenth century, amassing some two hundred thousand precious volumes that had formed the basis of the first ever public library in Europe.

Marcus was sitting at one of the tables in the reading room – known as the Salone Vanvitelliano, after the architect who had renovated the complex in the eighteenth century – surrounded by wooden shelves crammed with books. You gained access to it through a vestibule adorned by portraits of members of the Arcadian Academy. It was here that that the catalogues were kept. A little further on was the strongroom that contained the most valuable miniatures.

Over the course of centuries, the Biblioteca Angelica had been involved in various religious controversies, due to the fact that its collections contained a large number of banned texts. These were the ones that interested Marcus, who had asked to examine some volumes on symbology.

He put on a white cotton glove, because contact with acids in the skin could damage the older books. The sound of hands turning pages, a sound like the beating of a butterfly's wings, was the only noise in the room. At the time of the Inquisition, Marcus would have paid with his life for reading these texts. In one hour of research, he managed to trace the origin of the triangular symbol.

Seen as the opposite of the Christian cross, it had quickly become the emblem of a number of Satanic cults. Its creation went back to the time of the Emperor Constantine's conversion. The Christians stopped being persecuted and abandoned the catacombs. The pagans, on the other hand, took refuge there.

Marcus was surprised to learn that it was from this old paganism that modern Satanism derived. Over the course of centuries, the figure of Satan had replaced the other deities, because he was the principal antagonist of the Christian God. The followers of these cults were regarded as outlaws. They met in isolated places, usually in the open air. They traced the walls of their temple on the ground with a stick, making it easy to erase them if they were discovered. The killing of innocents was used to seal pacts of blood between the followers. But, as well as possessing a ritualistic purpose, it also had a practical one.

If I make you kill someone, Marcus thought, you are bound to me for life. Anyone leaving the sect risked being denounced as a murderer.

In the catalogue he had found books that explained the historical evolution of these practices, right up to the present day. As these were recent publications, he took off the glove.

In a volume on criminology, he learned that there were many murders with a Satanic element. In most cases, though, Satanism was merely a pretext for sexual perversions. Some psychopathic killers claimed that a superior force was trying to communicate with them. Indulging in a ritual of blood was a way of responding to the call. The corpses became messengers.

The best-known case was that of David Richard Berkowitz – best known as the Son of Sam – the serial killer who had terrorised New York at the end of the 1970s. When they finally captured him, he told the police that he had been ordered to kill by a demonic presence speaking to him through his neighbour's dog.

Marcus ruled out the idea that the murder of Valeria Altieri was a pathological crime. There had been more than one perpetrator, which suggested that the killers were in full possession of their mental capacities.

Group homicides, however, were a constant in cases of Satanism. In a group, individuals often found the courage to carry out heinous acts of which they would not otherwise have been capable. Acting in concert helped to overcome the normal inhibitions, and when responsibility was divided there was less of a sense of guilt.

There was also so-called 'acid Satanism', among whose followers drug use was common. Such groups were easily recognisable by their clothes, which made extensive use of the colour black and Satanic symbols. Their inspiration came less from sacrilegious texts than from heavy metal music.

The word EVIL on the wall of Valeria Altieri's bedroom could point to this kind of thing, Marcus thought. But it was rare for such groups to go as far as murdering human beings: they usually limited themselves to sacrificing poor animals in their imitation black masses.

True Satanism was not so overtly dramatic. It depended on total secrecy. There was no actual evidence of its existence, only deceptive and contradictory clues. There were, though, a few cases of Satanic murders not attributable to fanatics or mentally ill people, and it was here in Italy that the most famous of these had taken place: the so-called Monster of Florence case.

Marcus read a brief summary of the case. Having realised that the eight double homicides that had taken place between 1974 and 1985 were the work not of a single hand but of a group of killers, the police had arrested the culprits, but had stopped there, even though there was a suspicion that the murders had been ordered by members of some kind of unidentified sect. The theory was that the purpose of the killings was to procure human body parts to be used in rituals.

Marcus found a passage in this account that he thought might turn out useful. It was in reference to the Monster of Florence's motive for always killing young couples. The most favourable death was that which came during orgasm, which was termed *mors justi*. The belief was that at that precise moment, certain energies were unleashed that were capable of increasing and reinforcing the effects of a malign ritual.

In some cases, the murders occurred on dates that preceded Christian festivals, with a preference for nights when there was a new moon.

Marcus checked the date of the murders of Valeria Altieri and her lover. They had occurred on the night of 24 March, the eve of the Annunciation. And it was a new moon.

The elements of a Satanic crime were all there. In the light of this information, Marcus would have to reopen an investigation that had been closed nearly twenty years before. He was convinced that someone who knew a lot had chosen to keep quiet over the years. He searched in his pocket and found the business card that he had taken from Raffaele Altieri's desk.

He would begin with Ranieri, the private detective.

Ranieri had an office on the top floor of a small building in the Prati area. Marcus watched as the detective got out of a green Subaru. He was much older than the photograph on his agency's website. It had struck Marcus as strange that someone doing a job based on discretion should display his own face to the world. But presumably Ranieri didn't care.

Before following him inside the building, Marcus noticed that the parked car was spattered with mud. Despite the constant rain of the last few hours, it was unlikely that it had got that way in Rome. He deduced that the detective had been outside the city.

The doorman of the building was intent on reading a newspaper and Marcus passed him undisturbed. Ranieri had avoided the lift, maybe not wanting to wait for it. Judging by the way he was climbing the stairs, he seemed to be in a great hurry.

As he entered his office, Marcus stopped on the first floor, where there was a recess in which he could hide and wait for the man to come out again. He would then get into the office and try to find out why he was in such a rush.

While he had been carrying out his research in the library that morning, Clemente, as promised, had acquired the file on the case for him – code number *c.g.* 796-74-8. It contained a detailed dossier on all the protagonists involved in the affair. He had left it for him inside a letter box in a large block of flats. It was a place they always used for exchanging documents: that particular box was not assigned to any of the occupants of the block.

Marcus had had plenty of time to study Ranieri's profile while waiting for the detective to arrive.

Ranieri did not have much of a reputation. But that was hardly surprising. He had been suspended from the list of licensed investigators for improper conduct. Apparently, this was not his only occupation: in the past he had taken part in various scams, and had even done time in prison for passing false cheques. His best client was Raffaele Altieri, from whom, over the years, he had managed to obtain a considerable amount of money, although their relations had broken off abruptly. The office in the wealthy Prati neighbourhood was a facade to attract unknowing clients he could exploit. He did not even have a secretary.

It was as Marcus was going over these things in his mind that a woman's scream echoed down the stairwell. It seemed to come from the top floor.

His training was clear: in cases such as this, he should leave immediately. Once in a safe place, he would be able to alert the police. The most important thing was anonymity, which had to be preserved at all costs.

I don't exist, he reminded himself.

He waited to see if anybody in the building had heard anything. But nobody appeared on the landings. Marcus couldn't help it: if a woman really was in danger, he would never forgive himself for not intervening. He was about to go up to the top floor when the door of the office opened and Ranieri started down the stairs. Marcus took shelter in the recess and the man passed without noticing him. He was carrying a leather briefcase.

When Marcus was sure that Ranieri had left the building, he raced up the stairs, hoping he was still in time.

When he reached the landing, he launched a kick at the door of the office. He found himself in a narrow waiting room. At the end of the corridor was a single room. Marcus rushed in that direction. When he got to the doorway, he stopped. He could hear a knocking sound from inside. He leaned in cautiously and saw that it was just an open window banging in the wind.

No woman.

But there was a second door, which was closed. He approached cautiously. He placed his palm on the handle and opened it abruptly, sure he would be faced with some terrible scene. It was nothing but a small bathroom. And it was empty.

Where was the woman he had heard screaming?

The doctors had warned him about auditory hallucinations. A side effect of his amnesia. It had happened before. Once he had thought he heard a telephone ringing incessantly in his attic room in the Via dei Serpenti. But he didn't have a phone. On another occasion, he had heard Devok calling him by name. He didn't know if it was really his voice, as he couldn't remember what it sounded like. But he had linked the sound to Devok's face, which gave him hope that one day his memory might come back. The doctors said no, amnesia linked to brain damage is always irreversible, and his wasn't a psychological condition. He still believed, though, that he might eventually retrieve some hidden, ancestral memories.

He took a deep breath, trying to get the woman's scream out of his ears. He had to figure out what had happened in that room.

He went to the open window of the office and looked down: the space where Ranieri had parked his green Subaru was empty. The fact that he had taken the car meant that he wouldn't be back soon, so Marcus had a little time.

He noticed an oil stain on the asphalt. Added to the mud he had noticed on the bodywork of the car earlier, it suggested that some time that morning Ranieri had been somewhere where the ground was uneven, soiling and damaging the Subaru in the process.

He closed the window and turned to the office.

Ranieri had stayed barely ten minutes. What had he come to do?

There was one way to find out. Marcus had a very clear memory of one of Clemente's lessons. Criminologists and profilers called it the enigma of the empty room. It started with the assumption that every event, even the most insignificant, left traces which, as the minutes passed, lost their latency. That was why, even if this place might seem empty, it wasn't. It contained a lot of information. Marcus, though, didn't have much time to locate the clues and use them to reconstruct what had happened.

The first approach was visual. So he looked around. A half-empty bookcase, with ballistics magazines and law books. Judging by the dust that covered them, they were there purely for appearance. A threadbare sofa, a couple of small armchairs in front of a desk with a swivel chair.

He noted also the anachronistic combination of a plasma television and an old video recorder. He didn't think anyone still used video recorders, and despite its presence he noticed that there were no videocassettes in the room.

He registered the detail and went on. Diplomas on the walls showing that he had taken part in specialist courses in investigative techniques. An out-of-date licence, hanging lopsidedly. Marcus moved it and discovered a small safe behind it, its door not fully shut. He opened it. The safe was empty.

He thought again of the leather briefcase Ranieri had been carrying when he left the office. He must have taken something with him. Money? Was he running away? From whom, from what?

He next considered the state of the place. When he had arrived, the window was open. Why had Ranieri left it that way?

To let some air into the room, he told himself. He sniffed. There was a slight but peculiar smell of burning. Chlorophyll, he thought. He rushed to the waste-paper basket.

There was a single sheet, crumpled by fire.

Ranieri had not only taken an item from the office, he had also got rid of something before he left. Marcus recovered what remained of the piece of paper from the bottom of the basket and placed it carefully on the top of the desk. He went back to the bathroom, checked the label on a bottle of liquid soap, and took it into the office. He poured some on his fingertips and, unfolding the sheet of paper as best he could, ran them over the darkest part, where there were traces of handwriting. Then he took a match from a box on the desk – Ranieri had probably taken one from the same box earlier – and got ready to set fire to the sheet. Before doing so, however, he stopped to think. He would have one chance at this, then everything would be destroyed forever.

Apart from the migraines, the sound hallucinations and the sense of confusion, the amnesia had produced at least one advantage: it had given him remarkable mnemonic skills. Marcus was convinced that his ability to learn and absorb things quickly was due to the empty space in his head. And he had realised that he also possessed a perfect photographic memory.

Let's hope it works, he told himself.

He struck the match, took the sheet of paper and passed it under the flame, from left to right.

The ink started to react to the glycerine in the soap and the characters on the paper fleetingly reformed. Marcus ran his eyes quickly over the numbers and letters as they appeared. The effect faded in a few moments, ending in a puff of grey smoke. He had his answer. The text was an address: 19 Via delle Comete. Before everything vanished, though, he had also noticed the three little dots that formed the symbol of the triangle.

Apart from the place, it was identical to the note received by Raffaele Altieri.

2.00 p.m.

'I don't think it's a good idea.'

On the telephone, De Michelis was quite direct. Sandra almost regretted involving him. The traffic in Rome was slowed by the rain, and the taxi she had taken at the station was advancing in fits and starts.

The inspector was perfectly willing to help, but he didn't understand why she had needed to go there in person.

'Are you sure you're doing the right thing?'

Sandra had packed a case with what she needed to be away from home for a few days; she also threw in the photographs from the roll in the Leica, the diary in which her husband had noted those unknown addresses and the two-way radio she had found in his bag.

'David had a dangerous job. By mutual agreement, he would never tell me where he was going on his travels. So why did he tell me that lie in the message he left me? Why did he have to say he was in Oslo? I've thought about it and I've realised I was an idiot. He wasn't trying to hide something, but to call my attention to it.'

'OK, so maybe he made a discovery and wanted to protect you. But now you're putting yourself in danger.'

'I don't think so. David knew he was taking a risk. If anything happened to him, he wanted me to investigate. That's why he left me clues.'

'You mean the pictures in that old camera?'

'Talking of which, have you figured out what painting the detail of the child running away is from?'

'From your description, no. I'd have to see it.'

'I emailed it to you.'

'You know what I'm like with computers. I'll ask one of the boys to download it for me and let you know as soon as possible.'

Sandra knew she could count on him. It had taken him five months to tell her how sorry he was that David had died, but all things considered he was a good man.

'Inspector . . .'

'Yes?'

'How long have you been married?'

De Michelis laughed. 'Twenty-five years. Why?'

Sandra had thought again about what Schalber had said. 'I know this is a personal question, but . . . have you ever doubted your wife?'

The inspector cleared his throat. 'One afternoon, Barbara told me she was going to see a girlfriend. I knew she was lying. You know that sixth sense we police officers have?'

'Yes, I think I do.' Sandra was not sure she wanted to hear this. 'But you don't have to tell me.'

Ignoring her, De Michelis continued with his story. 'Well, I decided to follow her, as if she was a criminal. She didn't notice a thing. But after a while, I stopped to think about what I was doing, and I decided to turn back. You can call it fear, if you like, but I know what it was. The fact is, I didn't care if she had lied to me. If I'd discovered she really was going to see her girlfriend, I would have felt that I'd betrayed her. Just as I had the right to a faithful wife, Barbara deserved a husband who trusted her.'

Sandra realised that the story her older colleague had just shared was one that he had probably never confided in anyone. So she summoned up the courage to carry on. 'Inspector, there's another favour I'd like to ask you.'

'What is it now?' he asked, pretending to be annoyed.

'Last night, an Interpol agent named Schalber called me. He thinks David was involved in something shady. I thought he was a pain in the arse.'

'I get it: you want me to check him out. Is that all?'

'Yes, thanks,' Sandra said, relieved.

De Michelis, though, had not finished. 'Tell me one thing. Where are you going now?'

Where everything ended, Sandra would have liked to say. 'The building David fell from.'

The idea that they should live together had been hers. But David had accepted it willingly. At least, that was what she had believed. They had known each other only a few months and she was not yet sure of her ability to figure out what he really thought. He could be complicated at times. Unlike her, David was never clear-cut in his emotions. When they disagreed, she was always the one who raised her voice, whereas he would remain detached and vaguely conciliatory. Sandra could not help thinking that this wasn't a lack of interest on David's part but a definite strategy: he would allow her to let off steam, then wait until she gave in out of sheer exasperation.

The proof of her theory was what had happened a month after he had moved into her apartment.

For a week, David had been in a strange, silent mood, and Sandra had the impression he was avoiding her, even when they were alone in the apartment. Although he was not working at the time, he was constantly busy. He would shut himself up in the study, or else he would mend a plug or clear a blocked sink. Sandra felt there was something wrong, but she was afraid to ask. She told herself that she had to give him time, that David was not only unaccustomed to having a place he could call home, but lacked any experience of living as a couple. Along with her fear of losing him, though, her anger at his evasive attitude also grew, until she was ready to explode.

It happened one night. As they were sleeping, she felt his hand shaking her to wake up. Realising that it was not even three in the morning, still dazed by sleep, she asked him what the hell he wanted. David switched on the light and sat her up in bed. His eyes wandered around the room as he searched for the words to tell her what had been churning in his head for some time. Which was that they couldn't carry on this way, that he felt uncomfortable and found the situation stifling.

Sandra struggled to understand the meaning of this speech, and the only explanation she could come up with was: the idiot is dumping me. Her pride wounded, and incredulous that he couldn't wait till the following morning to ditch her, she got out of bed and started hurling insults at him. In her anger, she flung to the ground any object that came to hand. One of these was the remote control that, as it fell, switched on the TV. It was the time of night when all that was broadcast was old black-and-white films. At that moment, they were showing *Top Hat*, with Fred Astaire and Ginger Rogers singing a duet.

The mixture of the sweet melody and Sandra's hysteria created a surreal scene.

To make matters worse, David didn't say a word, just bore her insults passively, his head bowed. When her fury was at its height, though, Sandra saw him put his hand under the pillow, take out a blue velvet case, and put it down on her side of the bed with a sly smile. Suddenly struck dumb, she looked at that little case, knowing full well what it contained. She felt such a fool, her mouth fell open in astonishment.

'I was only trying to tell you,' David said, 'that we can't go on like this and that, in my humble opinion, we ought to get married. Because I love you, Ginger.'

He said this to her – it was both the first time he had told her what he felt and the first time he had called her Ginger – as Fred sang 'Cheek to Cheek'.

Heaven, I'm in heaven,
and my heart beats so that I can hardly speak;
and I seem to find the happiness I seek
when we're out together dancing, cheek to cheek.

Sandra, without even realising it, started to cry. She threw herself in his arms, needing to be held tight. Sobbing on his chest, she started to undress, driven by an urgent desire to make love to him. They had carried on until dawn. There were no words to describe what she had felt that night. Pure joy.

It was at times like those that she knew she would never have a calm, quiet time with David. They both needed to live their lives with passion. But for that very reason, there had also been a fear that everything could burn out itself out quickly.

And that was what had happened.

Now, three years, five months and a handful of days after that unrepeatable night, Sandra found herself on an abandoned building site, standing at the exact spot where the body of David – her David! – had come crashing to the ground. There was no blood; it had long since been washed away by the bad weather. She'd thought about bringing flowers, but was afraid of being overcome with emotion. The main reason she had come here was to understand.

After his fall, David had lain here all night, dying, until a man on a bicycle who happened to be passing by noticed him and raised the alarm. Too late, however. David had died in hospital.

When her colleagues in Rome had told her, Sandra hadn't asked herself too many questions. For example, whether he had remained conscious all that time. She preferred to think that he had died immediately, rather than later from his many fractures and from internal bleeding. Above all, she had dismissed from her mind the most terrible question.

If someone had noticed David lying there earlier, could he have been saved?

That slow death agony supported the theory that this had been an accident. If someone had pushed him, they would certainly have finished the job.

Sandra noticed a flight of stairs to her right. She put down her bag and started to climb, taking great care because there was no handrail. On the fifth floor the dividing walls were completely missing, and there were just pillars supporting the floors. She approached the edge from which David had slipped. He had gone there after dark. She recalled the conversation on the telephone with Schalber the previous night.

'According to the police, Signor Leoni was on that construction site because it offered an excellent vantage point for a photograph . . . Have you been there?'

'No,' she had replied irritably.

'I have.'

'What are you trying to tell me?'

'Your husband's camera was destroyed in the fall,' he had said drily. 'A pity we'll never see that photograph.'

When Sandra saw what David had seen that night – a vast open space, surrounded by apartment buildings – she understood the reason for Schalber's sarcasm. Why would he have wanted to take a photograph of it? And in the dark, to boot.

She had brought with her one of the five images contained on the roll from the Leica. She had not been mistaken: it was a photograph of this building site, but by day. Her first thought on developing it was that he had come here to look the place over.

Sandra looked around: there must have been a purpose. The site was abandoned, it didn't seem to be of any importance, at least on the surface.

So why had David come here?

She had to think in other terms, to shift focus, as her forensics instructor used to say.

The truth is in the details, she repeated to herself.

And it was in the details that she had to look for answers. So she did what she always did at the crime scenes she photographed. She got ready to read the scene. From top to bottom. From the general to the particular. As a point of comparison, she had the photograph taken by David with the Leica.

I have to compare the reality with the picture, she told herself.

Like those puzzles where you have to find the differences between two apparently identical pictures.

Keeping strictly to what was shown within the frame of the photograph, she began with the floor. She let her eyes move over what she had in front of her, foot by foot, then raised them to the ceiling. She was looking for a sign, something written in the concrete. There was nothing.

She looked at the pillars, one at a time. Some had suffered a little damage in the course of those five months, due partly to the fact that they didn't have plaster on them and so were more exposed to wear and tear.

When she reached the one furthest to her left, towards the edge, she noticed that it was different from the way it looked in the photograph. It was a small detail, but it might be significant. When David had been here, the pillar had had a horizontal cavity at its base. It wasn't there now.

Sandra bent to get a closer look. The difference lay in a strip of plasterboard that covered the base of the pillar. It seemed to have been put there specifically to conceal something. Sandra moved it away and what she saw left her stunned.

The cavity was still there, and in it lay David's voice recorder. The one she remembered not finding in his bag, even though it was included on the list that her husband had used to pack his bags.

Sandra took it out and blew on it to get the dust off. It was four inches long, thin, and with a digital memory. It was the kind that had replaced the old tape models.

Looking at it in the palm of her hand, Sandra realised she was scared. God alone knew what could be on it. It was possible that David had hidden it here and had taken that photograph to indicate the hiding place. Then, later, he had come back to pick it up and had fallen. Or else he had brought it here to make a recording, maybe the very night he had died. Sandra recalled that the device could be activated from a distance. All it took was a noise and the recording started.

She had to decide, she couldn't wait any longer. But she hesitated, aware that what she heard might change for ever her certainty that

David had been the victim of an accident. The result of that would be that she wouldn't be able to resign herself, that she would have to keep looking for the truth – with the risk that she would never find it.

Without further hesitation, she started the machine and waited.

Two coughs. Probably just to start the recording from a distance. Then David's voice, dim, distant, blurred by surface noise, and fragmentary.

' . . . be alone . . . I've been waiting since then . . . '

His tone was calm. Sandra, however, felt quite uncomfortable, hearing his voice again after so long. She had got used to the idea that he would never again talk to her. Now she was afraid the emotion would overwhelm her, just when she needed to keep a clear head. This was an investigation, she told herself, and she needed to approach it as a professional.

' . . . doesn't exist . . . had to imagine it . . . disappointment . . . '

The sentences were too broken up to be able to understand the drift of what he was saying.

' . . . I know . . . everything . . . all this time . . . it isn't possible . . . '

None of this made any sense to Sandra. But then came a complete sentence.

' . . . I looked for a long time, and in the end I found it . . . '

What was David talking about, and who to? There was no way of knowing.

Maybe she could copy the recording and have a sound technician listen to it and get rid of the surface noise. That was all she could think of at this point. She was about to switch off the machine when she heard another voice.

' . . . yes, it's me . . . '

Sandra felt a sudden chill. Now she had confirmation that David had not been alone. That was why he had wanted to record that dialogue. What followed were a series of agitated phrases. The situation, for some reason, had changed. Now her husband's tone was scared.

' . . . wait . . . it isn't possible . . . really believe . . . I don't . . . what I can . . . no . . . no . . . no! . . . '

The noise of a struggle. Bodies rolling on the ground.

'. . . Wait . . . Wait! . . . Wait! . . .'

And then a last desperate scream that gradually faded into the distance before ending abruptly.

The recorder fell from her hands. Sandra put both her hands flat on the concrete. She retched violently, then vomited, twice.

David had been killed. Someone had pushed him over the edge.

Sandra would have liked to scream. She would have liked not to be here. She would have liked not to have known David, not to have ever met him. Not to have loved him. It was a terrible thing to think, but it was the truth.

The sound of footsteps approaching.

Sandra turned towards the recorder. The machine hadn't finished with her, it still claimed her attention. It seemed as if the killer had known the location of the microphone.

The footsteps stopped.

A few seconds passed, then a voice. Not a speaking voice this time. No, it was singing.

> *Heaven, I'm in heaven,*
> *and my heart beats so that I can hardly speak;*
> *and I seem to find the happiness I seek*
> *when we're out together dancing, cheek to cheek.*

3.00 p.m.

The Via delle Comete was on the outskirts of the city. It took Marcus a while to get there by public transport. After the bus dropped him at a stop, he had to continue on foot for two hundred yards or so. Around him, uncultivated fields, industrial warehouses, and a number of apartment blocks, well spaced out, forming an archipelago of concrete. In the middle, an ugly modern church, very different from those that had graced the centre of the city for centuries. Traffic flowed by on the avenues.

Number 19 was an abandoned-looking warehouse. But this was

certainly the address written on the sheet of paper with the triangular symbol that he had found in Ranieri's office. Before going in, Marcus stopped to look around. He didn't want to run any pointless risks. On the other side of the street there was a petrol station with an adjoining car wash and a café. There was a constant coming and going of customers. Nobody seemed interested in the warehouse. Marcus slowly walked towards the petrol station, pretending that he was waiting for someone who was late. He stood there, watching, for half an hour, until he was convinced the place wasn't under surveillance.

In front of the warehouse there was an open space. The rain had turned it into a quagmire. He could see the furrows left by tyres. Probably those of Ranieri's green Subaru, Marcus immediately thought, remembering how muddy they had been.

The detective had been here. Then he had rushed back to his office to destroy that paper. Finally he had left, taking with him an item from the safe.

Marcus tried to put these elements together to form a complete picture. But the one thing uppermost in his mind was how much of a hurry Ranieri had been in.

The urgency of a man afraid. What had he seen that had thrown him into such a panic?

Deliberately avoiding the main entrance to the warehouse, Marcus looked for a side door. He made his way through the brushwood surrounding the low rectangular building. With its bulging roof made out of sheet metal, it resembled a hangar. He found a fire exit. Ranieri might well have come this way, because the door was ajar. With a little effort, pulling the door with both hands, he managed to open it enough to slip in.

He entered a vast, dimly lit space, empty except for a few stacked machines and some pulleys hanging from the ceiling. Rain dripped through the roof, forming dark, stagnant puddles on the floor.

As Marcus moved, his steps echoed. At the far end, an iron staircase led up to a mezzanine, where there was a small office. As he approached it, he was immediately struck by something. There was no dust on the handrail. Someone had taken the trouble to clean it, perhaps to erase his own fingerprints.

Whatever this place hid, it must be up there.

He started climbing, taking care where he put his feet. Halfway up the stairs, the smell reached him. It was unmistakable. Once you had smelt it, you could recognise it anywhere. Marcus couldn't remember where and when he had first encountered it. But something inside him had not forgotten it. That was the kind of trick amnesia played on you. He would have preferred to remember the smell of roses or his mother's breast. But what he remembered was the smell of a dead body.

Covering his nose and mouth with the sleeve of his raincoat, he climbed the last steps. He could see the bodies from the doorway of the office. They were close together. One on its back, the other on its stomach, both with bullet holes in the head. An execution, Marcus concluded.

Their already advanced state of decomposition was made worse by fire. Somebody had tried to burn them with alcohol or petrol, but the flames had attacked only the upper parts of the bodies, leaving the lower parts intact. Whoever had done it had merely succeeded in making them unrecognisable. Then Marcus noticed something that told him the two men must have been criminals: if they didn't have records, why take the trouble to remove their hands?

Trying not to retch, Marcus went closer to get a better look.

The hands had been removed at the wrists. The fibres were torn, but there were regular scratches on the bones. The kind usually left by a jagged instrument, such as a saw.

He lifted the trousers of one of the two, uncovering the calf. There were no burns on the skin at this point of the body. Judging by the lack of colour, he estimated that death had occurred a little under a week earlier. And from the swollen but flabby appearance of the skin, he also judged that they had both been over fifty.

He didn't know who they were, and would probably never know. But he strongly suspected that they were the killers of Valeria Altieri and her lover.

What he had to do now was figure out who had killed them, and why so long after the event.

Just as Raffaele had been drawn to Lara's apartment by an

anonymous letter, so Ranieri had been summoned to this warehouse with the note that Marcus had found in his office.

Here, he had discovered the two men, who might have been led there by a similar ploy, and killed them.

No, Marcus didn't buy it.

Ranieri had been here just a few hours ago. If the two had been dead a week, what had he come back for? Maybe to set fire to them or remove their hands, or simply to check the condition of the bodies. But why take such a risk? And why was he scared? Who was he running away from?

No, someone else killed them, Marcus thought. And if that someone hadn't got rid of the bodies, it was because he had wanted them to be found.

These two were probably of little account. Maybe they'd simply done as they were told. He still favoured the theory that the Altieri murder had been ordered by someone. Or maybe by more than one person. Although he didn't like this last possibility, it couldn't be ruled out. Given the apparently ritualistic nature of the killings, the hypothesis that it could have been a sect seemed stronger than ever. An occult group capable of eliminating anyone who might incriminate them, even two of their own members.

Marcus sensed the presence of two entities in this case, working in opposing directions: one intent on exposing the secret by sending anonymous notes, the other determined to protect it at all costs.

The link between them had to be Ranieri.

The detective had known something, Marcus was sure of it. Just as he was convinced that in the end he would find a link with Jeremiah Smith and Lara's disappearance.

Obscure forces were at work. Marcus felt like a pawn at the mercy of events. He had to define his own role, which meant that it was necessary to confront Ranieri.

He decided he had had enough of the stench of corpses. Before leaving, he instinctively raised his hand to make the sign of the cross, then thought better of it. These two probably didn't deserve it.

*

Ranieri had been summoned to the warehouse by an anonymous message. He had gone there this morning and seen the bodies. Then he had returned to his office, destroyed the note, and run away, taking with him whatever it was he had been keeping in the safe.

Marcus continued to ruminate on this sequence of events. He was sure he was missing some important detail.

In the meantime, it had started raining again. He left the warehouse and headed across the open space, taking care not to get himself too muddy. As he did so, he spotted something he hadn't noticed earlier.

It was a dark patch on the ground. There was another one a bit further on. They were similar to the one he had seen that morning outside Ranieri's office, on the asphalt where the green Subaru had been parked.

The fact that the rain had not washed it away suggested it was some kind of oily substance. Marcus bent down to check. It was motor oil.

Clearly, the car had been parked outside the abandoned warehouse. That much he had already deduced from the muddy bodywork. At first, Marcus had thought the two things were linked: Ranieri had damaged and dirtied the car at the same time. But he looked around and did not see any potholes or protruding stones that might have caused damage. So that must have happened earlier, somewhere else.

Where had Ranieri been before coming here?

Marcus lifted a hand to the scar on his temple. His head was throbbing, another migraine was on the way. He needed a painkiller and something to eat. He felt as if he had come to a dead end and needed to find a way to continue. When he saw his bus approaching the stop, he hurried to catch it. Once aboard, he made his way to one of the seats at the back, next to an elderly lady with a shopping bag, who looked askance at his swollen cheek and split lip, both souvenirs of the attack by Raffaele Altieri. Ignoring her, Marcus folded his arms across his chest and stretched his legs under the seat in front. He closed his eyes, trying to forget the hammering in his head and drifted into a kind of half-sleep, still vaguely aware of the voices and other noises around him, and unable to dream. There had been many times he'd got on a bus like this one or an underground carriage and fallen half-asleep, aimlessly going back and forth between termini, trying to escape the recurring dream in which he and Devok both died. The motion cradled him, creating the impression that an invisible force was taking care of him, making him feel safe.

He opened his eyes again because he had stopped feeling the peaceful rocking of the bus and the passengers around him had suddenly become agitated.

The bus had, in fact, ground to a halt and some of the passengers were complaining about the time they were wasting. Marcus looked out of the window to see where they were. He recognised the buildings lining the ring road. He got up from his seat and made his way to the front of the bus. The driver had not switched off the engine, but was sitting there with his arms folded.

'What's happening?' he asked.

'An accident,' the driver replied. 'I think we'll be moving soon.'

Marcus looked at the vehicles in front of them. One by one, they were driving across a space that had been cleared at the side of the road in order to avoid the scene of the accident, which seemed to have involved several cars.

The bus advanced in fits and starts. When their turn finally came, a traffic policeman motioned them to hurry up. Marcus was still on his feet next to the bus driver when they passed a mass of twisted and burnt metal. The firemen had only just managed to put out the flames.

He recognised Ranieri's green Subaru from part of the bonnet that had been spared by the flames. Inside, the body of the driver had been covered with a sheet.

At last Marcus understood the reason for the oil stains the detective's car had left behind everywhere it stopped. He had been wrong: they were not linked to a place Ranieri had visited and where he had damaged the Subaru. The oil must have been leaking from the brakes, because someone had tampered with them.

This was no accident.

The song was for her. A message. Drop the investigation, in your own interest.

Or else the exact opposite. Come and get me.

The water from the shower poured down her neck and back. Sandra stood there without moving, her eyes closed, her hands pressed against the tiled wall. In her head, she again heard the melody of 'Cheek to Cheek' mixed with David's last words on the recorder.

'Wait! Wait! Wait!'

She had decided she would not cry again until this was all over. She was afraid, but she would not turn back. Now she knew.

Someone was involved in her husband's death.

That death was irreversible, she knew, but she wasn't going to let that stop her. The idea that she could do something, something that could make up, at least partly, for an absurd, unjust loss, was one she found strangely consoling.

She had settled for a modest one-star hotel near the Termini station, used mainly by groups of pilgrims who had come to visit the Christian sites.

David had stayed here when he had been in Rome. Sandra had asked for the same room and fortunately it had been available. In order to carry out her own investigation, she needed to reproduce the conditions in which he had operated.

Why, after her discovery of the recording, hadn't she immediately gone to the police and told them what had happened? It wasn't that she didn't trust her colleagues. The husband of one of their own had been murdered. They would have given priority to the case. That was the unwritten rule, a kind of code of honour. She could at least have told De Michelis. She continued to tell herself that she preferred to put together enough evidence to facilitate his work. But that wasn't the real motive. The real motive was one she wouldn't even admit to herself.

She came out of the shower and wrapped herself in the bath towel. Dripping, she came back to the room, put her case on the bed and started emptying it until she came to an item she had put right at the bottom.

Her service gun.

She checked the magazine and the safety catch, then placed it on the chest of drawers. From now on, she would always carry it with her.

She put on just a pair of knickers and started sorting through the other things she had brought with her. She removed the small TV set from the shelf where it stood and replaced it with the two-way radio, David's diary with those strange addresses, and the voice recorder. With adhesive tape, she stuck the five photographs she had developed from the Leica to the wall. The first was that of the building site, and she had already used it. Then there was the one that had come out completely dark, which she had decided to keep all the same. Then the one of the man with the scar on his temple, the detail from the painting, and, finally, the image of her husband waving and simultaneously taking a photograph while standing bare-chested in front of the mirror.

Sandra turned towards the bathroom. That was where this last photograph had been taken.

At first sight it appeared to be one of those humorous gestures typical of him, like when he had sent her a photograph of himself lunching on roast anaconda in Borneo or another where he was covered with leeches in a swamp in Australia.

But, unlike those photos, in this one David was not smiling.

Maybe what she had at first thought of as a sad farewell from a ghost concealed another message for her. Maybe Sandra ought to search the room, because David had hidden something there and wanted her to find it.

She shifted the furniture, looked under the bed and the wardrobe. She carefully felt the mattress and pillows. She took the cover off the telephone and the TV set and looked inside. She checked the floor tiles and the skirting board. Finally, she carefully inspected the bathroom.

Apart from proof that it wasn't cleaned very often, she didn't find anything.

Five months had gone by. Whatever it was might well have been removed. She cursed herself again for waiting so long before checking what was in David's bags.

Sitting on the floor, still without any clothes on, she started to feel cold. She pulled the faded bedspread around herself and stayed there, trying not to let her frustration overcome her powers of reasoning. Just then, her mobile phone began vibrating.

'So, Officer Vega, did you follow my advice?'

It took her a moment or two to recognise that irritating, German-accented voice.

'Schalber, I was hoping I'd hear from you.'

'Is your husband's luggage still in the police storeroom, or can I take a look at it?'

'If there's an investigation in progress, you can submit a request to the examining magistrate.'

'You know as well as I do that Interpol can only work alongside a country's official police force. I wouldn't like to bother your colleagues, it might be embarrassing for you.'

'I have nothing to hide.' The man really did have the ability to get on her nerves.

'Where are you now, Sandra? I can call you Sandra, can't I?'

'No, and it's none of your business.'

'I'm in Milan, we could meet for a coffee, or whatever you prefer.'

Sandra absolutely had to avoid him finding out that she was in Rome. 'Why not? How about tomorrow afternoon? Then we can clear up this whole thing.'

Schalber gave a loud laugh. 'I think the two of us are going to get along very well.'

'Don't delude yourself. I don't like the way you operate.'

'I assume you asked one of your superiors to check me out.'

Sandra said nothing.

'You did the right thing. He'll tell you I'm the kind of person who doesn't easily let go.'

That phrase sounded to her like a threat. She wouldn't let herself be intimidated. 'Tell me, Schalber, how did you end up in Interpol?'

'I was in the police in Vienna. Murder squad, antiterrorism, drug squad: a bit of everything. I got noticed and Interpol called me.'

'And what do you deal with for them?'

Schalber made a pregnant pause, and when he spoke his jocular tone had vanished. 'I deal with liars.'

Sandra shook her head. 'You know what, I should slam the phone down on you, but I'm still curious to hear what you have to tell me.'

'I'd like to tell you a story.'

'If you really think it's necessary . . .'

'I had a colleague in Vienna. We were investigating a gang of Eastern European smugglers, but he had a bad habit. He didn't like to share information, because he was desperate to advance his career. He took a week's leave, telling me he was taking his wife on a cruise. Instead of which, he infiltrated this gang. But they found out who he was. They tortured him for three days and three nights, knowing nobody would come and look for him, then killed him. If he'd trusted me, he might still be alive today.'

'That's a nice anecdote,' she said sarcastically. 'I bet you tell it to all the girls.'

'Give it some thought. We all need somebody. I'll call you tomorrow about that coffee.'

He hung up. She sat there, wondering what he had meant by that last phrase. The only person she needed was no longer here. And what about David? Who had he needed? Was she sure she was the target of the clues he had disseminated before leaving forever?

When he was still alive, he had kept her out of the investigation, he had not told her he was running any risks. But had he been alone in Rome? On David's mobile phone there was no record of calls received from or sent to unknown numbers. He didn't seem to have been in contact with anyone. But maybe he had received help of some kind.

Her eyes came to rest on the two-way radio. She had wondered what David was doing with it. What if he had used it to communicate with someone?

She got up, went to the shelf, picked up the radio and examined it now with different eyes. It was tuned to channel 81.

Maybe she should keep it on, maybe someone would try to contact her.

She switched it on and raised the volume. Of course she was not expecting to hear anything. She put it back on the shelf and turned back to her case to get her clothes.

At that moment, a transmission began.

It was the cold, monotone voice of a woman reporting that a fight between drug dealers was in progress in the Via Nomentana. Patrol cars in the area were asked to intervene.

Sandra turned to look at the radio. It was tuned to the frequency used by the headquarters of the Rome police to communicate with patrol cars.

And with that realisation, she also understood the meaning of the addresses in David's diary.

7.47 p.m.

Marcus went back to his attic room in the Via dei Serpenti. Without turning on the light or taking off his raincoat, he lay huddled on the bed with his hands between his knees. His sleepless night was catching up with him, and he could feel another migraine coming on.

Ranieri's death had brought his investigation crashing to a halt. All that effort for nothing!

What had the detective taken from the safe in his office that morning?

Whatever it was, it had probably been destroyed with him in the Subaru. Marcus took the file on case number *c.g. 796-74-8* from his pocket. He didn't need it any more. He threw it down, and the papers scattered across the floor. The moonlight shone on the faces of those involved in a murder that had occurred nearly twenty years ago. Far too long ago to get at the truth now, he thought. If he couldn't have justice, he had to be satisfied with that conclusion. Now, though, he had to start again from the beginning. His priority was Lara.

Valeria Altieri looked up at him from a newspaper cutting, smiling in a photograph of a New Year's Eve party. She looked very elegant, her blonde hair and shapely body perfectly set off by the dress she was wearing. There was a unique magnetism in her eyes.

She had paid for so much beauty with her life.

If she had been a less striking woman, her death might not have interested anybody.

Marcus found himself involuntarily thinking about the reason the killers had chosen her. Just like Lara, who for some obscure reason had been selected by Jeremiah Smith.

Up until that moment, he had thought of Valeria as Raffaele's mother. After seeing the bloody footprints of his little feet on the white carpet in the bedroom, he hadn't been able to focus on her.

There's always a reason we attract other people's attention, he told himself. It didn't happen to him, of course, he was invisible. But Valeria was a woman who was very much in the public eye.

The word EVIL written on the wall behind the bed. The numerous stab wounds on the victims' bodies. The murder taking place within a domestic environment. Everything seemed to have been done in order to be noticed. The homicide had captured the public's imagination not only because it had involved a member of high society and her equally well-known lover, but also because of the way it had happened.

It seemed to have been staged specially for the scandal magazines, even though no paparazzo had photographed the crime scene.

Horror as spectacle.

Marcus sat up in bed. Something was germinating in his mind. *Anomalies.* He switched on the light and retrieved the profile of Valeria Altieri from the floor. That fine-sounding surname belonged to her husband: before she was married her name was Colmetti, a name less suited to the jet set. She came from a small middle-class family, her father a clerk. She had attended teacher training college, but her true talent was beauty. That, and a natural propensity to drive men wild. At twenty she had tried to make it as a film actress, but had only managed to obtain a few walk-on parts. Marcus could imagine how many men had tried to get her into bed by promising her an important role. Maybe at first Valeria had yielded. How many compliments with a double meaning, how many unwanted fumblings, how many faked orgasms had she had to endure in order to realise her dream?

And then, one day, Guido Altieri had come into her life. A handsome man, a few years older than her, from a well-known and highly respected family. A lawyer with an assured future. Valeria knew she wasn't able to love anyone exclusively. Guido in his heart was aware that this woman would never belong to anybody – she was too selfish and too beautiful for one man alone – and yet he asked her to marry him.

It was there that everything started, Marcus told himself, getting up to look for a pen and paper to take notes. The wedding had been only the beginning, the first act in a chain of apparently happy events that would inevitably lead to the slaughter in the bedroom.

He found a notebook. On the first page he drew the symbol of the triangle. On the second he wrote EVIL.

Valeria Altieri represented everything that men might want, but that nobody could have. Desire, especially when it is uncontrollable, makes us do things we wouldn't believe ourselves capable of. It corrupts, undermines, and occasionally it can be a motive for murder. Especially when it is transformed into something else, something dangerous.

An obsession, like the one tormenting Raffaele Altieri.

But if Raffaele was obsessed by a mother he had barely known, then perhaps someone else had felt a similar obsession. And what is the only solution in such cases? Marcus was afraid to answer his own question. He said it in a low voice. A single word.

'Destruction.'

Annihilating the object of our obsession, rendering it incapable of hurting us any more. And making sure it stays that way forever. To achieve that aim, death sometimes isn't enough.

Marcus tore the pages with the symbol and the word from the notebook. He held them in his hands, looking from one to the other, hoping to find the key to this mystery.

He sensed someone behind him, looking at him insistently. He turned and saw who it was: his own reflection in the windowpane. Although he hated looking at himself in mirrors, this time he didn't move.

He read the word reflected there – EVIL – but the other way around.

'Horror as spectacle,' he repeated to himself. And he realised that the woman's scream he thought he had heard coming from Ranieri's office was not an acoustic hallucination. It was real.

The large red-brick villa was situated in the exclusive Olgiata area. It was surrounded by a luxuriant garden with an English lawn and a swimming pool. The two-storey house itself was well lit.

Marcus walked along the drive. The privilege of entering the gates of these dwellings was limited to a select few. But it hadn't been difficult for him to get in. No alarm had gone off, no private guard had come running. And that could mean only one thing.

Someone inside the villa was expecting a visit.

The glass-fronted door was open. He went in and found himself in an elegant living room. No voices, no other noises. To his right was a staircase. He started climbing. The lights were out on the upper floor, but through the doorway of a room at the end of the corridor he could see the dancing reflections of a fire. He followed them, sure that at the end of his journey he would find what he was looking for.

The man was in his study. Sunk in a leather armchair beside a lighted fire, with his back to the door and a glass of cognac in his hand. Facing him – just as in Ranieri's office – the jarring combination of a plasma TV and a video recorder.

He realised that he was no longer alone.

'I sent everybody away. There's nobody else in the house.' Guido Altieri seemed to be confronting his fate pragmatically. 'How much do you want?'

'I don't want money.'

Altieri made as if to turn. 'Who are you?'

Marcus stopped him. 'If you don't mind, I'd prefer you not to look at my face.'

Altieri humoured him. 'You won't tell me who you are, and you haven't come for money. So what brings you to my house?'

'I want to understand.'

'If you've come this far, you already know everything.'

'Not yet. Do you intend to help me?'

'Why should I?'

'Because, apart from saving your own life, you can also save that of an innocent girl.'

'I'm listening.'

'You also received an anonymous message, didn't you? Ranieri's dead, the two killers have been shot and then burnt. And now you're wondering if I was the person who sent all those notes.'

'The one I received announced a visitor for this evening.'

'Not me, and I'm not here to harm you.'

The crystal glass in Altieri's hand reflected the flames of the fire.

Marcus paused before coming to the point. 'When an adulterous woman is murdered, the first suspect is always the husband.' He had quoted Clemente's words, even though at first that motive had seemed too obvious. 'The murder on the eve of a religious festival, the night of the new moon . . . All coincidences.' Men sometimes let themselves be guided by superstition, he thought. And to fill the void of doubt, they are ready to believe in anything. 'There was no ritual, no sect. The word written behind the bed, "Evil", wasn't a threat, it was a promise . . . Read the other way round, it says "Live". A joke maybe, or maybe not . . . A message that had to go all the way to London, where you were: the job had been carried out as requested, you could go home . . . Those marks on the carpet, the occult triangle, weren't a symbol. Something had been placed in the pool of blood next to the bed and then moved to the other side. As simple as that. A creature with three paws and a single eye. A video camera on a tripod.'

Marcus thought again of the woman's scream he had heard coming from Ranieri's office. It hadn't been an acoustic hallucination. It was the voice of Valeria Altieri, and it came from the video cassette Ranieri kept in his safe, the cassette he had viewed before taking it away with him in the leather briefcase.

'Ranieri arranged the murder, you simply commissioned it. But after the anonymous note and those bodies in the warehouse, he was certain somebody knew the truth. He felt hunted, he was scared they wanted to pin it all on him. He was paranoid. He ran back to his office and burned the note. If someone had managed to track down the killers after nearly twenty years, then they were quite capable of replacing the tape in the safe with a fake, that was why he checked it before taking it away with him . . . Tell me, was the one Ranieri owned the original or a copy?'

'Why do you ask that?'

'Because it was destroyed when his car crashed. And without it, there'll never be justice.'

'A sad twist of fate,' Altieri commented, sarcastically.

Marcus looked again at the video recorder beneath the plasma TV. 'It was at your request, wasn't it? You couldn't be content with your wife's death. No, you had to see it. Even at the risk of becoming a laughing stock: the husband betrayed by his wife while he was on a trip abroad, in the family home, in the marriage bed. You would be the butt of everyone's jokes, but in the end you would have your revenge.'

'You couldn't possibly understand.'

'You may be surprised. For you, Valeria was an obsession. A divorce wouldn't have been enough. You wouldn't have been able to forget her.'

'She was one of those women who can make you lose your reason. Some men are attracted by creatures like that. Even though they know that, in the end, they'll be led to their own destruction. These women seem sweet and loving, but they only grant you the leftovers of their affection. After a while you realise that you can still save yourself, have another woman who loves you truly, children, a family. But at that point you have to choose: either you or her.'

'Why did you want to see it?'

'Because then it'd be as if I'd killed her myself. That was what I wanted to feel.'

'And so, every now and again, when you were alone in the house like now, you sat down in that lovely armchair, poured yourself some cognac and put on that tape.'

'Obsessions are difficult to get rid of.'

'And whenever you saw it, what did you feel? Pleasure?'

Guido Altieri lowered his eyes. 'Regret ... that I hadn't done it myself.'

Marcus shook his head: he felt anger, and he didn't like to feel anger. 'Ranieri hired the killers. The word written in blood was an amateur touch, but the symbol on the carpet was a stroke of luck. A mistake that might have revealed the presence of the video camera, instead of which it turned into an unexpected advantage, by complicating everything.' Marcus laughed at himself for having thought of Satanism as a motive, when the reality was much more banal.

'But you understood everything.'

'Dogs are colour blind, did you know that?'

'Of course, what has that to do with it?'

'A dog can't see a rainbow. And nobody will ever be able to teach it what colours are. But you know as well as I do that red, yellow and blue exist. Who's to say that isn't true of people, too? There may be things that exist, even though we can't see them. Like evil. We know it's there only when it manifests itself, by which time it's too late.'

'Do you know evil?'

'I know men. And I see the signs.'

'What signs?'

'Bare little feet walking in blood ...'

Altieri made a bad-tempered gesture. 'Raffaele wasn't supposed to be there that night. He was meant to go and stay with Valeria's mother, but she was sick. I didn't know that.'

'But he was there, in the house. And he stayed there for two days. Alone.'

Altieri fell silent, and Marcus realised that the truth hurt him. He was pleased to see that part of the man at least could still experience a recognisably human feeling.

'For all these years, Ranieri had the task of putting your son off the scent as he continued to investigate his mother's death. But at a certain point, Raffaele started receiving strange anonymous notes that promised to lead him to the truth.' One of them led him to me, Marcus told himself, even though he didn't know why someone had wanted to involve him in the case. 'First your son dismissed Ranieri. A week ago he managed to track down the killers, lured them to an abandoned warehouse and killed them. He killed Ranieri, too, by tampering with his car. Which means he's the one who's coming here. I just got here before him.'

'If it wasn't you, then who plotted all this?'

'I don't know. What I do know is that less than twenty-four hours ago a serial killer named Jeremiah Smith was found dying, with two words written on his chest: *Kill me*. In the ambulance team that came to his rescue was the sister of one of his victims. She could have taken the law into her own hands. In my opinion, Raffaele has been offered the same opportunity.'

'Why are you so interested in saving my life?'

'Not just you. That serial killer kidnapped a young student named Lara. He's keeping her prisoner somewhere, but he's in a coma and can't talk.'

'Is she the innocent girl you mentioned a while ago?'

'If I find out who arranged all this, I may still save her.'

Altieri raised the glass of cognac to his lips. 'I don't know how I can help you.'

'Raffaele will be here in a little while, probably looking for revenge. Call the police and turn yourself in. I'll wait for your son and try to persuade him to talk to me. There's every chance he knows something that may be useful to me.'

'You want me to confess everything to the police?' From his derisory tone, it was obvious he had no intention of doing any such thing. 'Who are you? How can I trust you if you won't tell me who you are?'

Marcus was tempted to reply. If that was the only way, he would contravene his rule. He was about to tell him when the shot rang out. He turned. Behind him stood Raffaele with a gun in his hand pointed straight at the armchair in which his father was sitting. The bullet had perforated the leather and the upholstery. Altieri slumped forward, dropping the glass with the cognac.

Marcus would have liked to ask the boy why he had opened fire, but he realised that Raffaele had chosen revenge over justice.

'Thank you for getting him to talk,' Raffaele said.

Marcus knew now what his role had been in the whole affair. It was why somebody had brought them together in Lara's apartment.

He was to provide Raffaele with the missing piece of the puzzle: his father's confession.

Marcus was on the verge of asking him a question, still hoping to find the link between this twenty-year-old case, Jeremiah Smith and Lara's disappearance. But before he could say anything, he became aware of sounds in the distance. Raffaele smiled at him. It was the police siren. He had called them, but he didn't make a move to escape. This time justice would be done, all the way. Even in this, he wanted to be different from his father.

Marcus knew that he only had a few minutes left. He had many questions, but he had to leave. They couldn't find him here.

Nobody was supposed to know that he existed.

8.35 p.m.

After putting what she needed in a bag, Sandra managed to get a taxi near the Via Giolitti. She gave the address to the driver, then sat back and went over the plan she had worked out. She was running an enormous risk. If they discovered her true purpose, she would certainly be suspended from the force.

The taxi passed the Piazza della Repubblica and turned into the Via Nazionale. She didn't know Rome very well. For someone like her, born and brought up in the North, this city was an unknown quantity. Too much beauty, maybe. A bit like Venice, which always seemed populated only by tourists. It was difficult to believe that people actually lived in such a place. That they worked, did their shopping, took their children to school, instead of spending all their time looking in awe at the splendours around them.

The taxi turned into the Via San Vitale. Sandra got out in front of Police Headquarters.

Everything will be fine, she told herself.

She showed her badge at reception and asked to speak to someone of equal rank in records. They told her to sit down in the waiting room while they tried to contact him by telephone. After a few minutes, a redheaded officer in shirtsleeves came to greet her, with his mouth full.

'What can I do for you, Officer Vega?' he asked, chewing. Judging by the crumbs on his shirt, he had been eating a roll.

Sandra gave him her most conciliatory smile. 'I know it's late, but my chief only sent me to Rome this afternoon. I should have warned you I was coming, but there wasn't time.'

Her redheaded colleague nodded, vaguely interested. 'What's it all about?'

'I have to do some research.'

'On a specific case or . . .'

'A statistical study on the incidence of violent crime within society and the police force's ability to intervene effectively, with particular emphasis on the differences of approach between Milan and Rome.' She had said all this in one breath.

The man frowned. On the one hand, he didn't envy her: it was the kind of mission that was usually assigned as a punishment or because your chief was really angry with you. On the other hand, he couldn't figure out what the point of it was. 'Who on earth's interested in all that?'

'I don't know. I think the Commissioner's going to a conference in a few days. He probably needs it for his presentation.'

The man had started to realise that this was going to take a long time, and he had no desire to ruin a quiet evening shift with all this hassle. Sandra could see it in his face.

'Can I see your service order, Officer Vega?' he said in a bureaucratic, authoritarian tone, as if to prepare her for his refusal.

But she had planned for this, too. She leaned towards him

conspiratorially and said in a low voice, 'Listen, between you and me, I really don't fancy spending the night in records just to keep my stupid chief, Inspector De Michelis, happy.' She felt tremendously guilty for depicting him in this way but, in the absence of a service order, she needed to mention her superior's name. 'Let's do something: I'll leave a list of things to look for and you give me what I need as soon as you can.'

Sandra handed him a printed sheet. Actually, it was a list of the tourist attractions of the city, provided by the porter at her hotel. She knew that her colleague only needed to see how long it was and all his objections would disappear.

He immediately gave her back the list. 'I really wouldn't know where to start. From what you tell me, it's quite tricky research. I think you'd be better suited to it.'

'But I don't know your cataloguing system.'

'No problem, I'll explain it to you. It's really very simple.'

Sandra exaggerated her annoyance, shaking her head and raising her eyes to heaven. 'Well, all right, but I'd like to get back to Milan tomorrow morning, or in the afternoon at the latest. So if you don't mind I'd prefer to start straight away.'

'Of course,' he said, suddenly more than willing to help. 'Follow me.'

A richly frescoed room with a high damasked ceiling, in which there were six desks, with a computer on each one. The records were all here. The paper records had all been transferred onto a database, the server being located two floors below, in the basement.

Police Headquarters dated from the nineteenth century. It was like working inside a work of art. One of the advantages of Rome, Sandra thought as she allowed herself a glance upwards.

She was sitting at one of the desks. The others were unoccupied. The only light came from the lamp on her desk, which spread a pleasant glow around her. In that silence, every noise echoed through the room. Outside, another storm could be heard rumbling.

She concentrated on the computer in front of her. Her red-headed colleague had taken a few minutes to explain to her how to get into the system, provided her with temporary security codes, then left.

Sandra took David's old leather-bound diary from her bag. Her husband had spent three weeks in Rome and, on the pages corresponding to that time, had written down some twenty addresses, then pinpointed them on a map of the city. That was why he had needed a radio tuned to the police frequency. Presumably, every time the operator had sent out a message to the patrol cars, David had proceeded to the scene.

Why? What had he been looking for?

Sandra went to the page of the diary on which the first address had been noted. She entered it together with the date in the search engine of the records department. Within seconds the result appeared on the screen.

Via Erode Attico. Homicide of a woman by her partner.

She opened the file and read a quick summary of the police report. It was a domestic quarrel that had degenerated. The man, an Italian, had stabbed his Peruvian companion and run away. He was still at large. Not at all sure why David had been interested in this story, Sandra decided to insert a second address, together with the date, in the search engine.

Via dell'Assunzione. Robbery and involuntary homicide.

An elderly lady's home had been broken into. The thieves had bound and gagged her, and she had died from suffocation. However hard she tried, Sandra could not grasp the connection between this and the affair in the Via Erode Attico. The people and the places were different, as were the circumstances of these violent deaths. She continued: another address, another date.

Corso Trieste. Homicide following a fight.

It had happened at night, at a bus stop. Two strangers had come to blows for some stupid reason. Then one of them had taken out a knife.

What has this one got to do with anything? she wondered, increasingly frustrated.

She could not find any link between the three episodes, nor with those she examined as she proceeded with her search. They were simply violent acts with one or more victims. A strange map of crimes. Some had been solved, others not.

All of them, though, had been documented by forensic photographers.

Her job was to understand the scene of the crime on the basis of images, which was why she was not so good at studying written documents. She preferred a visual approach and, given that there were photographs relating to all these cases, she decided to concentrate on them.

It wasn't a simple task: twenty homicides meant hundreds of photographs. She started to view them on the computer. But given that she didn't know what she was looking for, it might take days and David hadn't left any further indications.

Damn it, Fred, why all this mystery? Couldn't you have written me a letter of instructions? Would it have cost you too much, darling?

She was nervous, she was hungry, she hadn't slept in more than twenty-four hours and, ever since she had arrived at Police Headquarters, she had been desperate to have a pee. Over the past day, an agent from Interpol had undermined the trust she had in her husband, she had discovered that David had not died in an accident but had been murdered, and his killer had threatened her, transforming a song linked to the most beautiful memory of her life into a macabre funeral dirge.

It was definitely too much for a single day.

Outside, it had started raining again. Sandra let herself go, putting her head down on the table. She closed her eyes and for a moment stopped thinking. She felt weighed down with an enormous responsibility. Bringing criminals to justice was never an easy matter, that was why she had chosen her profession. But it was one thing to be part of the mechanism, to contribute to the result with her work. It was quite another matter when the result depended entirely on her.

I can't do it, she said to herself.

At that moment, her mobile phone began vibrating. The noise echoed in the empty room, making her jump.

'De Michelis here. I know everything.'

For a moment, she feared that her superior had been informed that she had used his name inappropriately and was there without official approval.

'I can explain,' she immediately said.

'Explain what? Wait, let me speak. I found the painting!'

The euphoria in the inspector's voice calmed her down.

'The boy running away in horror is a figure in a painting by Caravaggio: *The Martyrdom of St Matthew*.'

Sandra had hoped this might tell her something, but it didn't. She had been expecting more, but she couldn't bring herself to put a damper on De Michelis's enthusiasm.

'It was painted between 1600 and 1601. It was commissioned as a fresco, but then the artist opted for an oil painting on canvas. It's part of a cycle about St Matthew, along with *The Inspiration* and *The Vocation*. The three paintings are in Rome, in the Contarelli chapel in the church of San Luigi dei Francesi.'

None of this helped her. She needed to know more. She opened the browser and looked for the picture on Google Images.

It appeared on the screen.

It depicted the scene of St Matthew's death. His executioner was looking at him with hatred, brandishing a sword. The saint was lying on the ground. He was trying to stop his killer with one arm, but had the other down by his side, almost as if accepting the martyrdom that awaited him. Around him were other people, among them the horror-struck boy.

'There's one unusual thing about the painting,' De Michelis said. 'Among those watching the scene, Caravaggio has painted himself.'

Sandra recognised the artist's self-portrait in the top left-hand corner. Suddenly she had a brainwave.

The painting showed a crime scene.

'Inspector, I have to go.'

'What? Aren't you even going to tell me how you're getting on?'

'Don't worry, everything's fine.'

The inspector muttered something.

'I'll call you tomorrow. And thank you, you're a friend.'

She hung up without waiting for him to reply. Now she knew what to look for.

Forensic photography required other things to be photographed apart from the crime scene itself: the state of the surroundings and, especially in cases where the culprit had not yet been brought to justice, the crowd of onlookers who usually gathered beyond the police cordon. In fact, the guilty party was sometimes among them, checking up on how the investigation was proceeding.

The maxim about the murderer always returning to the scene of the crime did sometimes hold true. A number of murderers had been caught that way.

These were the pictures Sandra now concentrated on as she skimmed through the photographs of the twenty crimes noted by David in the diary. She was looking for a face among the onlookers. Someone who, like Caravaggio in the painting, was concealing his identity in the multitude.

She lingered over the murder of a prostitute. The photograph showed the moment when her body had been fished out of the little lake in the EUR area. The woman's scanty, colourful clothes were in marked contrast to the deathly pallor that had already settled over her young skin like a patina. In the expression on her face, Sandra seemed to glimpse embarrassment and shame at being exposed in this way to both the pitiless light of day and the gaze of a handful of onlookers. Sandra could imagine their dismissive comments: she'd asked for it, if she'd chosen another life she wouldn't have ended up like this.

Then she saw him. The man was standing a little way back from the others. He was on the pavement, watching in a neutral, non-judgemental way as the mortuary staff got ready to take away the body.

Sandra immediately recognised that face. It was the man in the fifth photograph from the Leica. Dressed in dark clothes, with a scar on his temple.

Who are you, you bastard? Was it you who threw my David off that building?

She looked for him in other photographs. His face cropped up on three more occasions. Always among the onlookers, but always standing somewhat apart.

David had been hoping to catch a glimpse of him in places where an act of violence had been committed. That was why he had kept his radio tuned to the police frequency and noted those addresses in his diary and on the map of the city.

Why had he been investigating him? Who was this man? In what way was he implicated in these cruel deaths? And in David's?

Now Sandra knew what to do. She would have to find him. But where? Maybe she had to use the same method, wait for radio transmissions to the patrol cars and then rush to the scene.

Suddenly, she started to consider an element she hadn't previously taken into account. It had nothing to do with the man she was looking for, but it was still a question that required an answer.

David hadn't photographed the whole of the Caravaggio painting, merely a detail. That didn't make sense: if he had meant it for her, why make things more complicated?

Sandra found the painting again on the computer. David could have found the image on the internet and photographed it from the screen. Instead of which, by photographing just the detail of the boy, he had been trying to tell her that he had been there in person.

'There are things you have to see with your own eyes, Ginger.'

She remembered what De Michelis had told her. The painting was in Rome, in the church of San Luigi dei Francesi.

11.39 p.m.

The first time he had been with Clemente at a crime scene, it had been here in Rome, in the EUR area. The first victim in whose eyes he had looked was a prostitute fished out of the little lake there. Since then there had been other bodies, and all had the same look in their eyes. A questioning look.

Why me?

Always the same surprise, the same astonishment. Incredulity mixed with the unrealisable desire to turn round, to wind back the tape, to have a second chance.

Marcus was sure that the surprise was not at death, but at the sudden terrible intuition of how irreversible it was. These victims hadn't thought, 'Oh God, I'm dying,' but rather, 'Oh God, I'm dying and I can't do anything to prevent it.'

Maybe the same idea had occurred to him, too, when someone had shot him in that hotel room in Prague. Had he felt fear or was it a comforting sense of inevitability? The amnesia had wiped out that last memory and everything before it. The first image that had fixed itself in his new memory was the wooden crucifix on the white wall facing his hospital bed. He had lain there looking at it for days, wondering what had happened to him. The bullet had not affected the areas of the brain that controlled language and movement, so he could still walk and talk. But he did not know what to say or where to go. Then Clemente had appeared: that smiling, clean-shaven face, that dark hair with the side parting, those benevolent eyes.

'I've found you, Marcus.' Those were his first words. A hope, and his name.

Clemente hadn't recognised him from his face, because he had never seen him before. Only Devok had known his identity, that was the rule. Clemente had simply followed his trail to Prague. It had been his friend and mentor Devok who had saved him, even as a dead man. That had been the bitterest news that Marcus had had to learn. He didn't remember anything about Devok, any more than he remembered anything else. But now he had discovered that Devok had been killed, and had realised that grief is the one human emotion that doesn't need to be linked to a memory. A child will always feel grief at the loss of a parent, even if that loss happened before it was born or when it was still too little to understand what death was. Raffaele Altieri was a good example of that.

We need memory only to be happy, Marcus had thought.

Clemente had been very patient with him. He had waited for him to recover, then had brought him back to Rome. In the months that had followed, he had tried to teach him the few things that he knew of his past: his country of origin, which was Argentina, his parents, who were now dead, the reason he was in Italy and, finally, his task – Clemente did not call it a job.

He had trained him, just as Devok had done many years earlier. It had not been difficult, all he had had to do was make him realise that certain things were already present in him, he simply had to bring them out again.

'That's your talent,' he would say.

Sometimes Marcus didn't want to be the way he was. Sometimes he would have preferred to be normal. But all he had to do was look at it himself in a mirror to know that he would never be normal, which was why he avoided mirrors. The scar was a grim memento. Whoever had tried to kill him had left him that souvenir on his temple, because death was the one thing he would never be able to forget. Every time Marcus saw a murder victim, he knew he had been in the same condition. He felt similar to them, he was doomed to feel the same solitude as them.

The prostitute fished out of the little lake was the mirror he had been trying to escape.

She had immediately reminded him of a painting by Caravaggio, *Death of the Virgin*, in which the Madonna was shown lying lifeless on what looked like a slab in a morgue. There were no religious symbols around her, and she was not enveloped by any kind of mystical aura. Far from being shown as a creature halfway between the divine and the human, which was usually the case, Mary was a pale, abandoned body with a swollen belly. It was said that the artist had been inspired by the corpse of a prostitute fished out of a river, that was why the painting had been rejected by its sponsors.

Caravaggio liked to take a scene from the horrors of everyday life and superimpose a sacred meaning on it, giving the people different roles, turning them into saints or dying virgins.

When Clemente took Marcus for the first time to the church of San Luigi dei Francesi, he told him to look at *The Martyrdom of St*

Matthew. Then he asked him to divest those figures of any holy element, as if they were ordinary people at a crime scene.

'Now what do you see?' he asked.

'A murder,' was the reply.

That was his first lesson. The training, for people like him, always started with that painting.

'Dogs are colour blind,' his new teacher had said. 'We humans, on the other hand, see too many colours. Take them away, leaving only black and white. Good and evil.'

But very soon Marcus had realised that he could see other shades, too. Shades that neither dogs nor men could perceive. That was his true talent.

Thinking about it now, he was overcome with a sudden nostalgia. He didn't even know for what. But it happened sometimes, this feeling things he had no reason to feel.

It was late, but he didn't want to go home. He didn't want to fall asleep and have that recurring dream that took him back in time, to Prague and the moment when he had died.

Because I die every night, he told himself.

Instead he wanted to stay here, in this church that had become his secret refuge. He often came back here.

Tonight he was not alone. He was waiting together with a group of people for it to stop raining outside. A concert had not long ended, but the priests and caretakers hadn't wanted to throw out the few spectators who had remained. So the musicians had started playing more pieces for them, unexpectedly prolonging the sweetness of that evening. As the storm attempted to drive them out, the music rose up against the roar of thunder, spreading joy through those present.

Marcus stood to one side, as always. For him, San Luigi dei Francesi also meant Caravaggio's masterpiece, *The Martyrdom of St Matthew*. For once he allowed himself to look at it with the eyes of a normal man. In the gloom of that side chapel, he noticed that the light illuminating the scene was already inside the painting. He envied Caravaggio's talent: to perceive light where others saw only shadows. Exactly the opposite of his own talent.

Just as he was savouring the results of that intuition, he happened to turn his eyes slightly to his left.

At the end of the nave, a young woman, soaking wet from the rain, was looking at him.

Immediately, an alarm was triggered inside him. For the first time, someone was violating his invisibility.

He turned away and headed quickly towards the sacristy. She moved to follow him. He would have to throw her off his trail. He remembered that there was another exit on this side. He walked faster in that direction, but could hear her rubber shoes squeaking on the marble floor as she tried to catch up with him. A roll of thunder echoed over his head, drowning out that other sound. What could this woman want with him? He entered the vestibule that led to the back of the church. There was the door. He went to it, opened it, and was about to step out into the shroud of rain when she spoke.

'Stop.' She said it without shouting. Her tone was cold.

Marcus stopped.

'Now turn round.'

He did so. The only light was the yellowish one from the street lamps, which stopped at the threshold of the church. But there was enough light to see that she was holding a gun.

'Do you know me? Do you know who I am?'

Marcus thought before replying. 'No.'

'What about my husband, did you know him? Did you kill him?' There was no anger in her voice, just despair. 'If you know something you have to tell me. Or I swear I'll kill you.' She seemed sincere.

Marcus said nothing. He had his arms down by his sides, motionless. He returned her gaze. He was not afraid of her. Rather, he felt compassion.

The woman's eyes turned watery. 'Who are you?'

At that moment there was a flash of lightning, followed by a deafening roll of thunder. The lights of the street lamps trembled for a moment, then went out. The street and the sacristy were plunged into darkness.

But Marcus did not run away immediately.

'I'm a priest.'

When the street lamps went on again, Sandra saw that he was no longer there.

ONE YEAR EARLIER
MEXICO CITY

The taxi advanced slowly in the heavy rush-hour traffic. The Latin music on the radio joined the music coming from the other cars, all with their windows open because of the heat. The result was an unbearable cacophony, but the hunter noticed that each of the drivers seemed to be following his own little tune. He had asked his driver to switch on the air conditioning, only to be told that it wasn't working.

It was thirty degrees centigrade in Mexico City, and the rate of humidity was due to rise that night. It would be made all the worse by the canopy of smog that covered the metropolis. That was why he had no wish to linger too long. He would do what he had to do and then leave immediately. Despite the discomfort, he was excited at the idea of being here.

He had to see with his own eyes.

In Paris, his prey had made a narrow escape and then, predictably, had wiped out all traces of himself. But this city represented a new hope. If the hunter was going to relaunch the chase, he needed to gain a better understanding of who he was dealing with.

The taxi dropped him outside the main entrance of the Hospicio de Santa Lucía. The hunter looked up at the white, somewhat dilapidated five-storey building. However striking its colonial architecture, the bars on the windows left no doubt as to the place's current use.

This was, after all, the destiny of psychiatric hospitals, he thought. Once you went in, you didn't come out.

Dr Florinda Valdez came to the reception desk to greet him. They had exchanged a few emails, in which, for the first time, he had assumed the identity of a lecturer in forensic psychology in Cambridge.

'Hello, Dr Foster,' she said with a smile, holding out her hand.

'Hello, Florinda.' The hunter had realised immediately that this plump woman in her early forties would easily be won over by the suave Dr Foster, if for no other reason than that she was still unmarried. He had done his research before contacting her.

'I hope you had a good trip?'

'Oh, yes, and I've always wanted to visit Mexico.'

'Well, I've thought of some very nice things we can see this weekend.'

'Good,' he said, feigning enthusiasm. 'Then I suggest we get straight down to work. That way we'll have more time to ourselves later.'

'Yes, of course. Come this way.'

The hunter had come across Florinda Valdez by chance while doing some internet research on psychiatric disorders. On YouTube, he had found a lecture she had given at a convention of psychiatrists in Miami. It had been a stroke of luck, the kind that made him believe that he would achieve his aim in the end and that his self-denial would be rewarded.

Florinda Valdez's lecture had been entitled *The case of the girl in the mirror.*

'Of course we don't allow just anybody to see her,' she hastened to say as they walked along the corridors of the hospital, implying that she might be expecting something equally flattering from him in return.

'You know, my scholarly curiosity got the better of me. I left my luggage at the hotel and came straight here. Perhaps we could go back there later before we go out to dinner? If you don't mind, of course.'

'No, of course not.' She blushed, imagining all kinds of developments that evening. But he did not have a hotel room. His flight was leaving at eight.

The woman's joy was out of place amid the moans emanating from the rooms of the hospital. As they passed them, the hunter managed to glance inside. Their occupants were no longer people: heavily sedated, their faces as white as the clothes they wore, their skulls shaved to deter fleas, they wandered barefoot, bumping into one another like drifting pieces of flotsam. Others were tied with leather straps to sweat-soaked beds, writhing and screaming with the voice of demons, or else lying motionless, waiting for a death that was mercilessly late in coming. There were old people who seemed like children, unless they were children old before their time.

As the hunter passed through this hell, the malign force that kept them locked up within themselves stared out at him with wide-open eyes.

They reached what Florinda Valdez called the special ward. It was in a wing isolated from the others, where the patients were kept two in a room at most.

'This is where we keep the violent patients, but also the most interesting clinical cases ... Angelina is one of them.' There was pride in her voice.

They came to an iron door like that of a cell, and Florinda gestured to a male nurse to open it. Inside, it was dark, with just a glimmer of light filtering through a small window high up on the wall. It took the hunter a while to make out a body as slender as a twig huddled in a corner between the wall and the bed. The girl could not have been more than twenty. A certain delicacy could still be glimpsed in a face hardened by suffering.

'This is Angelina,' Florinda announced with a dramatic flourish, as if presenting a fairground freak.

The hunter took a few steps forward, eager to find himself face to face with the reason that had brought him here. But the patient did not even seem to be aware of them.

'The police discovered her when they raided a brothel in a village near Tijuana. They were looking for a drug trafficker, and instead they found her. Her parents were alcoholics and her father sold her into prostitution when she was barely five years old.'

She must have been a valuable asset at first, the hunter thought, to be reserved for clients ready to pay for their own little vice.

'As she grew up, she lost her value and the men could have her for a few pesos. The people who ran the brothel kept her for drunken peasants and lorry drivers. She probably had sex with dozens of men every day.'

'A slave.'

'She never left the place, they kept her prisoner. The woman who had charge of her mistreated her. She never spoke. I doubt she really understood what was happening around her. As if she was in a catatonic state.'

The perfect escape valve for the worst instincts of those perverts, the hunter was about to remark, but he held back. He had to make sure his interest seemed purely professional. 'Tell me when you first noticed her . . . talent.'

'When they brought her here, she shared a room with an elderly patient. We'd thought of putting them together because both were disconnected from the world. And in fact they didn't communicate with each other at all.'

The hunter looked from the girl to Florinda Valdez. 'What happened then?'

'At first Angelina developed strange motor symptoms. Her joints were stiff and painful, and she moved with difficulty. We thought it was some kind of arthritis. But then she started to lose her teeth.'

'Her teeth?'

'Not only that: we ran tests on her and discovered a serious weakening of her internal organs.'

'And when did you finally realise what was happening?'

A shadow passed over Florinda Valdez's face. 'When her hair turned white.'

The hunter turned to look at the patient again. From what he could see, her almost shaven hair was unmistakably black.

'To reverse the symptoms, all we had to do was take the old lady out of the room.'

The hunter looked closely at the girl, trying to sense whether there was still anything human hidden deep in her inexpressive eyes. 'The chameleon syndrome,' he said.

For a long time, Angelina had been forced to be what the men who violated her wanted her to be. An object of pleasure, nothing else. So she had adapted. The result was that she had lost her own self. One little piece at a time, it had been taken away from her.

Many years of abuse had wiped out all traces of identity. So she borrowed one from the people around her.

'We're not dealing with a case of multiple personality,' Florinda Valdez said, 'or the kind of patient who claims to be Napoleon or the Queen of England. Subjects affected by chameleon syndrome tend to imitate perfectly whoever they meet. Faced with a doctor they become doctors, faced with a cook they say they know how to cook. Questioned on their profession, they respond in a general but appropriate manner.'

The hunter remembered reading about a patient who identified with the cardiologist he was talking to and, when the doctor asked him a trick question on the diagnosis of a particular cardiac anomaly, answered that he couldn't give an opinion without careful clinical examination.

'But Angelina doesn't simply emulate other people. When she was in contact with the old woman, she actually began to age. Her mind was causing her body to change.'

A transformist, the hunter told himself. 'Have there been other manifestations?'

'Some, but insignificant ones, lasting barely a few minutes. Subjects affected by the syndrome are the way they are because they've undergone brain damage or, as in the case of Angelina, some kind of shock that produces the same effects.'

The hunter was both disturbed and fascinated by the girl's abilities. This was the proof he needed to demonstrate to himself that he had not been labouring under a delusion all this time. The theories he had formulated about his prey had been confirmed.

The hunter knew that all serial killers suffer from a crisis of identity: when they kill they are reflected in the victim and recognise themselves, they don't need to pretend any more. While the murder is happening, the monster deep inside them appears on their faces.

But the man he was hunting – his prey – was much more than that. He had no true identity, which was why he had constantly to borrow one from somebody else. He was a unique example, an extremely rare psychiatric case.

A transformist serial killer.

He didn't just take another person's place and imitate his behaviour, he actually *became* that person. That was why nobody, apart from the hunter, had ever identified him.

It was impossible to predict his moves. The transformist had exceptional learning skills, especially as regards languages and accents. Over the years he had perfected his method. First of all he chose an appropriate individual. A man similar to himself: nondescript features, the same height, easily reproducible distinguishing marks. As in the case of Jean Duez in Paris. The most important thing was that he had no past, no ties, and a monotonous daily routine, and preferably worked from home.

The transformist took over his life.

The modus operandi was always the same. He would kill the person and wipe out his face, as if wanting to remove his identity for ever, then assume that identity for himself.

Angelina wasn't merely a confirmation. She was a second example. Looking at her, the hunter realised that he hadn't been deceiving himself all this time. But he still needed a demonstration, because the most difficult challenge was in trying to imagine such a talent combined with an instinct to kill.

Florinda Valdez's mobile phone started to vibrate. She excused herself and went out to answer the call. This was the opportunity the hunter had been waiting for.

He had done some research before coming here. Angelina had a younger brother. They had lived together for a very short time, given that she had been sold at the age of five. But perhaps that had been sufficient for some trace of him to remain in her.

For the hunter, it was the key he needed to enter the prison of her mind.

Alone now with the girl, he went and placed himself in front of her, kneeling in such a way that she could see his face properly. Then he started to speak slowly.

'Angelina, I want you to listen to me. I've taken your brother. Little Pedro, do you remember? He's a lovely boy, but now I'm going to kill him.'

The girl did not react.

'Did you hear what I said? I'm going to kill him, Angelina. I'm going to tear his heart from his chest and hold it in my hand until it stops beating.' The hunter held out his open palm towards her. Can you hear it beating? Pedro is dying. And nobody will save him. And it'll really hurt, I swear. He'll die, but first he'll have to suffer terribly.'

All of a sudden, the girl lunged forward and bit the hand the hunter was holding towards her. Caught off guard, he lost his balance, and before he knew it Angelina was on top of him, pressing down on his chest. She was not heavy; he yanked at her and managed to pull free of her. He watched as she crawled back into her corner, her mouth filled with blood, her sharp gums stained red. Even though she had no teeth, she had managed to inflict a deep wound.

Dr Valdez came back in and saw Angelina sitting calmly in her corner and her visitor using his shirt to try and stem the blood gushing from his hand.

'What happened?' she cried in alarm.

'She attacked me,' the hunter hastened to say. 'It isn't serious, but I'll probably need a few stitches.'

'She's never done that before.'

'I don't know what to say. All I did was try and talk to her.'

Florinda Valdes accepted that explanation, perhaps because she was afraid to spoil her chances with Dr Foster. As for the hunter, he had no further reason to stay here: in provoking the girl, he had got the answer he was looking for.

'I think it's best if I have this seen to,' he said, exaggerating his grimace of pain.

Dr Valdez was all at sea, she didn't want him to go, but she didn't know how to detain him. She offered to accompany him to Emergency, but he politely declined the offer. In sudden desperation, she said, 'I wanted to talk to you about the other case ...'

Her words had the hoped-for effect. The hunter stopped in the doorway. 'What other case?'

'It happened many years ago, in the Ukraine,' Dr Valdez replied. 'A boy named Dima.'

THREE DAYS AGO

3.27 a.m.

The corpse started screaming.

Only when his lungs were empty and he was forced to catch his breath did he realise that he had come back from the dream. Devok had been killed, again. How many more times would he have to witness his death? This was the earliest memory he possessed, and it was repeated every time he closed his eyes to sleep.

Marcus put his hand under the pillow and searched for his felt-tip pen. When he found it, he wrote on the wall next to the bed: *Three shots.*

Another glimmer of his past. But this new element changed many things. Like the detail of the smashed window the night before, the perception had been an auditory one. But he was convinced that this time it was really important.

He had heard three distinct shots. Previously, he had always counted two. One for himself, one for Devok. But in the latest version of the dream there had been a third shot.

His unconscious could have been playing tricks on him, arbitrarily modifying the scene in the hotel in Prague. Sometimes it inserted unlikely or incongruous sounds or objects: a jukebox, a piece of pop music. Marcus had no control over its quirks.

But this time it was as if he had always known it.

This third shot now joined the other fragments of the scene. He was sure it, too, would prove useful in reconstructing what had happened and, above all, in helping him to see the face of the man who had killed his master and had forced him to forget himself.

Three shots.

A few hours earlier, Marcus had again found himself facing the threat of a gun. But that had been different. He hadn't been afraid. The woman in San Luigi dei Francesi would have pulled the trigger, he was sure of it. But there was no hate in her eyes, there was desperation. Only the momentary blackout had saved him. At that point, he could have escaped. Instead, he had stayed and revealed to her who he was.

I'm a priest.

Why had he done that? Why had he felt the need to tell her? He had wanted to give her something, some kind of compensation for all her suffering. His identity was his greatest secret, he should have defended it at all costs. The world would not understand. That was the litany Clemente had repeated to him from the first day. And he had failed in that commitment. With an unknown woman, as well. This woman, whoever she was, had a reason to kill him, that reason being, apparently, the murder of the man she had loved. And yet Marcus felt unable to consider her an enemy.

Who was she? In what way could she and her husband have been part of his previous life? What if she held some clue to his past?

Maybe I should look for her, he told himself. Maybe I should talk to her.

But that wasn't wise. And besides, he didn't know anything about her.

He wouldn't say anything to Clemente. He was sure he wouldn't approve such an impulsive act. They both served a sacred oath, but in different ways. His young friend was a faithful, devout priest, whereas in Marcus's heart spirits moved that he was unable to comprehend.

He looked at his watch. Clemente had left him a message. They had to meet before dawn. A few hours earlier, the police had suspended their search of Jeremiah Smith's villa.

Now it was their turn to visit the house.

The road wound between the hills to the west of Rome. A few miles away were Fiumicino, the coast, the turbulent estuary of the Tiber. The old Fiat Panda laboured up the slope, its headlights barely illuminating a portion of the road. Around them, the countryside was starting to wake up. Dawn was near.

Clemente was leaning forward as he drove to see where he was going. He was often forced to shift gears noisily. Marcus, who had climbed in near the Ponte Milvio, had given him an account of what had happened the previous evening in Guido Altieri's house. His friend, however, was much more interested in the version that had appeared on television, which failed to mention the presence of a third man at the scene. He was relieved by that: for now, their secret was safe.

Marcus made no reference to what had happened later, the episode of the armed woman in San Luigi dei Francesi. Instead he went straight on to how the events of the last few hours reflected on the disappearance of young Lara.

'Jeremiah Smith didn't have a heart attack. He was poisoned.'

'The toxicological tests didn't reveal the presence of any suspicious substances in his blood,' Clemente retorted.

'Well, I'm convinced that's what happened. There's no other explanation.'

'Then someone must have taken the words on his chest seriously.'

Kill me, Marcus thought. Someone acting in the shadows had offered both Monica, the sister of Jeremiah Smith's first victim, and Raffaele Altieri the opportunity to redress the terrible wrongs they had suffered. 'When justice is no longer possible, there remains only one choice: forgiveness or revenge.'

'An eye for an eye,' Clementi said.

'Yes, but there's something else.' Marcus paused, trying to formulate an idea that had been maturing in him since the previous evening. 'Someone was expecting our intervention. Do you remember the Bible with the red satin bookmark I found in Lara's apartment?'

'The page with St Paul's Epistle to the Thessalonians: "the day of the Lord will come like a thief in the night".'

'Somebody knows about us, Clemente,' he said with ever greater conviction. 'Think about it. He sent Raffaele an anonymous letter, for us he chose a sacred text. A message appropriate to men of faith. I was involved for one reason, and it's the reason Raffaele was summoned to Lara's apartment. In the end, I was the one who led him to the truth about his father. It's my fault that Guido Altieri was killed.'

Clemente turned for a moment to look at Marcus. 'Who can have arranged all this?'

'I don't know. But whoever it is has not only been putting the victims' relatives in contact with the killers, he's also been trying to involve us.'

Clemente sensed that this wasn't mere hypothesis, and that troubled him. At this point, the visit to Jeremiah Smith's villa had become of vital importance. They were convinced they would find a sign there that would lead them to the next level of the labyrinth. It was their one hope of saving Lara. Without that objective, they would have been less motivated to continue. And whoever was behind this enigma knew that, which was why he was offering the young student's life as a prize.

There were still police patrolling in front of the main gate. But the property was too large to be watched in its entirety. Clemente parked the Panda on a side road half a mile away. Then they got out and continued on foot, trusting that the darkness would hide them.

'We have to be quick,' Clementi said as they hurried across the uneven ground. 'In a couple of hours the forensics team will be back to continue their work.'

They got into the villa through a back window, removing the seals. They had others, fake ones, which they would put on when they left. Nobody would suspect a thing. Having put on overshoes and latex gloves, they lit the torches they had brought with them, keeping the beams of light partially covered with the palms of their hands so that they could orient themselves without being noticed from outside.

The house was a kind of refurbished Art Nouveau, with a few modern concessions. They went into a study with a mahogany desk and a large bookcase. The furnishings bore witness to a comfortable past. Jeremiah had grown up in an upper middle-class family, and his parents had built up a decent fortune in the textile trade. Their dedication to business had prevented them having more than one child. They had probably assumed he would carry on with the company and preserve the good name of the Smiths. But they must soon have realised that their sole heir was not cut out for that.

Marcus shone his torch over a series of framed photographs neatly arranged on an oak table. The story of the family was condensed into those faded images. A picnic in a meadow, a very young Jeremiah on his mother's lap, his father embracing both of them in a protective hug. On the villa's tennis court, in immaculate sportswear, clutching wooden rackets. At Christmas, dressed in red, posing in front of a decorated tree.

Waiting stiffly for the camera's self-timer to go off, always composed in a perfect triptych, like ghosts from another era.

At a certain point, though, these photographs lost one of their protagonists. A teenage Jeremiah and his mother, smiling sadly and formally: the head of the family has left them after a brief illness and they continue the tradition, not so much to perpetuate his memory as to distance themselves from the shadow of death.

One image in particular aroused Marcus's curiosity. It struck him as rather macabre that they had found a way to include the dead man in the pose. Mother and son stood on either side of a large sandstone fireplace above which hung a rather austere portrait of the father.

'They haven't found anything to link Jeremiah Smith to Lara,' Clemente said behind him.

In the room, marks of the police search were evident. Objects had been moved, furniture inspected.

'So they still don't know he was the one who took her. They won't search for her.'

'Stop it,' Clemente said, his tone suddenly hard.

Marcus was surprised: it wasn't like him.

'I can't believe you still don't get it. You're not a detective, and you're not allowed to intervene. You've been trained to do what you do, and that's it. Do I have to spell it out for you? There's every chance the girl will die in the end. In fact, I'd say it's almost certain she will. But it won't depend on anything we do or don't do. So stop feeling guilty.'

Marcus concentrated again on the photograph showing a solemn twenty-year-old Jeremiah Smith posing beneath his father's portrait.

'Where do you want to start?' Clemente asked.

'In the room where they found him dying.'

It was clear that the forensics team had been hard at work in the living room: there were halogen lamps on stands, deposits of residue from the reagents they used to detect organic liquids and prints, and numbered stickers marking the positions of finds that had been photographed and then taken away.

It was in this room that a blue hair ribbon, a coral bracelet, a pink knitted shoe and a red roller skate – items belonging to Jeremiah Smith's four victims – had been found. These souvenirs indisputably proved that he had been involved, and keeping them had been a risk. But Marcus could imagine how the killer had felt every time he touched these trophies. They were the symbols of what he did best: killing. Having them in his hands, he absorbed their energy, as if violent death had the power to reinvigorate the person who dispenses it.

They were kept in the living room, because Jeremiah wanted them next to him. That way the girls were always there. Souls in torment, prisoners of that house together with him.

But among the objects there wasn't one that belonged to Lara.

Marcus entered the room, while Clemente remained in the doorway. The furniture was covered with white sheets, apart from the sofa in the middle of the room and the old television set. A small table had been overturned, and on the floor were a broken bowl, a pool of milk, now dry, and crumbled biscuits.

Jeremiah had knocked them over when he had felt ill, Marcus thought. In the evening he had milk and biscuits while watching TV. The image of solitude. The monster didn't need to hide, other people's indifference was shelter enough. If only the world had paid any attention to him, he might have been stopped earlier.

Jeremiah was an unsociable character, and yet he transformed himself in order to lure his victims. *Apart from Lara, he took the others by day*, Marcus recalled. What method did he use to approach them and gain their trust? It must have been convincing, because the girls didn't fear him. Why didn't he use the same tricks to make friends? The one thing that drove him was murder. His success was down to evil. Because evil somehow made him seem a good person, someone you could trust. But Jeremiah Smith had overlooked one important fact: there is always a price to be paid. The greatest fear of every human being, even of those who have chosen to live as hermits, is not death, but dying alone. There is a subtle difference. And it's one that you don't realise until you experience it.

The thought that nobody will mourn us, that nobody will feel our loss or remember us. It's the same thing that was happening to me, Marcus thought.

He was looking at the part of the room where the ambulance team had tried to resuscitate Smith. Sterile gloves, pieces of gauze, syringes and cannulas: everything was still there, as if frozen in that moment.

Marcus tried to focus on what had happened before Jeremiah Smith started to feel the symptoms. 'Whoever poisoned him knew his habits – he did to Jeremiah exactly what Jeremiah had done to Lara. He introduced himself into his life, into his house, and observed him. He didn't choose sugar to conceal the drug, but maybe he put something in the milk. It was a kind of retaliation.'

Clemente watched as his pupil entered completely into the psyche of the person who had done all this. 'That's why Jeremiah felt bad and telephoned Emergency.'

'The Gemelli is the nearest hospital – it was only natural for the call to be directed there. Whoever did this to Jeremiah Smith knew that Monica, the first victim's sister, was the doctor on duty in Emergency last night and that she'd go with the ambulance.' Marcus seemed impressed with the skill of the person who had orchestrated this opportunity for revenge. 'He doesn't act randomly, he's meticulous.' He had taken the crime scene apart, piece by piece, revealing the conjuring trick that had been played. 'Yes, you're good,' he said, addressing his adversary as if he were present. 'And now let's see what else you have in store for us.'

'Do you think there are any clues that could lead us to the place where Lara's being kept prisoner?'

'No, he's too clever for that. Even if there had been, he would have removed them. The girl is a prize, don't forget that. We have to deserve her.'

Marcus started moving around the room, convinced there was something he was still missing.

'What do you think we should be looking for?' Clemente asked.

'Something that has no connection with anything else. Something the police wouldn't notice, but that only we could grasp.'

He needed to find the precise point to start his examination of the scene. He was sure that from there, the anomaly would be evident. The most logical spot was right here, where Jeremiah had been found dying.

'The shutters,' he said. Clemente went and closed the shutters over the two large windows that looked out on the back of the house. Now Marcus let the beam of his torch wander over the room. The shadows of the objects rose in turn, like obedient little soldiers, as he aimed at them. The sofas, the sideboard, the dining table, the armchair, the fireplace with the painting of tulips above it. Marcus was struck by a feeling of déjà vu. He turned back and again shone his torch at the painting.

'That shouldn't be here.'

Clemente did not understand. But Marcus had a clear memory of the sandstone fireplace as he had seen it in one of the photographs in the study: the photograph of mother and son standing beneath an oil portrait of Jeremiah's late father.

'It's been moved.'

The portrait wasn't there now. Marcus went up to the painting of the tulips, shifted the frame and ascertained that the mark left on the wall over the years was a different size. He was about to put it back into position, when he noticed a number on the back, in the bottom left-hand corner of the canvas: the number 1.

'I've found it,' Clemente called to him from the corridor.

Marcus joined him and saw the painting of Jeremiah's father on the wall next to the door.

'The pictures have been swapped round.'

He took the painting from the wall and checked the back. The number this time was 2. They both looked around, with the same idea in their minds. They separated, and started taking every painting off the wall, trying to find the third one.

'Here it is,' Clemente announced. It was a landscape painting hanging at the end of the corridor, at the foot of the staircase that led to the upper floor. They started climbing and, halfway up, found the fourth painting. They knew now they were on the right track.

'He's showing us the way,' Marcus said. But neither of them could imagine where it would lead them.

On the second-floor landing they located the fifth painting, then the sixth in a little passage, and the seventh in the corridor that led to the bedrooms. The eighth was very small: a tempera painting of an Indian tiger. It was next to a little door in what must have been Jeremiah Smith's bedroom as a child. A battalion of lead soldiers on a shelf, a Meccano set, a catapult, a rocking horse.

We often forget that even monsters were children once, Marcus thought. There are things we carry with us from childhood. But God knows where the urge to kill comes from.

Clemente opened the little door to reveal a steep flight of stairs that probably led to the attic.

'Maybe the police haven't yet had a good look up there.'

They were both sure that the ninth painting would be the last in the series. Cautiously they climbed the uneven steps. The ceiling was low, forcing them to stoop. At last they came out into a large room crammed with old furniture, books and trunks. A few birds had made their nests between the rafters. Startled by the presence of the two men, they began whirling around, desperate for a way out, which they found in an open dormer window.

Clemente looked at his watch. 'We can't stay too long, it's almost dawn.'

So they immediately started looking for the painting. There were various canvases piled up in a corner. Clemente looked through them. 'Nothing,' he announced after a moment or two, shaking the dust from his clothes.

Marcus caught a glint of gold from behind a chest. He stepped around it and saw a richly decorated frame hanging on the wall. There was no need to turn it to realise that this was indeed the ninth picture. The content was unusual enough to confirm that they had reached the end of this strange treasure hunt.

It was a child's drawing.

Done with coloured pencils on a sheet from an exercise book, it had subsequently been put in this frame that was much too elaborate for it, the very incongruity calculated to attract attention.

It depicted a day in summer or spring, with the sun casting a pleasant glow over a luxuriant scene. Trees, swallows, flowers, a small river. There were two children in the picture, a little girl in a red polka dot dress and a little boy clutching an object in his hand. Despite the gaiety of the colours and the innocence of the subject, Marcus felt a curious sensation.

There was something malign in that drawing.

He took a step forward to get a better look at it. Only then did he realise that what he saw on the little girl's dress were not polka dots but bleeding wounds. And that the little boy was holding a pair of scissors.

He read the date written in the margin: it went back twenty years. Jeremiah Smith was already too old at the time to be the artist. No, this picture was part of somebody else's sick fantasy. He remembered Caravaggio's *Martyrdom of St Matthew*: what he had in front of him was the depiction of a crime scene. But, when it had been drawn, the crime had not yet been committed.

Even monsters were children once, he repeated to himself. The one in the drawing had grown up in the meantime. And Marcus realised that he would have to find him.

6.04 a.m.

The first day in forensics they teach you that in a crime scene there is no such thing as coincidence. Then they continue to repeat it to you at every opportunity, in case you forget it. They tell you that coincidences are not only misleading but could turn out to be harmful and counter-productive. And they cite various extreme cases in which this had compromised investigations irrevocably.

Thanks to this conditioning, Sandra didn't much believe in coincidences. But in real life, she admitted that these accidental connections between events could sometimes be useful, at the very least to call our attention to things we wouldn't see otherwise.

She had come to the conclusion that some of them were of little importance. These were the ones that could be dismissed with the words: 'Oh, it's just a coincidence.' Others, though, seemed designed to point our lives in a different direction. These were given a different name: 'signs'. These make us feel we are receiving an exclusive message, as if the cosmos or a superior entity has chosen us. In other words, they make us feel special.

Sandra recalled that Jung had called this second kind of coincidence *synchronicity*. He had enumerated the fundamental characteristics of these coincidences. They were absolutely acausal, in other words unconnected to the nexus of cause and effect. They coincided with profound emotional experiences. And they possessed a strong symbolic value.

Jung maintained that certain individuals go through life looking for deeper meanings in every unusual event that happens to them.

Sandra was not one of those people. But she had been forced to re-evaluate her position. And this turnaround had been brought about by David's story of the extraordinary chain of events that had led to their meeting.

It was two days before the August bank holiday and he was in Berlin. He was supposed to join a few friends on Mykonos, where they would board a sailing boat for a cruise around the Greek islands. That morning, however, his alarm clock had not gone off; he had woken up late, yet still managed to get to the airport moments before check-in closed. He remembered thinking: What luck! He hadn't known what was in store for him.

To get to his destination, he needed to catch a connection in Rome. But before he could get on this second plane, the airline told him there had been a problem and his luggage had been left behind in Berlin.

Having no intention of giving up, he quickly bought a new suitcase and new clothes in the airport shops and presented himself punctually at the check-in for his flight to Athens – only to discover that, due to the large numbers travelling over the holiday weekend, he was double-booked.

At eight in the evening, when he should have been sitting in the stern of a three-master sipping ice-cold ouzo with a gorgeous Indian model he had met two weeks earlier in Milan, he found himself in a departure lounge packed with tourists, filling out insurance forms to reclaim his baggage.

He should have waited until the following day and taken the first available flight, but he didn't think he could bear that. So he rented a car with the intention of going to the port of Brindisi and there embarking on a ferry for Greece.

After driving all night, a journey of over three hundred miles, he saw the sun begin to emerge over the coast of Apulia. The road maps indicated that he was not far from his destination, but just then his car developed a fault. After chugging along for a while, it finally broke down completely.

Pulling up at the side of the road, David got out and instead of cursing his bad luck looked at the landscape around him. To his right, a white town on a plateau. To his left, a few hundred yards away, the sea.

He walked to the beach, which was deserted at that hour of the morning. On the foreshore, he took out one of his aniseed cigarettes, lit it, and celebrated the rising sun.

It was then that he looked down and saw some small, perfectly symmetrical footprints in the wet sand. Instinctively, he attributed them to a woman jogging. The coast in that direction was full of inlets, so whoever had left them had already disappeared from sight. But one thing was certain: not much time had passed, or the backwash would have erased the prints completely.

Whenever he told the story subsequently, he always found it difficult to describe what had gone through his head at that moment.

He had suddenly felt that he absolutely had to follow those foot-prints, and had broken into a run.

At this point in the story, Sandra would always ask him how he knew it was a woman.

'I didn't know, I could only hope. I mean, it could have been a little boy, or even a short man.'

She was never entirely convinced by this explanation. Her instinct as a police officer drove her to ask, 'And how did you know they were jogging?'

But David was prepared for this, too. 'The prints in the sand were deeper at the front, which meant the person was running.'

'I guess that's plausible.'

And David would resume the story from where she had inter-rupted him. He said that he had gone a hundred yards, climbed a dune, and from the top spotted the figure of a woman. She was wearing shorts, a figure-hugging T-shirt and trainers, and her blonde hair was gathered in a ponytail. He couldn't see her face. He felt an urge to call out to her, which was stupid, because he didn't even know her name.

At this point, he put on speed.

What would he say once he had caught up with her? The closer he got, the more he realised that he had to come up with something so as not to appear a complete idiot. But he couldn't think of any-thing.

After much effort, he managed to come up alongside her. She was very beautiful – when Sandra heard him say this, she usually smiled. He apologised to the woman and asked her to stop. She did so, but reluctantly, and stared at this madman standing there trying to catch his breath. He couldn't have made a great impression on her. He had been wearing the same clothes for twenty-four hours, he hadn't slept all night, he was sweating from his run, and he probably didn't smell particularly good.

'Hi, I'm David,' he said, holding out his hand. She looked at it in disgust, without taking it, as if he had offered her a rotten fish. Then he continued, 'Do you know what Jung said about coinci-dences?' And he launched into an account of all the things that had happened to him since he had left Berlin the previous day. She stood there listening to him without saying a word, trying perhaps to figure out where he was going with all this.

She let him finish, then said that their meeting couldn't exactly be called a coincidence. Because, although the chain of events that had led him to this beach had been independent of his will, he had decided of his own volition to follow her footprints. Which meant that the theory of synchronicity didn't apply.

'Who says so?'

'Jung says so.'

David considered this an excellent objection, and fell silent. Not knowing what else to add, he bade her goodbye and sadly turned away. On the way back, he thought how wonderful it would have been if that girl had indeed turned out to be a special woman, maybe the love of his life. It would have been memorable to fall in love like that and have that story to tell in years to come. It would have transformed a series of small misadventures into a great romantic epic.

All because of some mislaid luggage.

The girl didn't run after him to tell him she had changed her mind. He had never even learned her name. But after waiting a month for the airline to find his case, he had gone to Police Headquarters in Milan to report the theft. There, in front of a coffee machine, he had met Sandra for the first time, they had exchanged a few words, had liked each other and, a few weeks later, had started living together.

Now, waking up in her hotel room in Rome with a weight on her soul – the recent discovery that David had been murdered and the knowledge that she had to find his killer – Sandra couldn't help smiling.

Every time David had told that story to a new friend, this friend had assumed that the girl on the beach would turn out to be her. But the amazing thing about it was that life sometimes takes the most banal way to offer us the greatest opportunities. Men and women don't need to look for 'signs'.

Sometimes, amid billions of people, they simply have to find each other.

If, when they were standing at that coffee machine, she hadn't had a five-euro note and David hadn't been able to change it for her with some coins he had in his pocket, they might not have had a reason to talk. They might have just stood there, waiting for their respective drinks, then walked away as two strangers, unaware of the love that they could have shared and – which was the most incredible thing of all – they wouldn't have suffered any regrets for a missed opportunity.

How many times a day does this kind of thing occur and we don't know it? How many people meet by chance and then separate as if nothing has happened, without knowing that they were perfect for each other?

That was why, although David was dead, she felt privileged.

And what of last night's events? she wondered. That encounter with the man with the scar on his temple had left her stunned. She still couldn't get over it. She thought she had met a killer, only to discover he was a priest. There was no doubt in her mind that he was telling the truth. He could have taken advantage of the blackout to escape, instead of which he had stayed and told her what he was. Faced with that unexpected revelation, she had wavered, unable to press the trigger. It was as if she had heard her mother's voice admonishing her: 'Sandra, my dear, you can't shoot a priest. It's simply not done.' It was ridiculous.

Coincidences.

How to figure out the relationship between David and that man? Sandra got out of bed and went to look at his photograph again. What did a priest have to do with the investigation? Instead of providing answers, that image complicated everything.

Her stomach rumbled. She hadn't eaten for hours. She also felt feverish. Last night, she had been soaked to the skin by the time she had got back to the hotel.

In the sacristy of San Luigi dei Francesi she had realised that what she was looking for went beyond justice. There was something else, something darker, that needed to be assuaged. Suffering produces strange effects. It weakens us, makes us more fragile. But, at the same time, it strengthens a desire we thought we could keep at bay. The desire to inflict the same pain on others. As if revenge is the only cure for our own pain.

Sandra realised she would have to come to terms with a dark side of herself that she had never been aware of until now. I don't want to become like that, she thought. But she feared that she had changed irrevocably.

She put to one side the photograph showing the priest with the scar on his temple and concentrated on the last two.

One of them was the dark photograph. The other was the one showing David in front of the mirror, waving sadly.

She held them both up in front of her, as if trying to grasp the connection. But they didn't suggest anything to her. As she put them down again, she froze, her gaze fixed to the floor.

There was a small card just inside the door.

She stood there for a few moments looking at it. Then, steeling herself, she picked it up, quickly, as if she was afraid. Someone must have slipped it in overnight, during the few hours she had yielded to sleep. She looked at the card. It was a holy picture, depicting a Dominican friar.

St Raymond of Penyafort.

The name was printed on the back, together with a prayer in Latin to be recited in order to obtain the saint's intercession. Some of the phrases were illegible, because someone had written a word across them in red ink. Only one word, but a word that sent a shiver down Sandra's spine.

Fred.

7.00 a.m.

He needed a crowded place. At this hour of the morning, the McDonald's near the Spanish Steps fitted the bill perfectly. Most of the customers were foreign tourists looking for more substantial fare than the usual Italian breakfast.

Marcus chose the place because he needed to feel the presence of other people. He needed to know that the world was capable of going on despite the horrors he witnessed every day, and that he wasn't alone in this struggle, because the families that surrounded him – bringing children into the world and raising them with love – played a role in the salvation of the human race.

He moved his cup of watery coffee, which he hadn't even touched, into a corner of the table, and put in the middle the file that Clemente had left for him half an hour earlier in a confessional: another of the places they used for exchanging information.

The child's drawing of the boy with the scissors that they had found in Jeremiah Smith's attic had immediately reminded Clemente of something that had happened three years earlier. He had given him a brief account of it while they were still in the villa. But after they had left, he had rushed to the archive to look for it. The code number on the cover was *c.g. 554-33-1*, but everybody had called it the Figaro case. Figaro was the name that the media had given to the perpetrator of the crime – catchy, but showing scant regard for the victims.

Marcus opened the file and started reading the account.

The scene that had greeted the police in a small house in the Nuovo Salario area one Friday evening was a truly horrifying one. A young man of twenty-seven was lying semi-conscious in a pool of his own vomit, at the foot of the staircase that led to the upper floor of the house. Some distance from him, a damaged wheelchair. Federico Noni was a paraplegic and, at first, the police had thought he had simply fallen and hurt himself. But then they had gone up to the first floor, and it was there that they had made their macabre discovery.

In one of the bedrooms lay the naked and mutilated body of his twenty-five-year-old sister, Giorgia Noni.

She had suffered multiple stab wounds. The fatal one had torn open her stomach.

Analysing the lesions, the pathologist had established that the murder weapon had been a pair of scissors. This had caused alarm bells to start ringing in the minds of the police, because three women had been attacked previously in the same manner by a maniac – hence the nickname Figaro. They had all escaped with their lives. But it was clear that the assailant had wanted to go one stage further. This time, he had killed.

Maniac was an imperfect definition, Marcus thought. This individual was much more than that. In his sick, twisted imagination, what he was doing with the scissors was necessary to give him pleasure. He wanted to smell his victims' fear, mixed with the smell of the blood gushing from their wounds.

For a moment, Marcus lifted his eyes from the papers. He needed a breath of normality. He found it in a little girl a few tables away who was licking her lips as she carefully opened a Happy Meal, her eyes shining with excitement.

When is it that we change? he asked himself. When do our lives become irreversibly modified? Not that it always happens. Sometimes, everything goes the way it should.

The sight of the little girl was sufficient to restore his faith in humanity. He could again immerse himself in the abyss opened up by the file in front of him.

He started reading through the police report.

The killer had got in through the main door, left carelessly open by Giorgia Noni when she had come back after doing the shopping. Figaro was in the habit of choosing his victims in hypermarkets and then following them home. The others, though, had always been alone when they were attacked. In the case of Georgia, her brother Federico was also in the house. He had been an athlete with great prospects, but a motorcycle accident had put an end to his career. According to the young man's testimony, Figaro had come up behind him and overturned his wheelchair, sending him crashing to the floor and knocking him out. Then he had dragged Georgia upstairs, where he had subjected her to the same treatment as his other victims.

When Federico regained consciousness, he had discovered that the wheelchair was irreparably damaged. From his sister's screams he had realised that something terrible was happening upstairs. After trying to call for help, he had attempted to drag himself up the stairs. But his body was long out of training, not to mention that he was still dazed from the blow on the head, and he had had to give up.

From where he was, he had been forced to listen, unable to do anything to help the person he loved most in the world: the sister who took care of him and would probably have continued to look after him for the rest of her life. He had lain there at the foot of those damned stairs, cursing, angry and powerless.

A neighbour who had heard the screams coming from the house had finally raised the alarm. Hearing the siren of a police car, the killer had run away through the back door, which led out into the garden. His shoe prints had been found in the soil of a flower bed.

When he finished reading, Marcus noticed that the little girl with the Happy Meal was now diligently sharing a chocolate muffin with her younger brother, while their parents looked on benevolently. His vision of this idyllic family picture was clouded by the questions rushing into his mind.

Was Federico Noni the victim appointed this time to carry out an act of revenge? Was somebody already helping him to find his sister's as yet unpunished killer? And was it his, Marcus's, task to stop him?

As he was considering this, Marcus came across a note at the end of the file. It was something that even his friend Clemente might not have known, because he had omitted it from the account he had given him while they were still in Jeremiah Smith's villa.

No revenge seemed possible, because Figaro had a name. He had even been arrested, and the case was officially closed.

7.26 a.m.

She had sat staring at the holy picture signed *Fred* for at least twenty minutes. First there had been the macabre singing of the song that symbolised her love for her husband, as left on the recorder hidden in the abandoned building site, with the voice of the man who had killed him. Now something else from their private lives had been defiled. The affectionate nickname she had used for David no longer belonged only to her.

It must have been his killer, she told herself. He slipped the card under the door. He knows I'm here. What does he want from me?

Sitting in her hotel room, Sandra tried to find an explanation. In addition to the picture of St Raymond of Penyafort and a prayer, the card also mentioned a place dedicated to the saint.

A chapel in the basilica of Santa Maria sopra Minerva.

Sandra made up her mind to call De Michelis and ask him for information. She picked up her mobile phone, but the battery had run out. She started recharging it and went to pick up the telephone in the room. But before she could dial the number, she stopped suddenly and looked at the receiver in her hand.

Since discovering that David had come to Rome to carry out a delicate investigation, she had been wondering whether he had contacted anyone during his stay in the city. But there were no emails on his laptop relating to that time, nor any calls in the memory of his mobile.

That had struck her as odd.

What she realised now was that she hadn't checked the hotel's phones.

We're so used to all this technology, she told herself, that we forget the most obvious things.

She dialled 9 to get through to reception, and asked to speak to the manager. When he came on the line, she asked him for a list of calls made by David during his stay at the hotel. Once again, she used her authority as a police officer, claiming that she was conducting an investigation into her husband's death. She didn't know if he entirely believed her, but he did as she asked. After a while, he sent somebody up to her room with a printout. There was only one number on it.

0039 328 39 56 7 XXX

She had been right: David had called somebody's mobile phone several times. She would have liked to know who that number belonged to, but the last three figures had been blocked out with Xs.

To safeguard guests' privacy, the hotel's switchboard did not record the complete numbers of incoming and outgoing calls. All that mattered from the hotel's point of view was that each call should be itemised on the bill, so they merely kept a tally of how many calls a guest made and whether they were local or long distance.

Since David had chosen to phone that number from his hotel room, that meant he didn't fear whoever was at the other end. Why should she?

She looked again at the card signed *Fred*.

What if it hadn't been her husband's killer who had sent it to her? What if it was the work of some mystery person who was helping her? Whoever it was, he must feel he was in danger after what had happened to David. So it was natural that he should be cautious. Maybe what she had found under the door was an invitation to go to the basilica of Santa Maria sopra Minerva, because there was something there that might help her. The only reason he had signed himself Fred was to reassure her that he had known David. When you thought about it, if this person had wanted to harm her, it would have been easy for him to wait and then attack her when she least expected it; he certainly wouldn't have left her a message.

Sandra knew there were no certainties, only questions and more questions. She realised she was at a crossroads. She could take the first train back to Milan and try to forget this whole business. Or else she could continue, whatever the cost.

She decided that she would carry on. But first she had to find out what was waiting for her in the chapel of St Raymond of Penyafort.

The basilica of Santa Maria sopra Minerva was not far from the Pantheon. It had been built in 1280 on the site of an ancient temple dedicated to the goddess Minerva.

Sandra's taxi pulled up in the square in front of the church. In the middle of the square was a curious statue, designed by Bernini: an obelisk on the back of a small elephant. According to legend, Bernini had deliberately positioned the elephant with its back turned to the nearby Dominican monastery, in a mocking reference to the friars' obtuseness.

Sandra was wearing jeans and a grey sweatshirt with a hood that she could pull up in case it rained. The previous night's storm seemed but a memory. The warmer air had dried the streets. The taxi driver had even apologised for that endless succession of rainy days, assuring her that in Rome the sun always shone. But black clouds were already spreading like gangrene across the golden sky.

Sandra entered the church and discovered that the Romanesque and Renaissance facade concealed a Gothic interior, with a few debatable Baroque touches. She stood for a few moments looking up at the blue vaulted ceiling adorned with the figures of apostles, prophets and doctors of the Church.

The basilica had only just opened its doors to worshippers. According to the calendar at the entrance, the first Mass of the morning would not be celebrated until ten. Apart from a nun arranging flowers on the main altar, Sandra was the sole visitor. She found the nun's presence reassuring.

She took out the card showing the picture of St Raymond of Penyafort and set off in search of the original. She walked past numerous chapels: the church had twenty of them in all. They were all luxurious, full of veined red jasper that pulsed with life, polychrome marble falling in soft curves like drapery, smooth and luminous ivory statues.

The chapel that interested her was the last one on the right, and it was the simplest of them.

It was no bigger than a hundred and fifty square feet, a dark alcove with bare, soot-blackened walls, filled with tombs.

Sandra took out her mobile phone, and proceeded to photograph it, just as she would a crime scene. From the general to the particular. From the bottom to the top. She devoted particular attention to the works of art.

St Raymond of Penyafort, in his Dominican habit, was shown next to St Paul in the altarpiece over the main altar. On the left was an oil painting of St Lucy and St Agatha. But Sandra was particularly struck by the fresco to the right of the chapel.

Christ the judge between two angels.

Beneath it were a large number of votive candles. Their little flames danced in unison at the slightest breath of air, giving the narrow space a reddish tinge.

Sandra photographed these works in the hope that they would supply her with the answer that had been promised to her, just as had happened with *The Martyrdom of St Matthew* in San Luigi dei Francesi. She was sure that everything would appear clearer to her through a camera lens, the way it always did at a crime scene. But she couldn't see anything here to help her solve the mystery. It was the second time this morning she'd hit a dead end, the first being the discovery of the mysterious mobile number catalogued by the hotel's switchboard but with the last three numbers missing. It was discouraging to know that she was so close to a truth and could not take that last, decisive step.

Was it possible there was nothing in David's photographs that referred to this place?

She thought of the two remaining images. As before, she ruled out the dark one and concentrated on the other: David bare-chested in front of the mirror in the hotel room. With one hand he was photographing himself, with the other waving at the camera. It might seem a cheerful pose, but because of his serious expression there was nothing comical in the image.

Abruptly, she stopped taking pictures and thought about what she had in her hand. A mobile phone taking photographs. She hadn't made the connection until now. Photographs and mobile phone. No, she said as if she had been struck by the most ridiculous of brainwaves. It couldn't be. The solution was within reach and she had not grasped it earlier. She looked in her bag for the printout with the mobile number they had given her at the hotel.

0039 328 39 56 7 XXX

David was not waving at the mirror. Instead, he was communicating a number to her with his raised hand. The very one that was missing from that telephone number. Sandra dialled the sequence on her mobile, replacing the three Xs with three 5s.

She waited.

Outside, the sky was again overcast. A greyish, sooty light had furtively penetrated the basilica through the windows. Gliding along the naves, it had filled every corner, every nook and cranny.

She was getting through.

A moment later, she heard the ringing of a mobile phone echoing through the church.

It couldn't be a coincidence. He was here. And he was watching her.

After three rings, the sound stopped and the line went dead. Sandra turned towards the main altar to see if the nun she had seen a little while earlier was still there. But she wasn't. She looked around, waiting for a presence to manifest itself. She didn't realise she was in danger until something whistled just above her head and then hit the wall. Recognising the sound as a shot fired from a gun with a silencer, she crouched, moving her hand to her service weapon. All her senses were alert, but she couldn't stop her heart from pounding. A second bullet missed her by a few feet. She was unable to establish the position of the sniper, but she was certain he couldn't see her. Confident as she was of this, she would need to move to get a better vantage point.

She had to get out of here.

Holding her gun out in front of her, she swivelled on her heels, exactly as she had been taught to do at the academy, all the while surveying her surroundings. She spotted another exit a few yards from where she was standing. To get to it, she would have to take shelter behind the columns of the nave.

She had been wrong to trust that card slipped under her door. How could she have been so careless, with David's killer still at large?

She gave herself ten seconds to get to the exit. She started counting, and simultaneously darted forward. One – no shot. Two – she already had a couple of yards advantage. Three – the dim light from a window fell on her for a moment. Four – she was again in the shadows. Five – a few more steps to go, she'd soon be out of here. Six and seven – she felt herself being seized by the shoulders, someone was pulling her to him from one of the chapels. Eight, nine and ten – the person was unexpectedly strong, and she couldn't resist. Eleven, twelve and thirteen – she struggled, trying to free herself from that embrace. Fourteen – she managed to get free, but only just. Her gun fell and, in her desperate attempt to start running again, she slipped. Fifteen – she realised that her head was going to hit the marble floor and, with a kind of sixth sense, she felt the pain one second before she touched the ground. She put her hands forward to cushion her fall, but it was useless. All she could do was turn her head in the hope of softening the blow. Her cheek hit the cold floor, which in a second became white hot. A shudder went through her like an electric shock. Sixteen – her eyes were open, but she felt as if she had already lost consciousness. It was a strange sensation, as if she was absent and present at the same time. Seventeen – she was aware of two hands grabbing her by the shoulders.

Then she stopped counting and darkness fell.

9.00 a.m.

Regina Coeli was a former convent, built in the second half of the seventeenth century. It had been a prison since 1881, but had kept its original name, which meant Queen of Heaven, a homage to the Virgin Mary.

The building, which could house up to nine hundred prisoners, was divided into various sections depending on the category of crimes committed. Section 8 held the so-called borderline cases. These were individuals who had lived normally for years, working, building relationships, sometimes families, and then suddenly had committed heinous crimes for no clear or explicit reason, arousing doubts concerning their mental health. They did not present the unmistakable signs of mental illness. Their abnormality was revealed solely through their criminal conduct and was not the result of morbid psychological manifestations: the only thing morbid about these people was their crimes. While waiting for a court to pronounce on whether or not they could be classed as criminally insane, they enjoyed different treatment from the rest of the prison population.

For more than a year, Section 8 had been the home of Nicola Costa, also known as Figaro.

Having undergone the normal checks, Marcus went in through the main entrance and proceeded down a long corridor punctuated from time to time by gates, gradually getting deeper into the heart of the prison. It was as if he was descending into the Underworld.

For the occasion, he had put on his priestly garb. He was not used to the white collar that constricted his throat, or to the cassock that fluttered around him as he walked. Never having worn it before, he thought of it less as a uniform than as a disguise.

A few hours earlier, after learning that Figaro was safely behind bars, he and Clemente had decided on a stratagem to get in to see him. Nicola Costa was waiting for a judge to decide whether he should continue to see out his sentence in prison or in a psychiatric hospital. In the meantime, he had set out on a path of conversion and repentance. Each morning he was accompanied to the little church inside the prison by the guards. He would make confession and follow the Mass in perfect solitude. Today, however, the chaplain had been summoned urgently to the Curia for an unspecified reason. It would take him a while to realise it was all a mistake. Clemente had arranged everything, even getting Marcus a permit to temporarily replace the chaplain, and thus gain unimpeded access to Regina Coeli.

Obviously, it was a risk, one that might undermine their secrecy. But the drawing found in Jeremiah Smith's attic suggested that the Figaro case might not be closed after all. Marcus was here to find out.

After walking down a long stone passageway, he came out into a high octagonal space, bounded by the three floors that housed the cells. The balconies were protected by metal nets that extended all the way to the ceiling, to stop prisoners committing suicide by jumping off.

A guard led him into the church and left him alone to prepare for the service. One of the priestly duties was to celebrate Eucharist: priests were expected to say Mass every day. Because of the particular ministry he carried out, Marcus had been given a dispensation relieving him of such duties. But since the events in Prague, he had celebrated a few Masses under Clemente's guidance, just to feel comfortable with the ritual. So he was well prepared now.

He had not had time to study the man he was to meet in any great depth, especially as far as his psychological state was concerned. But the definition 'borderline' was an excellent way of expressing the idea that there was a tissue-thin membrane between good and evil. Sometimes, that membrane was elastic, allowing brief incursions into the dark side, but also the possibility of coming back. In some instances the barrier broke, leaving the way open for individuals to go back and forth with ease. They might appear completely normal, but one step to the other side was all it took to transform them into dangerous psychopaths.

According to the psychiatrists, Nicola Costa belonged to this latter category.

Marcus was preparing the altar, with his back to the deserted congregation area, when he heard the clink of handcuffs. Costa entered the church escorted by the guards. He was wearing jeans and a white shirt buttoned to the collar. He was bald apart from a few scattered tufts of hair, and he moved in an awkward way. But the most noticeable thing about him was his cleft palate, which gave his face a fixed and very sinister smile.

Costa dragged himself to one of the pews. Supporting him by his arms, the guards helped him to sit down, then went and stood sentry outside the door, where they would remain for the duration of the service, in order not to invade the sanctity of Mass.

Marcus waited another few minutes, then turned.

Costa was startled and clearly dismayed. 'Where's the chaplain?' he asked.

'He wasn't feeling well.'

Costa nodded and said nothing. Holding a rosary in his hands, he started muttering incomprehensibly. Every now and again he was forced to take a handkerchief from the breast pocket of his shirt and wipe the saliva from the split on his lip.

'Before we proceed with the service, do you want to confess?'

'With the other priest I've been embarking on a kind of spiritual journey. I tell him my doubts and anxieties and he teaches me the Gospels. Perhaps I ought to wait until he's back.'

He was as meek as a lamb, Marcus noted. Or maybe he was just playing his part well.

'I'm sorry, I thought you liked it,' he said, turning his back on him again.

'What?' Costa asked, confused.

'Confessing your sins.'

The phrase evidently upset him. 'What's happening? I don't understand.'

'It doesn't matter, don't worry.'

Costa appeared to calm down and started praying again. Marcus put on his stole, as if to begin the service.

'I don't suppose someone like you ever weeps for his victims. Mind you, with that deformed lip of yours it'd probably look grotesque anyway.'

These words hit Costa like a punch, but he made an effort to absorb the blow. 'I always thought priests were kind-hearted people.'

Marcus went close to him until their heads were almost touching. 'I know what happened,' he whispered.

Costa's face became a wax mask. The fixed smile was belied by the harsh expression in his eyes. 'I've confessed my crimes and am ready to pay for them. I wasn't expecting gratitude, I know I did a bad thing. But at least I deserve a bit of respect.'

'Oh, yes,' Marcus said, sarcastically. 'You gave a full and detailed confession of the assaults you carried out and of the murder of

Giorgia Noni. But none of the victims you assaulted before you committed that murder was able to provide a single detail about you.'

'I always wore a balaclava.' Costa had swallowed the bait, feeling it his duty to support the theory of his guilt. 'And besides, Giorgia Noni's brother identified me.'

'He only recognised your voice,' Marcus retorted.

'He said the attacker had a speech defect.'

'He was in a state of shock.'

'That's not true, it was because of my . . .' Costa did not complete the sentence.

'Your what? You mean that twisted lip of yours?'

'Yes,' Costa said, struggling to restrain himself. He was clearly taken aback by the offensive way this man referred to his handicap.

'It's always the same, isn't it, Nicola? Nothing's changed since you were a child. What did your classmates call you? They had a nickname for you, didn't they?'

Costa shifted on the pew and emitted a sound that resembled a laugh. 'Leper face. Not very inventive. They could have made a bit more effort.'

'You're right, Figaro is better.'

Nervously, Costa wiped his mouth again with a handkerchief. 'What do you want from me?

'I shan't absolve you of your false sins, Costa.'

'I want to leave.' He turned to call the guards.

But Marcus put a hand on his shoulder and looked him straight in the eyes. 'When you've always been called a monster, it's easy to get used to the idea. And as time passes, you start to realise it's the one thing that makes you really special. You're no longer a nonentity. Your face is in the papers. When you appear in court, people stare at you. It's one thing for people not to like you, quite another for them to fear you. You were used to everybody's indifference or scorn, but now they're forced to pay attention to you. They can't turn away, because they need to see what they fear the most. Not you, but people like you. And the more they look at you, the more different they feel. You've become their alibi for thinking they're better than they are. After all, that's what monsters are for.'

Marcus put his hand in the pocket of his cassock and took out the drawing he had found in the attic. He carefully unfolded it and placed it on the pew next to Nicola Costa. The boy and the girl smiling amid lush vegetation. The girl with her little dress stained with blood and the boy with the scissors in his hand.

'Who drew this?' the prisoner asked.

'The real Figaro.'

'I'm the real Figaro.'

'No, you're a compulsive liar. You only confessed to give your insipid existence some meaning. You're playing your part well, I have to say. The religious conversion is a nice touch, it makes you seem more credible. And I think the police were only too happy to close a case that risked exploding in their faces: three women assaulted, one killed and nobody behind bars.'

'So how do you explain the fact that there haven't been any more victims since I was arrested?'

Marcus had foreseen this objection. 'Barely a year has gone by, but it's just a matter of time before he strikes again. It's convenient for him, knowing you're inside. I wager he's even thought of stopping, but he won't be able to resist for much longer.'

Nicola Costa sniffed, his eyes darting restlessly from one side of the church to the other. 'I don't know who you are, or why you came here today. But no one's going to believe you.'

'Admit it: you don't have the courage it takes to be a monster. You're taking the credit for someone else's work.'

Costa seemed on the point of losing his temper. 'Who says so? Why couldn't I be the boy in this drawing?'

Marcus went closer to him. 'Look at his smile and you'll understand.'

Nicola Costa looked down at the sheet of paper and saw that the little boy's lip was perfectly normal. 'That doesn't prove a thing,' he said in a thin voice.

'I know,' Marcus replied. 'But it's enough for me.'

Sandra was woken by an intense pain in her left cheek. She opened her eyes slowly, almost afraid to look. But she was lying on a bed, with a soft red quilt beneath her. Around her, IKEA furniture and a window with dark shutters. It must still be day, because a glimmer of sunlight still filtered through.

She was not tied up, as she might have expected. She was wearing her jeans and sweatshirt, although someone had taken off her trainers.

There was a door at the back of the room. It was slightly ajar. That was a kind gesture, she had to admit. They hadn't wanted to wake her by closing the door.

Her hand went to her side, feeling for her gun. But the holster was empty.

She tried to sit up, but immediately felt dizzy. She collapsed back on the bed and lay there looking up at the ceiling until the furniture and objects stopped spinning.

I have to get out of here.

She moved her legs to the edge of the bed and dropped first one, then the other, to the floor. When she was sure both feet were steady, she tried to push herself up into a vertical position, keeping her eyes open in order not to lose her balance. She managed to sit up. Reaching out her hands to the wall to support herself and then using a chest of drawers to give herself the necessary impetus, she was able to get to her feet. But it did not last. She felt her legs giving way. An invisible wave passed over her, making her totter. She tried to resist, but it was hopeless. She closed her eyes, and was about to fall when someone grabbed her from behind and laid her back down on the bed.

'Not yet,' a male voice said.

Sandra grabbed hold of two powerful arms. Whoever it was had a good smell. She found herself lying on her stomach, with her head sunk in a pillow. 'Let me go,' she murmured.

'You're not ready. How long is it since you last had something to eat?'

Sandra turned. Her eyes were no more than cracks, but she could make out a male figure in the half darkness. Ash-blond hair, worn long. Delicate yet masculine features. She was sure he had green eyes, like a cat's, because of the light that emanated from them. She was about to ask him if he was an angel when she realised where she had heard that oddly boyish voice with the German accent.

'Schalber,' she said, disappointed.

He smiled at her placidly. 'I'm sorry, I couldn't hold you and you slipped.'

'Damn, so it was you in the church!'

'I tried to hold you, but you were kicking.'

'I was kicking?' Her anger made her forget her grogginess.

'The sniper would have got you if I hadn't intervened and stopped you walking right in front of him. You would have been an easy target.'

'Who was he?'

'I have no idea. Luckily I was following you.'

Now she was really furious. 'You were what? Since when?'

'I got here last night. This morning I went to the hotel where David stayed when he was in Rome. I was sure I'd find you there. I saw you come out and take a taxi.'

'So the idea of meeting for a coffee today in Milan ...'

'I was bluffing. I knew you were in Rome.'

'The persistent calls, the request to look at David's bags ... All this time you've been leading me on.'

With a sigh, Schalber sat down on the bed, facing her. 'I had to.'

Sandra realised he had been using her. 'What's behind all this?'

'Before I explain, I need to ask you a few questions.'

'No. Right now you have to tell me what's going on.'

'I will, I promise. But first I need to know if we're still in danger.'

Sandra looked around, and spotted what looked like a bra – definitely not hers – draped over the arm of a chair. 'Just a minute, where am I? What is this place?'

Following the direction of her gaze, Schalber went and removed the undergarment. 'Sorry for the mess. It belongs to Interpol, we use

178

it as a guest apartment. People come and go constantly. But don't worry, we're safe.'

'How did we get here?'

'I had to fire a few shots, I doubt I hit the sniper, but we did get out of the basilica unharmed. It wasn't easy to carry you outside on my back. Luckily, it was pouring with rain and I managed to put you in my car without anybody seeing. It would have been rather complicated trying to explain it to a passing policeman.'

'Oh, so that was your only worry, was it?' Then she stopped to think. 'Hold on a minute, why should we still be in danger?'

'Because whoever tried to kill you will certainly try again.'

'Someone slipped a card under the door of my hotel room. It's what sent me to that church. What's so important about the chapel of St Raymond of Penyafort?'

'Nothing, it was a trap.'

'How do you know that?'

'David would have mentioned it in the clues he left you.'

These words stopped her dead in her tracks. 'You know about David's investigation?'

'I know many things. But all in good time.'

He stood and went into the next room. Sandra heard him rattling dishes. Soon afterwards he came back in with a tray bearing scrambled eggs, toast and jam, plus a steaming coffee pot.

'You have to get something in your stomach if you're to feel better.'

It was true: she hadn't eaten for more than twenty-four hours. The sight of the food awakened her appetite. Schalber helped her to sit up with her back propped against a couple of pillows, then placed the tray on her lap. As she ate, he sat down next to her, stretched his legs out on the bed and folded his arms. Until a few hours earlier, their relations had been formal, now they seemed intimate. The man's intrusiveness got on her nerves, but she said nothing.

'You took a big risk this morning. The one thing that saved you was that the ringing of my mobile phone disturbed the sniper.'

'So it was you . . .' she said with her mouth full.

'How did you get hold of the number? I always used another phone to call you.'

'It was the number David called from the hotel.'

'Your husband was stubborn. I really didn't like him.'

Sandra was upset to hear him talk about David in that way. 'You don't know what kind of man he was.'

'He was a pain in the arse,' he insisted. 'If he'd listened to me, he'd still be alive.'

Irritably, Sandra put the tray aside and tried to stand up. Her anger had made her forget her dizziness.

'Where are you going?'

'I can't bear a stranger saying these things.' Still swaying, she walked around the bed, looking for her trainers.

'All right, you're free to go,' he said, indicating the door. 'But give me the clues David left you.'

Sandra looked at him in astonishment. 'I'm not going to give you anything!'

'David was killed because he'd tracked someone down.'

'I think I met him.'

Schalber stood up and went to her, forcing her to look at him. 'What do you mean, you met him?'

Sandra was lacing up her shoes, but stopped. 'Last night.'

'Where?'

'What a question! What's the most likely place to run into a priest? A church.'

'That man isn't just a priest.' He had recaptured her full attention. 'He's a *penitenziere*.'

Schalber went to the window, opened the shutters wide, and looked out at the black clouds preparing to invade Rome again. 'What's the biggest criminal records archive in the world?' he asked her.

Sandra was taken aback. 'I don't know . . . The one at Interpol, I suppose.'

'Wrong,' Schalber retorted, turning with a smug smile.

'The FBI?'

'Wrong again. It's in Italy. In the Vatican, to be precise.'

Sandra still did not understand. But she had the impression she would have to worm it out of him. 'Why does the Catholic Church need a criminal records archive?'

Schalber motioned her to sit down again. 'Catholicism is the only religion that includes the sacrament of confession: men tell their sins to a minister of God and in return receive forgiveness. Sometimes, though, the sin is so serious that a mere priest cannot give absolution. That's the case with the so-called mortal sins.'

'Murder, for example.'

'Precisely. In such cases the priest transcribes the text of the confession and submits it to a higher authority: a college of high-ranking prelates called together in Rome to pronounce on such matters.'

Sandra was surprised. 'A court to judge the sins of men.'

'The Tribunal of Souls.'

The name reflected the gravity of its task, Sandra thought. What secrets must have passed through that institution! She could see why David might have been driven to investigate it.

'It was established in the twelfth century,' Schalber continued, 'under the name *Paenitentiaria Apostolica*. Its scope was a smaller one then. At the time there was a great influx of pilgrims into Rome, not just to visit its basilicas but also to obtain absolution for their sins.'

'This was the period of indulgences.'

'Precisely. There were dispensations and pardons that the Pope alone could grant. But it was a huge task for him. So he began delegating it to certain cardinals, and they set up the *Paenitentiaria*.'

'I don't quite see the relevance of all this today . . .'

'At first, once the tribunal pronounced judgement, the texts of the confessions were burnt. But after a few years, the members of the *Paenitentiaria*, known as penitenzieri, decided to create a secret archive . . . and their work has never stopped.'

Sandra was starting to understand the significance of this undertaking.

'For nearly a thousand years,' Schalber went on, 'the worst sins committed by mankind have been preserved there. Including crimes that never came to light. You have to remember that confession is undertaken voluntarily by penitents, which means they always tell the truth. So the *Paenitentiaria Apostolica* isn't simply a database of criminal cases, the kind that any police force in the world would have.'

'What is it, then?'

Schalber's green eyes gleamed. 'It's the largest and most up-to-date archive of evil in the world.'

Sandra was sceptical. 'Do you mean it has something to do with the devil? What are these priests, exorcists?'

'No. The penitenzieri aren't interested in the existence of the devil. Their approach is a scientific one. They're more like profilers. Their experience has matured over the years, thanks to the archive. After a while, in addition to confessions, they started collecting detailed records of all criminal cases. They study them, analyse them and try to decipher them, the same way a modern criminologist would.'

'You mean they even solve cases?'

'Sometimes, yes.'

'And the police don't know?'

'They're good at protecting their secrecy. They've been doing it for centuries.'

Sandra went to the tray with the food and poured herself a large cup of coffee. 'How do they operate?'

'As soon as they discover the solution to a mystery, they find a way to communicate it anonymously to the authorities. Sometimes they intervene personally.'

Schalber went and fetched a briefcase from a corner of the room and opened it to look for something. Sandra remembered the addresses in David's diary, derived from listening to the police frequency: that was why her husband had been looking for that priest at crime scenes.

'Here it is,' Schalber announced, holding a file in his hands. 'The case of little Matteo Ginestra from Turin. The boy went missing, and his mother thought his father had taken him. The couple were separated, and the man wasn't satisfied with the amount of access the judge had granted him. It took the police a long time to track him down, but when they did he denied kidnapping his son.'

'Who was it, then?'

'While the police were following that lead, the child reappeared unharmed. It turned out he'd been taken by a group of older boys, all of good family. They'd kept him shut away in an abandoned house, intending to kill him. Purely for fun, or out of curiosity. The child said he'd been saved by someone who'd broken into the house and got him out.'

'That could have been anybody, why specifically a priest?'

'Not far from the place where he was found, some papers containing a detailed account of what had happened were discovered. One of the teenagers involved had started getting a bad conscience and had confessed to the priest of his parish. That confession was what was on the papers. Someone had apparently mislaid it.' Schalber handed her the document. 'Read what's written in the margin.'

'There's some kind of serial number: *c.g. 764-9-44*. What is it?'

'The penitenzieris' method of classification. I don't think the numbers mean anything in particular, but *c.g.* stands for *culpa gravis.*'

'I don't understand. How did David come to be investigating them in the first place?'

'Reuters had sent him to Turin to cover the case. He was the one who found those documents while he was taking photographs. That's how it all started.'

'And where does Interpol fit into this?'

'Although you may think what the penitenzieri are doing is a good thing, it's actually illegal. Their activities have no rules or limits.'

Sandra poured herself another cup of coffee and sipped at it, looking at Schalber. Perhaps he was expecting her to say more. 'It was David who put you on to it, wasn't it?'

'We met years ago, in Vienna. He was pursuing an investigation, and I passed him a few tips. When he started investigating the penitenzieri, he realised that their activities extended beyond Italy and so might interest Interpol. He called me a couple of times from Rome, telling me what he'd found out so far. Then he died. But if he arranged things so that you could get my telephone number, that means he wanted you to meet me. I can complete his work. So where are the clues?'

Sandra was sure that, just as Schalber had taken away her gun while she was unconscious, he must also have searched her things. So he must already know she didn't have the clues with her. She certainly had no intention of handing them over to him just like that. 'We need to join forces.'

'No way, forget it. You'll take the first train back to Milan. Someone wants you dead and you're not safe in this city.'

'I'm a police officer: I can look after myself and I know how to conduct an investigation, if that's what you're worried about.'

Schalber started to walk nervously about the room. 'I work better alone.'

'Well, this time you'll have to rethink your methods.'

'You're really pig-headed, you know?' He came and stood in front of her, and raised his index finger. 'On one condition.'

Sandra raised her eyes to heaven. 'Yes, I know: you're the boss and we always do what you say.'

Schalber was taken aback. 'How did you . . . '

'I know how men's egos work. So, where do we start?'

Schalber went to a drawer, pulled out the gun he had taken from her and handed it back to her. 'They're interested in crime scenes, right? When I arrived in Rome last night, the first place I went to was a villa outside the city where a police search was in progress. I placed bugs in the house, hoping that the penitenzieri would show up as soon as forensics had cleared the place. Before dawn, I recorded a conversation between two of them, I don't know who they were. They were discussing a killer named Figaro.'

'All right, I'll show you the clues David left me. And then we'll try to dig up more on this Figaro.'

'I think that's an excellent idea.'

Sandra, no longer on the defensive, looked closely at Schalber.

'Somebody killed my husband and they tried to do the same to me this morning. I don't know if it was the same person or what any of this has to do with the penitenzieri. Maybe David knew too much.'

'If we find them, they'll tell us.'

12.32 p.m.

Pietro Zini's only companions were cats. He had six of them. They would stay in the shade of an orange tree, or else go wandering amid the pots and flower beds in the little garden of his house in the heart of Trastevere.

Through the open French windows of his study came the strains of Dvořák's Serenade for Strings on an old record player, making the curtains dance – not that Zini was aware of this last detail. He was in a deckchair, enjoying the music and the warmth of a sunbeam that seemed to have got through the clouds just for him. He was a sturdy sixty-year-old, with the prominent belly typical of certain brawny men from the early twentieth century. The big hands with which he usually explored the world rested in his lap. His white stick lay at his feet. His dark glasses reflected a reality that had become superfluous to him.

Ever since he had lost his sight, he had given up on human contact. He divided his days between the little garden and the house, blissfully immersed in his record collection. Silence bothered him more than darkness.

One of the cats jumped on to the deckchair and curled up in his lap. Zini ran his fingers through its thick fur and the animal purred in gratitude.

'Nice, this music, isn't it, Socrates? I know you're the same as me: you prefer a sweet tune. Your brother likes that pretentious fellow Mozart.'

The cat was grey and brown, with a white stain on its muzzle. Something must have drawn its attention, because it raised its head. It deserted its master and followed the flight of a bluebottle. After a few minutes, it lost interest in the insect and again huddled on Zini's lap and let him stroke its fur.

'Come on, ask me what you need to.'

Calmly, Zini reached out his hand to take a glass of lemonade from the small table next to him and sipped at it.

'I know you're here. I realised it as soon as you arrived. I was wondering when you would speak. So, have you made your mind up yet?'

One of the cats rubbed against the intruder's calf. Marcus had been here for at least twenty minutes. He had got in through a side door and had been watching Zini all this time, looking for the right way to approach him. He was good at understanding people, but didn't know how to communicate with them. The fact that the retired policeman had lost his sight had led him to believe that it would be easier to talk to him. In addition, there was the advantage that he wouldn't be able to recognise his face: his invisibility was safe. And yet the man had somehow seen him better than anyone else.

'Don't be deceived. I haven't gone blind. It's the world around me that's gone dark.'

There was something about him that inspired trust. 'It's regarding Nicola Costa.'

Zini nodded, then smiled. 'You're one of *them*, aren't you? No, don't try and think up an answer. I know you can't tell me.'

Marcus found it hard to believe that the former policeman knew.

'There are stories that circulate in the force. Some people think they're myths. But I believe them. Many years ago, I was assigned a case. A married woman had been kidnapped and killed. The details were unusually horrible. One evening I got a phone call. The man at the other end told me why we shouldn't be looking for a random kidnapper and pointed me in the direction of the real perpetrator. It wasn't the usual anonymous call, it was very convincing. The woman's killer had been a rejected suitor of hers. We arrested him.'

'Figaro is still at large,' Marcus said.

But the man was wandering off the point. 'Did you know that in ninety-four per cent of cases the killer is known to his victim? There's more chance of our being killed by a close relative or an old friend than by a perfect stranger.'

'Why won't you answer me, Zini? Don't you want to finish with the past?'

The Dvořák had come to an end, but the needle kept bouncing on the last groove of the vinyl. Zini leaned forward and crossed his hands, forcing Socrates to slide to the ground and join his companions. 'The doctors told me well in advance that I was going blind. So I had plenty of time to get used to the idea. I said to myself: when it starts interfering with my work, I'll stop immediately. In the meantime, I prepared myself. I studied Braille, I sometimes wandered through the house with my eyes closed, training myself to recognise objects by touch, or else I went around with a stick. I didn't want to depend on other people. Then one day things started to appear out of focus. Some details vanished, others became incredibly clear, almost iridescent. It was unbearable. Whenever that happened, I prayed that the darkness would come quickly. Then one year ago my wish was granted.' Zini took off his dark glasses, exposing his motionless pupils to the glare of the sun. 'I thought I would be alone down here. But you know what? I'm not alone at all. In the darkness there are all the people I wasn't able to save in the course of my career. Their faces stare at me, lying in their own blood or their own shit, at home or in the street, in an empty field or on a slab in a morgue. They're all here, they were waiting for me. And now they live with me, like ghosts.'

'I'll bet Giorgia Noni is one of them. What does she do, does she talk to you? Or does she look at you without saying anything, making you feel ashamed?'

Zini flung the glass of lemonade down on the ground. 'You don't understand.'

'I know you rigged the investigation.'

Zini shook his head. 'It was the last case I worked on. I had to hurry, I didn't have much time left. Her brother Federico deserved a result.'

'Is that why you sent an innocent man to prison?'

Zini looked straight at Marcus, as if he could see him. 'That's where you're wrong. Costa isn't innocent. He had previous convictions for stalking and molesting women. We found hardcore pornography in his apartment, illegal stuff downloaded from the internet. The theme was always the same: violence against women.'

'Fantasies aren't enough to condemn a man.'

'He was preparing to act. You know how his arrest came about? He was on the list of suspects in the Figaro case, we had our eye on him. One evening we saw him stalking a woman outside a supermarket, he had a gym bag with him. We didn't have any proof, but we had to decide quickly. We could let him make his move, taking the risk that he'd harm the woman, or else stop him immediately. I chose the second option. And I was right.'

'Did he have scissors in the bag?'

'No, only a change of clothes,' Zini admitted. 'But they were identical to the ones he was already wearing. And you know why?'

'To change in case he got blood on his clothes. Perfectly logical.'

'And besides, he confessed. That's enough for me.'

'None of the victims of his attacks provided a description that could identify him. They simply stated *after the fact* that it was him. Women who are subjected to violence are often so upset that when the police show them a suspect, they immediately say it's him. They're not lying, they want to believe it, in fact they're convinced of it. They couldn't live with themselves, knowing that the monster who harmed them is still at large. The fear that it'll happen again is stronger than any feeling of justice. So one guilty party is as good as another.'

'Federico Noni recognised Costa from his voice.'

'Really?' Marcus said angrily. 'Was he in his right mind when he fingered him? Think of all the traumas he'd suffered in his life.'

Pietro Zini did not know how to reply. The old mettle was still there, but something had snapped in his heart. The man who once had been capable of striking terror in a criminal with his eyes now seemed incredibly fragile. And it wasn't merely because of his blindness. In fact, his blindness had made him wiser. Marcus was convinced he knew more and, as was so often the case, all he needed to do was to let him talk.

'After they told me I was going blind, I made sure never to miss a sunset. Sometimes I would go up on to the terrace of the Janiculum and stay there until the light had completely faded. There are things we take for granted and forget to look at. The stars, for example. I remember when I was a child I used to lie in the grass and imagine all those distant worlds. Before I went blind, I started doing it again, but it wasn't the same. My eyes had seen too many terrible things. One of the last things I saw was the body of Giorgia Noni.' He held out his hand to summon his cats to him. 'It's hard to accept that someone could have put us in this world just to see us suffer. They say that if God is good then He can't be omnipotent, and vice versa. A good God wouldn't let His children suffer, which means He must be powerless to prevent it. If on the other hand He's foreseen everything, then He isn't as good as He'd have us believe.'

'I wish I could tell you there's some greater design that we can't understand, that it's beyond the comprehension of any one of us. But the truth is, I don't know the answer.'

'At least you're honest. I appreciate that.' Zini got to his feet. 'Come, let me show you something.'

He took his stick and went into the study. Marcus followed him. The room was extremely neat and tidy, a sign that Zini was perfectly self-sufficient. The ex-policeman went to the record player and started the Dvořák LP again. As he did so, Marcus noticed a rope, some six feet long, lying in a corner of the room. He wondered how many times Zini had been tempted to use it.

'My mistake was to give up my weapons licence,' Zini said, as if he had guessed his visitor's thoughts. Then he went and sat down at a desk with a computer on it: not a normal computer but a Braille display. 'You won't like what you're going to hear.'

Marcus tried to imagine what it could be.

'But first let me tell you that Federico Noni has already suffered enough. Years ago he lost the use of his legs. Becoming blind at my age is a blow you can learn to accept, but losing the use of your legs when you're a young athlete! Then his sister was brutally murdered, practically in front of his eyes. Can you even imagine something like that? Think how powerless he must have felt, think of the guilt he must still feel, even though he didn't do anything wrong.'

'What does this have to do with what you're going to tell me?'

'Federico has a right to justice. Whatever that justice is.'

Pietro Zini fell silent, waiting for Marcus to demonstrate that he had understood. 'You can live with a handicap,' Marcus said. 'You can't live with doubt.'

That was enough for Zini, who began tapping at the keyboard. Technology was a great boon to blind people. It allowed Zini to carry on activities like surfing the internet, chatting, or else sending and receiving emails.

'I had an email a few days ago,' he said. 'Let me play you this . . .'

On Zini's computer there was a program that read his email messages for him. He activated it and sat back in his chair, waiting. A synthesised voice first recited an anonymous Yahoo address. The message had no subject. Then came the text.

'He-is-not-like-you . . . Look-in-Vil-la-Glo-ri-Park.'

Zini pressed a key to stop the voice. Marcus was stunned: the person responsible for the enigmatic message had to be the unknown guide who had led him here. Why had he written to a blind ex-policeman?

'"He is not like you." What does that mean?'

'Frankly, I'm more interested in the second part: "Look in Villa Glori Park."'

Zini got up from his chair, came to him and grabbed him by the arm. He almost seemed to be begging him. 'Of course I can't go. But you know what you have to do now. Go and see what's in that park.'

2.14 p.m.

In the months since David's death, solitude had been like a shell. It was not a state, it was a place. The place where Sandra could continue talking to him, without feeling that she was going mad. She had shut herself up in an invisible bubble of sadness, and let things bounce off it. Nothing and nobody could touch her if she remained there. Paradoxically, her grief protected her.

Until the pistol shots meant for her that morning in the chapel of St Raymond of Penyafort.

She had been afraid to die. At that moment, the bubble had burst. She wanted to live. And that was the reason why she felt guilty towards David. For five months, life had been suspended. Though time had passed, she had stood still. But now she wondered how loyal a wife had to be to her husband. Was she wrong to want to live when he was dead? Could it be considered a kind of betrayal? It was stupid, she knew. But for the first time, she had moved away from David.

'Very interesting.'

Schalber's voice broke the spell of her thoughts. They were in Sandra's hotel room and he was sitting on the bed, holding the photographs David had taken with the Leica. He had looked at them over and over again.

'Are you sure there are only four? No others?'

Sandra feared that he had guessed her little deception: she had decided not to show him the photograph of the priest with the scar on his temple. But Schalber was still a policeman, and she knew how policemen thought. They never allowed themselves the benefit of the doubt.

'Even though you may think it's a good thing, what the penitenzieri are doing is illegal. There are no limits or rules to their activities.' That was what he had said when he had told her about them. Which meant that, as far as he was concerned, that priest was a criminal. Nothing would make him change his mind.

In the academy, she had been taught that everybody was guilty until proven innocent, not the other way round. Plus, you should never believe anybody. For example, during an interrogation a good police officer should question every word. She remembered once giving the third degree to a hiker who had discovered a woman's body in a ditch. It was obvious that the man had nothing to do with the death, he had simply raised the alarm. But she had bombarded him with pointless questions and made him repeat his answers, pretending she had not understood, all with the intention of making him contradict himself. The poor man had submitted to this relentless onslaught, innocently thinking that it could help to throw light on the woman's death, unaware that if he had shown the slightest uncertainty he would have ended up in real trouble.

I know what you're thinking, Schalber. And I won't let you. At least until I know I can trust you completely.

'Just four photographs,' Sandra confirmed.

Schalber looked at her for several moments, either weighing up her reply or hoping she would betray herself. She managed to sustain his gaze. He looked away and started examining the photographs again. She thought she had passed the test, but she was wrong.

'You told me before that you met one of them last night. I wonder how you managed to recognise him if you had never seen him before.'

Sandra realised she had made a mistake. She blamed herself for supplying him with that information while they were in the Interpol guest apartment, but it had come out spontaneously.

'I went to San Luigi dei Francesi to see the Caravaggio painting David had photographed part of.'

'You already told me that.'

'I saw a man standing in front of it. I didn't know who he was. He was the one who recognised me. He immediately moved away and I followed him. I pointed my gun at him, until he told me that he was a priest.'

'You mean he knew who you were?'

'I don't know how, but he gave me the impression he knew me. So yes, I think he did know.'

Schalber nodded. 'I see.'

Sandra was sure he hadn't swallowed her lies. But for the moment he had preferred to let it go. In any case, it was all right: this way he would be forced to include her in the investigation. She tried to change the subject. 'What about the dark photograph, what do you think it means?'

He had been distracted for a moment, but he immediately recovered. 'I don't know. For the moment, it doesn't mean anything.'

Sandra got up from the bed. 'All right, so what do we do now?'

Schalber gave her back the photographs. 'Figaro,' he said. 'They caught him. But if the penitenzieri are interested in the case, there must be a reason.'

'What do you plan to do?'

'The attacker became a killer: his last victim died.'

'You want to begin with her?'

'With her brother: he was there when she was killed.'

'The doctors were convinced I'd walk again soon.'

Federico Noni kept his hands flat on his thighs, and his eyes bowed. He had not shaved for a while and his hair was long. Beneath his green T-shirt, the muscles of the athlete he had once been could still be glimpsed. But his legs were thin and motionless in the track-suit trousers. His feet were raised up on the foot rests of the wheelchair. He was wearing a pair of Nikes with clean soles.

Looking at him, Sandra catalogued these details. Those Nikes encapsulated his whole tragedy. They looked new, but he may well have had them for years.

She and Schalber had presented themselves at the door of the little villa in the Nuovo Salario area a few minutes earlier. They had rung the bell several times before the door was opened. Federico Noni lived like a recluse and did not want to see anyone. To persuade him, Schalber had had Sandra give him an Italian police badge and had shown it to Noni through the video entry phone. He had passed himself off as an inspector. However reluctantly, she, too, had lied. She hated Schalber's methods, his arrogance, the way he used other people for his own ends.

The house was untidy. There was a musty odour and the blinds had not been raised in ages. The furniture was positioned in such a way as to create routes for the wheelchair. You could see the tracks of the wheels on the floor.

Sandra and Schalber were sitting on a sofa, with Federico facing them. Behind him were the stairs that led to the upper floor, where Giorgia Noni had been killed. But her brother, obviously, never went up there. There was a camp bed for him in the living room.

'The operation was a success. I'd been assured that with a bit of physiotherapy I'd recover. It wouldn't be easy, but I could do it. I was used to physical effort, it didn't scare me. And yet . . .'

Federico was trying to respond to a blunt question from Schalber on the cause of his paraplegia. The Interpol agent had deliberately started with the most uncomfortable subject. Sandra knew that technique, it was the one some of her colleagues used when they questioned crime victims. Compassion often made them clam up, whereas if you wanted to get useful answers you had to be cold and unsympathetic.

'When you had your accident, were you speeding on the motor-bike?'

'Not at all. It was a stupid fall. I remember that at first, despite the fractures, I could still move my legs. After a few hours I couldn't feel them any more.'

On a cabinet was a photograph of Federico Noni standing in his motorcycle gear next to a bright red Ducati. He was holding a wrap-around helmet and smiling at the camera. A handsome, happy, fresh-faced young man. Quite a heartbreaker, Sandra suspected.

'You were an athlete. What was your speciality?'

'Long jump.'

'Were you good?'

Federico merely pointed at the display case filled with trophies. 'Judge for yourselves.'

Obviously, they had seen it when they arrived. But Schalber was using the subject to gain time. He was trying to provoke Noni. He had a plan, although Sandra couldn't yet understand what he was hoping to obtain.

'Giorgia must have been proud of you.'

The mere mention of his sister's name made Federico stiffen. 'She was all I had left.'

'What about your parents?'

He was clearly reluctant to talk about them, and quickly disposed of the question. 'My mother left home when we were still young. My father brought us up. But he never got over her leaving him, he'd loved her too much. He died when I was fifteen.'

'What kind of person was your sister?'

'The most cheerful person I've ever known: nothing hurt her, and her mood was contagious. After the accident she took care of me. I knew what a burden I would become over the years and that it wasn't right for her to take it on, but she insisted. She gave up everything for me.'

'She'd been a veterinarian . . .'

'Yes, and she also had a boyfriend. He dumped her when he realised the kind of responsibility she'd assumed. I know you must have heard this a hundred times, but Giorgia didn't deserve to die.'

Sandra wondered what divine plan could possibly be behind the chain of tragic events that had destroyed the lives of two good young people. Abandoned by their mother, orphaned by their father, the brother confined to a wheelchair, the sister brutally murdered and killed. For some reason, what came into her mind was the girl David had met on the beach. That encounter after a whole series of mishaps – the lost suitcase, the double booking, the hire car breaking down a few miles short of the destination – could have ended differently. If that unknown jogger had found David even slightly interesting or attractive, he and Sandra might never have met, and there might now be another woman mourning him. Fate sometimes seemed really determined for things to work out in a particular way, a way that had some kind of meaning. But in the case of Federico and Giorgia Noni that meaning was elusive.

Federico tried to move the conversation away from these painful memories. 'I don't quite understand why you're here.'

'There's a possibility your sister's killer, Nicola Costa, may get a big reduction in his sentence.'

The news clearly upset him. 'I thought he confessed.'

'Yes, but apparently he's now claiming insanity at the time of the murder,' Schalber lied. 'That's why we need to prove that he was always in full possession of his faculties. During the three assaults and above all during the murder.'

Federico shook his head and clenched his fists. Sandra felt sorry for him and upset about the way they were deceiving him. She hadn't yet said a word, but her mere presence here supported every one of Schalber's lies, so she felt complicit.

Federico looked at them, his eyes glowing with anger. 'How can I help you?'

'Tell us what happened.'

'Again? It's been a long time, my memory may not be what it was.'

'We're aware of that. But we have no choice, Signor Noni. That bastard Costa will try to distort the facts, and we can't allow him to do that. It was you who identified him.'

'He was wearing a balaclava, I only recognised his voice.'

'That makes you our sole witness. You do realise that?' Schalber took out a notebook and pencil, pretending that he wanted to write down every word.

Federico stroked his bristly beard. He took a few deep breaths, his chest rising and falling, as if he might hyperventilate. He started to reconstruct what had happened. 'It was seven o'clock in the evening, Giorgia always came home at that hour. She'd been shopping, and had bought the ingredients for a cake. I like sweet things.' He sounded apologetic, as if that was the reason for what had happened later. 'I was listening to music on headphones. I didn't pay any attention to her. She used to say I was becoming a slob, that she was prepared to wait for a bit but then she'd make damn sure I became more active ... The fact is, I was refusing to do physiotherapy. I'd lost hope of ever walking again.'

'Then what happened?'

'All I remember is being thrown to the ground and passing out. The bastard had come up behind me and tipped my wheelchair over.'

'Hadn't you noticed that someone had got into the house?'

'No.'

They had reached a critical point. From now on, the story would become more difficult.

'Please go on.'

'When I recovered consciousness, I was dazed. I couldn't keep my eyes open and my back hurt. I didn't understand straight away, but then I heard the screams coming from upstairs ...' A tear welled up, ran down his cheek and ended up in his beard. 'I was on the floor, my wheelchair was five or six feet away, but it was damaged. I tried to get to the phone, but it was on a cabinet, and I couldn't reach it.' He looked down at his legs. 'When you're like this, even the simplest things become impossible.'

But Schalber was unmoved. 'What about your mobile phone?'

'I didn't know where it was, and anyway I was in a panic.' Federico turned to look at the stairs. 'Giorgia was screaming and screaming ... She was asking for help, begging for mercy, as if that bastard would give her either.'

'And what did you do?'

'I dragged myself to the stairs, and tried to climb them, using my arms to support me. But I didn't have the strength.'

'Really?' Schalber gave a smug smile. 'You were a trained sportsman. I find it hard to believe it could have been so difficult for you to get up the stairs.'

Sandra turned and glared at him, but he ignored her.

'You don't know how I felt after banging my head on the floor,' Federico Noni retorted, his manner hardening.

'You're right, I'm sorry.' Schalber said it without conviction, deliberately letting his scepticism shine through. He looked down and made a note. In reality, he was waiting for Federico to take the bait he had held out.

'What are you getting at?'

'Nothing, go on,' he said with an irritating movement of his hand.

'The killer escaped through a back door when he heard the police coming.'

'You recognised Nicola Costa from his voice, is that right?'

'Yes.'

'You stated that the killer had a speech defect, which is perfectly compatible with his deformation.'

'Yes, what of it?'

'At first, though, you had taken the effect of his cleft palate for an Eastern European accent.'

'It was you police who made the mistake, what does it have to do with me?' Federico Noni was on the defensive now.

'All right, goodbye.' Taking Federico – and Sandra – by surprise, Schalber held out his hand to the young man and made as if to leave.

'Wait a minute.'

'Signor Noni, I have no time to waste. There's no point being here if you won't tell us the truth.'

'And what is that?'

Sandra saw that Federico was quite shaken. She didn't know what game Schalber was playing, but she took the risk of butting in. 'I think it's best if we go.'

Schalber again ignored her. He went and stood in front of Noni and started pointing his finger at him. 'The truth is, you only heard Giorgia's voice, not the killer's. Forget about an Eastern European or a speech defect.'

'That's not true.'

'The truth is that when you came to, you could have climbed up there and tried to save her. You're an athlete, you could have done it.'

'That's not true.'

'The truth is that you stayed down here, while that monster finished the job.'

'That's not true!' Federico Noni cried, bursting into tears.

Sandra stood up, took Schalber by the arm, and tried to pull him away. 'That's enough now, leave him alone.'

But Schalber wouldn't let go. 'Why don't you tell us what really happened – why you didn't intervene to help Giorgia?'

'I, I . . .'

'What? Come on, be a man for once.'

'I . . .' Federico Noni was stammering through his tears. 'I didn't . . . I wanted . . .'

Schalber kept going. 'Show me some balls, not like you did that evening.'

'Please, Schalber,' Sandra said.

'I . . . I was scared.'

Silence descended on the room, broken only by Federico's sobs. Schalber at last stopped tormenting him. He turned his back on him and headed for the door. Before following, Sandra stood for a moment looking at Federico Noni, who was shaking with sobs, his eyes bowed over his useless legs. She would have liked to console him, but she could not find the words.

'I'm sorry for what happened to you, Signor Noni,' Schalber said as he walked out. 'Good day to you.'

As Schalber hurried to the car, Sandra ran after him and forced him to stop.

'What were you thinking? You didn't have to treat him that way.'

'If you don't approve of my methods, you can always let me work on my own.'

He was contemptuous of her, too, and she couldn't accept that. 'You can't treat me this way!'

'I told you: my speciality is liars. I can't do anything about it, I hate them.'

'Were we so honest in there?' she asked, pointing to the house behind them. 'How many lies did you tell? Or have you lost count?'

'Haven't you ever heard of the ends justifying the means?' Schalber stuck his hand in his pocket, took out a packet of chewing gum and slipped one into his mouth.

'And what was the end that justified humiliating a cripple?'

He shrugged. 'Listen, I'm sorry Federico Noni has been dealt a bad hand by fate, he probably didn't deserve it. But bad things happen to everybody, that shouldn't absolve us of our responsibilities. You more than anyone should know that.'

'Because of what happened to David, you mean?'

'Precisely. You don't use his death as an alibi.'

He chewed the gum with his mouth open, which jarred on her nerves. 'What do you know about that?'

'I know you could spend all your time crying and nobody would blame you. Instead, you're fighting. They kill your husband, they

199

shoot at you, and yet you don't give up.' He turned his back on her and continued towards the car. It was starting to rain again.

Not caring if she got wet, Sandra waited where she was. 'You really disgust me.'

Schalber stopped, turned and retraced his steps. 'With his fake testimony, that little arsehole Federico Noni let an innocent man go to prison rather than admit that he was a coward. Doesn't *that* disgust you?'

'I get it. You're the one who establishes who's guilty and who isn't. How long have you been working like that, Schalber?'

He snorted and waved his arms. 'Listen, I don't want to stand arguing in the middle of the street. I'm sorry if I was harsh, but that's the way I am. Don't you think I feel bad about David's death? Don't you think I feel partly to blame for not preventing it?'

Sandra fell silent. She hadn't considered that. Maybe she had judged Schalber too hastily.

'We weren't friends,' he went on, 'but he trusted me, and that's enough to make me feel guilty.'

Sandra calmed down, and when she spoke again it was in a reasonable tone. 'What do we do about Noni? Should we inform anyone?'

'Not now. We still have a lot to do. I think we can assume by now that the penitenzieri are looking for the real Figaro. We have to get to him before they do.'

3.53 *p.m.*

A persistent drizzle had slowed the Rome traffic. When he finally got to the park, Marcus stood at the gate for a few moments, thinking again about the email Zini had received.

He is not like you. Look in Villa Glori Park.

Who was the real Figaro? And who would the role of avenger fall to this time? The answer might be here.

Although not the biggest park in Rome, Villa Glori nevertheless covered some sixty acres: too large to explore in its entirety before

sunset. Not that he had any idea what he was supposed to be looking for anyway.

The message was addressed to a blind man, he thought.
Therefore it must be an obvious sign, maybe an auditory one. But
then he thought again: no, the message was addressed to the penitenzieri. The fact that it was sent to Zini was completely accidental.

It was meant for us.

He went through the large black gate and started up the slope:
Villa Glori was on a hill. He immediately passed a foolhardy jogger
in shorts and a waterproof jacket, followed by a boxer dog keeping
perfect pace with him. It was starting to get cold and Marcus lifted
the collar of his raincoat. He looked around, hoping that something
would attract his attention.

Anomalies.

The vegetation was much thicker in Villa Glori than in Rome's
other parks. Tall trees stood out against the sky, creating strange
interplays of light and shade. The undergrowth was made up of
small shrubs and bushes, and the ground was covered in branches
and dead leaves.

A blonde was sitting on a bench. In one hand she held an
umbrella, in the other an open book. A Labrador was circling her
restlessly. It probably wanted to play, but its mistress continued
to ignore it, absorbed as she was in her reading. Marcus tried to
avoid her eyes as he came towards her, but she looked up from
her book, wondering perhaps if this stranger constituted a potential danger. He passed her without slowing down and the dog
started following him, with its tail wagging. It wanted to make
friends. Marcus stopped and let it come to him. He stroked its
head.

'Good boy, now go back to her.'

The Labrador seemed to have understood and turned back.

He needed to orientate his search somehow. It had to be concealed in the very nature of the place.

A wood with thicker vegetation than in the other parks in Rome.
Not really ideal for picnics, but excellent for jogging or riding a
bike . . . and perfect for letting your dog run free.

Dogs: that was the answer. If there's something here, they must have scented it, Marcus told himself.

He climbed up the path that led to the top of the hill, carefully scrutinising the ground that lapped against the asphalt. After a hundred yards, he saw a kind of trail on the muddy ground.

A trail made up of dozens of paw prints.

They hadn't been left by just one animal. Many dogs had come running here towards the wood.

Marcus left the main path and entered the shrubbery. The only sounds were the drizzle and his footsteps on the soggy leaves. He went on for about a hundred yards, trying not to lose sight of the paw prints, which, despite the recent storms, were still quite visible. That meant the dogs had come here over many days, one set of prints replacing another. But he still couldn't see any sign.

The single trail broke off suddenly. From here on, the prints were scattered over a fairly broad area, as if the dogs had lost the scent. Or as if the smell was so pervasive that they couldn't locate its source.

The sky was overcast. The sounds and lights of the city had vanished beyond the curtain of foliage. Marcus felt as if he was a long way from civilisation, somewhere dark and primeval. He took the torch from his pocket and lit it. He moved the beam around, cursing his bad luck. He would be forced to retrace his steps now and come back the following morning. But there would probably be more people in the park then, and it might be impossible to see his task through to the end. He was about to give up when his torch caught something about six feet from where he was standing. At first he took it for a fallen branch. But it was too straight, too perfect. He aimed the torch directly at it, and knew what he had to do.

It was a shovel, propped against one of the trees.

He put the torch down on the ground, so that it lit the area around. Then he put on the rubber gloves he always carried with him and started digging.

The noises of the wood were amplified by the darkness. Every sound became threatening, passing him like a ghost and vanishing with the wind that rustled the branches. The shovel sank into the soft earth. As he dug, Marcus flung aside the mixture of mud and foliage that came up, without bothering where it landed. He was in a hurry to see what was buried down there, although part of him already knew the answer. It was harder work than he had expected. He was sweating, his clothes were sticking to him and he was getting out of breath. But he didn't stop. He wanted to be refuted.

Lord, let it not be what I think it is.

But soon afterwards he became aware of the smell. It was pungent and sickly, filling his nostrils and lungs with every breath he took. It had an almost liquid consistency, it was as if he could drink it. Coming in contact with his gastric juices, it made him retch, and Marcus had to pause to lift the sleeve of his raincoat to his mouth. Then he set to work again. At his feet there was a small hole, nearly two feet wide and three feet deep. But the shovel continued to sink into the muddy ground. Another foot or so. More than twenty minutes had gone by.

At last he saw a blackish liquid, as viscous as petroleum. A residue of decomposition. Marcus knelt by the hole and started digging with his bare hands. The dark oil stained his clothes, but he didn't care. He started to feel something more solid than earth beneath his fingers. Something smooth and partly fibrous. He was touching a bone. He cleared a space around it and discovered a patch of pale flesh.

There was no doubt about it, it was human.

He took the shovel again and tried to free as much of the body as he could. A leg emerged, then the pelvis. It was a woman, and she was naked. The process of putrefaction was at an advanced stage, but the body had been well preserved. Marcus could not have said how old she was, but he was sure she was young. There were deep cuts all over the chest and in the pubic area, caused by a sharp weapon.

Scissors.

At last, Marcus stopped. Breathing in deep mouthfuls of air he crouched to look at that obscene display of violence and death.

He made the sign of the cross, then put his hands together and started praying for this unknown woman. He could imagine her young dreams, her zest for life. At her age, death must have seemed distant and undefined. Something that only concerned other people. Marcus implored God to receive her soul, without knowing if anyone was listening to him or if he was talking to himself. The terrible truth about Marcus was that, along with his memories, the amnesia had taken away his faith. He did not know how a man of the cloth should feel. But saying a prayer for that poor girl's soul was comforting to him. Because right now, with all the evil he was facing, the existence of God was his one consolation.

Marcus could not have determined with any certainty when death had occurred. But the nature of the burial site and the state of preservation of the body suggested it was not so long ago. He came to the conclusion that the corpse he had in front of him was proof that Nicola Costa was not Figaro, because the man with the cleft palate was already in prison when this girl had been killed.

Somebody else was Figaro.

There are people who taste human blood and recover an old predatory instinct, a legacy of the fight for survival, the echo of an ancestral need to kill that has been lost in the course of evolution. With the murder of Giorgia Noni, the serial attacker had discovered a new pleasure. Something that was present in him, without his knowing it.

He would kill again. Marcus was sure of it.

The telephone was ringing at the other end. He hoped it would be answered soon. He was in one of the safe houses, not far from Villa Glori.

At last, Marcus heard Zini's voice. 'Hello?'

'It's as I thought,' he said immediately.

Zini muttered something, then asked, 'How long ago?'

'A month, maybe more. I couldn't say with any certainty, I'm not a pathologist.'

Zini weighed up this information. 'If he took the trouble to hide the body this time, he'll do it again soon. I think I should report it.'

'Let's try to figure it out first.' Marcus wished he could tell him what he knew, communicate his anxieties. What he had discovered would

not be enough to bring the guilty party to justice. Whoever had sent
Zini the anonymous email and placed the shovel in Villa Glori to indicate the exact point to start digging would give Federico Noni the
opportunity to avenge himself. Or else the opportunity would be
offered to one or other of the three women attacked before Giorgia's
murder. Marcus knew he didn't have much time left. Should they tell
the police so that they could contact the other victims and prevent the
worst from happening? He was convinced that someone was on the
trail of the real Figaro. 'Zini, I need to know one thing. The first part
of the message you received: "He is not like you." What does it mean?'

'I have no idea.'

'Don't play games with me.'

Zini paused for a few seconds. 'Okay, come here late this evening.'

'No, now.'

'Now I can't.' Zini turned to someone who was with him in the
house. 'Pour yourself some tea, I'll be right there.'

'Who's there with you?

Zini lowered his voice. 'A policewoman. She says she wants to ask
me some questions about Nicola Costa, but she hasn't told me the
whole truth.'

The situation was becoming complicated. Who was this woman?
Why were the police suddenly taking an interest in a case that was
apparently closed? What was she really looking for?

'Get rid of her.'

'I think she knows a lot.'

'Then keep her there and try to find out the real reason she came
to see you.'

'I don't know if you'll agree, but there's something I think you
have to do. Can I give you a piece of advice?'

'Go on, I'm listening.'

5.07 p.m.

She poured herself a large cup of tea and held it in her hands, enjoying the warmth. From the kitchen she could see Pietro Zini's back.

He was talking on the telephone in the hall, but she couldn't hear what he was saying.

She had managed to persuade Schalber to wait for her in the guest apartment. It made more sense for her to meet Zini on her own. After all, he was a former policeman, and he wouldn't be so easy to trick as Federico Noni. She would ask a lot of questions, making it clear that there wasn't any official investigation in progress. And besides, the police didn't like people from Interpol. Presenting herself at his door, she had simply told him that the Milan police were dealing with a case similar to the Figaro case. Zini had believed her.

As she waited for the end of the phone call, Sandra glanced at the file that Zini had given her. It was a duplicate of the official file on Nicola Costa. She hadn't asked him how he had come by it, but he had been at pains to tell her that, when he was on the force, he was in the habit of keeping copies of all material relating to his cases.

'You never know when an idea might come to you that helps you solve a case,' he had said by way of justification. 'So you always have to have everything within reach.'

Leafing through the pages, Sandra realised that Zini was a meticulous type. There were many annotations. The last reports, though, revealed a certain haste. It was as if he had wanted to speed things up, knowing that his blindness was catching up with him. At times, especially in his handling of Costa's confession, he had been quite slapdash. There was a lack of corroborating evidence and, without the confession, the legal case would have collapsed like a house of cards.

She looked through the material gathered by the forensic photographers at the various crime scenes. First of all, the assaults that had preceded the murder. The three victims had all been alone in their homes. It had always happened in the late afternoon. The maniac had stabbed them repeatedly with the scissors. The wounds, which were concentrated in the breasts, legs and pubic area, were never deep enough to cause death.

According to the psychiatric report, the assaults had a sexual origin. Figaro's aim, however, was not to reach orgasm, as was the case with those sadists who could only gain satisfaction through coercion. He was after something else: to prevent these women from ever being attractive to men again.

If I can't have you, nobody else will.

That was the message the lesions conveyed. And such behaviour was perfectly compatible with Nicola Costa's personality. Because of his cleft palate, the opposite sex rejected him. That was why he did not penetrate his victims. Even if he had obtained physical contact through force, he would still have felt their revulsion, and that would merely have echoed his experience of rejection. The scissors, though, constituted an excellent compromise. They allowed him to feel pleasure but, at the same time, to keep a safe distance from the women who had scared him all his life. The male orgasm was replaced by the gratification of seeing them suffer.

But if, as Schalber maintained, Nicola Costa was not Figaro, then they had to completely revise the perpetrator's psychological profile.

Sandra went on to the photographs of the murder of Giorgia Noni. The corpse presented the unmistakable signs that the maniac had left on the other women. But this time he had wounded to kill.

As in the previous cases, he had broken into the victim's home. But this time a third person had been present: Federico. According to his statement, the killer had escaped through a back door as soon as he had heard the police siren.

Figaro's steps as he escaped were imprinted in the soil of the garden.

The crime-scene photographer had shot some close-ups of the shoe prints. For some reason, Sandra remembered David's encounter with the unknown girl jogging on the beach.

Coincidences, she thought.

Guided by an instinct, her husband had followed those steps in the sand, eager to find out who they belonged to. Suddenly, those actions seemed to her to have a meaning. Even though she did not yet understand what it was. As she was focusing on this idea, Zini finished his phone call and came back into the kitchen.

'You can take it with you if you want,' he said, referring to the file. 'I don't need it any more.'

'Thank you. I really should go now.'

Zini sat down facing her and placed his arms on the table. 'Stay a while longer. I don't get many visitors, it's nice to have a bit of a chat.'

Before the phone call, Zini had seemed anxious to get rid of her as soon as possible. Now he was actually asking her to stay. It didn't seem to be a simple gesture of politeness, so she decided to humour him in order to discover what he had in mind.

And to hell with Schalber, he could wait a while longer. 'All right, I'll stay.' Zini reminded her of Inspector De Michelis. She felt she could trust this man. With his big hands, he was a solid as a tree.

'How was the tea?'

'Very nice.'

Zini poured himself a cup, even though the water in the teapot was no longer as hot as it had been. 'I always used to have tea with my wife. On Sundays when we got back from Mass, she'd make tea and we'd sit down here and talk. It was like a date.' He smiled. 'I don't think we ever skipped that teatime conversation in twenty years of marriage.'

'What did you talk about?'

'Everything. We didn't have one subject in particular. That was the good thing: being able to share everything. Sometimes we argued, we always laughed a lot, we conjured up memories. Not having been lucky enough to bring children into the world, we knew we had a terrible enemy to confront every day. Silence can be hostile. If you don't learn to keep it at bay, it gets into the cracks of a relationship and makes them wider. With time, it creates a distance between you, and you don't even realise it.'

'I lost my husband not long ago.' The words came out spontaneously, without her thinking. 'We were only married for three years.'

'I'm sorry, I know how hard that can be. Despite everything, I feel lucky. Susy went the way she always wanted: suddenly.'

'I still remember when they came to tell me that David was dead.' Sandra didn't want to think about it. 'How did you find out?'

'One morning I tried to wake her.' Zini did not go on, but it was sufficient. 'It may seem selfish, but an illness is an advantage for those who have to remain behind. It prepares you for the worst. Whereas this way ...'

Sandra knew what he meant. The sudden emptiness, the irreversibility, the unassuaged need to talk about it before everything becomes final. The mad temptation to pretend it didn't happen. 'Zini, do you believe in God?'

'What are you really asking me?'

'Just that. You say you used to go to Mass, so you must be a Catholic. Aren't you angry with God for what happened?'

'Believing in God doesn't necessarily mean loving Him.'

'I don't follow.'

'Our relationship with Him is based solely on the idea that there's life after death. But if there wasn't, would you still love the God that created you? If you weren't going to get the reward you were promised, would you still be capable of kneeling and praising the Lord?'

'What about you?'

'I believe in a creator, but not in an afterlife. So I feel justified in hating Him.' Zini burst into a laugh that was as loud as it was bitter. 'This city is full of churches. They represent men's attempts to prevent the inevitable and, at the same time their failure. Yet each one contains its own secret, its own legend. My favourite is the Sacro Cuore del Suffragio. Not many people know it, but it houses the Museum of Purgatory.' Zini's voice grew sombre. He leaned towards her, as if to confide something important. 'In 1897, a few years after it was built, there was a fire. When the flames were overcome, a few of the faithful noticed that a human face had appeared in the soot on the wall behind the altar. Immediately the rumour spread that this image belonged to a soul in Purgatory. A priest named Victor Jouet was so impressed, he started hunting for other traces left by the dead as they wander in pain, trying desperately to ascend to Paradise. What he collected is in that museum. You're a forensic photographer, you should go there and take a look at it. Do you know what he discovered?'

'No.'

'That if a soul has to try and get in contact with us, it wouldn't do it with sounds, but with light.'

Sandra thought of the photographs David had left her in the Leica, and shuddered.

Not hearing any response from her, Zini apologised. 'I didn't mean to scare you, please forgive me.'

'It's nothing. You're right, I should go there.'

'Then you'd better get a move on. The museum only opens one hour a day, at the end of Vespers.'

From Zini's tone, Sandra realised it wasn't just a casual piece of advice.

The water was bubbling up from the drains, as if the belly of the city could no longer contain it. Three days of heavy rain had stretched the sewerage system to its limits. But it was over.

Now the wind had arrived.

It had risen without any warning, and had started to blow through the streets in the centre. Loud and unpredictable, it had invaded Rome, its alleys and squares.

Sandra was making her way through an invisible multitude, as if battling an army of ghosts. The wind was trying to force her to change direction, but she carried on regardless. She felt the vibration of the mobile phone in the bag she kept with her. Frantically, she searched for it, simultaneously thinking about what she would tell Schalber, because she was sure it was him. It hadn't been easy to persuade him to stay in the guest apartment, so she could imagine the objections he would raise on hearing that she wouldn't be coming straight back to tell him the outcome of her conversation with Zini. But she had an excuse all ready.

At last she dug the phone out from amid the jumble of objects she carried with her and looked at the screen. She was wrong, it was De Michelis.

'Vega, what's all that noise?'

'Just a minute.' Sandra took shelter in a doorway. 'Can you hear me now?'

'That's better, thanks. How are you?'

'There have been some interesting developments,' she said, although she had decided not to tell him that someone had shot at her that morning. 'I can't tell you too much now, but I'm putting the pieces together. David had discovered something big here in Rome.'

'Don't keep me in suspense. When are you coming back to Milan?'

'I need a couple of days, maybe even more.'

'I'll see if I can extend your leave.'

'Thanks, Inspector, you're a friend. How about you, any news for me?'

'Thomas Schalber.'

'So you managed to find out something?'

'Of course. I talked to an old acquaintance who used to work for Interpol but who's now retired. You know what they're like, they're a bit suspicious when you ask them about their colleagues. I couldn't be too direct, couldn't come straight out with it, so I had to invite him to lunch. Quite a long lunch, as it turned out . . . '

De Michelis had a bad habit of wandering off the point. 'What did you find out?' Sandra prodded him.

'My friend doesn't know him personally, but when he was working for Interpol he heard that Schalber's quite a tough nut. He doesn't have many friends, he prefers to work alone, and his superiors don't like that. But he gets results. He's stubborn and argumentative, but everybody agrees he's honest. Two years ago he carried out an internal investigation into corruption. Obviously, that didn't make him very popular, but he did nail a group of agents who were in the pay of a drugs gang. He's one of the Untouchables!'

De Michelis's description, however ironic and exaggerated, made her think. Why should an agent like that be bothering with the penitenzieri? Judging by his past, Schalber generally seemed drawn to cases where the crime was a more obvious one. Why was he so determined to hunt down these priests who were performing a positive task and weren't actually harming anyone?

'So, Inspector, what's your overall impression of Schalber?'

'From what I've heard, he seems to be a real pain in the arse. But I'd say he can be trusted.'

De Michelis's words reassured Sandra. 'Thanks, I'll bear that in mind.'

'If you need me again, don't hesitate to call.'

She hung up and, with renewed determination, plunged back into the invisible river of the wind.

In his farewell to her, Pietro Zini had been trying to give her a message. The visit to the Museum of Purgatory wasn't one she could put off. Sandra didn't know what to expect, but she was sure she had understood what the former policeman had been telling her. There was something there, something she absolutely had to see as soon as possible.

Within a few minutes, she was outside the church of the Sacro Cuore del Suffragio. Its neo-Gothic style immediately reminded her of Milan Cathedral, even though the building only dated from the late nineteenth century. Inside, Vespers was coming to an end. The congregation was not large. The wind beat at the doors, got in through a few cracks and whistled down the naves.

Sandra followed the sign to the Museum of Purgatory.

She soon discovered that it was a collection of strange relics – at least ten – crammed into a single display case in the passageway leading to the sacristy. Among them, an old prayer book opened at the page on which the print of a hand appeared, a hand that was said to belong to a dead man. Or the marks left in 1864 on the cover of a cushion by the tormented soul of a dead nun. Or those present on the habit and shift of an abbess who had received a visit from the spirit of a priest in 1731.

When she felt a hand coming to rest on her shoulder, Sandra was not afraid. She knew now why Pietro Zini had sent her here. She turned and saw him.

'Why are you looking for me?' the man with the scar on his temple asked.

'I'm a police officer,' she said immediately.

'That's not the reason. There's no official investigation, you're acting in a personal capacity. I realised that after we met in San Luigi dei Francesi. You weren't there to arrest me last night, you wanted to shoot me.'

Sandra did not reply: it was all too obvious that he was right. 'You really are a priest,' she said.

'Yes, I am.'

'My husband was David Leoni. Does that name mean anything to you?'

He seemed to give it a moment's thought. 'No.'

'He was a photojournalist. He died a few months ago, falling off a building. He was murdered.'

'What does that have to do with me?'

'He was investigating the penitenzieri. He took a photograph of you at a crime scene.'

Hearing the penitenzieri mentioned, the priest gave a start. 'And is that the only reason he was killed?

'I don't know.' Sandra paused. 'That was you on the phone to Zini, wasn't it? Why did you want to meet me again?'

'To ask you to drop this.'

'I can't. I have to discover why David died and find his killer. Can you help me?'

He took his sad blue eyes off her and turned his gaze to one of the objects in the display case, a small wooden table on which a cross was imprinted. 'All right. But you have to destroy the photograph of me. That's all your husband found out about the penitenzieri.'

'I'll do that once I've got the answers I want.'

'Does anybody else know about us?'

'No,' she lied. She didn't have the courage to tell him Schalber and Interpol were also involved. She was afraid that, if he realised he was in danger of being exposed, he would disappear forever.

'How did you discover I was investigating the Figaro case?'

'The police know – they intercepted a conversation in which you discussed it.' She hoped he would be content with that version. 'Don't worry, they don't know who they're dealing with.'

'But you do.'

'I knew how to find you. David showed me.'

He nodded. 'It seems to me there's nothing else to say.'

'What if I want to see you again?'

'I'll find you.'

He turned to go, but Sandra stopped him. 'How do I know you're not deceiving me? How can I trust you if I don't know who you are or what you're doing?'

'That's nothing but curiosity. And people who are too curious commit the sin of pride.'

'I'm only trying to understand.'

The priest moved his face closer to the case containing the unlikely relics. 'These objects are examples of superstition. Man's attempt to look into a dimension that isn't his. Everyone wants to know what happens when our time on earth is over. They don't realise that every answer they get contains within itself a new question. So even if I explain to you what I do, it wouldn't be enough.'

'Then at least tell me why you do it . . . '

The penitenziere was silent for a few moments. 'There is a place where the world of light meets the world of darkness. It is there that everything happens: in the land of shadows, where everything is vague, confused, undefined. We are the guardians appointed to defend that border. But every now and again something manages to get through.' He turned to look at Sandra. 'I have to chase it back into the darkness.'

'Maybe I could give you a hand with Figaro,' she said instinctively, and saw an expectant look come into his eyes. From her bag, she took the file on the case that Zini had given her. 'I don't know if it'll be of any use to you, but I think I've discovered a clue that was overlooked in the murder of Giorgia Noni.'

'Go on,' he said, with a gentleness that surprised her.

'Federico Noni is the sole witness to what happened. According to his statement, the killer continued stabbing his sister until he heard the police siren. Only then did he run away.' Sandra opened the file and showed him a photograph. 'These are the prints that Figaro left in the garden after he ran out through the back door.'

The priest leaned forward to get a better look at the image of the shoe prints in a flower bed. 'What's strange about it?'

'Federico Noni and his sister Giorgia were victims of a series of tragic events. Their mother abandons them, their father dies, the boy has an accident, the doctors tell him he'll walk again but it doesn't happen, and finally, the girl is killed. Too many things.'

'What does that have to do with the prints?'

'There was a story that David liked to tell. He was fascinated by coincidences, or synchronicity as Jung called it. He believed in them so much that once, after a series of incredibly unfortunate events that had led him to a beach, he started following the prints left in the sand by a girl who was jogging. He was convinced that once he found her it would make sense of all the bad things that had happened to him along the way. In fact, he was sure he would meet the love of his life.'

'Very romantic.'

He wasn't being sarcastic. Sandra could tell from the way he was looking at her that he was perfectly serious. So she continued with her story. 'David was wrong only about that last detail. The rest was true.'

'What are you trying to say?'

'That if I hadn't recently recalled that story, I mightn't be able to give you the solution you're looking for ... Like all police officers I'm a sceptic when it comes to coincidences. So whenever David told me that story, I always tried to pull it apart. "How could you be sure that the prints belonged to a girl?" I'd ask him. Or: "How did you know she was jogging?" And he'd reply that those feet were too small to be a man's – or at least he hoped so – and that the prints were deeper at the soles than at the heels, because she was running.'

As Sandra had expected, this last statement triggered a reaction. The priest looked again at the photograph of the garden.

The prints seemed deeper at the heels.

'He wasn't running ... he was walking.'

He had got there. Now Sandra was sure she hadn't been mistaken. 'There are two possibilities. Either Federico Noni was lying when he said that the killer ran away when the police arrived ...'

'. . . or else someone, after the murder, had all the time in the world to prepare the crime scene for the police.'

'Those prints were left deliberately, which can mean only one thing.'

'Figaro never left the house.'

8.38 p.m.

He had to hurry. Getting there by public transport would have taken too long, so he had hailed a taxi. He asked the driver to drop him a short distance from the house in Nuovo Salario and continued on foot.

As he approached, he thought again about the policewoman's words, the intuition that had allowed her to reach the solution of the mystery. Even though he hoped he was wrong, he was pretty sure now that things had happened exactly as she had said.

It was still windy, and plastic bags and scraps of paper whirled around Marcus, accompanying him to his destination.

There was nobody in the vicinity of Federico Noni's house. All the lights were off inside. He waited a few minutes, huddling inside his raincoat, then went inside the house.

Everything was quiet. Too quiet.

He decided not to use the torch.

There was no sound.

Marcus reached the living room. The blinds were down. He lit the lamp next to the sofa and the first thing that leapt to his eyes was the wheelchair, abandoned in the middle of the room.

Now he could see clearly what had happened. His talent was to enter into objects, identify with their mute souls, and look at the past through their invisible eyes. This scene revealed the meaning of a phrase in the anonymous email received by Zini.

He is not like you.

It referred to Federico. It meant they weren't both suffering from physical handicaps. The boy was simulating his.

But where was Figaro now?

If Federico lived like a recluse, he could not have left the house through the front door. The neighbours might have seen him. How did he manage to get out undisturbed to attack his victims?

Marcus continued his search. As he approached the staircase leading to the first floor, he noticed that there was a door under the stairs, and that it was ajar. He opened it and went in. As he did so, his head knocked against something hanging from the low ceiling. A lamp with a short rope next to it. He pulled on the rope and the light came on.

He found himself in a narrow cubbyhole that stank of mothballs. Old clothes were kept here, divided into two rows. Men's clothes on the left, women's clothes on the right. They had probably belonged to the boy's dead parents, Marcus thought. There was also a shoe rack and boxes piled up on shelves against the wall.

He noticed two dresses on the floor, a blue one and a red flowery one. Maybe they had slipped off their hangers, or maybe someone had dropped them. Marcus put a hand between the hangers and moved the clothes aside, revealing a door.

He deduced that the cubbyhole had originally been a passageway.

He opened the door. He took the torch out of his pocket and shone it at a short corridor with peeling, damp-stained walls. He walked along it until he reached a place into which a number of large boxes and a few items of furniture no longer in use were crammed. The beam of light fell on an object lying on a table.

An exercise book.

He took it and started leafing through it. The drawings on the first pages were clearly the work of a child. The same elements recurred endlessly.

Female figures, wounds, blood. And scissors.

A page was missing, clearly torn out. Presumably the one they had found hanging, framed, on the wall of Jeremiah Smith's loft. He had come full circle.

The subsequent pages of the exercise book, however, bore witness to the fact that this practice had not ended with his youth. The drawings continued, more precise, more mature in their line. The women were much more defined, the cuts ever more realistic. A sign that the monster's sick, twisted imagination had grown as he had grown.

Federico Noni had always harboured these violent fantasies. But he had never realised them. It was probably fear that had stopped him. Fear of ending up in prison, or of being pointed out by everyone as a monster. He had created the mask of the good athlete, the good boy, the good brother. He had even believed it himself.

Then the motorcycle accident had happened.

That event had released everything. Marcus recalled the policewoman telling him that she had heard Federico Noni say the doctors believed he would recover the use of his legs. But then he had refused to continue with his physiotherapy.

His condition was the perfect camouflage. At last, he could let his true nature emerge.

Reaching the last page of the exercise book, Marcus discovered that it contained an old press cutting. He unfolded it. It went back to more than a year before and reported the news of Figaro's third assault. Across the article, someone had written in black felt-tip pen the words *I know everything*.

Giorgia, Marcus thought immediately. That was why Federico killed her. And that was when he discovered that he liked the new game more.

The assaults had begun after the accident. The first three had been useful as preparation. They were a kind of exercise, although Federico may not have been aware of it at the time. What awaited him was another kind of satisfaction, one that was much more gratifying. Murder.

The killing of his sister had been unplanned but necessary. Giorgia had understood everything and had become an obstacle, as well as a danger. Federico couldn't allow her to tarnish his clean image, or to cast doubt on his precious disguise. That was why he had killed her. But it had also helped him to understand something.

Taking a life was much more gratifying than a mere assault.

And so he had not been able to restrain himself. The dead girl in

Villa Glori Park was the demonstration of that. But this time he had been more cautious. Having learned from experience, he had buried her.

Federico Noni had deceived everyone. Starting with Pietro Zini. All it had taken was a false confession by a compulsive liar, a confession he had confirmed. An inadequate investigation, based on the assumption that only an obvious monster could have committed such a crime, had done the rest.

Marcus put down the exercise book because he had caught sight of an iron door half hidden behind a sideboard. He went and opened it.

A raging wind burst into the little room. He looked out and saw that the door led to a deserted side street. Nobody would notice who went in or out. It had probably fallen into disuse over the years, but Federico Noni had learned to use it.

Where is he now? Where has he gone? The question echoed again in Marcus's head.

He closed the door and hurriedly retraced his steps. Coming back into the living room, he started rummaging around. He didn't care if he left prints, his one concern was that he might be too late.

He looked at the wheelchair. On one side there was a kind of pocket for keeping things. He put his hand in and found a mobile phone.

He's clever, he told himself. He left it here because he knows that, even if it's off, it might help the police to establish his location.

That meant that Federico Noni had left home to commit a crime.

Marcus checked the last calls. There was one incoming one, from an hour and a half earlier. He recognised the number because he had dialled it himself that afternoon.

Zini.

He pressed the recall button, waiting for the blind ex-policeman to reply. He heard the ringing, but nobody answered. Marcus hung up and, with a chilling sense of foreboding, rushed out of the house.

As she looked in the mirror in the bathroom of the Interpol guest apartment, Sandra thought again of what had happened that afternoon after her meeting with the penitenziere.

She had wandered for nearly an hour through the streets of Rome, letting herself be carried by the wind and her thoughts, heedless of the risk she ran after the ambush by the sniper that morning. As long as she was among people, she felt safe. When she had had enough she'd returned here. She had waited a while on the landing before knocking, trying to put off for as long as possible Schalber's reprimands for her long absence. But as soon as he had opened the door to her, she had seen the relief on his face. It had surprised her: she hadn't expected him to be worried about her.

'Thank God nothing's happened to you,' were his only words.

She was stunned. She had expected a million questions, instead of which Schalber had been content with her brief summary of her visit to Pietro Zini. Sandra had handed him the file on the Figaro case and he had leafed through it in search of any clue that might lead them to the penitenzieri.

But he had not asked her why she had taken so long to get back.

He had invited her to wash her hands because dinner would soon be ready. And then he had gone into the kitchen to get a bottle of wine.

Sandra turned on the tap in the wash basin and stood there looking at her own reflection for another few seconds. She had deep eye sockets and her lips were chapped, because of her habit of biting them when she was tense. She ran her fingers through her dishevelled hair, then looked for a comb in the cabinet. She found a brush in which some long, brown hairs were trapped. A woman's, she thought, remembering the bra she had seen on the arm of the chair in the bedroom of the guest apartment that morning. Schalber had justified its presence by saying that the apartment was used by many people, but she had noticed his embarrassment. She was sure he knew the provenance of that undergarment. There was no reason for it to bother her that another woman had been in the bed in which she had woken up, maybe even just a few hours earlier. What irritated her was that Schalber had tried to justify himself. As if it was of any interest to her!

At that moment, she felt like an idiot.

She was envious, there was no other explanation. She could not bear the thought that people had sex. The very word was liberating, even if only in the privacy of her own head. Sex, she repeated to herself. Maybe because that possibility was denied her. There was nothing actually stopping her, but part of her knew that this was how it had to be. Once again she seemed to hear her mother's voice: 'Darling, who would ever want to go to bed with a widow?' Her mother had made it sound like a kind of perversion.

No, she really was being an idiot again, wasting time on such thoughts. She had to be practical. She had been in the bathroom for too long and Schalber might start to get suspicious, so she had to hurry up.

She had made a promise to the priest, and she had every intention of keeping it. If he helped her to locate David's killer, she would wipe out all traces that led to the penitenzieri.

In any case, it was better to put the clues in a safe place for the moment.

Sandra turned towards the bag she had brought into the bathroom and placed it on the cistern. She took out the mobile phone and checked that there was sufficient space in the memory. She was about to erase the photographs she had taken in the chapel of St Raymond of Penyafort, but then she thought better of it.

Someone had tried to kill her there, and these images might help her discover who it had been.

Then she took from the bag the photographs from the Leica, including the one of the priest with the scar on his temple, which Schalber did not know about. She placed them in a row on a shelf and photographed them one by one with the mobile: it was better to possess copies, just as a precaution. She took a transparent plastic bag that could be hermetically sealed and put in the five photographs, lifted the ceramic lid over the cistern and dropped the bag in the water.

*

She had been sitting for ten minutes in the little kitchen of the apartment, looking at the laid table, while Schalber toiled at the stove, his shirtsleeves rolled up to his elbows, an apron round his waist and a dishcloth thrown over his shoulder. He was whistling. He turned and found her lost in thought. 'Risotto in balsamic vinegar, mullet in foil, and a radicchio and green apple salad,' he announced. 'I hope you approve.'

'Yes, of course,' she said, surprised. That morning he had made breakfast, but making scrambled eggs didn't exactly mean knowing how to cook. This menu, though, suggested a passion for food. She was full of admiration.

'You'll sleep here tonight.' It was a statement of fact, not a suggestion. 'It's unwise to go back to your hotel.'

'I don't think anything will happen to me. And besides, I left all my things there.'

'We can go and get them tomorrow morning. There's a very comfortable sofa in the other room.' He smiled. 'Of course I'll be the one to make the sacrifice.'

Soon afterwards, Schalber put the risotto on the plates and they ate, mostly in silence. The fish was delicious, and the wine helped her relax. It was a change from all those evenings she had spent alone at home since David's death, knocking back glass after glass of red wine until she fell into a stupor. This time it was different. She hadn't thought she was still capable of sharing a decent meal with someone.

'Who taught you to cook?'

Schalber swallowed a mouthful of food and took a sip of wine. 'You learn to do a lot of things when you're alone.'

'Never been tempted to get married? The first time on the telephone, you told me you came close a couple of times . . .'

He shook his head. 'Marriage isn't for me. It's a matter of perspective.'

'What do you mean?'

'We all have a vision of our lives. It's like a painting: there are some elements in the foreground, others in the background. The background elements are at least as necessary as the foreground ones, or there wouldn't be any sense of perspective and everything would be flat and unrealistic. Well, the women in my life are background elements. They're indispensable, but not so indispensable as to be moved into the foreground.'

'So what is there in your life? Apart from you, obviously.'

'My daughter.'

She hadn't been expecting that reply. Schalber was delighted to see that he had surprised her.

'Do you want to see her?' He took out his wallet and began looking in the pockets.

'Don't tell me you're one of those fathers who go around with a photograph of their little girl in their pocket! Damn it, Schalber, you're really going all out to astonish me.' Her tone was ironic, but actually she found it rather touching.

He showed her the creased photograph of a little girl with ash blonde hair, exactly like his. She even had his green eyes.

'How old is she?'

'Eight. Gorgeous, isn't she? Her name's Maria. She loves dancing. In fact, she attends ballet school. Every Christmas or birthday she asks for a puppy. Maybe this year I'll give in.'

'Do you get to see her often?'

Schalber's face clouded over. 'She lives in Vienna. I'm not on good terms with her mother, who resents the fact that I wouldn't marry her.' He laughed. 'But whenever I get the time, I go and see Maria and take her riding. I'm teaching her to ride, the way my father taught me when I was her age.'

'That's very good of you.'

'Every time I go to see her, I'm scared it won't be the same. That during my absence, our relationship will have cooled. Maybe she's still too young now, but what'll happen when she wants to go out with her friends? I don't want to become a burden to her.'

'I don't think that'll happen,' Sandra said. 'Daughters usually reserve that treatment for their mothers. My sister and I were crazy about our father, even though his work often took him away. In fact, that was probably why we doted on him. Whenever we knew he was coming home, there was this really happy atmosphere in the house.'

Schalber nodded, grateful for the reassurance. Sandra stood up and gathered the plates, ready to put them in the dishwasher. He stopped her. 'Why don't you go to bed? I'll clear up.'

'If we do it together it'll only take a moment.'

'Please, I insist.'

Sandra stopped. All this attention made her uncomfortable. She'd got out of the habit of having someone take care of her. 'When you called me on the phone, I immediately hated you. I could never have imagined that two nights later we'd actually be having dinner together, let alone that you'd cook for me.'

'Does that mean you don't hate me any more?'

Sandra turned red with embarrassment. He burst out laughing.

'Don't joke with me, Schalber.'

He raised his hands in surrender. 'I'm sorry, I didn't mean to.'

At that moment, he seemed genuinely sincere, and a very long way from the disagreeable image she'd had of him. 'Why are you so keen to stop the penitenzieri?'

Schalber turned serious. 'Don't make that mistake, not you too.'

'What do you mean, "you, too"?'

He seemed to regret having expressed himself badly, and tried to correct it. 'I've already explained: what they're doing is against the law.'

'I'm sorry, I don't buy that. There's more to it, isn't there?'

From the way he hesitated, she knew that the stuff he'd told her about the penitenzieri that morning was only part of the story.

'All right . . . It isn't much of a revelation, but I think what I'm about to tell you might explain why your husband died.'

Sandra stiffened. 'Go on.'

'The fact is, the penitenzieri shouldn't exist any more. After Vatican II, the Church disbanded their order. In the 1960s, the *Paenitentiaria Apostolica* was reorganised with new rules and new people in charge. The archive of sins was marked as confidential, and the priest-criminologists were told to put a halt to their activities. Some went back into the ranks, others objected and were suspended *a divinis*. Those who refused outright were excommunicated.'

'So how is it possible that—'

'Wait, let me finish,' Schalber interrupted her. 'Just when history seemed to have forgotten them, the penitenzieri reappeared. It happened a few years ago, which made some people in the Vatican suspect that many of them had simply feigned obedience to the Pope's dictates while continuing their work covertly. And it was true. At the head of this closed group was a simple Croatian priest: Luka Devok. It was he who ordained and taught the new penitenzieri. It's possible that he in his turn answered to somebody in the upper echelons of the Church who had decided to reconstruct the penitenzieri. In any case, he was the sole depository of a great many secrets. For example, Devok was the only person who knew the identities of all the penitenzieri. Everyone answered to him alone, and they had no idea who the others were.'

'Why do you talk of him in the past tense?'

'Because Luka Devok is dead. He was shot in a hotel room in Prague about a year ago. That was when the truth came out. The Vatican stepped in to put an end to a situation that might have become a serious embarrassment.'

'I'm not surprised: there's nothing the Church hates more than scandal.'

'It wasn't just that. The mere idea that someone high up in the Church had covered for Devok all those years frightened a lot of people. Disobeying a Papal order is tantamount to creating an irreconcilable schism.'

'So how did they regain control of the situation?'

'Well done,' Schalber said. 'I see you're starting to understand how these things work. They immediately replaced Devok with someone they trusted, a Portuguese priest named Augusto Clemente. He's very young but very good. The penitenzieri are all Dominicans, whereas Clemente is a Jesuit. The Jesuits are much more pragmatic and less inclined to sentimentality.'

'So this Father Clemente is the new head of the penitenzieri?'

'His task is to track down all the penitenzieri ordained by Father Devok and bring them back to the Church. So far, he's discovered only one: the man you saw in San Luigi dei Francesi.'

'So the ultimate aim of the Vatican is to pretend that there hasn't been any violation of the rules?'

'Precisely. They always try to heal any splits. Look at the followers of Archbishop Lefebvre, who've been negotiating for years to be allowed back into the mainstream of the Church. The same holds true for the penitenzieri.'

'The duty of a good shepherd is not to abandon the stray sheep and try to bring it back to the fold,' Sandra said ironically. 'But how do you know all these things?'

'The same way David did. But we had different visions, that's why we quarrelled. When I asked you to not make the same mistake, not to think of the penitenzieri too leniently, I was referring to what David thought.'

'Why makes you right and David wrong?'

'Someone killed him because of what he had discovered, whereas I'm still alive.'

This wasn't the first time Schalber had said something disrespectful about her husband, but Sandra had to admit that it was the truth. His version of the facts was convincing. She couldn't help feeling guilty. This lovely evening had helped to relieve the tension, and it was thanks to Schalber. Not only had he opened up to her about his personal life, he had also answered her questions without asking anything in return. She, on the other hand, had lied to him, omitting to mention her second encounter with the priest.

'How come you never asked me why it took me so long to come back here after seeing Zini?'

'I told you, I don't like liars.'

'Were you afraid I wouldn't tell you the truth?'

'Questions give liars an excuse to lie. If you'd had anything to tell me, you would have done so of your own accord. I don't like forcing things, I prefer you to trust me.'

Sandra looked away. She walked to the dishwasher and turned on the tap. The sound of the water running filled the room. For a moment she was tempted to tell him everything. Schalber was a few steps behind her. As she got ready to wash the dishes, she became aware of him coming closer, casting his protective shadow over her.

Then he put his hands on her sides and moved even closer so that his chest touched her back. Sandra let him. Her heart was pounding and she had the temptation to close her eyes. If I close them it's over, she said to herself. She was scared, but she couldn't summon the strength to push him away. He leaned over her and moved her hair away from her neck. She felt the warmth of his breath on her skin. Instinctively, she tilted her head back, as if to welcome that embrace. Her hands were motionless under the jet of water. Without realising it, she raised herself slightly on tiptoe. Her eyelids yielded to a gentle lethargy. With her eyes closed, and her body quivering, she leaned in to him, searching for his lips.

Over the last five months, she had lived with memories.

Now, for the first time, Sandra forgot she was a widow.

11.24 p.m.

The door of the house was open and banging. Not a good sign.

He put on his rubber gloves and pushed open the door. Zini's cats came to greet their new visitor. Marcus understood why the blind ex-policeman had chosen cats to keep him company.

They were the only animals who could live with him in darkness.

He closed the door behind him, shutting out the storm. After all that noise, he expected silence. Instead, he heard a shrill, intermittent electronic sound, somewhere close by.

He went further in, following the sound. After a few steps, he saw a cordless telephone, standing on its base, next to the refrigerator. That was where the signal was coming from, an indication that the battery was running out.

The same telephone had rung unanswered when he had called Zini's number from Federico Noni's house. But it wasn't its constant ringing that had exhausted the battery: somebody had cut off the current.

What reason did Figaro have to turn the lights out in a blind man's house?

'Zini!' Marcus called. But there was no answer.

He advanced along the corridor that led to the other rooms. He was forced to take out his torch. As soon as he lit it, he saw that there were some items of furniture barring the way, as if someone had put them there while trying to run away.

Had there been a chase?

He tried to reconstruct what had happened. Blindness had opened Pietro Zini's eyes: he had understood. It had been the anonymous email that had put him on the right track, perhaps reviving an old suspicion.

He is not like you.

The body at the Villa Glori had provided confirmation of that. So he had phoned Federico Noni. Perhaps there had been an argument, and Zini had threatened to turn him in.

Why hadn't he done so? Why had he given him the time to come there and kill him?

Zini had tried to escape, but obviously Federico – who, as a former athlete, was not only stronger, but also, and above all, sighted – hadn't let him get away.

Marcus knew for certain that someone had died here.

Preceded by the cats, he headed for the study. He was about to go in when he noticed that the cats all gave a little jump as they entered the room. He aimed the torch and saw something shining a few inches from the floor.

It was a nylon cable stretched across the doorway. Only the cats could see it in the dark.

He had no idea why that obstacle was there. He stepped over it and entered the room.

The wind was blowing hard outside the house, looking for a crack through which to enter. As Marcus moved the torch around the study, the shadows danced. All except one.

But it wasn't a shadow. It was a man lying on the floor with a pair of scissors in one hand and another pair planted in his neck. One cheek lay in a pool of dark blood. Marcus bent over Federico Noni, who stared up at him with lifeless eyes, his mouth twisted in a grimace. Suddenly he realised what had really happened within these walls.

Zini – a man of justice – had chosen revenge.

It was Zini who had insisted on Marcus meeting the police-woman. While they had been at the Museum of Purgatory, Zini had taken advantage of their absence to put his plan into operation. He had telephoned Federico Noni and told him that he knew the truth. But it was basically an invitation. And Federico had fallen for it.

While waiting for him to arrive, Zini had prepared obstacles, including the nylon cable. By cutting off the electricity he had put them both on an equal footing. Neither would be able to see the other.

Zini had acted like a cat. And Federico had been the mouse.

Zini was bigger and more capable in the dark. He knew the place, he knew how to move about in it. In the end, the advantage had been his. Federico had tripped over the cable, and Zini had plunged the scissors into him. It was a kind of retaliation.

An execution.

Marcus stood for a while longer looking at the corpse's hypnotic gaze. He had made another mistake. Once again he had been the one to provide the missing piece of the puzzle, leading to an act of revenge.

He turned and looked back, but realised that the cats had gathered in front of the French window that led to the little garden.

There was something outside.

He opened the window wide and the wind rushed into the room. The cats ran to the deckchair on which Pietro Zini was sitting, just as he had been the first time Marcus had met him.

Marcus aimed his torch at the absent eyes. He wasn't wearing his dark glasses. He had one hand in his lap, still clutching the gun with which he had shot himself in the mouth.

He should have been angry with Zini. The man had used him, had led him on a wild goose chase.

Federico Noni has already suffered enough. Years ago he lost the use of his legs. Becoming blind at my age is a blow you can learn to accept, but losing the use of your legs when you're a young athlete! Then his sister was brutally murdered, practically in front of his eyes. Can you even imagine something like that? Think how powerless he must have

229

felt, think of the guilt he must still feel, even though he didn't do any-
thing wrong.

The ex-policeman could have turned Federico Noni in, established the truth, released the innocent man imprisoned in Regina
Coeli. But Zini was convinced that Nicola Costa had been on the
verge of taking a fatal step when they had arrested him. He wasn't
just a compulsive liar, he was a dangerous psychopath. The attention he had received since his arrest had appeased his instinct for the
moment. But when you came down to it, it was merely a palliative.
There were several sides to his character. The narcissistic side would
eventually lose out to the homicidal side.

And for Zini it was also a matter of pride. Federico Noni had
played with him, striking him in his weak spot. Because of his own
imminent blindness, Zini had felt empathy with the young man. It
had been his compassion that had led him astray. He had forgotten
the first rule of every policeman: never believe anyone.

In addition, Federico had committed the most outrageous of
crimes by killing his own sister. What kind of creature strikes his
own nearest and dearest? The young man would stop at nothing.
That was why, according to Zini's law, he deserved to die.

Marcus closed the French window, as if drawing a curtain over
that spectacle. In the study, he immediately located the Braille display. Although there was no electricity, it was on. It was being fed by
a generator.

It was a sign.

That afternoon, thanks to the voice program, he had listened to
the contents of the anonymous email that Pietro Zini had received
a few days earlier. But Marcus was sure that there had been more in
that message and that Zini had switched it off before he had heard
everything.

That was why, after locating the right key, Marcus again activated
the device. The cold and impersonal electronic voice resumed those
mysterious words that he was now in a position to decipher.

'He-is-not-like-you . . . Look-in-Vil-la-Glo-ri-Park . . . '

That was the part he knew. But as he had foreseen, there was
more.

'. . . The-boy-de-ceived-you . . . You-will-soon-have-a-vis-i-tor.'

This second fragment referred directly to Federico Noni and, indirectly, to Marcus, telling Zini in advance that he was coming.

But it was the last verse of this electronic dirge that most struck him.

'It-hap-pened-be-fore . . . it-will-hap-pen-a-gain . . . c.g. 925-31-073.'

It was partly the prophecy it announced – *It happened before, it will happen again* – partly the code number referring to another unsolved crime – *925-31-073* – but above all it was the two letters that preceded the number.

Culpa gravis.

At last Marcus knew the truth.

There is a place where the world of light meets the world of darkness. It is there that everything happens: in the land of shadows, where everything is vague, confused, undefined. We are the guardians appointed to defend that border. But every now and again something manages to get through . . . I have to chase it back into the darkness.

Whoever was putting victims and murderers in contact with one another was a penitenziere like himself.

ONE YEAR EARLIER
KIEV

'The great dream ended when we traded our integrity for a bit of consensus. We went to sleep with hope and we woke up with a whore whose name we couldn't even remember.'

This was how Dr Norzhenko summarised Perestroika, the fall of the Berlin wall, the breakup of the republics, the rise of the oligarchs: in other words, twenty years of Soviet history.

'Look at this . . . ' He stabbed his index finger at the front page of the *Kharkovskii Kurier*. 'Everything's going to pieces and what do they say? Nothing. So what was the point of freedom?'

Nikolai Norzhenko gave a sidelong glance at his visitor, who was nodding, apparently interested, even if not sharing as fully in this invective as he would have liked. Then he stared at the man's bandaged hand. 'Did you say you were American, Dr Foster?'

'Actually I'm English,' the hunter replied, trying to distract Norzhenko's attention from the bandage. Beneath it was the bite he had received from young Angelina in the psychiatric hospital in Mexico City.

The office in which they were sitting was on the second floor of the administration building of the State Centre for Child Assistance, in the western part of Kiev. Through the large window there was a view of the grounds, the birch trees bright with the colours of early autumn. In the room, Formica predominated: everything was covered in it, from the desk to the walls. On one of the walls you could still see three lighter rectangular patches where portraits of Lenin, Stalin and whichever Secretary of the Communist Party was then in power must once have hung. The stale smell of cigarettes hung in the room: the ashtray in front of Norzhenko was filled with cigarette ends. Although he was probably only in his early fifties, his scruffy appearance and the unhealthy cough that punctuated his sentences made him seem much older. The man seemed to be seething with resentment and a sense of humiliation. The empty photo frame on a side table and the folded blankets at the end of a leather sofa suggested a marriage that had ended unhappily. In Soviet days, he must have been a respected man. Now he was a sad parody of a State functionary, with the salary of a street cleaner.

Norzhenko picked up the sheet of paper with the fake references that the hunter had shown him on his arrival and looked at it again.

'It says here that you're the editor of a review of forensic psychology at the University of Cambridge. That's remarkable at your age, Dr Foster, congratulations.'

The hunter had known these particulars would attract his attention. He wanted to appeal to Norzhenko's wounded ego and he was succeeding.

Pleased, Norzhenko put the paper down. 'You know, it's strange. You're the first person who's ever come here to ask me about Dima.'

The hunter's presence here was all down to Dr Florinda Valdez. Back in Mexico City, she had shown him an article Norzhenko had published in a minor review of psychology in 1989. It concerned the case of a child: Dmitry Karolyszin – Dima. Perhaps Norzhenko had hoped that the article would open doors for him, lead to a new career, at the very moment when everything around him was falling apart. But that hadn't happened. The story had remained buried, along with his expectations and ambitions – until now.

It was time to bring it back to the surface.

'Tell me, Dr Norzhenko, did you know Dima personally?'

'Of course.' Dr Norzhenko formed a pyramid with his hands and raised his eyes as if searching for a memory. 'At first he seemed like any other boy; sharper, perhaps, but very quiet.'

'What year was that?'

'The spring of 1986. At the time, this centre was at the forefront of childcare in the Ukraine, perhaps in the whole Soviet Union.' Norzhenko's tone as he said this was full of self-satisfaction. 'Unlike orphanages in the West, we didn't just take care of children who had nobody in the world, we prepared them for the future.'

'Everyone knew your methods. You were an example.'

Norzhenko was happy to accept the flattery. 'After the disaster at

Chernobyl, the authorities in Kiev asked us to take care of the children who had lost their parents through radiation sickness. It was thought likely that they, too, would develop symptoms. Our task was to care for them until relatives could be found who might be able to take them in.'

'Did Dima arrive with these children?'

'Six months after the disaster, if I remember rightly. He was from Prypiat. The city was in the exclusion zone around the reactor and had been evacuated. He was eight years old.'

'Was he with you for a long time?'

'Twenty-one months.' Norzhenko paused, frowning, then stood up and went to a filing cabinet. After a brief search, he came back to the desk with a file in a beige cover. He started leafing through it. 'Like all the children from Prypiat, Dmitry Karolyszin suffered from bed wetting and mood swings, common results of shock and forced separation. His case was followed by a team of psychologists. During the interviews, he told us about his family: his mother Anya, a housewife, and his father Konstantin, who had worked as a technician at the Chernobyl plant. He described details of their life together . . . details that would turn out to be accurate.' He emphasised these last words.

'What happened?'

Before answering, Norzhenko took a cigarette from the packet he had in the breast pocket of his shirt and lit it.

'Dima had only one relative still living, a brother of his father: Oleg Karolyszin. After a long search, we managed to track him down in Canada. He was perfectly happy to be given the chance to take care of his nephew. He only knew Dima from the photographs Konstantin used to send him. So when we sent him a recent image so that he could confirm the boy's identity, we had no idea of what would come next. It was little more than a formality.'

'Instead of which, Oleg told you the child wasn't his nephew.'

'Precisely . . . and yet even though Dima had never met him, he knew many things about his uncle, even anecdotes about his childhood that his father had told him. He remembered the presents he sent him every year for his birthday.'

'So what did you think?'

'At first, that Oleg had changed his mind and no longer wanted to take care of Dima. But when he sent us some of the photographs of the child that his brother had sent him over the years, we were astonished . . . We were dealing with a completely different person.'

For a few moments, there was an awkward silence in the room. Norzhenko studied the hunter's face as if to see whether he considered him mad.

'You hadn't realised this before?'

'There were no pictures of Dima prior to his arrival at the centre. The population of Prypiat had been forced to abandon their houses in a hurry, taking with them only what was strictly necessary. The child arrived here with nothing but the clothes he was wearing.'

'What happened next?'

Norzhenko took a deep drag on his cigarette. 'There was only one explanation: the child, whoever he was, had taken the place of the real Dima. But there was more . . . it wasn't simply a case of assumed identity.'

The hunter's eyes gleamed, and at the same time there was a flash of something in Norzhenko's eyes, too. Almost certainly fear.

'The two children were not simply similar,' Norzhenko went on. 'The real Dima was short-sighted, so was this boy. Both were lactose intolerant. Oleg told us that his nephew had no hearing in his right ear because of an inflammation that had been badly treated. We subjected our Dima to audiometric tests, without telling him why. He turned out to have exactly the same defect.'

'He could have been pretending. Audiometric tests rely on the answers provided by the patient. Maybe your Dima knew that.'

'Maybe . . . ' The rest of the sentence died on Norzhenko's lips. 'A month after our discovery, the boy disappeared.'

'Had he run away?'

'Not so much run away as . . . vanished.' Norzhenko's face turned sombre. 'We looked for him for weeks, with the help of the police.'

'And the real Dima?'

'No trace of him, or of his parents: we only knew they were dead because our Dima had told us. These were chaotic times, and it was impossible to check the facts. Everything connected with Chernobyl was kept under wraps, even the most trivial information.'

'Immediately after that, you wrote your article.'

'But nobody took any notice.' Norzhenko shook his head bitterly and looked away, almost as if ashamed of himself. But then he regained his composure and looked straight at the hunter. 'The boy wasn't simply trying to pass himself off as someone else, believe me. At that age, the brain isn't capable of structuring such an elaborate lie. No, in his mind he really was Dima.'

'When he disappeared, did he take anything with him?'

'No, but he left something behind . . .'

Norzhenko leaned down and opened one of the desk drawers. After searching for a moment, he extracted a little toy and placed it on the table in front of his visitor.

A stuffed rabbit.

It was blue, dirty and tattered. Someone had mended its tail and it lacked an eye. It had a smile that was both blissful and sinister.

The hunter looked at it. 'It doesn't seem like much of a clue.'

'I agree with you, Dr Foster,' Norzhenko admitted, his eyes lighting up as if he had something else in reserve. 'But you don't know where we found it.'

It was getting dark. Norzhenko led his supposed colleague across a corner of the grounds and into another building belonging to the centre.

'This used to be the main dormitory.'

They did not head for the upper floors, but down to the basement. Norzhenko activated a series of switches and the fluorescent lights came on, illuminating a vast area. The walls were dark with damp. Pipes of every size ran across the ceiling, many of them in poor repair.

'One of the cleaners made the discovery some time after the boy disappeared.' He went no further, almost as if he wanted to enjoy his younger colleague's surprise once they got there. 'I've tried to keep this place exactly as we found it. Don't ask me why, I simply thought that one day it would help us to understand. And besides, nobody ever comes down here.'

They walked along a narrow, high-ceilinged corridor lined with steel doors through which the noise of the boilers could dimly be heard. Then they came to a second room, used as a store room for old furniture: beds and rotting mattresses. Norzhenko made his way through it and invited his colleague to do the same.

'We're almost there,' he announced.

They turned a corner and found themselves in a narrow badly ventilated box room under the stairs. It was dark, but Norzhenko managed to illuminate the place with his cigarette lighter.

In the amber light of that little flame, his visitor took a step forward, incredulous at what he was seeing.

It resembled a gigantic insect's nest.

The hunter's first reaction was one of disgust, but then, as he went closer, he saw that it consisted of many small pieces of wood, held together with scraps of material of various colours, ropes, clothes pegs, drawing pins, and bits of papier mâché. Everything had been assembled with great care and meticulousness.

It was a child's makeshift refuge.

He had built similar things himself when he was small. But this one was different.

'The rabbit was in there,' Norzhenko said, and watched as his visitor leaned into the narrow opening and touched the floor. He looked over his shoulder and saw him examining a ring of small dark stains.

For the hunter, it was a startling revelation.

Dried blood. He had seen the same thing in Paris, in Jean Duez's apartment.

The false Dima was the transformist.

But he mustn't appear too excited. 'Do you have any idea where these stains come from?' he asked.

'I'm afraid not.'

'Do you mind if I take a sample?'

'Go ahead.'

'And I'd also like the stuffed rabbit, it may be linked to the false Dima's past.'

Norzhenko hesitated. He was trying to figure out whether his colleague was really interested in the story. This might be the last chance he would get to redeem his own existence.

'In my opinion, the case still has scientific value,' the hunter said, to convince him. 'It's worthy of further study.'

At these words, a naïve gleam of hope appeared in Norzhenko's eyes, as well as a silent request for help. 'So what do you think? Could we write another article, maybe the two of us together?'

At that moment, the furthest thing from Norzhenko's mind was that he would probably be spending the rest of his days in this institution.

The hunter turned and smiled. 'Of course, Dr Norzhenko. I'm flying back to England tonight, but I'll be in touch as soon as possible.'

In reality, he had another destination in mind. He would go where everything had started. To Prypiat, on the trail of Dima.

TWO DAYS AGO

The corpse said, 'No.'

The exclamation hung in the air between dream and waking. It came from the past, but it had somehow got through into the present an instant before the portal that connected the two worlds closed and Marcus was again awake.

He had uttered that 'no' in a loud but fearful voice, staring into the impassive barrel of a gun. Already knowing, as do all those about to die, that it would be no use, that the word was the final, futile barrier put up against the inevitable, the prayer of those who knew they had no way out.

Marcus did not immediately look for the felt-tip pen with which he recorded the fragments of his dreams on the wall next to the camp bed. He lay there breathing heavily, his heart thumping in his chest, contemplating what he had seen. This time he would not forget it.

He could still clearly see the image of the faceless man who had shot him and Devok. In the previous versions of the dream, the man had been a vague shadow that vanished every time he made an effort to focus on it. But now he possessed an important detail about the killer. He had seen the hand with which he was holding the gun.

He was left-handed.

It wasn't much, but for Marcus it was some kind of hope. Perhaps one day he would see past that outstretched arm and look into the eyes of the man who had condemned him to wander in search of his own identity, leaving him only the awareness of being alive and nothing more.

He thought again of Federico Noni and the drawings in the exercise book he had found in his house. They recounted the genesis of a monster. The most disturbing fact about these violent fantasies was that they went back to childhood. In this whole tangled web, there was one question that predominated. If some people were good and some bad, some evil and some compassionate, was it because they were born like that or did they become that way? How could a child contemplate evil so lucidly and let himself be infected by it?

Some might have blamed a series of events that had scarred Federico's psyche, such as his being abandoned by his mother or his father's premature death. But that was too simplistic an explanation. Many children lived through worse tragedies and didn't turn into killers when they grew up.

Marcus was fully aware that this question was of deep personal significance to himself. His amnesia may have wiped out his memories, but his past still existed somewhere. What had it been before that moment? In Federico's exercise book there was perhaps a glimmer of an answer. In every individual there exists something innate, which goes beyond the consciousness of the self, the experience accumulated while growing up. A spark that identifies each man more than his name and appearance.

One of the first steps in his training had consisted in liberating himself from the deceptiveness of appearance. Clemente had made him examine the case of Ted Bundy, the serial killer who to all appearances had been a perfectly pleasant young man. Bundy had committed twenty-eight murders, and yet he had a steady girlfriend and his friends described him as an affable, generous man. Before being unmasked as what he really was, he had even been awarded a medal for saving a little girl from drowning in a lake.

We are always in a battle, Marcus had told himself, and the choice of sides is never clear cut. In the end the only arbiter is man himself, who decides to follow his own spark, whether positive or negative, or else to ignore it.

That was true of the guilty, but also of their victims.

The last three days had been very instructive from that point of view. Monica – the sister of one of the girls killed by Jeremiah Smith – Raffaele Altieri and Pietro Zini had all found themselves at a crossroads, and had made their choice. They had been given not just the truth, but also the opportunity to choose between forgiveness and revenge. Monica had chosen the first, the other two had opted for the second.

And then there was the policewoman who was investigating her husband's death. What was she looking for: a truth that liberated her or the opportunity to inflict punishment? Marcus had never heard of David Leoni, who, according to his wife, had been killed while he was investigating the penitenzieri. He had promised that he would help her to solve the mystery. Why? He feared that she, too, might yet be offered the change to take revenge, even though at this stage he couldn't see how. He had done it, above all, to gain time. He felt there was something that linked her to the others.

All the people involved so far had suffered a wrong that had changed their lives for ever. Evil had not merely struck them, it had sown seeds. In some cases these seeds had taken root, infecting their whole existence. Like a silent parasite, they had grown into a festering hatred and resentment, transforming the host body. Individuals who had never thought they could take the life of another human being suffered terrible losses, which, over time, transformed them into dispensers of death.

Part of Marcus, though, did not feel able to condemn anyone who, rather than being content to learn the truth and move on, had decided to inflict punishment. Because he himself had much in common with these people.

He turned to the wall next to the camp bed and re-read the last two details of the scene in the Prague hotel that he had marked there.

Shattered window. Three shots. Now he added: *Left-handed.*

What would he do if he found himself face to face with Devok's killer, the man who had tried to kill him and had deprived him of his memory? He did not think of himself as a just man. How could you forgive someone who has not paid for his sins? That was why he was unable to completely blame anyone who, to remedy a misdeed, had committed a crime in his turn.

These people had been granted an immense power. *And it was a penitenziere who had given it to them.*

After that discovery, Marcus had felt conflicting emotions. He had seen it as a betrayal, but he had also felt an enormous relief in discovering that he was not the only one to possess that obscure talent. Even though he didn't yet know what exactly drove this mystery penitenziere, the fact that behind every revelation there was a man of God gave him hope that Lara might still be saved.

I won't let her die, he told himself.

All the same, Marcus could feel the threads of the investigation slipping through his fingers. His priority had to be Lara, and yet he had almost forgotten her. He had let himself be carried along by events, trusting that, whatever the mystery man's plan might be, it somehow involved the missing student. But now the words of his last message, as contained in the email he had sent Pietro Zini, echoed in Marcus's head.

It happened before. It will happen again.

What if the plan entailed his getting very close to freeing Lara and then failing? He would have to live with the remorse, which would be a heavy burden for his new memory to bear.

I have to see this through, I have no choice. But I have to get there just before it's all over. Otherwise I won't be able to save her life.

For the moment he put aside any sense of foreboding. It was a more imminent danger he had to consider.

c.g. 925-31-073.

The code number at the end of the email announced another crime that had remained unpunished, more blood that had been spilt without anyone paying the price. Somewhere out there, someone was getting ready to choose whether to remain a victim or become an executioner.

Two months after beginning his training, Marcus had asked Clemente about the archive. Having heard so much about it, he was curious to know when he could see it. Late one night, his friend had come to his attic room in the Via dei Serpenti and said, 'The moment has come.'

Marcus had let himself be led across Rome without asking any questions. They had done part of the journey by car and continued on foot. After a while, they had come to an old building in the centre. Clemente had invited him to descend into the basement. Then he had led him along a frescoed corridor until they came to a small wooden door. As Clemente opened it with the key he had brought with him, Marcus looked at him uneasily. Now that he had reached this final frontier, he did not feel ready. He had never imagined it could be so easy to get here. Ever since he had first heard of the archive, it had filled him with a degree of fear. Over the centuries this place had been called many things, some quite disturbing. The library of evil. The devil's memory. Marcus had imagined it as a tangle of dark cloisters, lined with shelves full of neatly arranged volumes. A vast labyrinth you could easily get lost in or that could drive you mad because of what it contained. But when Clemente opened the door, Marcus had looked inside in astonishment.

It was a small room with bare walls and no windows. In the middle stood a table and one chair. On the table was a file.

Clemente had motioned him to sit down and read. It was the confession of a man who had committed eleven murders. The victims were all little girls. He had killed the first one at the age of twenty, and after that he hadn't been able to stop. He couldn't explain what obscure force guided his hands as he dealt each terrible death. There was an inexplicable urge within him to repeat the act.

Marcus immediately thought of a serial killer and asked Clemente if he had been stopped in the end.

Yes, his friend had reassured him. Only the events went back more than a thousand years.

Marcus had always assumed that serial killers were a product of the modern era. Over the last century, mankind had made enormous strides in the realm of ethics and morality. Marcus considered the existence of serial killers one of the prices to be paid for progress. But, reading that confession, he had had to think again.

On each of the following evenings, Clemente led him to that little room and submitted a new case to him. Very soon, Marcus started to wonder why he took him there. Couldn't he have brought him the files in his attic room? The answer, however, was simple. That isolation was necessary for Marcus to learn an important lesson.

'I'm the archive,' he said to Clemente one day.

Clemente confirmed that, apart from this secret place where the testimonies of evil were kept, the penitenzieri themselves were the archive. Each one knew a different part of it, preserved that experience and took it out into the world with him.

But from the death of Devok up until the previous evening at Zini's house, Marcus had always thought he was the only one.

This thought gave him no peace as he walked through the narrow streets of the Jewish ghetto to the Portico of Octavia, situated behind the great synagogue. In ancient Rome, it had housed the temples of Juno Regina and Jupiter Stator. Over the ruins was a modern pier of steel and wood, from which there was a view of the Circus Flaminius.

Clemente was holding on to the balustrade with both hands. He already knew everything.

'What's his name?'

'We don't know,' Clemente said, without turning.

This time, Marcus would not be fobbed off. 'How can you not know the identity of a penitenziere?'

'I wasn't lying when I told you that only Father Devok knew all your names and faces.'

'But you lied about something,' he insisted.

'All this began a long time before Jeremiah Smith.'

'So you knew that somebody was violating the secrecy of the archive.' He would clearly have to get there by himself.

'"That which has been done will be done again." You wanted to know what that means? Ecclesiastes, Chapter 1, Verse 9.'

'How long have these revelations been going on?'

'Four months. There have been too many deaths, Marcus. It isn't good for the Church.'

Clemente's words made him uncomfortable. He had imagined that all their efforts were for Lara. Now he had to accept that this was not the case. 'So that's what interests you,' he said angrily. 'Plugging up the leaks in the archive, stopping it getting out that somebody has started taking the law into his own hands. What's Lara, then, just an accident? Will her death be classed as collateral damage?'

'The reason you were brought in was to save her.'

'That's not true.'

'What the penitenzieri were doing ran contrary to the decisions of the Church hierarchy. They were dismissed, their order abolished. But someone wanted to continue.'

'Devok.'

'He maintained that it was wrong to stop, that the penitenzieri had a vitally important role to play. The knowledge of evil contained in the archive had to remain at the world's disposal. He was convinced that his mission was just. You and other priests followed him in that mad undertaking.'

'Why did he come to Prague to look for me? What was I doing there?'

'I don't know, I swear.'

Marcus let his eyes wander over the remains of Imperial Rome. He was starting to understand his own role. 'Every time he reveals one of the secrets, the penitenziere leaves clues for his colleagues. He wants to be stopped. The reason you trained me up again was to find him. You've been using me. Lara's disappearance gave you the excuse you needed to bring me on board without my suspecting anything. In reality, you don't care about her ... or even about me.'

'Oh, but I do. How can you say that?'

Marcus went closer to Clemente so that he was forced to look him in the eyes. 'If the archive wasn't in danger, you'd have left me without a memory in that hospital bed.'

'No. We would have provided you with memories so that you could carry on. I went to Prague because Devok was dead. I found out that when he was shot there was someone with him. I had no idea who it was, all I knew was that this unknown person was in hospital and had amnesia.'

At first, Marcus had had Clemente tell him this story many times, to convince himself of his own identity. Searching among his things in the hotel room, Clemente had found a Vatican City diplomatic passport with a false identity and his notes, a kind of diary in which Marcus talked about himself in broad terms, perhaps fearing that, if he had died, he would have remained a nameless corpse. It was from that diary that Clemente had deduced who he was. But the confirmation had come later, after he had been discharged from hospital, when he had taken him to a crime scene and seen how Marcus had been capable of describing, with a remarkable degree of accuracy, what had happened.

'I communicated the discovery to my superiors,' Clemente continued. 'They were reluctant to pursue the matter. I insisted, maintaining that you were the right person, and I managed to convince them. We haven't been using you, as you put it. But you do represent an opportunity.'

'If I find this penitenziere who's been betraying the secrets of the archive, what will become of me?'

'You'll be free, don't you understand? Not because of someone else's decision, but your own. You could even leave now if you wanted to – it's all down to you. You're under no obligation. But I know that, deep in your heart, you feel the need to know who you really are. And even though you won't admit it, what you're doing is helping you to understand that.'

'And when it's all over, the penitenzieri will be history again. And this time you will all be sure they'll never return.'

'There's a reason the order was abolished.'

'What is it? Come on, tell me.'

'There are things that neither you nor I can understand. Decisions that come from on high. Our duty as men of the Church is to obey without asking questions, knowing that there is someone over us who's acting for our benefit.'

Birds circled between the ancient columns, singing in the crisp morning air. The day had begun with sunshine, but that brightness did not correspond to Marcus's frame of mind. However hard he fought against it, the thought that he could live differently was an attractive one. Ever since he had discovered his own talent, he had felt somehow obligated. As if the solution to all this evil lay with him. Now, though, Clemente was leaving an exit route open for him. But he was right: they needed what he was doing. Only if he found Lara and stopped the penitenziere would he feel he had the right to leave, to lead his own life.

'What do I have to do?'

'Find out if the girl is still alive, and save her.'

The only way, as Marcus knew perfectly well, was to follow the trail left by the penitenziere. 'He's managed to solve cases that were classified as unsolved in the archive. He's good.'

'So are you. Otherwise you wouldn't have discovered the same things. You're like him.'

Marcus didn't know if that comparison cheered or depressed him. But he had to carry on. He had to see this through. 'The code number this time is *c.g. 925-31-073.*'

'You won't like it,' Clementi warned him, taking an envelope from the inside pocket of his raincoat. 'Someone is dead, but we don't know who. His killer has admitted his crime, but we don't know his name.'

Marcus took the file from Clementi's hands. It was unusually light and thin. He opened it, to reveal a single handwritten sheet of paper.

'What is this?'

'A suicide's confession of his sins.'

7.40 a.m.

She was awoken by a hand stroking her cheek. She opened her eyes, expecting to see Schalber next to her. But she was alone. And yet the sensation had been quite vivid.

Her partner from that strange night had already got up. She could hear the water running in the shower. Better that way. Sandra was not sure she wanted to see him yet. She needed a little time to herself. Because now the pitiless honesty of the day gave her a completely different sense of what had happened between the sheets. Indifferent to her embarrassment, the sun filtered through the blinds, revealing her clothes and underwear strewn on the floor, the crumpled blankets at the foot of the bed, her own naked body.

'I'm naked,' she said, as if to convince herself.

At first she blamed the wine. But then she realised this was hardly a sufficient excuse. Who was she trying to kid? Women never make love by chance, she told herself. Men, yes: they see an opportunity and they seize it with both hands. Women need preparation. They want to be smooth to the touch, to smell nice. Even when it seems as if they're just throwing themselves into a one-night stand, the reality is that they've planned it. She might not have foreseen this particular encounter, but, physically speaking, she hadn't let herself go over the past few months. She had continued taking care of herself. Part of her had refused to let grief gain the upper hand. And then there was also her mother. Before David's funeral she had sent Sandra into the bedroom to do her hair. 'A woman can always find two minutes to brush her hair,' she had said. Even when she's suffering and can hardly breathe, Sandra herself had added. It was a concept that had nothing to do with beauty. It was a matter of identity. A gesture that men might dismiss as pointless and affected at such a moment.

But now Sandra felt ashamed. What if Schalber thought she had given in too easily? She feared his judgement. Not of her, but of David. Had he felt sorry for him, seeing how ready his widow was to sleep with another man?

Suddenly, she realised that she was looking for a reason to hate him. And yet Schalber had been affectionate last night. It had not been a moment of wild passion, it had all happened with almost maddening slowness. She remembered how he had held her tight, without saying a word. Every now and again he had kissed her hair. She had felt the kiss coming by the warmth of his breath.

She had been attracted to him from the first moment. Perhaps that was why he made her angry. She recognised it for the cliché it was. First two people hate each other, then, inevitably, they fall in love. She felt as trite as a fifteen-year-old. All she needed now was to make a comparison between her new boyfriend and David. She dismissed that idea irritably and summoned the strength to get out of bed. She picked up her knickers from the floor and quickly put them on. She didn't want Schalber to come out of the shower and find her defenceless.

She sat down on the bed, waiting for the bathroom to be free so that she could go and take a shower herself. Of course it would be strange passing him with her knickers on. He might interpret it as her belatedly having second thoughts. But the fact was, Sandra didn't feel sorry at all. She ought to be crying, and yet she felt an unconscious joy.

She still loved David.

But it was in the word 'still' that the difference lay. The word concealed a trap: the trap of time. That word had been inserting itself into the middle of the phrase for some time now, without Sandra even realising it. Operating a *de facto* separation. Slyly anticipating what was bound to happen eventually. Everything changes and is transformed, sooner or later even that feeling would change. What would she feel for David in twenty or thirty years? Assuming she was granted all that time. She was twenty-nine, so she was obliged to carry on, even though he had stopped. Every time she turned back, her husband would be ever smaller. Until, one day, he would disappear beyond the horizon. They had been together a lot. But it was no time at all compared with the future that awaited her.

She was scared of forgetting him. That was why she clung so desperately to memories.

Looking now at her own reflection in the mirror next to the wardrobe and seeing not a widow but a young woman still capable of giving her energy and passion to a man, she remembered the countless times she had made love with David. Two of them, in particular.

One, predictably, was the first time of all, which had been also the least romantic. After their third date, in the car, as they were going home, where a comfortable bed and all the privacy a moment like that needs was waiting for them. Instead of which, they had stopped at the side of the road, and literally thrown themselves on to the back seat. Unable to let their lips separate for one second. Frenziedly removing each other's clothes. They had needed to find each other, urgently, almost as if they foresaw that they would lose each other all too soon.

The second, though, was less obvious. It was not the last time.

In fact, Sandra had only a vague memory of that last time. She had often noticed something that, instead of making her sad, made her smile: every time a loved one dies, for those who remain the last time they saw them becomes an instrument of torture. I could have said this, done that. She and David had no unsettled accounts. He knew how much she loved him, and vice versa. Sandra had no regrets. A sense of guilt, yes. And it arose precisely from that time she remembered now, a few months before her husband had been killed. In many ways, that night had been no different from any other. They had their courtship rituals, which required him to say nice things to her all evening. She would let him approach slowly, refusing him his reward until the very last moment. Even though they did that every time, they never lost the habit. It wasn't simply a game to make everything more interesting. It was a way of renewing the promise that they would never take each other for granted.

That day, however, something had happened. David had come back from an assignment that had lasted a couple of months. He could not have imagined what had happened in his absence. Nor could she let on. She wouldn't lie, but she would pretend. An easy compromise to make. All you have to do is repeat a routine. As if everything is normal. Including the habit of making love.

She had never told anyone. She actually forbade herself to think about it. David didn't know and, if one day she had confessed it, he would have left her, she was sure of it. There was a word that defined her guilt, but she had never uttered it.

'Sin,' she said out loud now to her own image in the mirror.

Would the penitenziere forgive her? The thought, meant humorously, didn't help to alleviate the sense of discomfort she felt.

She looked towards the closed door of the bathroom. What's going to happen now? she wondered. She and Schalber had made love, or was it only sex? And how would they behave towards each other? She hadn't thought of that before, and now it seemed a bit late to start. She didn't want him to be the first to speak. But the truth was, she didn't want to stop. She felt suddenly self-conscious. If he was cold to her, she didn't want her disappointment to be too obvious. But she didn't know how to avoid it. To distract herself from that thought, she looked at her watch. She had been awake for twenty minutes and Schalber still hadn't come out of the bathroom. She could hear the shower, but now she realised for the first time that there was no variation in the sound, as there ought to be when a body moves under a jet of water. The noise was constant, as if there was no resistance.

She leapt to her feet, and rushed to the bathroom. The door opened easily and she was overwhelmed by a blanket of steam. Trying to disperse it with her hand, she looked at the shower cubicle: there was no silhouette beyond the opaque sheet of glass. She pulled the shower door open.

The water was running, but there was no one under it.

There was only one reason why Schalber would have thought up a trick like that. Sandra turned immediately towards the toilet. She went to it and moved the lid of the cistern. The waterproof bag she had hidden was still there. She took it out to check the contents. Instead of David's clues, there was a train ticket for Milan.

She sat down on the damp floor and put her head in her hands. Now she really did feel like crying. And even screaming. It would be liberating, but she didn't do it. She refused to think of the night they had spent together, or to wonder if the affection he had shown her had been part of the deception or not. Instead, she remembered that time she had made love with David even though she knew she was hiding something from him. For a long time she had tried to dismiss that secret. Now it welled up from her conscience and she could no longer silence it.

Yes, I'm a sinner, she admitted. And David's death was my punishment.

She tried several times to contact Schalber on his mobile phone. But all she got was a recorded voice telling her that the number was unobtainable. She had little hope that he would let her find him. And anyway there was no time for recriminations, or for wondering if she had made a mistake. She had to get back to work.

She had made a pact with the priest with the scar on his temple. But now that Schalber had the photograph that David had taken of him, it would be easier for him to track him down. And if he arrested him, that would be the end of it for her. The trail that led to her husband's killer broke off abruptly with the dark photograph, and that priest was her last remaining hope.

She had to warn him before it was too late.

Sandra had no idea how to find him and she couldn't wait for him to reappear, as he had promised he would. She had to come up with a plan.

She started pacing the apartment, trying to think through the latest events. Her anger did not help, but she tried to keep it at bay. She had conflicting feelings about Schalber. But she wouldn't let her anger get the better of her.

She would have to go back to the Figaro case.

The previous evening, at the Museum of Purgatory, she had provided the priest with a plausible solution to the mystery. He had listened to her and then had run away, saying that he had to hurry before it was too late. He hadn't given her any other explanation, and she hadn't had time to insist.

She wondered whether the situation had changed overnight. And the answer might come from the television. She went into the kitchen and switched on the small set that was on the dresser. After hopping between channels, she came across a news bulletin, just as the newsreader was announcing that a woman's body had been discovered in Villa Glori Park. This item was followed by another crime report: a combined homicide and suicide in Trastevere. The names Federico Noni and Pietro Zini were mentioned.

Sandra couldn't believe it. What had her role been in this tragic outcome? Might she have contributed, in however small a way, to these deaths? When she heard the chronology of the events, she realised the answer was no. The timetable did not match: while the tragedy was taking place, she was talking to the priest. Which meant that he hadn't been present while it was happening either.

Nevertheless, the Figaro case seemed to be over, and it wouldn't be of any help to her in getting back in contact with the penitenziere.

It was frustrating. She didn't know where to start.

Wait a minute, she told herself. How did Schalber find out that the penitenzieri were interested in the Figaro case?

She went over what he had told her about the case until she found what she was looking for: Schalber had become aware of the penitenzieris' interest by bugging a conversation. He had placed listening devices in a villa outside Rome where the police were carrying out a search.

What villa? And why were they there?

She recovered her mobile phone from her bag and dialled the number of the last call she had received the previous day. De Michelis replied at the sixth ring.

'What can I do for you, Vega?'

'Inspector, I need your help again.'

'That's what I'm here for.' He sounded in a good mood.

'Do you know if the police here have been searching a villa in the last few days? It's probably in connection with a major case.' Sandra deduced that from the fact that Schalber had gone straight there to place his bugs.

'Don't you read the papers?'

She was taken aback. 'What have I missed?'

'A serial killer was captured the other day. You know how crazy people get over that kind of thing.'

It must have been an item on the TV news, but she had missed it. 'Bring me up to speed.'

'I don't have much time.' She could hear voices around De Michelis. He moved to somewhere a little more private. 'Here goes: Jeremiah Smith, four victims in six years. He had a heart attack three days ago. An ambulance team went to his aid and that's when they discovered the kind of man he is. He's in hospital now, more alive than dead. Case closed.'

Sandra paused for a moment to think this over. 'I need a favour.'

'Another one?'

'A big one this time.'

De Michelis muttered something incomprehensible. 'Go on,' he said.

'A service order to work on that case.'

259

'You're joking, I hope.'

'Would you prefer it if I started investigating without any cover? You know I'd do it.'

De Michelis only took a moment. 'You'll explain all this one of these days, won't you? Otherwise I'll feel like an idiot for believing you.'

'I promise.'

'Okay, I'll send the service order via fax to police headquarters in Rome in an hour. I have to invent a plausible reason, but I have a vivid imagination.'

'Do I need to tell you I'm grateful?'

De Michelis laughed. 'Obviously not.'

Sandra hung up. She felt as if she was back in the game. She wished she could forget what Schalber had done to her, but had to make do with venting her anger on the train ticket he had left her, tearing it into very small pieces and scattering them over the floor. She doubted that Schalber would be back here to receive that message. She was convinced they would never see each other again. And the thought hurt her a little. Best not to think about it. Sandra vowed that she would cast aside what had happened. She had other things to do. For a start she had to go to Headquarters to collect the service order. Then she would ask to be given a copy of the material on Jeremiah Smith. She would look through it, guided by one insight: if the case was of interest to the penitenzieri, then it wasn't closed at all.

8.01 a.m.

Marcus was sitting at one of the long tables in a soup kitchen run by Caritas. There were crucifixes on the walls as well as posters proclaiming the Word of God. An all-pervading smell of beef stock and fried onions hung in the air. At this hour of the morning, the homeless people who usually frequented the place had left and the kitchen staff were starting to prepare lunch. For breakfast, people usually started lining up about five in the morning. By seven they were back on the streets, except when it was cold or rainy, when some lingered a while longer. Marcus knew that many of them, although probably not the majority, were no longer capable of being shut in and so they refused accommodation, even a dormitory for one night. This was especially true of those who had spent a lot of time in prison or a psychiatric institution. The temporary loss of freedom had disorientated them, and now they no longer knew where they were coming from or where their homes were.

Don Michele Fuente would always greet them with a welcoming smile, dispensing both hot meals and human warmth. Marcus watched him as he gave instructions to his colleagues to make things ready for the next wave that would come flooding in silently within a few hours. Compared with this man and the mission he had set for himself, Marcus felt incomplete as a priest. Many things had vanished, not only from his memory, but also from his heart.

When he had finished, Don Michele came and sat down opposite him. 'Father Clemente told me you'd be coming. All he said was that you're a priest and that I shouldn't ask your name.'

'If you don't mind.'

'I don't mind.'

Don Michele was a plump man of about fifty, with puffy red cheeks, small hands and unkempt hair. His cassock was dotted with crumbs and oil stains. He wore a pair of glasses with round black frames, a plastic watch that he looked at constantly, and shapeless Nikes.

'Three years ago, you heard a confession,' Marcus said. It was not a question.

'I've heard a great many since then.'

'You should remember this one, though. I don't suppose you hear somebody planning to commit suicide every day.'

Don Michele did not seem surprised, but all the cordiality abruptly drained from his face. 'As usual, I transcribed the penitent's words and submitted it to the *Paenitentiaria*. I couldn't absolve him, the sin he confessed was too awful.'

'I read the account, but I'd like to hear it directly from you.'

'Why?' It was clear that this was a subject Don Michele would have preferred not to revisit.

'Your first impressions are important to me. I need to grasp all the nuances of that conversation.'

Don Michele let himself be persuaded. 'It was eleven at night, and we were closing. I remember noticing the man standing on the other side of the street. He had been there all evening. I realised he'd been trying to summon up the courage to come in. When the last visitor left, he finally made up his mind. He came straight to me and asked me to hear his confession. I had never seen him before. He was wearing a heavy coat and a hat, and he didn't take them off the whole time. It was as if he was in a hurry to get away. Our conversation didn't in fact last very long. He wasn't looking for solace or understanding, he merely wanted to relieve himself of a burden.'

'What did he tell you, exactly?'

Don Michele scratched at his straggly grey beard. 'I realised immediately that he was thinking of doing something extreme. There was a kind of torment in his gestures, in his voice, which made me think his intentions were serious. He knew that there was no forgiveness for what he was about to do, but he hadn't come to be absolved of the sin he hadn't yet committed.' He paused. 'He wasn't asking pardon for the life he was planning to take – his own – but rather for the one that he had already taken.'

Don Michele Fuente was a streetwise priest, constantly in contact with the ugly side of life. But Marcus did not blame him for his discomfort: what he had listened to that night was the confession of a mortal sin. 'Who had he killed, and why?'

The priest took off his glasses and started wiping them on his cassock. 'He didn't tell me. When I asked him, he was evasive. He said he thought it was best I shouldn't know, or I might be in danger myself. All he wanted was to be absolved. When I told him that, due to the gravity of his sin, a mere priest wouldn't be able to absolve him, he seemed upset. He thanked me and went away without another word.'

Terse as this account was, it was all that Marcus had to go on. In the archive, the confessions of murderers were kept in a separate section. The first time he had set foot there, Clemente had given him a single piece of advice: 'Don't forget that what you will read is not a statement in a police database, where objectivity acts as a kind of protective barrier. In these confessions, the vision of what happened is subjective, because it is always the murderer himself telling the story. Sometimes you may feel that you are in his place. Don't let evil deceive you, remember that it's an illusion, it can be dangerous.' Reading those accounts, Marcus had often been struck by tiny details. There was always some element in the stories that seemed incongruous. One killer, for example, remembered that his victim had been wearing red shoes, and the priest had included that in his transcription. It wasn't important, it wouldn't influence the judgement. But it was as if, in a list of horrific acts of violence, they wanted to create a way out, an emergency exit. Red shoes: a splash of colour interrupted the narrative for a moment, allowing whoever was reading it to catch his breath. In Don Michele's account there were no details of that kind. And Marcus suspected that the transcription was incomplete. 'You know who the penitent was, don't you?'

Don Michele hesitated a fraction too long, and Marcus knew he was right. 'I recognised him a few days later, in the newspapers.'

'But when you submitted his confession, you omitted the name.'

'I consulted the bishop, and he advised me to conceal the man's identity.'

'Why?'

'Because everyone thought he was a good man,' he said laconically. 'He built a big hospital for the poor in Angola. The bishop convinced me that there was no need to tarnish the memory of a great benefactor, that it was better to preserve it intact as an example to others. Any judgement to be made on him was no longer our concern.'

'What was his name?' Marcus insisted.

Don Michele sighed. 'Alberto Canestrari.'

Marcus sensed that there was something else, but he did not want to force the other man's hand. He sat watching him in silence, waiting for him to speak again.

'There's another thing,' Don Michele said, with some trepidation. 'The newspapers wrote that he died of natural causes.'

Alberto Canestrari was not only a world-famous surgeon, a luminary of medical science and an innovator in his profession. He was above all a philanthropist.

That much was clear from the plaques that adorned the walls of his office in the Via Ludovisi, along with the framed press cuttings that described his many innovations in surgical technique and praised his generosity in exporting his skills to the developing world.

His greatest achievement had been the building of a large hospital in Angola, where he often went and performed operations.

Those same newspapers that had celebrated his work had later reported the news of his sudden death from natural causes.

Once Marcus got into what had been Canestrari's surgery, located on the third floor of a prestigious building near the Via Veneto, he let his eyes wander over these relics, examining the doctor's smiling face in photographs in which he was posing with various celebrities, as well as the patients – many of them very poor – who owed their recovery and, in some cases, their lives to him. They were his family. Having devoted his entire existence to his profession, Canestrari had never married.

If he'd had to judge the man from the paeans of praise displayed on that wall, Marcus would have had no hesitation in calling him a good Christian. But experience had taught him to be cautious in his judgements. All that might have been a facade. Especially in the light of the words Canestrari had uttered a few days before his death, in his last confession.

As far as the world was concerned, Alberto Canestrari had not killed himself.

But Marcus found it difficult to believe that that he could actually have died from natural causes so soon after announcing his intention to commit suicide. There had to be more to it.

The surgery consisted of a large waiting room, the secretary's office, and the doctor's own office, a room with a large mahogany desk surrounded by a vast collection of medical books, many of them bound. Behind a sliding door was a small consulting room, with a couch, various pieces of apparatus and a compact medicine cabinet. Marcus concentrated on Canestrari's office. Part of it was a reception area with leather sofas and a swivel chair, also of leather, in which – according to the media – the surgeon had been found dead.

Why am I here? he asked himself.

Even if the man really had committed a murder, the case was now closed. There was nothing left for Marcus to do. The killer was dead, and this time the mystery penitenziere wouldn't be able to give anyone the chance to take revenge. But he had led him here, which meant the truth couldn't be as simple as that.

One thing at a time, he told himself. The first step was to ascertain the facts, and the first anomaly to deal with was the suicide.

Canestrari had no wife or children, and after his death his nephews and nieces had disputed the inheritance. That was why the surgery, which was one of the contested assets, had remained unchanged over the last three years. The windows were shuttered and there was a thick layer of dust over everything. The dust also hovered like gleaming fog in the thin beams of light that filtered through the shutters. Although time, in its indifference, had preserved the room as it had been, the place certainly didn't resemble a crime scene. Marcus almost regretted that there hadn't been a violent death here. Such deaths always left traces on which he could hang his own deductions. Amid the chaos generated by evil it was easier to detect anomalies. Here, though, in the false tranquillity of this office, they would be much harder to find. This time, the challenge required him to change his methods drastically. He would have to identify with Alberto Canestrari.

What counts most for me? he asked himself. Fame interests me, but it's not essential: unfortunately you don't become famous by saving lives or giving to charity. Then my profession. But my talent is more important to other people, so it's not what is most dear to me.

The solution came spontaneously as he looked again at the wall celebrating the doctor's life. My name, that's what really counts. My reputation is the most valuable thing I possess.

Because I'm convinced that I'm a good man.

He went and sat down in Canestrari's armchair. He put his hands together under his chin and asked himself one essential question.

How can I kill myself while making everyone believe I died from natural causes?

What Canestrari had feared most was scandal. He would never have tolerated the idea of people remembering anything bad about him. So he must have thought up a method. Marcus was convinced that the answer was very near.

'Within reach,' he said. He swivelled the chair round towards the bookcase.

Simulating a natural death should not have been a problem for someone so versed in the secrets of life. He was sure there was a simple method that would not arouse suspicion. Nobody would investigate, nobody would dig deeper, because it was such an upright man who had died.

Marcus stood up and started examining the titles of the books lined up on the shelves. It took him a while to find what he was after. He took out the volume.

It was a handbook of natural and artificial poisons.

He started to leaf through the lists of essences and toxins, mineral and vegetable acids, caustic alkalines. Everything was here, from arsenic to antimony, from belladonna to nitrobenzene, phenacetin and chloroform, with an indication of the fatal dosage, the active ingredients, and the uses and side-effects. At last he came across something that might be the answer he was looking for.

Succinylcholine.

It was a muscle relaxant used in anaesthaesia. Being a surgeon, Canestrari would have been familiar with it. In the book it was compared to a kind of synthetic curare, because it possessed the ability to paralyse patients for the duration of an operation, thus avoiding the risk of spasms or involuntary movements.

After studying the drug's properties, Marcus came to the conclusion that Canestrari would have needed a one-milligram dose to stop his respiratory muscles from working. A few minutes, and he would choke. It would have felt like an eternity, and made for a terrible death, but it would certainly be highly effective, because the paralysis of the body would make the process irreversible. Once the drug was injected, there would be no time for second thoughts.

But there was another reason why Canestrari had chosen it.

Marcus was surprised to learn that the principal quality of succinylcholine was that it did not show up in toxicological tests because it was composed of succinic and choline acids, two substances normally present in the human body. Death would seem to be from natural causes. No pathologist would think of looking for a very small hole caused by the insertion of a syringe, between the toes for example.

His good name would be safe.

But what of the syringe? If someone had found it next to the body, the idea of simulating a natural death would have gone out of the window. That didn't quite fit with the rest.

Marcus mulled it over. Before coming here, he had read on the internet that it was Canestrari's nurse who had found his body, when she opened up the clinic in the morning. Maybe she had been the one to get rid of the embarrassing evidence that it had not been a natural death.

Too risky, Marcus told himself: what was there to guarantee that the nurse would do that? Canestrari must have been sure that the syringe would be removed. Why?

Marcus looked around at the place where the famous doctor had decided to take his own life. This surgery was the centre of his universe. But that wasn't the reason he had chosen it. He must have been certain that someone would see his plan through to its conclusion. Someone who had an interest in getting rid of the syringe.

He did it here because he knew he was being watched.

Marcus leapt to his feet. There had to be a device in the room. Where could they have put it? In the electrical wiring, was the answer.

He looked at the light switch on the wall. He went up to it and noticed that there was a small hole in the box. To remove it, he used a paper knife he found on the desk. First he loosened the screws, then slowly prised the box off the wall.

It took one glance to recognise a transmitter cable among the electric wires.

Whoever had hidden this spy camera had been good.

But if someone was watching the clinic at the time of Canestrari's suicide, why was the device still there? Marcus realised he was in imminent danger. By now, his presence in the clinic must already be known.

They've left me alone so far to see who I am. But now they're on their way.

He had to get out immediately. He was heading for the door when he heard a noise coming from the corridor. Cautiously, he peered out through the doorway and saw a big, thuggish-looking man in a suit and tie trying to manoeuvre his huge frame along the narrow corridor without making a noise. Marcus retreated before the man could see him. There was no way out. His one escape route was occupied right now by that human mountain.

He looked around and saw the sliding door that led to the consulting room. He would be able to hide there. If the man came into the office, he might be able to slip out. After all, he was more agile than his adversary, and once he was out he would run.

The man stopped in the doorway. His head turned slowly on his massive neck, and two tiny eyes peered into the semi-darkness without seeing anything. Then he noticed the sliding door leading to the consulting room. He went to it, put his fat fingers in the gap, quickly pulled the siding door across, and burst into the consulting room. He had barely had time to see that it was empty when the sliding door closed behind him.

Marcus congratulated himself on having changed the plan at the last moment. He had hidden under Canestrari's desk and as soon as the man had fallen into the trap had jumped out and rushed to the sliding door to shut him in. But just as he was feeling smug about his own cleverness, he realised that the key did not turn in the lock. The sliding door started to vibrate as the man hammered on it. Marcus dropped the key and started running. He was in the corridor and could hear the thug behind him: the man had freed himself and was gaining ground. He slammed the main door of the surgery behind him, to slow his pursuer down, and ran to the landing. He was about to continue his escape down the main stairs when it struck him that the man behind him might not be alone, that he might have an accomplice downstairs, keeping an eye on the front door of the building. He spotted an emergency exit and decided to use it. The stairs were narrower and the steps themselves shorter, and he was forced to jump them to keep his head start. The thug was much more agile than he had anticipated and had almost caught up with him. The three floors separating him from the street seemed to take forever. Behind the last door lay salvation. When he flung it open, he found himself not in the street but in an underground car park. It was deserted. At the far end of the vast space, he saw a lift whose doors were opening. When they did so, instead of offering him a new way out, they revealed the existence of a second man in a jacket and tie, who recognised him and started running towards him. With two pursuers on his heels he wouldn't make it. He was getting out of breath. He was afraid he might collapse at any moment. He started climbing the ramp that led out of the garage. A few cars came towards him in the opposite direction. Some almost grazed him, and the drivers hooted their horns in protest. By the time he came out on the street, the two men had almost caught up with him. But then they stopped suddenly.

Ahead of them, a party of Chinese tourists formed a human barrier.

Marcus took advantage of them to get away. Soon, he was watching from a corner as his pursuers, having lost him, bent double from their exertions and tried to catch their breath.

Who were these two? Who had sent them? Could someone else have been involved in the death of Alberto Canestrari?

11.00 a.m.

Her badge hanging around her neck, she presented herself to the police officers standing guard outside the gate of Jeremiah Smith's villa and showed them the service order that De Michelis had sent her. As the officers checked her credentials, they exchanged know-ing glances. Sandra had the impression that the male race had suddenly started taking an interest in her again. And she knew why. That night spent with Schalber had removed the stench of sadness from her. She bore the procedure with resignation. At last, the offi-cers let her pass, apologising for detaining her.

She walked along the drive leading to the Smith residence. The garden was in a state of abandonment. The grass had grown until it had covered the big stone planters. Here and there, statues of nymphs and Venuses, some without limbs, saluted her with incom-plete, though still graceful, gestures. There was a fountain covered with ivy, the pool around it brimming with green, stagnant water. The house was a monolith made grey by time. Access to it was via a flight of steps that was wide at the bottom but narrowed towards the top. Instead of making the front of the house look thinner, it seemed to be supporting it like a pedestal.

Sandra climbed the steps, some of which were crumbling. As she went in through the main door, the light of day suddenly vanished, absorbed by the dark walls of a long corridor. It was a strange sen-sation, as if a black hole had sucked everything in.

Forensics were still at work, although they had nearly finished. Right now they were examining the furniture, pulling out the draw-ers, tipping them out on the floor and sifting through the contents, taking the lining out of the sofas and emptying the cushions. Some were probing the walls with phonendoscopes in search of cavities that might have been used as hiding places.

A tall thin man was giving instructions to the officers of the canine unit, pointing them in the direction of the garden. He noticed Sandra and gestured to her to wait. Sandra nodded and waited in the hall. The officers with the dogs left the house, the ani-mals pulling them towards the garden. Now the thin man came towards her.

'I'm Superintendent Camusso.' He held out his hand. He was wearing a purple suit and a striped shirt of the same colour, with a yellow tie as the finishing touch. A real dandy.

Sandra refused to let herself be distracted by her colleague's eccentric costume, even though it offered some much-needed light relief amid all this darkness. 'Vega.'

'I know who you are, they told me. Welcome.'

'I don't want to get in your way.'

'Don't worry. We're nearly finished here. The circus is taking down the tents this afternoon. You've come a bit late for the show, I'm afraid.'

'You already have Jeremiah Smith and the evidence linking him to the four killings – what are you still looking for?'

'We don't know where his playpen is. The women weren't killed here. He kept them prisoner for a month. He didn't rape them. They'd been tied up, but he didn't torture them. After thirty days he cut their throats. But he must have needed a secluded spot to do all that in peace. We were hoping to find some clue that might lead us to it, but we've drawn a blank so far. And what are *you* looking for?'

'My chief, Inspector De Michelis, wants me to write a detailed report on the killer. Cases such as this don't turn up every day. It's an excellent opportunity for a forensics person like me to get some experience.'

'I see,' Camusso said, apparently unconcerned as to whether or not she had told him the truth.

'What's the canine unit still doing here?'

'The dogs are going to take another sniff around the garden. A body may yet turn up – it wouldn't be the first time that's happened. With all the rain there's been in the last few days, we haven't had a chance till now. Though I doubt they'll be able to pick up a scent. When the ground is damp, there are too many smells. The animals get confused.' The superintendent signalled to one of his subordinates, who approached with a case file. 'Here, this is for you. Everything you need to know: reports, profiles of Smith and the four victims, and obviously all the photographs. If you want a copy, you'll need make a request to the examining magistrate. This one has to come back to me when you've finished with it.'

'That's fine, I won't need it for long,' Sandra replied, taking the file.

'I think that's everything. You can go wherever you want, I don't think you'll need a guide.'

'I'll manage, thanks.'

Camusso handed her overshoes and latex gloves. 'Well, have fun.'

'Yes, I think this place must put everyone in a good mood.'

'We love it. We're like children playing hide and seek in a cemetery.'

Sandra waited for Camusso to walk away, then took out her mobile phone, intending to take some photographs of the house. She opened the file and scanned through the last report. It referred to the way the killer had been identified. As she read it, she had difficulty believing that things had happened as they were described.

She headed for the room where Jeremiah Smith had been found dying by the ambulance crew.

In the living room, the forensics team had already finished their work, and Sandra found herself alone. Looking around, she tried to imagine the scene. The ambulance people arrive and find the man lying on the floor. They try to revive him, but he's in a critical condition. They're stabilising him in order to take him away when one of them – the doctor who's come in the ambulance – notices an object in the room.

A red roller skate with gold trimmings.

The doctor's name is Monica and she's the sister of one of the victims of a serial killer who has been kidnapping and murdering young women for the past six years. The skate belonged to her twin sister. Its pair was found on the foot of her corpse. Monica realises she has the murderer lying in front of her. The paramedic who is with her knows the story, as does everybody at the hospital. Sandra knew how it was: the police were the same. Your workmates become a kind of second family, because it's the only way to deal with the pain and injustice you come across every day. Out of that bond come new rules and a kind of solemn pact.

So at this point, Monica and the paramedic could let Jeremiah Smith die, as he deserves. He's in a desperate condition, nobody would accuse them of negligence. Instead, they decide to keep him alive. Or rather, Monica is the one who decides to save him.

Sandra was sure that was the way it had happened, as were the police who were in the villa now, even though it was quite incredible.

Fate had played a strange trick in this house. The coincidence was so perfect, it was hard to imagine it had happened any other way. After all, you couldn't stage something like that. But there were aspects of the matter she found hard to swallow.

The words on Jeremiah Smith's chest. *Kill me.*

In the file, together with a photograph of these words, there was a report from a handwriting expert, confirming that he had carved them there himself. Although it could be explained as an indication of Smith's sadomasochistic tendencies, it was strange that this invitation should correspond so exactly to the choice Monica had found herself faced with.

Sandra took a series of photographs of the room. Jeremiah Smith's armchair, the smashed bowl on the floor, the antiquated TV set. When she had finished, she felt a sudden sense of claustrophobia. Accustomed as she was to crime scenes, death seemed to her all the more tangible, all the more obscene, amid these familiar objects.

It was so unbearable, she needed to get out of the house.

There are objects that connect the dead to the world of the living. You just have to find them and liberate them.

A hair ribbon, a coral bracelet, a scarf . . . and a roller skate.

Sandra went over the brief list of keepsakes found by the police in Jeremiah Smith's house, linking him to the victims. In a way, the four murdered girls had become synonymous with those objects.

She ran out of the house, past her colleagues, and took refuge in the garden to avoid their glances. She sat down on a stone seat to catch her breath. It was pleasant to be there, caressed by the morning sun, with the trees swaying in the wind, the rustling of the leaves like laughter.

Four victims in six years, Sandra told herself. All had had their throats cut.

Monica's sister was called Teresa. She was twenty-one years old and loved roller skating. One Sunday afternoon, she disappeared.

Actually, the skating was a pretext: there was a boy at the rink she liked. That afternoon, she'd waited for him, but he didn't show. Perhaps that was when Jeremiah spotted her, sitting all alone at a table by the drinks kiosk. He approached her on some pretext and offered to buy her a drink. Forensics had found traces of GHB in a glass of orange juice. One month later, Jeremiah left her body on the banks of a river in the same clothes she had been wearing the day she had disappeared.

Everyone in the fast food restaurant remembered the blue satin ribbon twenty-three-year-old Melania used to gather her blonde hair. The waitress's uniforms weren't much to look at, so she decided to brighten hers up with that decidedly retro, Fifties touch. One afternoon she was abducted as she was on her way to work. The last time anyone saw her, she had been waiting for a bus. Her body turned up a month later in a car park. She was fully dressed, but the ribbon had disappeared from her hair.

At the age of seventeen, Vanessa was obsessed with the gym. She went there every day for a spinning class. She never missed a training session, even when she wasn't feeling well. The day she disappeared, she had a cold, and her mother had tried to persuade her to skip the class for once. As she couldn't get her to change her mind, she had given her a pink woollen scarf so that she could at least be a bit more covered. To please her, Vanessa had put it on. Her mother couldn't have known that the scarf wouldn't be enough to protect her from the danger that awaited her. This time, the drug had been concealed in a little bottle of mineral supplement.

Cristina hated her coral bracelet, but the only person who knew that was her sister: the same sister who noticed it wasn't on her wrist when she identified the body in the morgue. Cristina only wore it because it had been a gift from her boyfriend. They were both twenty-eight and were planning to get married. Maybe that was why she was a little tense. All those preparations to make, and so little time. So she had looked for quick and easy methods to relax her nerves. Alcohol helped. She would start in the morning and continue through the day, a little at a time, without ever getting really drunk. Nobody realised that it was becoming a problem. But

Jeremiah Smith did. All he had to do was follow her into some bar or other, and he soon realised that it would be easier with her than it had been with the others.

Cristina had been the killer's last victim.

These portraits had been put together from the testimonies of relatives, friends and boyfriends. Everyone had added an intimate detail or two, giving colour to a cold recital of events, letting these girls appear for what they really were.

People, not objects, Sandra told herself. Even though, since their deaths, objects – a hair ribbon, a coral bracelet, a scarf and a roller skate – had replaced them in the imaginations of those who had loved them.

But there was a strange contradiction that emerged from these profiles. The four girls were not naive. They had families, friends, rules of conduct, examples to follow. And yet they had let themselves be approached by someone as insignificant as Jeremiah Smith. A man in his early fifties, far from handsome, who had offered them a drink. Why had they accepted? He had acted in broad daylight and had captured their trust. How did he do it?

Sandra was convinced that the answer was not in those items. She closed the file, looked up and let her face be caressed by the breeze. For a time, she, too, had identified David with an object.

An awful green tie.

She smiled at the thought. It was even uglier than the yellow tie worn by the superintendent who had greeted her a little earlier. David never wore smart clothes, he didn't care for dressing up.

'You should get tails, Fred,' she would tease him. 'All tap dancers have them.'

So he only had one tie. When the undertakers had asked her what clothes to put on him in the coffin, it had been a shock. She had never imagined she would have to make such a decision at the age of twenty-nine. She had had to choose something that represented David. She started to rummage desperately through his clothes. She selected a safari jacket, a blue shirt, khaki trousers and trainers. That was how everybody remembered him. But it was at that moment that she realised that the green tie had disappeared. She couldn't find it anywhere but she wouldn't give up. She turned the house upside down. It became a kind of obsession. It might seem like madness, but she had already lost David and couldn't bear the idea of giving up anything else. Even an awful green tie.

Then one day she remembered exactly where it had ended up. It came into her mind suddenly, when she was thinking about something else. How could she have forgotten?

The tie was the only remaining proof of the time she had lied to her husband.

Sitting now in the garden of Jeremiah Smith's house, it struck Sandra that the warmth of the sun and the caress of the wind were undeserved. She opened her eyes, which she had half closed, and saw a stone angel gazing down at her. With its silence and stillness, the statue reminded her that she had something to be forgiven for. And that time doesn't always give us the opportunity to remedy our mistakes.

What would have happened if the sniper who had shot at her in the chapel of St Raymond of Penyafort had managed to kill her? She would have died with that weight on her conscience. What object would have remained to her family and friends to remember her? Whatever it was, it would have hidden the truth from them. Which was that she did not deserve David's love, because she had been unfaithful to him.

The girls Jeremiah Smith kidnapped felt safe, she told herself. Just as I did before I entered that church. That was why they died. He was able to kill them because their hunger for life prevented them from understanding what was about to happen to them.

Behind the stone angel, Sandra saw her colleagues from the canine unit searching a portion of the garden with their dogs. It was as Camusso had said: the animals appeared disorientated by the smells given off by the soil. The superintendent had told her they were only doing it in order to leave nothing untried. 'A body may yet turn up, it wouldn't be the first time that's happened,' he had said. But she was experienced enough to know when a colleague was trying to throw her off the scent. It was a cautious attitude that police officers adopted when they were afraid they had overlooked some detail that might come back to haunt them.

At that moment Superintendent Camusso himself came up behind her. 'Is everything okay?' he asked. 'I saw you run out of the villa and—'

'I needed a bit of air,' Sandra cut in.

'Found anything interesting? I wouldn't want you to go back to your superior empty-handed.'

It was obvious he was saying it to be kind. But Sandra decided to take advantage of the opportunity. 'There is something, something a bit odd. Maybe you could help me to understand . . . '

The superintendent stared at her in surprise. 'Go on.'

Sandra noticed a shadow pass across his eyes. She opened the file and showed him the profiles of Jeremiah Smith's four victims. 'I noticed that the murderer struck on average every eighteen months. Seeing that when you found him nearly eighteen months had already gone by and that you know for certain that he took the girls to another place, I was wondering if by chance he wasn't preparing to strike again. As I'm sure you know, with serial killers the intervals of time are crucial. If every crime is divided into three phases – incubation, planning and action – then I'd say that when he was taken ill, Jeremiah must have been in the middle of the third.'

The superintendent did not say a word.

'So I wonder,' Sandra went on, 'if somewhere out there, there isn't another girl being kept prisoner right now.'

She waited for this last sentence to sink in.

Camusso's face darkened. 'It's possible,' he said, at the cost of some effort.

Sandra guessed that she was not the first person to formulate this hypothesis. '*Has* another girl disappeared?'

Camusso stiffened. 'You know how these things are, Officer Vega: there's always a risk of confidential information getting out and compromising the outcome of an investigation.'

'What are you afraid of? Media pressure? Public opinion? Your superiors?'

Camusso took his time. Realising that she wouldn't let it go, he finally said, 'A young architecture student went missing nearly a month ago. At first, everything pointed to the likelihood that she had run away of her own free will.'

'My God.' Sandra could not believe that she had guessed correctly.

'It's as you were saying: the times coincide. But there's no evidence, only suppositions. You can imagine what fuss there'd be, though, if people found out that we'd downplayed this until Jeremiah Smith turned up.'

Sandra found it hard to blame her colleagues. Sometimes the police acted under pressure and made mistakes. Except that they were not forgiven. Which was natural: people wanted answers, security, justice.

'We are looking for her,' Camusso said.

And you're not the only ones, Sandra thought, at last understanding the role of the penitenzieri in this affair.

The stone angel cast its shadow over the superintendent.

'What's the name of this student?'

'Lara.'

11.26 a.m.

Lake Nemi had a surface area of less than a square mile and was situated in the Colli Albani to the south of Rome.

It had originally been the crater of a volcano. For many centuries it was reputed that the wrecks of two huge ships, so richly appointed as to be floating palaces, built on the orders of the Emperor Caligula, lay at the bottom of the lake. The fishermen in the area had brought up a number of finds over the years. After many attempts, it wasn't until the twentieth century that the lake was partly drained and the vessels recovered and moved to a museum. Here, they had been destroyed by fire during the Second World War. German troops had been blamed, but there had never been any definite proof.

This information was contained in a tourist leaflet that Clemente had left for him in the letter box they used for exchanging documents. Into its pages he had inserted a brief dossier on Dr Alberto Canestrari. There was nothing especially remarkable in it, apart from one fact that had led Marcus to make this short trip outside the city. As he sat on the coach, looking out at the lake, he reflected on the singular link between this area and fire.

As if in echo of the tragic fate of those ships, the clinic that Canestrari owned in Nemi had been destroyed in an act of arson. Those responsible had never been identified.

The coach climbed along the narrow scenic road, spluttering and leaving a trail of dark smoke behind it. Through the window, Marcus spotted the flame-blackened building, which still enjoyed an enviable view of the landscape. When the coach came to a halt, he got off and continued on foot until he came to a gate. Alongside it was a sign with the name of the clinic, although the ivy that covered it made it illegible. He went through the gate and then along an avenue that cut through a little wood. The vegetation had grown unchecked, overrunning the space. The clinic was composed of two floors plus a basement. It must originally have been somebody's holiday home before being converted to its new purpose.

This had been Alberto Canestrari's little kingdom, Marcus thought, as he looked at the building, made unrecognisable by the soot. Here, the doctor who considered himself a good man had given the gift of life.

Marcus went in through what remained of an iron door, and found himself in a corridor. The interior was as ghostly as the exterior. The columns surrounding the foyer, corroded as they were by the flames, were so thin that it was difficult to believe they could still support the weight of the roof. The floor had risen in several places and grass had grown in the cracks. There was a gaping hole in the ceiling, through which the upper floor could be seen. Ahead of him was a double staircase.

Marcus walked through the rooms, starting with the second floor. The place reminded him of a hotel: single rooms, equipped with all the comforts. From what remained of the furnishings, it could be assumed that they had been pretty luxurious.

Canestrari's clinic must have been very lucrative. In the operating theatres, of which there were three, the fire had been especially fierce: fed by the oxygen equipment, the flames had melted everything, leaving a carpet of surgical instruments and other metallic objects that had tried to withstand them. The ground floor was in the same state as the upper one. The fire had gone from one room to another: the fleeting shadows of its passing could still be seen on the walls.

The clinic had been empty when the fire broke out. After Canestrari's death, the patients had all left. After all, what had brought them there was an absolute faith in his skills.

An idea had been growing in Marcus's mind over the last hour. The fact that someone had destroyed the clinic after the doctor's suicide suggested there might have been something incriminating hidden there. That could also be the reason why spy cameras had been placed in his surgery and why those two thugs had been after him this morning. They weren't ordinary burglars: they wore elegant dark suits, they had the look of professionals. Someone had hired them.

Marcus hoped that the fire had spared something. A premonition told him it must have, otherwise the penitenziere who had preceded him would have broken off his investigation.

If he got to the truth, so can I.

In the basement, Marcus found a room where, according to the notice on the door, the clinic's waste had been stored. He assumed that it would subsequently have been sent to a special facility for disposal. The room was filled with metal drums, partly melted by the heat. The floor was composed of little blue-tinted majolica tiles, many of which had come loose, again because of the heat, and all of which were blackened.

All except one.

Marcus crouched down to get a better look at it. He had the impression that someone had moved it, cleaned it and put it back in its original place in the corner of the room. He realised that it was not fixed to the floor, and he had no difficulty shifting it.

It hid a shallow cavity, which extended under the wall. He put his hand in and, after feeling around for a while, took out a metal box, roughly a foot in length.

It was not locked. He lifted the lid. It took him a while to realise that the long whitish object inside the box was a bone.

He took it out and examined it, holding it with both hands. From its shape and dimensions, he established that it was a human humerus. He had the feeling this was something he had always known, even though he had no idea where in his past that knowledge came from. For the moment he dismissed the question, because he realised that wasn't the only thing he knew about that bone.

From the state of the calcification, the victim had not yet reached puberty.

Was the death Alberto Canestrari had on his conscience a child's? A shudder went through Marcus, taking his breath away and making his hands tremble. He didn't know if he had the strength to bear it. Whatever test God was subjecting him to, he was not worthy of it. He was about to make the sign of the cross when he noticed something else.

There was a tiny inscription carved on the bone with a sharp instrument. A name. *Astor Goyash.*

'Sorry, I'm taking that.'

Marcus turned and saw the gun in the man's hand. He recognised him: it was the first of the two thugs in suits who had tried to attack him in Canestrari's Rome surgery a few hours earlier.

He had not expected to see him again. The situation in which they found themselves – in an abandoned building surrounded by woods, miles from any built-up area – put him at a clear disadvantage. He would die here, he was sure of it.

But he didn't want to die again.

The scene suddenly seemed familiar to him. He had already experienced the same fear, staring down the barrel of a gun in the hotel room in Prague, the day Devok had been killed. Suddenly, along with the fear, there came another part of his memory of those events.

He and his master had not been mere spectators. There had been a struggle. And he had fought the third man, the left-handed killer.

So, as he held out the humerus to the thug, Marcus leapt up and threw himself on him. The man had not expected such an abrupt reaction. He instinctively drew back, hit one of the drums, and fell to the floor, dropping his gun.

Marcus picked it up and held it out in front of him. A new sensation was throbbing inside him, one he had never felt before. He could not control it. It was hatred. He aimed the gun at the man's head. He did not recognise himself, all he wanted to do was press the trigger. It was the other man's shout that stopped him firing.

'Get down here!'

Marcus realised that the second thug he had glimpsed that morning was up above. He looked towards the stairs: he had only a few seconds at his disposal. The humerus was closer to the man on the floor. It was risky to pick it up, the man might try to disarm him. And Marcus now no longer had the strength to shoot him. He fled.

He climbed the stairs without encountering any obstacles and headed for the back of the building. When he was outside, he looked for a moment at the gun he was holding, then threw it away.

The only escape route was over the ridge of the hill. He started to climb, hoping that the trees would make pursuit difficult. All he could hear was his own heavy breathing. After a while he noticed that nobody was following him. He did not have time to consider why: a bullet hit a branch, mere inches from his head.

He had become a target.

He started running again, looking for shelter behind the shrubs. His feet sank into the earth and he almost fell on his back.

A few more yards and he would come to a road. He was almost crawling on all fours. More shots. Almost there. He grabbed a root to pull himself up and found himself on tarmac. He lay there on his stomach, thinking he wouldn't be seen if he kept low. He realised he was bleeding from his right side, but the bullet must have gone straight through and he didn't feel any burning. If he hadn't moved so quickly, they would have got him.

A light blinded him. It was the reflection of the sun on the windscreen of a vehicle coming towards him. He saw a familiar face at the wheel.

It was Clemente in his old Panda. He pulled up. 'Get in!'

Marcus did as he was told. 'What are you doing here?'

'After you told me about the attempted attack at the surgery,' Clemente said as he accelerated, 'I decided to come and check that everything was all right. I saw a suspicious car outside the clinic, and was going to call the police.' He noticed the wound in Marcus's side.

'Don't worry,' Marcus said, 'I'm all right.'

'Are you sure?'

'Yes,' he lied. In fact, he wasn't all right at all. But it wasn't the fault of the bullet that had grazed him. He had managed to survive another encounter with death. But he regretted not losing his memory a second time, because now he knew something about himself he didn't like: he, too, would have been capable of killing. He immediately changed the subject. 'I found a bone in the clinic. A humerus. I think it belonged to a child.'

Clemente seemed shaken by this, but said nothing.

'In my hurry to get away, I left it there.'

'Don't worry, saving yourself was more important.'

'There was a name on the bone,' Marcus said. 'Astor Goyash. We have to find out who he was.'

Clemente looked at him. 'Who he *is*, you mean. He's still alive and he certainly isn't a child any more.'

1.39 p.m.

The first lesson Sandra Vega had learned was that houses and apartments never lie.

That was why she had decided to inspect Lara's apartment in the Via dei Coronari. She was hoping to re-establish contact with the penitenziere with the scar on his temple, because she wanted to know if Lara really was Jeremiah Smith's fifth victim.

The girl might still be alive, she told herself. But she lacked the courage to imagine what might be happening to her right now. In an effort to remain detached, she approached the task following the standard procedure for a forensic photographer.

It was a pity she did not have her proper camera with her. Once again, she would have to make do with her mobile phone. Taking photographs was more than a necessity, it was a frame of mind.

I see what my camera sees.

She had considered making space in the phone's memory by erasing the photographs she had taken in the chapel of St Raymond of Penyafort. It was pointless keeping them, seeing that the chapel had nothing to do with the case. But then she'd had second thoughts: those photos would be a useful memento of the day death had come close to her. It was an experience she ought to preserve, in order not to fall into that kind of trap again.

Walking into the apartment in the Via dei Coronari, she was greeted by a smell of damp and mustiness. The place really needed a thorough airing. She hadn't needed keys to get in: the door had been taken off its hinges by the police when the girl's family had reported her disappearance. The officers hadn't found anything unusual in what was officially the last place Lara had been before she had vanished into thin air. At least, that was what the friends who had been with her on the day of her disappearance had stated, and the phone records appeared to confirm it: she had made two calls from that apartment before eleven.

Sandra made a mental note of that detail: if she had been abducted, it had happened after those calls; in other words, when it was completely dark. And that went against Jeremiah Smith's habit of always acting by day. He had changed his modus operandi for Lara, she told herself. He must have had a good reason for that.

She put her bag down on the floor, took out her mobile phone, activated the screen and prepared to take her photographs. In order to follow the manual to the letter, she started by giving her own details, plus date and time, exactly as she would have done if she'd had her recorder with her. She would make a detailed description of what she saw as she photographed it.

'The apartment is on two levels. On the first floor there is a living room and kitchen. The furniture is modest but decent. The typical apartment of a student living away from home. Except that this one is well looked after.' Too well looked after, she thought.

She took a series of pictures. When she turned to photograph the front door, she was taken aback.

'There are two locks. One is a chain and can only be opened and closed from the inside. But it's been broken.'

How could her colleagues not have noticed it? Lara was inside the apartment when she disappeared. It didn't make any sense.

She was anxious to get to the bottom of the mystery, but this discovery risked distracting her. Registering the incongruity, she reminded herself to focus on completing her survey of the upper floor.

The second lesson that Sandra Vega had learned was that, like people, houses and apartments die.

But Lara isn't dead, she tried to convince herself.

Sandra noticed immediately that, if the student had been abducted in her sleep, Jeremiah had taken the trouble to make the bed and take away a rucksack and some clothes together with her mobile phone. It had to look as if she had run away voluntarily. But the chain on the door contradicted that. And yet he'd had all the time in the world to cover his tracks. How had he managed to come in and go out if the door was locked from the inside? That question nagged at her.

In rapid succession, she photographed the teddy bear on the pillows, the chest of drawers with the photograph of Lara's parents, the desk with the unfinished plan for a bridge, the architecture books lined up in the bookcase.

There was an anomalous symmetry in that room. That must be typical of architects, she thought. I know you're hiding something, if that monster chose you it's because he knew you. Tell me where you're keeping a clue that'll lead me to him. Let me have some confirmation that I'm right and I swear to you I'll move heaven and earth to find you.

As she appealed for a sign from Lara, Sandra continued to describe out loud everything she was seeing. She didn't notice anything unusual, apart from that fanatical tidiness. She went back through the last pictures on the screen of her phone, hoping that some detail would strike her.

Under the desk, there was a waste-paper basket filled with used tissues.

The care that Lara devoted to her apartment had led Sandra to assume that she was rather a fussy kind of person. Compulsive, was the word that came to mind. Her sister was identical. There were things that could easily drive her mad: for example, the cigarette icon on the lighter in her car always had to be upright, the ornaments in her apartment always had to be in descending order of height. From the obsessiveness with which she approached such things, anyone would have thought the future of mankind was at stake. Lara was the same – the symmetry that Sandra had noted a little earlier was no accident. So the fact that she hadn't emptied that waste-paper basket, even though it was full, struck Sandra as strange. She put down her phone and bent to have a better look at the contents. In the middle of lots of used handkerchiefs and old notes, she found a sheet of paper rolled into a ball. She opened it. It was a receipt from a pharmacy.

Fifteen euros ninety, she read. There was no indication of what item had been purchased. The date of the receipt was a couple of weeks before Lara disappeared.

For a moment, Sandra abandoned her photography. She started going through the drawers, in search of the medication that might correspond to that receipt. She didn't find any. Then, still clutching the paper, she went back down to the lower level and headed for the bathroom.

It was small, but included a little broom cupboard. There was a cabinet over the mirror. Sandra opened it. It was filled with medicines and cosmetics. She started pulling them out and checking the prices stamped on them.

As she proceeded, she placed them in the wash basin, one by one. There was nothing that cost fifteen euros ninety.

But Sandra knew that this information was important. She sped up the operation, more out of nervousness than out of necessity. When she was finished, she leaned with both hands on the edge of the basin. She needed to calm down. She took a deep breath, but was forced to expel the air because the smell of damp was stronger here than in the rest of the apartment. Even though the toilet seemed clean, she flushed it and turned to go back upstairs. It was then that she noticed the calendar hanging behind the door.

Only a woman knows why another woman needs to keep a calendar in the bathroom, she told herself.

She took it off the nail on which it was hanging and started going through it, in reverse chronological order. On every page, certain consecutive days had been circled in red. More or less the same days every month.

But on the last page, these days were clear of circles.

'Shit,' she exclaimed.

Sandra had understood from the start. She hadn't needed that confirmation. Lara had thrown the receipt from the pharmacy in the waste-paper basket, but then hadn't had the strength to empty it in the refuse. Because there had been something else with the receipt and the Kleenex. Something that had a particular meaning for Lara, something she couldn't throw away.

A pregnancy test.

But Jeremiah had taken it when he had kidnapped Lara, Sandra told herself. After the hair ribbon, the coral bracelet, the pink scarf and the roller skate, was it the monster's latest fetish?

Sandra walked into the living room with the mobile phone in her hands, ready to inform Superintendent Camusso of her discovery. Maybe the information that Lara was pregnant would give a new impetus to the investigation. But she held back, wondering what else she had neglected.

The door closed from the inside, was the answer.

That was the one obstacle to the theory that someone had taken Lara from her apartment. If she could demonstrate with certainty that the student had not left of her own free will, there would be no more doubt about the fact that she was Jeremiah Smith's fifth victim.

What am I missing?

The third lesson she had learned is that houses and apartments have a smell.

What was the smell of this apartment? Damp, Sandra thought immediately, remembering what she had smelled on first entering. But, paying closer attention, she realised she had smelled it above all in the bathroom. It might be sewage. There were no obvious leaks, and yet the smell was really pervasive. She went back to the bathroom, switched on the light, and looked around. She checked the pipes in the shower and under the wash basin, and flushed the toilet again. Everything seemed to be in perfect working order.

She bent down because the smell came from below. She looked carefully at the mosaic tiles under her feet and noticed that one looked chipped. As if something had been stuck into it to lever it up. She looked around and grabbed some scissors she found on a shelf. She slipped the point into the crack, and to her great surprise found she could lift a portion of the floor. She shifted it to one side and saw what it concealed.

Beneath her there was a stone trapdoor that someone had left open.

That was where the smell came from. Travertine steps led down to an underground gallery. That in itself wasn't enough to demonstrate that Jeremiah had come this way. She needed further proof. There was only one way to get it.

Sandra summoned up her courage and went down.

When she reached the bottom of the steps, she took her mobile phone from her pocket, intending to use the light from the screen to orientate herself. She lit up both sides of the tunnel, but from the right she had the impression she could feel a draught. And from that same side there also came a distant booming sound.

She walked on, taking care where she put her feet. The ground was slippery and if she fell she might do herself serious harm. Nobody would find me down here, she thought.

After going twenty yards, she saw a glimmer of light and realised that she was coming to an exit that led directly to the Tiber. The river was swollen by the rainfall of the past few days and the muddy water carried detritus of every kind with it. It wasn't possible to go any further, because of a thick metal grille. Too difficult for

Jeremiah, she thought. So he must have gone in the other direction. Still using the light from the mobile phone she turned back, went past the stone staircase that led up to Lara's bathroom, and soon discovered that on the other side, the gallery turned into a maze of tunnels.

Sandra checked that there was still a network and used the phone to contact Headquarters. After a few minutes, they put her through to Superintendent Camusso.

'I've been in Lara's apartment. It's as we feared: Jeremiah kidnapped her.'

'What proof do you have?'

'I've found the passage he used to take her away without being seen. It's hidden under a trapdoor in the bathroom.'

'He's been really clever this time,' he said. But from Sandra's tone he sensed there was more. 'Anything else?'

'Lara's pregnant.'

Camusso fell silent. Sandra could guess his thoughts. The pressure on them had increased: now there were two lives at stake.

'Listen, Superintendent, send someone immediately.'

'I'm coming myself. We'll be right there.'

Sandra hung up. She made to turn back, aiming the light from the phone at the viscous ground, as she had done when coming. But she must have been lost in thought earlier and had not noticed the second row of footprints in the mud.

There was someone down here with her.

Whoever it was, he was hiding now in the maze of tunnels in front of her. Sandra was frozen with fear. Her breath condensed in the cold air of the gallery. She put her hand on her gun, but immediately realised that, where she was standing, she was too easy a target if her pursuer was armed.

He *is* armed. She was sure he was, especially after her experience with the sniper. It was him.

She could turn and start running to the stone steps. Or else fire blindly into the darkness, hoping to hit him before he hit her. Both solutions, though, were risky. She was aware of two eyes watching her. There was nothing in those eyes. She had felt the same sensation listening to the recorded voice of David's killer singing 'Cheek to Cheek'.

It's over.

'Officer Vega, are you there?' The call echoed behind her.

'Yes, I'm here,' Sandra cried, her voice transformed by terror into a ridiculous high-pitched scream.

'Police,' the voice went on. 'We were on patrol in the area when Superintendent Camusso called us.'

'Please, come and get me.' Without her realising it, her tone had turned imploring.

'We're in the bathroom, give us time to get down.'

It was then that Sandra clearly heard the footsteps of someone moving away in the opposite direction along the gallery.

The invisible eyes that had terrified her were escaping.

2.03 p.m.

They had gone to one of the safe houses the penitenzieri used, one of the many Vatican properties spread throughout the city. In it, there was a first-aid kit, as well as a computer to connect to the internet.

Clemente had got hold of a change of clothes and some sandwiches. Marcus, standing bare-chested in front of the mirror in the bathroom, was stitching his wound with needle and thread – another skill he didn't know he had – and as always was concentrating on what he was doing, and avoiding his own reflection.

This would not be only his second scar. In addition to the one on his temple he had other marks on his skin. The amnesia prevented him from finding memories in his mind, so he had looked for them on his body. Traces of small traumas in the past, like the pinkish nick he had on his calf, or the incision in the hollow of his elbow. Maybe they came from a fall from a bicycle when he was a child, or a trivial domestic accident when he was older. But they hadn't helped him to remember. It was sad not to have a past. The child whose bone he had found, though, would not have a future. In any case, both of them had died. Except that for Marcus death had worked in a strange way, proceeding in reverse.

On the ride from Canestrari's clinic to the safe house, Clemente had told him about Astor Goyash.

He was a seventy-year-old Bulgarian, who had lived in Rome for the last twenty of those years. His business interests, legal and illegal, ranged from construction to prostitution. He was known to have connections with organised crime.

'What does someone like that have to do with Alberto Canestrari?' Marcus asked once again, after listening to Clemente's story, unable to find a satisfactory explanation.

His friend, who was holding cotton wool and disinfectant for him, said, 'First we should try to find out who left that bone there, don't you think?'

'It's the mystery penitenziere,' Marcus stated with certainty. 'When he first looked into the case, after Canestrari's confession, he found the remains of the little boy in the storeroom. Maybe Canestrari, feeling guilty, had been hesitant to get rid of it. Luckily the penitenziere hid the humerus, first writing the name Astor Goyash on it. He wanted us to find it. If he hadn't hidden it, it would have been destroyed in the fire at the clinic.'

'Let's try and put the events in chronological order,' Clemente suggested.

'All right ... Canestrari kills a child. A major criminal named Astor Goyash is also involved. But we don't yet know why.'

'Goyash doesn't trust Canestrari: the doctor is conscience-stricken and could easily make a false move. So Goyash decides to keep an eye on him: that would explain the spy camera concealed in his surgery.'

'When Canestrari killed himself, it must have set alarm bells ringing in Goyash's mind.'

'That's why, immediately afterwards, his men set fire to the clinic, in the hope of wiping out for once and all any possible proof of the child's murder. They had already got rid of the syringe that Canestrari had used to inject the poison, to avoid an investigation being opened into the death.'

'Right,' Marcus agreed. 'But one fundamental question remains: what's the connection between a highly regarded philanthropist like Canestrari and a criminal like Goyash?'

'Frankly,' Clemente said, 'I can't see any. They belonged to different worlds.'

'And yet there must be something that unites them, I'm sure of it.'

'Listen, Marcus, time is running out for Lara. Maybe you should drop this Canestrari business and concentrate on finding her.'

The suggestion struck Marcus as strange. For a moment, he pretended to concentrate on medicating his wound, all the while examining Clementi's expression in the mirror. 'You may be right, I realised that today. It was lucky you came to the clinic: if you hadn't got me out of there, those two would have killed me.'

As he said this, his friend lowered his eyes.

'You were keeping an eye on me, weren't you?'

'What are you talking about?' Clemente said, feigning indignation.

Marcus turned to look at him. 'What's going on? What are you hiding from me?'

'Nothing.' Clemente was clearly on the defensive.

'Don Michele Fuente reports the confession of the would-be suicide Alberto Canestrari but, at the request of the bishop, omits the penitent's name. What are you all trying to safeguard? Who above us wants to keep this quiet?'

Clemente did not reply.

'I knew it,' Marcus said. 'The link between Canestrari and Astor Goyash is money, isn't it?'

'Canestrari didn't seem to be short of money,' Clemente objected, although without much conviction.

Marcus grasped his difficulty. 'The thing Canestrari prized above all else was his name. He believed himself to be a good man.'

Clemente realised that he could not continue much longer with this deception. 'The hospital Canestrari built in Angola is a wonderful thing. We mustn't run the risk of destroying it.'

Marcus nodded. 'Whose money did he use to build it? Astor Goyash's?'

'We don't know.'

'It seems plausible, though, doesn't it?' Marcus was angry now. 'The life of one child in exchange for thousands of lives.'

There was nothing Clemente could say: his pupil had understood everything.

'So we choose the lesser evil,' Marcus went on. 'But when we do that, we embrace the same logic that led Canestrari to accept such an unholy pact.'

'The logic of it doesn't concern us. But the lives of thousands of people do.'

'What about the child? Didn't that life count?' He paused to control his rage. 'How would the God in whose name we act judge all this?' He looked Clemente in the eyes. 'Someone will avenge that child's life, as the mystery penitenziere planned. We can decide to stand and watch while it happens, or we can try and prevent it. If we opt to do nothing, we'll be accessories to murder.'

Clemente knew Marcus was right, but he still hesitated. At last, he broke the silence. 'If Astor Goyash still feels the need to bug Canestrari's surgery three years after the event, it's because he's afraid of being implicated. That means there's evidence that can connect him to the murder.'

Marcus smiled: his friend was on his side, he wouldn't abandon him. 'We have to identify the child who was killed,' he said immediately. 'And I think I know how.'

They went into the adjoining room, where the computer was. After connecting to the internet, Marcus went on the police website.

'Where do you want to look for him?' Clemente asked over his shoulder.

'The mystery penitenziere is offering someone the possibility of revenge, so the young victim must be from Rome.'

He opened the page devoted to missing persons and clicked on the link for minors. The faces of children and teenagers appeared. There were an extraordinary number of them. Many were children contested in custody cases who had been taken by one of the parents, so the solution to the mystery was simple and their names soon disappeared from the list. Just as frequent were cases where the children had run away from home: these usually ended after a few days with a family reunion and a telling-off. But some of these minors had been missing for years, and would remain on this page until it was known what had happened to them. They smiled out from old, blurred photographs, a violated innocence in their eyes. In some cases, the police were able to take the image and make an identikit showing how their faces might have changed as they got older. The hope that these children could still be alive was a slim one. The photograph on the site was often a substitute for a headstone, a way to keep their memory alive.

By a process of elimination, Marcus and Clemente concentrated on the minors who had disappeared in Rome three years earlier. They narrowed the choice down to two. A boy and a girl.

Filippo Rocco had vanished one afternoon after leaving school. His classmates who were with him hadn't noticed anything. He was twelve years old and had a cheeky grin which displayed a gap where an upper incisor was missing. He was wearing the smock of the religious school he attended, a pair of jeans, and an orange sweater with a blue polo shirt and trainers. His satchel was covered with Scout badges, as well as the emblem of the football team he supported.

Alice Martini was ten years old and had long blonde hair. She wore glasses with pink frames. She had disappeared while she was in the park with her family: father, mother and younger brother. She was wearing a white Bugs Bunny sweatshirt, a pair of shorts and canvas shoes. The last person who had seen her was a balloon seller: he had spotted her near the toilets talking to a middle-aged man. But it had been a fleeting glimpse and he had not been able to provide the police with a description.

Marcus gathered other information from the websites of the newspapers that had reported the two disappearances. Both Alice's parents and Filippo's had put out appeals, taken part in talk shows and given interviews to keep interest in the two cases alive. But neither investigation had led anywhere.

'Do you think the child we're looking for is one of these two?' Clemente asked.

'It's likely, but I would've preferred there to be only one. Time isn't on our side. Up until now the penitenziere has calculated everything, planning for one act of revenge to be carried out every day. First, the sister of one of Jeremiah Smith's victims finds him dying in his house and discovers the truth. The following evening, Raffaele Altieri kills his father, the person responsible for the murder of his mother twenty years ago. Yesterday, Pietro Zini killed Federico Noni, guilty of assaulting a number of women and of killing first his sister Giorgia to silence her and then a girl buried in Villa Glori. Have you noticed that in these last two cases the messages from the penitenziere to the avengers arrived with split-second timing? He left us just a few hours to discover and stop the mechanism he'd set in motion. I don't think this case will be any different. So we have to hurry: someone will try to kill Astor Goyash by tonight.'

'It won't be easy getting to him. You've seen the kind of bodyguards he uses. He never goes anywhere without them.'

'In that case I need you, Clemente.'

'Me?' Clemente said, surprised.

'I can't keep an eye on the families of both missing children, so we have to divide the tasks. We'll use voicemail to communicate: as soon as one of us finds out something, he leaves a message.'

'What do you want me to do?'

'Find the Martinis, I'll deal with the parents of Filippo Rocca.'

Ettore and Camilla Rocca lived in Ostia, in a small one-storey house facing the beach. It was a decent-looking house, bought with savings.

Theirs was a normal family.

Marcus had often asked himself what that adjective really meant. It could mean a whole lot of small dreams and expectations that had become fixed over time and constituted a protection against any misfortune. For some, the greatest aspiration was to live a quiet life without too many upsets. It was a tacit pact with destiny, renewed every day.

Ettore Rocca was a travelling salesman and was often away from home. His wife Camilla was a social worker in a centre providing support to disadvantaged families and young people in difficulty. She spent her life helping others, even though she herself had become someone who needed help.

The couple had chosen to live on the coast because Ostia was quieter and less expensive. It meant commuting to Rome to work, but it was a sacrifice worth making.

When he entered their house, Marcus felt for the first time that he was an intruder. There were bars on the doors and windows, but he had had no difficulty in opening the main lock, closing it once he had entered. He found himself in a combined living room and kitchen. The dominant colours were white and blue. Not much furniture, all of it in a nautical style. The dinner table seemed to have been made out of the planks of a boat and above it hung a fisherman's lamp. On the wall was an old tiller with a clock face inlaid in it, and a fine display of shells stood on a shelf.

The sand came in with the wind and crackled under his shoes. Marcus moved further into the room, hoping to see some sign that might lead to the penitenziere. First of all, he looked at the refrigerator, on which a sheet of paper was held in place by a magnet in the shape of a crab. It was a message from Ettore Rocca to his wife.

See you in ten days. Love you.

So the man was away on business, although it might also be a lie for the benefit of his spouse. He might be preparing to kill Goyash. Given the risks involved, he wanted to leave her out of it, to protect her. A week to prepare, shut up in a motel outside the city. But Marcus couldn't indulge in speculation. He needed confirmation. He continued to search the room and, as he proceeded, he felt that something was lacking.

There was no sense of grief here.

Perhaps naively, he had expected that Filippo's disappearance would have created a kind of fracture in his parents' lives. Like a wound that, instead of being on the flesh, was on the objects, and you would just have to touch them to see them bleed. No, the boy seemed to have vanished even here. There were no photographs of him, no mementoes. But perhaps it was in that void that the grief manifested itself. Marcus wasn't able to perceive it, because only a mother and a father could see it. Then he understood. When he had looked at little Filippo's face surrounded by other missing children on the police website, he had wondered how their families managed to carry on. It wasn't the same as when a child died. When one disappeared, you had to learn to live with doubt. Doubt could insinuate itself everywhere, corroding everything from inside, without your being aware of it. It consumed the days, the hours. Years might pass without an answer. By comparison, Marcus had thought, how much better to know for certain that your child had been killed.

Death took hold of your memories, even the most beautiful ones, and inseminated them with grief, making them unbearable. Death became the master of the past. But doubt was worse, because it took away your future.

He entered Ettore and Camilla's bedroom. On the double bed, their pyjamas were laid out on the respective pillows. The blankets were smooth, the slippers matched. Everything in its place. As if all that order could compensate for the madness of grief, the upheaval caused by a tragedy. Domesticating everything. Training the objects to carry on a charade of normality, making them repeat the comforting news that everything is fine.

And in that idyllic little picture, he at last found Filippo.

The boy was smiling out of a framed photograph, together with his parents. He had not been forgotten after all. He, too, had his place here: on a chest of drawers, beneath a mirror. Marcus was about to leave the room when his eye fell on an object and he realised he had been mistaken.

On the bedside table, on the side of the bed where Camilla slept, was a baby monitor.

There was only one explanation for the presence of that object.

Struck by the discovery, Marcus continued to the next room. The door was closed. Opening it, he discovered that, in what had once been Filippo's room, next to his bed there was now a crib. The space was divided equally. On one side, posters of Filippo's favourite team, the desk where he had done his homework, on the other a changing table, a high chair, a heap of games for infants, even a music box with little bees playing ring-a-ring-a-roses.

Filippo didn't know it yet, but he had a little brother or sister.

Life is the one antidote to grief, Marcus told himself. And he understood how the Roccas had found a way to take back their future and sweep away the fog of doubt. But then something nagged at him. Would this family really endanger their attempt to regain some kind of peace of mind in order to carry out an act of revenge? How had they reacted to the news that their firstborn was dead? Always assuming that Filippo really was Canestrari's victim, he reminded himself.

He was on his way out of the house, intending to track down Camilla Rocca at the centre where she worked and follow her for the rest of the day, when he heard the throbbing of a car engine. He moved the curtain away from a window and saw a runabout that had just parked on the path. Camilla was in it.

Taken by surprise and unable to leave, he looked frantically for somewhere to hide. He found a room that was used as both a laundry and a store room. He went and stood in the corner behind the door and waited. He heard the front door being unlocked, Camilla coming in and closing the door, the sound of the keys being placed on a shelf, her heels clicking on the floor. She took off her shoes and dropped them, one after the other. Marcus peered through the crack in the door. She was walking barefoot and carrying a couple of cardboard boxes. She had been shopping and had come back home earlier than expected. But her son, or daughter, was not with her. She came into the laundry to hang a new garment on a hook. She did not turn. The thin wooden door was the only thing separating them. If the woman had moved it, she would have seen him. But instead she turned and made for the bathroom, shutting the door behind her.

Marcus heard the water running in the shower and left his refuge. He passed in front of the closed door and, coming back into the living room, saw a gift-wrapped package on the table.

In this house, life had somehow resumed.

Instead of heartening him, the thought made him uneasy. He was overcome with a sense of panic. Clemente, he murmured: it seemed likely that the family they were looking for was the one he had sent his friend to keep an eye on.

Taking advantage of the fact that Camilla Rocca was in the shower, he took the telephone attached to the wall of the kitchen and dialled the voicemail number. There was a message from Clemente. He sounded excited.

'Get here as soon as you can. Alice Martini's father is loading his car with luggage. I suspect he's getting ready to leave the city. And there's something else I discovered: the man owns an unlicensed gun.'

5.14 p.m.

She had not said anything to Superintendent Camusso about the danger she had been in while in the gallery under Lara's apartment. It doesn't have anything to do with the girl, she had told herself. It concerns only me and David.

And besides, she was not afraid any more. She had realised that her pursuer had an ulterior motive. He didn't want to kill her. At least not yet. He'd had the opportunity in that tunnel, before she made the call to Camusso. It wasn't that he had missed his chance; he'd held back deliberately.

He was checking up on her.

Sandra had a sense that Camusso suspected she was not telling him the whole story. She wondered if she was imagining it, blaming her lack of sleep and the fact that she hadn't eaten. So she had accepted the inspector's invitation to join him at Francesco's, a typical Roman trattoria in the Piazza del Fico. Although it was already mid-afternoon, they'd eaten pizza at a table in the open air, enjoying the smells and sounds of the neighbourhood. Around her, Rome with its stone streets, its buildings with their rough facades, its ivy-covered balconies.

Then they had come straight back to Headquarters. Camusso had shown her around the fine building he was lucky enough to work in, and Sandra had omitted to tell him that she already knew it from having got round one of his colleagues to do some research in records.

They made themselves comfortable in the superintendent's office. Here too, there was a high frescoed ceiling, but the furnishings did not reflect the man's eccentric taste. They were very sober and minimal, unlike Camusso, who moved like a splash of colour through the room. As he arranged his purple jacket on the chair behind the desk, Sandra noticed that he wore turquoise cufflinks. She couldn't help breaking into a smile.

'Are you absolutely sure Lara is pregnant?' Camusso asked.

They had already tackled the subject at the restaurant. The superintendent could not resign himself to the thought that women possessed a sixth sense for certain things, even though Sandra had excellent evidence to support her theory.

'Why do you doubt it?'

Camusso shrugged. 'We've spoken to her friends and her colleagues at university: nobody mentioned a boyfriend, even a casual one. Judging from her phone records and her emails, she didn't seem to be in any kind of relationship.'

'You don't have to be in a relationship to get pregnant,' she said, as if it was the most obvious thing in the world. But she could understand his objections: Lara didn't seem the type to sleep around. 'I was wondering about Jeremiah Smith. In every case except this one, he lured his victims in broad daylight, somehow persuading them to have a drink with him. How did a man like that manage to attract these girls?'

'I've been following this case for six years now and I still can't explain it,' Camusso said, shaking his head. 'Whatever trick he used, it was certainly effective. Every time it was the same story: a girl disappeared, and we put everything we had into finding her, knowing we had just one month. Thirty days during which we recited a script for the sake of the family, the press and public opinion. Always the same lines, the same lies. Then our time was up and we found a body.' He paused for a long time. 'When I realised the other night that this fellow in a coma was the killer, I heaved a sigh of relief. I was happy. You know what that means?'

'No.'

'I was enjoying the fact that another human being was dying. I said to myself: God, what's happening to me? What that man did was terrible, but he's made us become like him. Because only monsters are happy at the thought of death. I tried to convince myself that, when you came down to it, his dying meant that other girls would be spared. It was saving lives. But what about ours? Who would save us from the joy we were feeling?'

'Are you trying to tell me that when you found out he had kidnapped another girl it was almost a consolation?'

'If Lara is still alive, obviously.' Camusso smiled bitterly. 'Even that's quite monstrous, don't you think?'

'Yes, it is. It's as if we're making her salvation dependent on Jeremiah Smith's recovery.'

'The man will probably be a vegetable for the rest of his life.'

'What do the doctors say?'

'Strangely, they're rather in the dark. At first they thought it was a heart attack, but after running a lot of tests, they've ruled that out. They're looking for neurological damage, although they still can't locate it.'

'It might be the action of a toxic agent, maybe a poison.'

'They're analysing his blood to trace the substance,' Camusso admitted grudgingly.

'But if that's the case, then someone else is involved. Someone who tried to kill him.'

'Or to have him killed by the sister of one of his victims ...'

The Figaro case, thought Sandra. There was a similarity between the way Federico Noni had been killed and what had happened to Jeremiah Smith. Both appeared to be executions. Both men had been punished for their crimes. Or for their sins, she said to herself.

'Wait a minute, I want to show you something.'

Sandra had been lost in thought and did not take in at first what Camusso had said.

The superintendent took a laptop out of a case, switched it on and placed it in front of her. 'One week before the disappearance, there was a graduation ceremony in the faculty of architecture. The father of the graduate filmed everything.' He clicked to start the video. 'These are the last images we have of Lara before she vanished.'

Sandra leaned in towards the screen. The camera was moving around a lecture hall. There were about thirty people present. They were milling around, chatting in small groups, some laughing. Drinks had been set out on a desk and many of the people were holding glasses. There was a cake, but only half of it remained. The person doing the filming was moving among the guests, inviting them to say a few words to the camera. Some waved, others made witty remarks. The camera lingered on a young man who launched into a sarcastic monologue about the latest events at the university. His friends laughed. Behind him, in the background, was a girl who seemed not to be taking part in the festivities. She was leaning on a desk, with her arms folded and her eyes staring into the distance, unaffected by the joy around her.

'That's her,' Camusso said, as if there was any need.

Sandra looked closely at Lara. She was swaying on her heels, biting her lip. She had the look of a creature in pain.

'Strange, isn't it? It makes me think of when the media publish the photograph of a crime victim. They always seem to have been taken at some event that has nothing to do with what happened to them later. A wedding, an excursion, a birthday. Maybe they didn't even like that photo. While they were posing they certainly never imagined that one day that image would end up in the newspapers or on TV.'

The dead smiling out of the photographs of their past: Sandra was very familiar with that.

'In the course of their lives it probably never occurred to them that they might become famous. Suddenly they die and people know everything about them. Weird, don't you think?'

While Camusso was still pondering this, Sandra, her instincts as a forensic photographer to the fore, noticed a slight variation in Lara's expression. 'Do you mind going back a bit?'

Camusso looked at her, then did as she asked without demanding an explanation.

'Now slow it down.' Sandra leaned forward, waiting for the miracle to appear again.

Lara's lips suddenly moved.

'She spoke,' Camusso said, surprised.

'Yes, she spoke,' Sandra confirmed.

'And what did she say?'

'Let me see it again.'

Camusso ran the video several times, while Sandra made an effort to catch every vowel and consonant.

'She's saying, "Bastard."'

Camusso looked at her. 'Are you sure?'

Sandra turned to him. 'Yes, I think so.'

'And who is she angry at?'

'Definitely a man. Go forward and let's try and see who it is.'

He started the video again. The cameraman had been a bit haphazard, rarely taking time to focus on any of the guests for very long. All at once, the camera moved abruptly to the right, almost as if following the direction of Lara's gaze. She wasn't staring into the distance, as Sandra had thought at first: she was looking at someone.

'Can you pause it for a moment?' she asked Camusso.

He did so. 'What is it?'

Sandra had spotted a smiling man of about forty, surrounded by a group of female students. He was wearing a blue shirt and his tie was loose. An irreverent air, brown hair, clear eyes: a charmer. He had his hand on the shoulder of one of the girls.

'Is that the bastard?' Camusso asked.

'He looks the type.'

'Do you think he's the child's father?'

Sandra looked at Camusso. 'There are some things you can't tell from a video.'

The superintendent realised his gaffe and tried to make a joke of it. 'I thought that sixth sense of yours might tell you.'

'Not really,' she said, pretending to regret what she had said. 'But it might be useful to have a chat with him.'

'Wait, I can tell you who he is.' Camusso walked around the desk to check a file. 'We made a list of all those present that day. You never know.'

Sandra was surprised at the efficiency of her Roman colleagues.

'Christian Lorieri,' the superintendent announced, after looking through the list. 'He's an assistant lecturer in art history.'

'Did you question him?'

'There was no reason to. He had no contact with Lara.' Camusso guessed what was going through her head. 'Even if he was the father of the baby she was carrying and knew it, I doubt he'd be prepared to talk to us: he's married.'

Sandra thought this over. 'Sometimes it's worth provoking a reaction,' she said, with a wicked gleam in her eyes.

'What do you intend to do?' asked Camusso, curious.

'First I have to print some photographs . . .'

The corridors of the faculty of architecture were filled with students coming and going. Sandra had always found it strange that university students started to bear a resemblance to one another, depending on the subject they studied. As if they answered to a kind of genetic code that identified the group they belonged to and brought out similar characteristics in everyone. For example, law students were undisciplined and competitive, medical students strict and lacking a sense of humour, philosophy students melancholy and always dressed in outsize clothes. Architects, on the other hand, were unkempt and went about with their heads in the clouds.

She had been directed by a porter to Christian Lorieri's office and now she was looking for his name on the plates next to the doors. At Headquarters she had printed the photographs stored in the memory of her mobile phone. There were the pictures of Jeremiah Smith's villa, but also copies of those from David's Leica, which luckily she had duplicated in the bathroom at the guest apartment. There were the images of Lara's apartment and, above all those of the chapel of St Raymond of Penyafort. And to think that she had wanted to erase them, believing they were no use to her! They might well prove vital now.

The door of Lorieri's office was open. He was sitting with his feet on the desk, reading a magazine. He was a handsome man, just as he had appeared in the video. The classic slightly rumpled forty-year-old who drove his female students crazy. The essence of his personality was summed up by the Converse All Stars he wore on his feet. They communicated a message of peaceful revolution.

Smiling, Sandra knocked at the door.

Lorieri looked up from his reading. 'The exam has been moved till next week.'

She sat down without being invited to come in, emboldened by the relaxed climate that prevailed in the room. 'I'm not here for an exam.'

'If you want to discuss your work, you have to come back on an odd-numbered day.'

'And I'm not a student.' She took out her badge. 'Sandra Vega, police.'

Lorieri did not seem surprised and did not lean forward to shake her hand. His one gesture towards politeness was to take his feet off the table. 'Then I should say: What can I do for you, Officer?' He smiled ingratiatingly.

Sandra hated his charm. He reminded her of Schalber, and the poor assistant lecturer could not have imagined at how much of a disadvantage this put him. 'I'm conducting an investigation and I need some advice relating to art. I was told you could help.'

Surprised, Christian Lorieri put his elbows on the table. 'Well, well. What's the case? Is it one I might have read about in the newspapers?'

'That's confidential.'

'I see. Well, I'm at your disposal.' He gave her another smile.

If he does that again, I'll stick my gun in his face, Sandra thought. 'Would you mind taking a look at these and telling me if you recognise the place.' She handed him the photos of the chapel of St Raymond of Penyafort. 'We found them in the pocket of a suspect, and we can't figure out where the photographs were taken.'

Lorieri put on a pair of glasses and started examining the images. He took the photographs from the pile one at a time and then lifted them up in front of him. 'There are tombs, so I'd definitely say a chapel. It's very likely to be in a church.'

Sandra was watching him, waiting for his reaction when the moment came.

'There are various styles, so it's difficult to establish where we are.' He had looked at more than ten images when he came across the first photograph of Lara's apartment. 'There's one here that doesn't seem to . . .' When he saw the second one and the third one, his smile vanished. 'What do you want from me?' he said, without having the courage to look her in the face.

'You've been in that apartment, haven't you?'

He put down the pile of photographs and folded his arms, on the defensive now. 'Only once. Maybe twice.'

'Let's say three times, and stop there. Is that right?' Sandra was being deliberately provocative.

Lorieri nodded.

'Were you there the night Lara disappeared?'

'No, not that night,' he said firmly. 'I'd already dumped her more than two weeks before.'

'Dumped?' Sandra said, horrified.

'I mean . . . Well, you know what I mean: I'm married.'

'Are you reminding me or yourself?'

Lorieri stood up and went to the window. He ran a hand nervously through his hair, keeping the other down by his side. 'When I found out she had disappeared, I wanted to go to the police. But then I thought of all the questions they would ask me and my wife, the rector, the university . . . I knew I wouldn't be able to keep the thing hidden any longer. It would be a tragedy for my career and my family. I thought the whole business was some whim of Lara's, I thought she'd run away to get my attention, and that she'd come back eventually.'

'Did it not occur to you she might have done something rash because of your rejection?'

Lorieri turned his back on her. 'Of course,' he admitted.

'Nearly a month has passed and you haven't said anything.' Sandra made no attempt to hide her disgust.

Lorieri was clearly under pressure now. 'I did offer to help her.'

'To have an abortion, you mean?'

Lorieri knew he was in trouble. 'What else could I have done? It was a fling, nothing more, and Lara knew that. We never went out together, didn't talk on the phone, I didn't even have her number.'

'The fact that you didn't speak up after her disappearance makes you a suspect in her murder.'

'Murder? What are you talking about?' He was beside himself. 'Have you found her body?'

'We don't need to. You have a motive. Sometimes that's all it takes to arrest someone.'

'I haven't killed anyone, damn it.' He was on the verge of tears.

Strangely, Sandra felt sorry for him. In the past she would have applied the law of the good policeman: never believe anyone. But she sensed he was telling the truth: it was Jeremiah Smith who had taken Lara; the way she had been taken from her apartment was too well thought out. If Lorieri had wanted to kill her, he could have simply lured her to an isolated place, Lara would have followed him without question. And even if he had killed her in a fit of madness, perhaps after a quarrel at her apartment, there would have been traces of the murder.

Death is in the details, she remembered. And there was nothing to suggest that Lara was dead.

'Get a grip and sit down, please.'

He looked at Sandra with reddened eyes. 'All right.' He sat down again, sniffing.

Sandra had a good reason to feel compassion for this cowardly adulterer. I'm no different from him, I've cheated too, she told herself, remembering the green tie.

But she had no desire to share that story with Lorieri.

Instead, she said, 'Lara didn't want to present you with a fait accompli. She told you she was pregnant to give you a chance. If she is alive and comes back, please listen to her.'

He was unable to say a word. Sandra quickly recovered the photographs from the desk because she wanted to get out of here. She was putting them back in her bag when she carelessly dropped them.

They scattered over the floor and Lorieri bent down with her to pick them up.

'Let me.'

'It's all right, I can manage.' She noticed that among the photographs that had ended up on the floor was the one of the priest with the scar on his temple.

'The penitenziere.'

She turned to Lorieri, not sure she had heard correctly. 'Do you know this man?'

'Actually I have no idea who he is. I wasn't referring to that one, but to this one.' He picked up another photograph and showed it to her. 'St Raymond of Penyafort. Did you want to know about the chapel, or was that just an excuse?'

Sandra looked at it. It was a photograph of the altarpiece in the chapel, the one that depicted St Raymond himself. 'What can you tell me about this?'

'About the painting, not much: it's from the seventeenth century and it's in the basilica of Santa Maria sopra Minerva. No, actually I was referring to the saint.'

Lorieri stood up, went to the bookcase, and confidently picked a volume from one of the shelves. He leafed through the pages, showed Sandra a reproduction of the painting, then read the caption: '"The *Paenitentiaria Apostolica* is a department of the Holy See dealing with sins. Father Raymond was one of its most prominent members. In the thirteenth century he was given the task of drawing up a text analysing cases of conscience as a guide to confessors. This text was the *Summa de Casibus Penitentiae*, which laid down criteria for evaluation and assigned a specific penitence to each sin."'

Sandra blamed herself for not having looked earlier for information about the chapel. Whoever had slipped that card with the word *Fred* on it under the door of her hotel room hadn't just been trying to draw her into a trap.

The place itself had a meaning.

Even though the idea of going back where a sniper had tried to kill her didn't exactly fill her with enthusiasm, she had to discover what that meaning was.

Clemente's talent was for finding information. In the last few days, Marcus had had more than one confirmation of his abilities. He had never asked him how he did it. He assumed he drew on the archive, but that wasn't the only source. Above him there must be a whole secret network that gathered information. Historically, the Church had always proved itself capable of infiltrating lay institutions and organised groups that might threaten it. It was a form of self-defence.

As Clemente often said, the Vatican was calm on the outside but always vigilant.

But this time his friend had surpassed himself. They were in a bingo hall from whose windows they could keep an eye on the front door of the apartment block where the Martini family lived. The place was full of players, each one concentrating only on his or her own game.

'Alice's father put two large suitcases in his car,' Clemente said, pointing to a Fiat Multipla parked on the other side of the street. 'He was very agitated. He's taken a week off work and withdrawn a considerable sum from the bank.'

'Do you think he's getting ready to escape?'

'It certainly looks suspicious, doesn't it?'

'And what about the gun? How do you know he has one?'

'Last year he shot a man who was trying to lure some children in an amusement park. The only reason he didn't kill him is because the police intervened in time. He ran away, but none of those present at the shooting wanted to testify against him, and the police were unable to charge him because when they searched his apartment they couldn't find the gun. It goes without saying that he doesn't have a licence, which means he must have bought it illegally.'

His name was Bruno Martini. And Marcus remembered that it was in a park that his daughter had disappeared. He shook his head. 'Just what we need. An avenger.'

'After that incident, his wife left him, taking their other child with her. The man has never recovered from Alice's disappearance. For three years he's been conducting a personal investigation, often clashing with the police. By day he works as a bus driver, at night he goes looking for his daughter. He scours places frequented by paedophiles, areas where prostitution is rife, certain he'll find her in the end.'

'I think what he wants to find more than anything is an answer that will give him some peace.' Marcus couldn't help comparing Martini's situation and that of the Roccas. Filippo's parents had not given up when faced with that darkness, they hadn't opened the door wide to it and allowed it to invade their lives. They hadn't tried to meet evil with evil. 'Bruno Martini is going to get himself killed.'

Clemente agreed with him. Astor Goyash was practically unapproachable. His bodyguards would open fire before the man could get anywhere near him. He was deluding himself if he thought he could escape unscathed.

As they waited for Martini to leave the building, Clemente brought Marcus up to date on the other news of the day. 'The police have started looking for Lara.'

He was incredulous. 'Since when?'

'They've linked the disappearance to the cases of Jeremiah Smith. It's partly down to a policewoman from Milan who's working with them.'

Realising this was the same woman with whom he had made a pact, Marcus made no comment. But he found the news encouraging.

'And there's something else: the doctors have ruled out the idea that Jeremiah had a heart attack. They're thinking now that he was poisoned and are carrying out toxicological tests. So you were right.'

'I even know what substance was used,' Marcus said. 'Succinylcholine. It paralyses the muscles, produces an effect similar to a heart attack, and doesn't leave any residue in the blood.' He couldn't help a somewhat self-satisfied expression appearing on his face. 'It seems my mystery colleague was inspired by the suicide of Canestrari.'

Clemente was full of admiration: his pupil was passing every test with flying colours. 'Have you already decided what you're going to do when this whole thing is over?'

What he most wanted was to help others, like that priest from Caritas. But all he said was: 'For now, I'm trying not to think about it.' He would have continued, but Clemente prodded his arm.

'He's coming out.'

They looked through the window and saw Bruno Martini walking towards his car.

Clemente handed Marcus the keys to his Panda. 'Good luck,' he said.

The city was emptying for the dinner hour and the Fiat Multipla kept up a regular speed in the traffic. Marcus managed to stay behind it without too much difficulty, although at a safe distance to avoid being noticed.

According to the road maps Marcus consulted as he drove, Martini was heading out of Rome. But first he stopped at an ATM, which immediately struck Marcus as odd: Clemente had told him Martini had withdrawn money from the bank earlier today. He saw him get back in his car and resume his journey. But after about ten minutes, he stopped again, this time to have a coffee in a bar filled with people watching a match. Bruno Martini didn't appear to know anyone, he didn't greet anyone and nobody seemed to recognise him. After finishing his coffee, he paid and set off yet again. He headed into a restricted traffic area: a sign indicated that the restriction was currently in operation but, heedless of the fine he would incur, he passed beneath the surveillance camera. Marcus had no choice but to follow him. At this point, Martini took the ring road that led to the northern outskirts of Rome. He pulled up at the toll-gate to the motorway and bought his ticket. After a few minutes, he made a third stop, this time for petrol. Marcus waited for him in the layby beyond the petrol station and watched in his rear-view mirror as Martini refuelled calmly at one of the pumps and paid with a credit card. Once again he set off, keeping a constant moderate speed.

'Where is he going?' Marcus wondered. He was starting to feel quite puzzled. The man must have some purpose in mind, but he couldn't work it out.

Martini was driving in the direction of Florence, but after going about six miles, he stopped at another service station. This time Marcus decided to follow him inside. He parked and went in. Martini was sitting at the counter: he had bought a packet of cigarettes and ordered another coffee. Marcus pretended to look through the magazines, all the while peering out from behind the display rack as Martini drank his coffee. When he had finished, he did something that Marcus found hard to interpret.

He looked up and into the lens of a security camera positioned above the cash register, and remained stock still for a few moments.

He's making sure he's being filmed, Marcus thought.

Then Martini put down his cup and took the stairs that led to the toilets, situated on the lower floor. Marcus followed him down. He entered the men's toilet as Martini was washing his hands. Making sure they were alone, he placed himself a couple of wash basins away and turned on the tap. Martini looked at him in the mirror, though without any particular curiosity.

'Is it an alibi you're after, Signor Martini?'

The words took him by surprise. 'Are you talking to me?'

'The ATM, the petrol station, the cafeteria here: all places watched by security cameras. With all those supporters in that bar for the match, someone's bound to have noticed you. And it was a clever idea to risk a fine. Even driving on the motorway: the toll booths record entrances and exits. You want your movements to be traced, you're making sure you're being recorded. But where exactly are you going?'

Martini leaned forward threateningly, anger in his eyes at having been unmasked. 'What do you want from me?'

Marcus held his gaze. 'I want to help you.'

The man was on the verge of hitting him, but held back. His irascible state of mind was obvious in the way he moved his powerful hands, as well as the posture of his shoulders: like a lion preparing to attack. 'Are you police?'

Marcus avoided the question. 'Alberto Canestrari, Astor Goyash. Do you know those names?'

312

Martini didn't have any reaction except bewilderment.

'Do you know them or not?'

'Who the hell are you, can you at least tell me that?'

'You're running away, aren't you? You're no different from me. You're also trying to help someone. Who?'

Bruno Martini took a step back as if he had been hit full in the face. 'I can't.'

'You have to tell me, otherwise everything will be pointless. That person won't get the justice he's looking for. He'll die tonight.' He went closer. 'Who is it?'

Martini leaned on one of the wash basins, and lifted a hand to his forehead. 'She came to me yesterday and told me that her missing son was dead and she knew how to find his killer.'

'Camilla Rocca.' Marcus hadn't expected that.

Martini nodded. 'What happened to both our families three years ago united us. After their disappearance, it was as if Alice and Filippo were brother and sister. Camilla and I met in a police station and since then grief has kept us together. Camilla was close to me when my wife left me. She was the only one who understood. So I couldn't say no when she asked for the gun.'

Marcus couldn't believe it. The family that had bounced back, even bringing a new child into the world: it was all an illusion. Camilla's plan became clear to him now. Taking advantage of the fact that her husband was away, she had kept him in the dark about what she was going to do, so that, if anything happened to her, there would at least be one of them left to look after their child. That was why the little one had not been with her that afternoon. She must have entrusted it to someone's care.

'Camilla knew about your unlicensed gun. You gave it to her and then tried to construct an alibi, in case something went wrong and the police connected the gun to you, given that you'd already used it before.' Marcus knew he had him, there was no way he could withhold the truth now. 'Did Camilla tell you what she was planning?'

'A few days ago she received a phone call. An anonymous voice told her that if she wanted to find the man who'd had her son

Filippo killed, she just had to go to a particular hotel room tonight. The man who ordered the murder is called Astor Goyash.'

'What room, what hotel?' Marcus asked.

Martini continued staring down at his feet. 'I thought it over. There was no guarantee it was the truth, not a joke in bad taste. But doubt makes you believe anything. That silence is unbearable. You just want it to stop. Nobody else can hear it, but for you it's a torture, it drives you mad.'

'Killing someone certainly isn't going to make it stop . . . Tell me where Camilla Rocca is now, I beg you.'

'Hotel Exedra, room 303.'

8.00 p.m.

It was a few degrees colder than it had been in the morning and the change had brought down a very fine mist, made orange by the street lamps. It was like going into a fire: Sandra expected to see the flames appear at any moment.

In the square with the obelisk and the elephant, the faithful were lingering at the end of the Mass. She passed through the middle of the crowd and entered Santa Maria sopra Minerva. Unlike the first time she had been here, the church was not deserted. Tourists and worshippers were still wandering through the basilica. Sandra felt reassured by their presence. She headed straight for the chapel of St Raymond of Penyafort. She needed to understand.

Once again in front of the bare altar, she looked at the portrait of the saint. To its right, the fresco of Christ the judge between two angels, with the votive candles. She wondered how many prayers were being offered up in those little flames, or what sins were being expiated. This time, Sandra understood the meaning of the symbols around her. They represented a court of justice.

The Tribunal of Souls, she thought.

The simplicity of this chapel compared with the others in the basilica conferred the right degree of austerity on the place. The iconography depicted a trial: Christ was the one judge, assisted at his side by the two angels, while St Raymond – the penitenziere – was expounding the case to him.

Sandra smiled to herself. It was clear to her now that the first time she had not been led here by chance. She was no ballistics expert, but she could now be objective about the previous morning's incident. The sound of the gunshots had been lost in the church's echo, preventing her from knowing where the sniper was positioned. But after what had happened in the gallery beneath Lara's apartment, she doubted that somebody had actually wanted to kill her. There in that tunnel she had been a perfect target, but the man hadn't taken advantage of the situation. Something inside her ruled out the possibility that it might have been two different people.

The person who had led her to the basilica had wanted to find out what she knew. David must have made some discovery here: an important piece of information that this person needed to know at all costs. He had used her, taking advantage of the false threat that hung over her life and simultaneously boasting of his friendship with her husband. Then he had betrayed her, with one purpose in mind: using her as bait to catch the penitenziere. That was why he had gone down into that gallery with her. Sandra turned and saw him, surrounded by a group of worshippers.

Schalber was looking straight at her. Although still keeping at a distance, there was no need for him to stay hidden now.

She put her hand on the holster beneath her sweatshirt, to let him know what would happen if he attempted anything. He raised his arms, as if to say he was harmless, and came slowly towards her. He didn't seem hostile.

'What do you want?' she asked.

'I assume you've understood everything by now.'

'What do you want?' she repeated, emphatically.

Schalber looked towards Christ the judge. 'To defend myself.'

'You were the one who fired at me.'

'I slipped that card under the door of your hotel room and drew you here because I wanted David's photographs. But when you set my mobile phone ringing, I realised I had to act or the game would be up. So I improvised.'

'What had my husband discovered about this place?'

'Nothing.'

'So you pretended to have saved my life, you betrayed my trust, you told me a lot of nonsense about the relationship between you and my husband.' She resisted the temptation to add, you slept with me and made me believe you were genuinely fond of me. 'All that, just to get hold of the picture of the priest with the scar on his temple.'

'Yes, I was playing a part, same as you were. I knew you were lying to me. I knew you hadn't shown me all the photographs. Liars are my speciality, remember? There's some kind of pact between you and the priest, isn't there? You're hoping he'll help you get to the truth behind David's murder.'

Sandra was furious. 'That's why you followed me: to see if I was meeting him again.'

'I also followed you to protect you.'

'Stop it!' Sandra's tone was sharp, her expression a mixture of revulsion and resentment. 'I don't want to hear any more lies.'

'There's one thing, though, that you really ought to hear.' Schalber's tone was equally harsh. 'It was a penitenziere who killed your husband.'

She was shaken, but tried not to let him see it. 'It's very convenient for you to tell me that now. Do you expect me to believe you?'

'Aren't you curious as to why the Vatican suddenly decided to abolish the order of penitenzieri? It had to have been serious for the Pope to take such a decision, don't you think? Whatever it was has never been revealed. A kind of . . . side effect of their activities.'

Sandra said nothing, hoping that Schalber would continue.

'The archive of the *Paenitentiaria Apostolica* is a place where evil has been studied, taken apart, analysed. But there's a rule that says each penitenziere only has access to part of it. That's to preserve secrecy, of course, but also so that nobody should have to bear the knowledge of so much wickedness.' Aware that he now had Sandra's full attention, he continued, 'They deluded themselves into thinking that, by putting together the broadest possible record of sins, they'd be able to understand the manifestations of evil in human history. But however hard they tried to classify it, to force it into specific categories, evil found a way to elude every pattern, every attempt to predict it. There were always *anomalies*: small imperfections that needed correcting. So the penitenzieri transformed themselves from mere researchers and archivists into detectives, intervening directly in pursuit of justice. The greatest lesson of the archive, one the priests set great store by, is that *evil generates evil*. Sometimes it's like an unstoppable epidemic, which corrupts men indiscriminately. What the penitenzieri didn't take into account was the possibility that, as human beings, they, too, might be caught up in that process.'

'Do you mean that, over time, evil lead them astray?'

Schalber nodded. 'You can't live in close contact with such a dark force without being influenced by it. There was a reason why the individual penitenzieri weren't allowed to know too much of the archive, a safeguard which unfortunately fell by the wayside over the centuries.' Schalber's tone became friendlier. 'Think about it, Sandra, you're a police officer. Can you always leave behind the things you see at crime scenes? Or does some of that pain, that suffering, that malignity follow you home?'

She remembered David's green tie. She realised that Schalber might be right.

'How many of your colleagues have you seen give up because of that? How many have gone over to the other side? Officers with an impeccable career suddenly taking a bribe from a drug dealer. Policemen you would have trusted with your life beating a suspect half to death to make him talk. Abuses of power, acts of corruption, all committed by men who surrendered, who realised they couldn't help it. No matter how hard they tried, evil always won.'

'They're exceptions.'

'I know, I'm a policeman too. But that doesn't mean it can't happen.'

'And you're saying it happened to the penitenzieri?'

'Father Devok refused to accept it. He continued recruiting priests in secret. He was convinced he could keep control of the situation, but he paid for that naivety with his life.'

317

'So you don't know exactly who killed David. It might even have been the priest with the scar on his temple.'

'I could say yes, but the truth is, I don't know.'

Sandra looked closely at him, trying to tell if he was sincere. Then she laughed and shook her head. 'What an idiot – I almost fell for it again.'

'Don't you believe me?'

She gave him a look filled with hate. 'For all I know, it could even have been you who killed my husband.' She emphasised the words *my husband* as if to mark the difference between him and David, even though that was something she had conveniently forgotten during the night they had spent together.

'What can I do to convince you otherwise? Do you want me to help you find the killer?'

'I've had enough of forming alliances. And besides, there's a simpler way.'

'Go on, tell me.'

'Come with me. There's a superintendent I trust, his name's Camusso. Let's tell him everything, and he can help us.'

Schalber fell silent for a moment as if thinking it over. 'All right, why not? Shall we go now?'

'Why waste time? Walk in front of me as we go out so that I can see you.'

'If that makes you feel any better.'

He set off along the nave. The basilica was about to close and the worshippers were moving towards the central exit. Sandra followed Schalber at a distance of a few feet. Every now and again, he turned to check that she was still behind him. He was walking slowly to let her keep up with him, but he was soon swallowed up by the little crowd that had formed near the door. Sandra kept her eyes on him the whole time. Schalber turned again towards her and made a gesture as if telling her that it wasn't his fault. Sandra, too, was immersed in the flow. She could see his head among the others. Then someone ahead of her fell to the ground. Voices rose in protest: someone had pushed that person. Realising what had happened, Sandra tried to force her way through. She could no longer see the back of Schalber's head. Elbowing her way to the front, she at last managed to get out of the church.

Schalber had vanished.

All it had taken to motivate Camilla Rocca was a phone call. She hadn't needed any proof.

She had a name, Astor Goyash, and that was enough for her.

The Hotel Exedra was in what had once been the Piazza dell'Esedra – so called because it followed the lines of the semi-circular recess, or *exedra*, in the vast baths of Diocletian, the ruins of which could still be seen a short distance away – and since the 1950s had been called the Piazza della Repubblica. But the Romans had never got used to the change and, despite all the time that had passed, continued to use the old name.

The Exedra was a luxury hotel situated on the left-hand side of the square, facing the large Fountain of the Naiads. From the motorway, it took Marcus half an hour to get to his destination. He still hoped he could intercept Camilla before she did something foolish.

He had no idea what might await him. He had not been able to discover the reason for little Filippo's death. This time the message from the mystery penitenziere had not been so clear. 'You're as good as he is,' Clemente had said. 'You're like him.' But it wasn't true. He had never stopped to wonder where his predecessor was currently hiding. Marcus was sure he was watching him, though, judging his every move from a distance. He'll show himself eventually, he thought. He was convinced that they would meet in the end and that the penitenziere would explain everything to him.

He entered the hotel, passing a porter in top hat and livery. The light from the crystal chandeliers was reflected on the precious marble, the furnishings were luxurious. He lingered in the foyer like any other guest, wondering how he could find Camilla.

He saw a large group of young people come in, all wearing

evening dress. At that moment, a bellboy carrying a large package with a red ribbon walked up to the reception desk.

'This is for Astor Goyash.'

The receptionist pointed to the far end of the foyer. 'The birthday party's up on the terrace.'

At last Marcus understood the meaning of the gift-wrapped package he had seen in Camilla Rocca's house, as well as the purchase of a new dress: they were ploys designed to get her into the Exedra without looking too conspicuous.

He saw the bellboy getting into line together with other guests in front of the lift leading directly to the terrace. The two thugs who had followed Marcus to Dr Canestrari's surgery and then to the clinic were there, keeping an eye on those going up.

Astor Goyash would be there this evening. With these security measures, it would be impossible to get close to him. But the mystery penitenziere had supplied Camilla with an alternative.

Marcus had to get to room 303 before she did.

The main door of the hotel opened and a large group of bodyguards came in, surrounding a shortish man of about seventy with grey hair, a tanned and heavily lined face and glacial eyes.

Astor Goyash.

Marcus looked around, afraid Camilla might appear at any moment. But it didn't happen. Goyash was escorted to another lift. When the doors closed behind him, Marcus realised he had to be quick. Very soon his presence would be noticed by the surveillance cameras and the hotel's security staff would approach him discreetly to find out why he was here. He went to the receptionist and asked for the room he had reserved a little earlier using Bruno Martini's mobile phone. Asked for identification, Marcus showed the false Vatican City diplomatic passport Clemente had given him at the beginning of his training.

'Is Signora Camilla Rocca here yet?'

The receptionist looked at him, unsure whether or not to give him this information. Marcus sustained his gaze and in the end the receptionist limited himself to admitting that the lady had checked in one hour earlier. For Marcus that was sufficient. He thanked him and was given an electronic key: his room was on the second floor. He walked to another row of lifts, one not being watched by Goyash's men. Once in the lift, however, he pressed the button for the third floor.

The doors opened to reveal a long corridor. He looked around, but there were no bodyguards in sight. That immediately struck him as strange. Reading the numbers of the rooms, he headed for 303. He turned a corner, and after another ten yards came to the room. There was no one on guard, which again struck him as odd. Maybe they were inside with Goyash. A DO NOT DISTURB sign hung on the electronic lock. Marcus, unsure what to do, knocked. After about twenty seconds, a female voice asked him who was there.

'Hotel security. Sorry to disturb you, but the smoke detector in your room has triggered an alarm.'

There was a click, and the door was opened, much to Marcus's surprise, by a young blonde girl, fourteen at most. She was half naked, wrapped in a sheet, and had the misty-eyed look of someone on drugs.

'All I did was light a cigarette,' she said. 'I didn't think I was doing anything wrong.'

'No need to worry, but I do have to check.' Without waiting for an invitation, he moved her aside and entered.

It was a suite. The first room was a reception room with a dark parquet floor. There was a lounge area with a huge plasma TV set and a cocktail cabinet. A number of gift-wrapped packages were piled in a corner. Marcus took a look around: apart from the girl there didn't seem to be anybody here.

'Is Signor Goyash about?'

'He's in the bathroom. I can call him if you like.'

Marcus ignored the suggestion and headed for the bedroom.

Disconcerted, the girl followed him, forgetting to close the main door of the suite. 'Hey, where are you going?'

There was a large unmade bed. On a coffee table he glimpsed a mirror with lines of cocaine and a rolled-up banknote. There was a TV in here, too. It was on, and playing music videos at high volume.

'Get out of here, now,' he said to the girl.

He put his hand over her mouth and looked straight at her to make it clear to her that there was no point protesting. Now she was scared. Marcus approached the door of the bathroom and pointed to it. The girl nodded: Goyash was in there. The volume of the TV prevented him from hearing what was happening on the other side.

'Is he armed?'

The girl shook her head. Marcus realised she was the reason the old Bulgarian had temporarily got away from his bodyguards. A little present of sex and cocaine before the birthday party.

He was about to ask the girl to leave, when he turned and saw Camilla Rocca standing in the doorway of the suite. At her feet was the open gift package. In her hands, a gun. In her eyes, a dark gleam of hatred.

Instinctively, he reached out his hand to stop her. The girl gave a scream that was drowned by the deafening rock music from the TV. Marcus pushed her aside and she went and took shelter behind a corner of the bed, terrified.

Camilla was taking deep breaths, as if trying to summon up strength. 'Astor Goyash?' Obviously, she knew he ought to have been a man of seventy.

Marcus tried to remain calm and make her see reason. 'I know your story. You won't solve anything this way.'

The woman noticed the light filtering under the door of the bath-room. 'Who's in there?' She raised the gun in that direction.

Marcus knew that, as soon as it was open, she would shoot. 'Listen to me. Think of your new child. What's its name?' He was trying to gain time, to shift her attention on to something that would make her hesitate. But Camilla didn't reply. She was still staring straight at the door. He tried again: 'Think of your husband. You can't leave the two of them alone in the world.'

The first tears welled in Camilla's eyes. 'Filippo was such a sweet child.'

Marcus decided to be blunt with her. 'What do you think will happen when you've pulled the trigger? How do you think you'll feel afterwards? I'll tell you: it won't change anything. Everything will be exactly the same as it is now. There's no relief in store for you. Things will still be hard. And what will you have gained?'

'There's no other way to get justice.'

Marcus knew the woman was right. There was nothing to link Astor Goyash and Canestrari to Filippo. The one piece of evidence – the bone he had found at the clinic – had been taken by Goyash's men. 'There'll never be justice,' he said in a firm but compassionate tone, with a tinge of resignation, because he feared he wouldn't be able to prevent the worst. 'But revenge isn't the only possibility left to you.' He recognised in her the same look he had seen in Raffaele Altieri's eyes when he shot his father, the same determination Pietro Zini had shown when he had executed Federico Noni instead of turning him in to the police. This time, too, it was all pointless – the door of the bathroom would open and Camilla would pull the trigger.

They saw the handle turning. The light inside went off and the door opened wide. The girl screamed from the bed. The target appeared in the doorway. He was wearing a snow-white dressing gown, he stared at the barrel of the gun in sudden confusion, and his icy eyes melted in an instant. But he wasn't an old man of seventy.

He was a boy of fifteen.

There was confusion and dismay all round. Marcus looked at Camilla, who stared at the boy. 'Where's Astor Goyash?' she asked.

He replied in such a thin voice that they couldn't make out what he was saying.

'Where's Astor Goyash?' Camilla repeated angrily, brandishing the gun in his direction.

The boy said, 'I'm Astor Goyash.'

'No, you aren't,' she replied, disbelieving.

'You must mean my grandfather . . . My birthday party's upstairs, he's there now.'

Camilla realised her mistake and for a moment she looked unsteady on her feet. Marcus took advantage of this to go to her, put his hand on the gun, and make her slowly lower it. The woman's exhausted eyes lowered at the same time. 'Let's go,' he said to her.

'There's nothing else to do here. You're not going to kill the boy just because his grandfather is somehow involved in your son's death, are you? That would be gratuitous cruelty, not revenge. And I know you're not capable of that.'

Camilla was thinking about this when she stopped suddenly. She had noticed something.

Marcus followed the direction of her gaze and saw that she was again looking at the boy, staring at his bare chest as revealed by the opening of his dressing gown. She advanced and he retreated, until he found himself with his back to the wall. Camilla gently moved aside the lapels, uncovering the long scar on his chest.

A shiver went through Marcus, taking his breath away for a moment. My God, what did they do?

Three years earlier, Astor Goyash's grandson had been the same age as Filippo Rocca. Alberto Canestrari was a surgeon. He had killed Filippo on commission in order to procure a heart for this boy.

Camilla couldn't have known that, Marcus told himself. But some premonition, maternal instinct, a sixth sense – had driven her to make that gesture, even though she didn't seem to fully understand why.

She put her hand on the boy's chest, and he let her. She stood there, feeling the throb of that heart. A sound coming from another place, another life.

Camilla and the boy looked at each other. Was she looking for something deep in his eyes, a light that told her that her son was still there? Or perhaps the revelation that Filippo, too, could somehow see her at that moment?

Marcus didn't know, but he realised that the only evidence that could link old Astor Goyash to the child's death was encased in his grandson's chest. A biopsy taken from the boy's heart and a DNA comparison with Filippo's family, and they could nail him. But Marcus was not sure that such justice would be any consolation to this poor mother. The grief would be agonising. So he decided to keep silent. All he wanted right now was to take Camilla out of the room. The woman had another child to think about now.

He summoned the courage to break the contact between her and young Goyash. He took her by the shoulders with the intention of leading her to the door.

She gently removed her palm from the boy's chest, as if in a last farewell.

Then she walked to the door with Marcus. They went along the corridor, heading for the lift. Unexpectedly, Camilla now turned to her saviour and seemed to see him for the first time. 'I know you. You're a priest, aren't you?'

Marcus was taken aback and didn't know what to reply. He simply nodded, waiting for the rest.

'He told me about you,' she went on.

Realising that she was referring to the mystery penitenziere, Marcus let her continue.

'A week ago on the telephone he told me I would meet you here.' Camilla tilted her head and looked at him with a strange expression: she seemed to be afraid for him. 'He asked me to tell you that the two of you will meet where it all began. *But this time you'll have to look for the devil.*'

10.07 p.m.

She had caught the number 52 bus from the terminus in the Piazza San Silvestro, and got off near the Via Paisiello. There she had taken the 911 to the Piazza Euclide. She had gone down into the station and caught the local train from Viterbo to Rome, which at that point went underground, connecting the northern zone of the city with the centre. She had got off at the only stop on that stretch of the line, Piazza Flaminio, and changed to the Metro in the direction of Anagnina. Getting off at Furio Camillo, she had come back out on to the surface and called a taxi.

Each transfer had taken only a few minutes and the route had been dictated by chance, just to throw any possible pursuers off the scent.

Sandra didn't trust Schalber. He had shown a certain skill in predicting her moves. Although he had managed to escape on the way out of Santa Maria sopra Minerva, she was sure he must still be lurking somewhere, trying to get back on her trail. But the tricks she had adopted should have been sufficient to throw him off. Because she still had one more thing to do tonight before she went back to her hotel.

She had to pay a visit to a new acquaintance.

The taxi dropped her in front of the main entrance of the Gemelli hospital. Sandra followed the signs until she reached the small building that housed intensive care – the department that the staff of the Gemelli knew as 'the border'.

She went through the first door, a sliding one, and found herself in a waiting room with four rows of plastic chairs, one joined to the other, as blue as the walls that surrounded them. Even the heaters were the same colour, as well as the coats of the doctors and nurses, and even the drinking water dispenser. The effect was an incomprehensible monotony of colour.

The second door was a security door. To get to the heart of the building – intensive care – you had to have a special magnetic card that opened the lock electronically. There was a policeman on guard here, a reminder that the department housed a number of dangerous individuals, even though they were currently unable to harm anyone. Sandra flashed her badge at her colleague, and a nurse showed her the procedure for visitors, making her put on overshoes, a white coat and a cap. Then she activated the door to admit her.

The long corridor that stretched out ahead of her reminded her at first of an aquarium, like the one in Genoa she had visited a couple of times with David. She loved fish, she could watch them for hours, letting herself be hypnotised by their movements. In front of her now she had a series of goldfish bowls, which were in fact the recovery rooms, each behind a glass partition. The lights were low, and there was a strange silence over everything. If you listened hard, you realised that it was in fact made up of sounds. As quiet as breathing and as rhythmic and constant as a submerged heartbeat.

326

The place seemed to be asleep.

She walked along the linoleum floor of the corridor and came to the nurses' station, where two nurses sat in the gloom in front of a console, their faces reflecting the gleam of the monitors tracking the patients' vital signs. Behind them, a young doctor was sitting at a steel desk, writing.

Two nurses and a doctor: that was all the staff needed to keep an eye on the ward at night. Sandra introduced herself and asked for directions, which they gave her.

As she passed the goldfish bowls, she looked at the men inside them, lying in their beds as if swimming in a sea of silence.

She headed for the last of them. As she approached it, she realised that someone was watching her from the other side. A short young woman, about the same age as her, in a white coat, stood up and came to the door. There were six beds in the room, only one of which was occupied. By Jeremiah Smith. He was intubated and his chest rose and fell regularly. He looked much older than his fifty years.

The young woman looked straight at the newcomer. Seeing her face, Sandra had a sense of déjà vu. After a moment, she remembered where she had seen her before, and the memory sent a shiver through her. The monster was being visited by the ghost of one of his victims.

'Teresa,' she said.

The young woman smiled. 'I'm Monica, her twin sister.'

This wasn't just the sister of one of the poor innocents killed by Jeremiah, this was also the doctor who had saved his life.

'My name's Sandra Vega, I'm with the police.' She held out her hand.

Monica shook it. 'Is this the first time you've come here?'

'Is it that obvious?'

'Yes, from the way you were looking at him.'

Sandra turned to look at Jeremiah Smith again. 'Why, how was I looking at him?'

'I don't know. Maybe the way you'd look at a goldfish in an aquarium.'

Sandra shook her head, amused.

'Did I say something wrong?'

'No, nothing. Don't worry.'

'I come here every evening. Before starting the night shift or when I've finished the day shift. I stay here for fifteen minutes, then go. I don't know why I do it. I want to, and that's it.'

Sandra admired Monica's courage. 'Why did you save him?'

'Why do all of you ask me the same thing?' Monica retorted, although not in an unpleasant way. 'The right question should be: why didn't I let him die? They're two different things, don't you think?'

'Yes.' She hadn't thought of it that way.

'If you asked me whether I'd like to kill him now, I'd reply that I'd do it if I didn't fear the consequences. But what would have been the point of letting him die without intervening? A normal person getting to the end of his life should pass away naturally. He's not a normal person. He doesn't deserve it. My sister didn't get that chance.'

Sandra was forced to reflect. She was looking for David's killer, and she kept telling herself that it was in order to get at the truth, to find some meaning in her husband's death. To get justice. But how would she have behaved in Monica's place?

'No,' Monica continued, 'my greatest revenge is to see him in that bed. No trial, no jury. No law, no technicalities. No psychiatric reports, no extenuating circumstances. True revenge is in knowing that he'll stay like this, imprisoned in himself. That's a prison he certainly won't escape from. And I'll be able to come and see him every day, look him in the face and tell myself that justice has been done.' She turned to Sandra. 'How many of those who've lost loved ones through other people's wickedness have been granted the same privilege?'

'Yes, you're right.'

'I was the one who gave him cardiac massage. I put my hands on his chest, on those words . . . *Kill me.*' She choked back her revulsion. 'The smell of his faeces, his urine, was on my clothes, his saliva was on my fingers.' She paused. 'In my job, you see many things. Illness is a great leveller. But the truth is that we doctors don't save anyone.

Each person saves himself. Choosing the right life to lead, the right path to go down. For all of us, the time comes when we're covered in faeces and urine. And it's sad if we don't discover who we are until that day.'

Sandra was surprised at so much wisdom. And yet Monica was more or less her age and seemed quite fragile. She wished she could stay and listen to her some more.

But Monica looked at her watch. 'I'm sorry I've kept you. I'd better go, my shift will be starting soon.'

'It was a pleasure to meet you. I've learned a lot from you tonight.'

Monica smiled. 'Even slaps in the face teach you to grow, as my father always says.'

Sandra watched her as she walked away down the deserted corridor. Once again an idea materialised in her head. But she continued to dismiss it. She was convinced that Schalber had killed her husband. And she had slept with him. But she had needed those caresses. David would have understood.

She took a mask from a sterile container and put it on, then went through the door into that little hell that contained only one damned soul.

She counted the steps as she approached Jeremiah Smith's bed. Six. No, seven. She stared at him. The goldfish was within reach. His eyes were closed, surrounded by an icy indifference. The man was no longer in a position to arouse either fear or compassion.

There was an armchair next to the bed. Sandra sat down in it. She placed her elbows on her knees, put her fingers together, and leaned towards him. She would have liked to read his mind, to understand what had driven him to evil. When you came down to it, that was what the penitenzieri's work consisted of: scrutinising the human heart in search of the underlying motives for every act. She, on the other hand, as a forensic photographer, examined the outward signs, the wounds that evil left on the world.

She was reminded of the dark photograph in the roll from the Leica.

That's my limit, she told herself. Without that image, irretrievably lost perhaps because of an error as it was being taken, she couldn't go any further along the path indicated to her by David.

God alone knew what there had been in that photograph.

Outward appearances were her source of information, but they were also her limitation. She realised how much good it would do her for once to be able to look inside and draw everything out, trying to find a path to forgiveness. If nothing else, a confession would be liberating. That was why, suddenly, she started talking to Jeremiah Smith. 'I want to tell you a story about a green tie.' She didn't know why she had said it, it had simply come out. 'It all goes back to a few weeks before my husband was killed. David had come back from a long assignment abroad. That evening seemed like all the other times we saw each other after a long absence. We celebrated, just the two of us. The rest of the world was shut out, and we were the last two members of the human race. Do you know what I mean, have you ever felt that?' She shook her head, amused. 'No, of course not. But that evening, for the first time since we had known each other, I had to pretend to love him. David asked me a routine question. 'How are you, everything all right?' How many times we ask each other that every day, and we never expect to get an honest answer. But when I told him that everything was fine, it wasn't just a polite phrase: it was a lie ... A few days earlier I had been in hospital having an abortion.' Sandra could feel the tears welling up in her eyes, but she held them back. 'We had everything it takes to be fantastic parents: we loved each other, we were sure of each other. But he was a reporter, always off photographing wars, revolutions and massacres. I was a policewoman working for forensics. You can't bring a child into the world if your work makes you risk your life, as was the case with David, or if you see all the things I'm forced to see, every day, at crime scenes. All that violence, all that fear: that wasn't good for a child.' She said this with great conviction, and without a trace of regret. 'And that's my sin. I'll carry it with me as long as I live. But what I can't forgive myself is that I didn't allow David to have a say in the matter. I took advantage of his absence to decide.' Sandra gave a sad smile. 'When I got back home after the abortion, I found in the bathroom the pregnancy test I had done on my own. My child, or the thing they had pulled out of me – I don't know what it was after barely a month – had stayed in that hospital. I'd felt it die inside me, and then I'd left it there alone. That's terrible, don't you think? In any case, I thought that creature deserved at least a funeral. So I took a box and in it I put the pregnancy test and a series of objects that had belonged to its mother and father. Among them, David's only tie. The green one. Then I drove from Milan to Tellaro, the village in Liguria where we used to spend our holidays. And I threw everything in the sea.' She took a deep breath. 'I never told anyone. And it seems absurd that you should be the person I'm telling it to. But now comes the good part. Because I was convinced that I'd be the only one to pay the price for what I'd done. Instead of which, without knowing it, I'd brought about a disaster that couldn't be remedied. I didn't realise until later, when it was too late. Together with the love I could have felt for my child, I'd also thrown away the love I felt for David.' She wiped away a tear. 'It just didn't work: I kissed him, I caressed him, I made love with him and I didn't feel anything. The nest that child had started to build inside me in order to survive had become a void. I only started loving my husband again when he was dead.'

She crossed her arms over her chest, and bowed her head. Sunk in that uncomfortable position, she started to sob. The tears came out of her in one great uninterrupted flow. But it was liberating. She couldn't stop. It lasted a few minutes, then, as she blew her nose and tried to compose herself, she laughed at herself. She was exhausted. But, incomprehensibly, she felt good here. Another five minutes, she told herself, only five. The regular beep of the cardiograph connected to Jeremiah Smith's chest, the cadence of the respirator that was keeping him alive, worked their hypnotic, relaxing spell on her. She closed her eyes for a moment and, without realising it, fell asleep. She saw David. His smile. His dishevelled hair. His kindly eyes. That grimace he made whenever he found her looking a bit sad or thoughtful, jutting out his lower lip and tilting his head to the side. David took her face in his hands and pulled her to him to give her one of his long kisses. 'It's all right, Ginger.' She felt relieved, at peace. Then he waved at her and walked away. Dancing and singing their song: 'Cheek to Cheek'. Even though the voice seemed like David's, in her dream Sandra didn't know that it belonged to someone else. And that it was quite real.

Someone was singing in the room.

10.17 p.m.

After seeing Camilla Rocca unexpectedly place her hand on the chest of the boy who had inherited her son's heart, Marcus, for the first time, sensed an invisible, compassionate force intervening in his life. We are so insignificant in the immensity of the universe that we don't seem to deserve the privilege of a God who might be interested in us. That was what he had always told himself. But now he was changing his mind.

We will meet where it all began.

He would see his antagonist face to face. He would receive the prize of Lara's salvation.

And the place where it had all begun was Jeremiah Smith's villa.

He parked the Panda outside the main gate. There were no longer any policemen guarding the entrance, and the forensics team had moved out a little while earlier. The place was desolate and melancholy, just as it must have been before it had revealed its secret. Marcus walked towards the house. Only the full moon fought the power of darkness.

The trees in the drive swayed in the cool night breeze. The rustling leaves were like fleeting laughter, mocking him as he passed then fading behind him. The statues that adorned the untended garden stared at him with their empty eyes.

He reached the villa. Seals had been placed on its doors and windows. He wasn't actually expecting the penitenziere to be waiting for him here. The mandate in the message was clear.

This time you'll have to look for the devil.

This was his last test. In return, he would obtain the answers.

Did those words mean that he would have to look for a supernatural sign? But he told himself once again that the penitenzieri were not interested in the existence of the devil, in fact they were the only people in the Church to doubt it. They had always considered him a convenient pretext, invented by human beings to evade responsibility for their own sins and to absolve the defects of their own nature.

The devil only exists because men are wicked.

He removed the seals from the door and entered the house. The moonlight did not follow him inside, but stopped at the threshold. There were no noises or presences.

He took the torch from his pocket and made his way along the dark corridor. He recalled his first visit, when he had followed the trail of the numbers behind the paintings. And yet he must have missed something if the penitenziere had wanted him to come back. He pushed on as far as the room where Jeremiah Smith had been found dying.

The devil doesn't live here any more, he told himself.

A few things were missing from the previous time. The overturned table, the broken cup and the crumbs had been removed by forensics. Along with the materials – sterile gloves, pieces of gauze, syringes and cannulas – used by the ambulance crew when they had tried to revive him. Also gone were the souvenirs – the hair ribbon, the coral bracelet, the pink scarf and the roller skate – with which the monster had invoked the ghosts of his young victims to keep him company during his long nights of solitude.

But if the objects were gone, the questions remained.

How had Jeremiah Smith – a limited, antisocial man, devoid of any kind of attraction – managed to gain the trust of these girls? Where had he kept them prisoner for a month before killing them? Where was Lara?

Marcus avoided asking himself if she was still alive. He had carried out his own task with the greatest devotion, so he wouldn't accept a different outcome.

He looked around. *Anomalies.* The sign isn't supernatural, he told himself, but some detail that only a man of faith could recognise. This time he had to call on a talent he was afraid he didn't possess.

His eyes roamed the room, looking for anything that stood out. A small crack that led into another dimension. The breach utilised by evil to spread.

There is a place where the world of light meets the world of darkness . . . I am the guardian appointed to defend that border. But every now and again something manages to get through.

His eyes came to rest on the window. Beyond it, the moon was showing him the way.

The stone angel, unfolding its wings and looking in his direction. Summoning him.

It was in the middle of the garden, together with the other statues. According to the Scriptures, Lucifer was an angel before he fell. The Lord's favourite. Remembering that, Marcus ran outside.

He stopped in front of the tall figure, which was lit by a pale glimmer of moonlight.

The police hadn't noticed a thing, he told himself, examining the ground at the foot of the angel. If there's something under here, the dogs ought to have scented it. But because of the persistent rain of the last few days the odours given off by the earth might have confused the animals' sense of smell.

Marcus put his hands on the base of the statue, pushed it, and the angel moved, revealing beneath it an iron trapdoor. It was not locked. All he had to do was lift the handle.

Darkness. A strong smell of damp rose like a fetid breath from that hole. Marcus aimed his torch: six steps led to the abyss. No voice, though. No noise.

'Lara!' he called. Then three more times. Then once again. But there was no answer.

He went down the steps.

The beam of light illumined a narrow space, with a low ceiling and a tiled floor that dipped at a certain point. It must have been a swimming pool once, but somebody had turned it into a secret room.

Marcus moved his torch around in search of a human presence. He feared now that he would find merely a silent corpse. But Lara was not here.

Only a chair.

That was another reason the dogs didn't scent anything, he told himself. But it was here that Jeremiah brought them. This was the lair where he kept them prisoner for a month before killing them. There were no chains on the walls, no devices for giving vent to his sadistic impulses, no alcoves in which to have sex. No torture, no violence, Marcus reminded himself: Jeremiah didn't touch them. Everything was reduced to that chair. Next to it was the rope he used to tie them up and a tray with the knife, some eight inches long, with which he cut their throats. That was the extent of his perverted imagination.

Marcus went closer to the chair and saw that there was a closed envelope on it. He picked it up and opened it. Inside were the original plans of Lara's apartment, including the location of the trapdoor in the bathroom, a list of her movements and timetable, notes that mentioned the plan to hide the drug in the sugar, and finally a photograph of Lara smiling. Over her face, a question mark had been scrawled in red. You're mocking me, Marcus said to himself, addressing the penitenziere. The contents of the envelope were incontrovertible evidence that Jeremiah really had taken the girl.

But of Lara herself there was no trace. Nor of his mysterious companion who had led him here.

Marcus was seething with rage. The penitenziere had failed at his task. He cursed him, and cursed himself. The mockery was unbearable. He didn't want to stay a moment longer in this place. He turned to go out again, but the torch slipped from his hands. As it fell, it lit up something behind him.

Someone was in the corner.

He had been watching the scene. And he wasn't moving. In the beam of light, all that could be seen was the outline of an arm, clad in black. Marcus bent down to pick up the torch and slowly lifted it to the stranger.

It wasn't a person, but a priest's cassock on a hanger.

335

Everything suddenly became clear. That was how Jeremiah Smith had approached his victims. The girls had not feared him because they had seen, not a monster, but a man of the cloth.

One of the pockets of the cassock was bulging. Marcus approached and put his hand in. He took out a small medicine bottle and a hypodermic syringe – *succinylcholine*.

He hadn't been mistaken. And yet the objects in that pocket told a different story.

Jeremiah did it all himself.

He had known that the sister of one of his victims was on duty that night. So he had called the emergency number describing the symptoms of a heart attack. He had waited for the arrival of the paramedics before he injected the poison. He could even have thrown the syringe in a corner of the room or under a piece of furniture: the ambulance team in their excitement wouldn't have noticed and forensics would have confused it with the waste material left by the doctor and paramedic after their intervention.

He didn't disguise himself as a priest. He is a priest.

The beginning of his plan must have gone back to about a week earlier, when he had sent the anonymous notes to those involved in the murder of Valeria Altieri. Then he had sent the email that had informed Pietro Zini about the Figaro case. And then he had called Camilla Rocca to inform her that Astor Goyash would be at the Hotel Exedra a few days later.

He is the penitenziere.

All the time they had had him in front of their eyes without knowing who he really was. Just like Dr Alberto Canestrari, Jeremiah had simulated a natural death with the succinylcholine. No toxicological test would locate it. All you needed was a one-milligram dose to block the respiratory muscles. A few minutes and you choked to death, as had happened with Canestrari. The drug provoked immediate bodily paralysis, leaving no room for second thoughts.

But Canestrari hadn't planned for any ambulance team to come to his aid. Whereas Jeremiah had.

What do the police see? A serial killer who no longer constitutes a threat. What do the doctors see? A patient in a coma. What did Marcus see?

Anomalies.

Sooner or later, the effects of the succinylcholine would wear off. At any moment Jeremiah Smith would wake up.

11.59 p.m.

Forward. Stop. Back. Then again. Forward, stop, turned back.

In the blue waiting room of the intensive care department, that was the only sound, loud and repetitive. Marcus looked around. The place was deserted. He advanced cautiously towards the source of the noise.

The sliding security door that led to the department moved forward, suddenly stopped, and turned back. Repeating the same movement over and over, without ever completing it. Something was stopping the door from closing. Marcus approached to see what it was.

It was a foot.

The policeman who had been on guard was lying on the floor, face down. Marcus looked at the body – the hands, the blue uniform, the rubber-soled shoes – and realised that something was missing. It was his head, he didn't have a head. The cranium had exploded after receiving a bullet at point-blank range.

He's only the first, Marcus told himself.

He leaned over the policeman and saw that his belt holster was empty. He uttered a rapid benediction and straightened up again. He walked slowly along the linoleum floor of the corridor, looking at the recovery rooms on either side. The patients all lay on their backs asleep, impassive and unconcerned. The machines were breathing for them. Everything appeared unchanged.

Marcus moved through that unreal stillness. Hell must be like this, he thought. A place where life is no longer life but nor is it death. Only hope kept it going. It was like a conjuring trick. The essence of the illusion was the question you asked yourself looking

337

at these individuals. Where are they? Because they were here, and yet they weren't.

When he got to the nurses' station, he came across three people who hadn't been as lucky as the patients they were looking after. Or maybe they had, depending on your point of view.

The first nurse was lying back on the control console. She had a deep wound in her throat, and the monitors were stained with her blood. The second was lying next to the door. She had tried to run away, but in vain: a bullet had hit her in the chest, sending her flying backwards. At the far end of the station, a man in a white coat sat slumped in his chair, his arms dangling, his head thrown back and his eyes staring up at the ceiling.

The room that housed Jeremiah Smith was the last one at the end. He headed towards it, sure he would find an empty bed.

'Come in.' The voice that had called to him was low and hoarse, the voice of someone who has been intubated for three days. 'You're a penitenziere, aren't you?' For a few seconds Marcus was unable to move. Then he pushed on slowly to the open door that awaited him. Passing the glass partition, he saw that the curtains had been drawn. But behind it he could see a shadow in the centre of the room. He took up a position next to the door, in the shelter of the wall.

'Come in. Don't be afraid.'

'You're armed,' Marcus replied. 'I know, I checked the policeman's holster.'

Silence. Then he saw something slide towards his feet through the door. It was a gun.

'Check it: it's loaded.'

Taken by surprise, Marcus didn't know how to react. Why had Smith handed over his gun? It didn't look as if he was surrendering. This is his game, he remembered. And I have no choice, I have to play it. 'Does that mean you're unarmed?'

The gunshot was deafening. The answer was an eloquent one. He was armed.

'How do I know you won't shoot me as soon as I come through the door?'

'It's the only way if you want to save her.'

'Tell me where Lara is.'

A laugh. 'I wasn't actually talking about Lara.'

Marcus froze. Who was with him? He decided to put his head in for a moment to check.

Jeremiah Smith was sitting on the bed, wearing a hospital gown that was too short for him. His sparse hair was combed straight across his head. He had the clown-like appearance of someone who had just woken up. With one hand he was scratching his thigh, while with the other he was holding a gun aimed at the back of the neck of a woman kneeling in front of him.

The policewoman was with him.

Knowing now where the second gun came from, Marcus stepped forward.

Sandra had on her wrists the handcuffs Jeremiah had taken from the policeman on guard after shooting him. Like an idiot, she had fallen asleep. She had been woken by three gunshots in rapid succession. She had opened her eyes and immediately searched for her gun in her holster, but it wasn't there.

It was only then that she had realised the bed was empty.

A fourth shot and the whole scene had flashed in front of her eyes, as if she were photographing it with her camera. Jeremiah gets up, steals her gun. He passes the nurses' station and executes the nurses and doctor on night shift. The policeman at the entrance hears the shots. In the time it takes him to open the security lock, Jeremiah is already at the door. As soon as it opens, he shoots the officer at point-blank range.

She had rushed out of the room, thinking she could somehow stop him even though she was unarmed. Though she knew it made no sense, she felt in some way responsible for yielding to her fatigue, for not staying alert. But perhaps there was also something else.

Why didn't he kill me, too?

She hadn't seen him in the corridor. She had rushed to the exit. It was as she passed the room where drugs were stored that she had spotted him. There he was, looking at her with a nasty smile. She had been taken aback. Then he had pointed the gun at her and thrown her the handcuffs.

'Put them on, we're going to have some fun.'

She had done as she was told and the waiting had begun.

Now, from the floor of the recovery room, Sandra looked up at the priest with the scar on his temple, telling him silently that she was fine and he shouldn't worry. He nodded to let her know that he had grasped the message.

Another laugh from Jeremiah. 'Well? Happy to see me? I've wanted for so long to meet another penitenziere. For a long time I thought I was the only one. I'm sure it was the same for you. What's your name?'

Marcus had no desire to grant him any concessions.

'Come on,' Jeremiah insisted. 'You know my name. It's only right I should know the name of the person who's been so clever as to track me down.'

'Marcus,' he said, and immediately regretted it. 'Let the woman go.'

Jeremiah turned grave. 'Sorry, Marcus, my friend. She's part of the plan.'

'What plan?'

'Actually, it was a pleasant surprise to get a visit from her. I had intended to take one of the nurses hostage, but given that she was here . . . What is it we call them?' He raised his forefinger to his lip and looked up, pretending that he couldn't remember. 'Oh yes: anomalies.'

Marcus said nothing, refusing to humour him.

'The presence of this young lady is the confirmation that the theory is correct.'

'What theory?'

'"Evil generates evil." Didn't anyone ever tell you that?' He gave a grimace of disapproval. 'You see, I never expected to meet her. Although I did meet her husband a while back.'

Sandra raised her eyes to look at him.

'David Leoni was a good reporter, there's no denying that,' Jeremiah went on. 'He had unearthed the story of the penitenzieri. I followed him from a distance, learning a lot from him. It was ... instructive getting to know all those details of his private life.' He looked at Sandra. 'While your husband was in Rome, I went to Milan to meet you: I got into your apartment, I searched among your things, and you didn't even notice.'

Sandra remembered the song sung by the killer on David's recorder: 'Cheek to Cheek'. She had always wondered how that monster had managed to learn such a private piece of information.

Guessing her thoughts, Jeremiah confirmed them. 'Yes, my dear, I was the one who made an appointment with your husband in that abandoned building site. The fool had been taking precautions, but he trusted me because he believed that all priests, basically, are good. I get the feeling he changed his mind just before he crashed to the ground.'

Sandra had suspected Schalber. Now the truth hit her. She seethed at the cavalier manner in which Jeremiah dismissed David's death and the realisation that she had confided her innermost secret to her husband's killer. He hadn't been in a coma and had heard the story of the abortion and how it had preyed on her conscience. Having already taken the rest, he now possessed yet another part of her and David.

'He had discovered the penitenzieri's archive,' Jeremiah said, in justification. 'You understand, Marcus, surely? I couldn't let him live.'

Now Sandra knew what the motive was, and if the man who was holding a gun at the back of her neck was a penitenziere, then Schalber had been right. He had told her it was one of them who had killed David, and she hadn't believed him. Over time, evil had corrupted them.

'Anyway, his wife came to Rome to avenge him. But she would never admit it. Isn't that right, Sandra?'

She looked at him with hate-filled eyes.

'I could have let you believe it was an accident,' Jeremiah said.

'Instead I gave you the opportunity to find out the truth and track me down.'

'Where's Lara?' Marcus interrupted him. 'Is she all right? Is she still alive?'

'When I planned all this I thought you'd come here once you found my hiding place at the villa and ask me that question.' He paused and smiled at him. 'Because I know where the girl is.'

'Then tell me.'

'All in good time, my friend. Alternatively, if you hadn't discovered my plan by tonight, I would have felt perfectly justified in getting up from this bed and disappearing forever.'

'I figured out your plan, I've been equal to the task. So why not let this woman go and hand over Lara?'

'Because it's not as simple as that: you have to make a choice.'

'What choice?'

'I have a gun, you have a gun. You have to decide who will die tonight.' With the barrel of his gun he stroked Sandra's head. 'If you let me shoot the policewoman, I'll tell you about Lara. On the other hand, if you kill me you'll save this woman's life, but you'll never know what happened to Lara.'

'Why do you want me to kill you?'

'Haven't you understood yet, Marcus?'

Jeremiah's tone and the look in his eyes as he asked this question conveyed an unexpected air of smugness. It was as if he was telling Marcus he really ought to know the answer.

'Why don't you tell me?' Marcus retorted.

'That old madman Father Devok had absorbed the lesson of the penitenzieri: he thought that the only way to stop evil was evil itself. But think about it. What presumption! In order to be acquainted with evil, we had to go into its dark territory, explore it from the inside, become one with it. But some of us lost the way back.'

'And that's what happened to you.'

'And others before me,' Jeremiah said. 'I still remember when Devok recruited me. My parents were very religious, that's where I got my vocation from. I was eighteen, and attending the seminary. Father Devok took me with him, taught me to see the world through the eyes of evil. Then he wiped out my past, my identity, relegating me forever to this ocean of shadows.' A tear slid down his cheek.

'Why did you start to kill?'

'I always thought I was on the side of the good people. And that this made me better than others.' There was a sarcastic tone in his voice. 'But at a certain point I had to be sure it wasn't all in my mind. The only way was to put it to the test. I kidnapped the first girl and took her to the hiding place. You saw it: there are no instruments of torture, because I couldn't feel pleasure in what I was doing. I'm not a sadist.' There seemed to be a touch of sadness in this self-defence. 'I kept her alive, looking for a good reason to let her go. But every day, I put it off. She'd cry, she'd plead with me to let her go. I gave myself a month to decide. In the end I realised I didn't feel any compassion. So I killed her.

'But I wasn't yet satisfied. I continued carrying out my task in the penitenzieri, identifying crimes and criminals, without Devok suspecting anything. I was at one and the same time a just man and a sinner. After a while, I repeated the test with a second girl. And then a third and a fourth. From each of them I took an object, a kind of souvenir, hoping that over time they'd help me develop a sense of guilt for what I'd done. But the result was always the same: I felt no pity. I was so accustomed to evil that I could no longer distinguish between what I was coming across in my investigations and what I was doing myself. And you want to know the absurd conclusion to this story? The more evil I did, the better I became at uncovering it. From that moment on, I saved dozens of lives, foiled many crimes.' He laughed bitterly.

'So if I kill you now, I'll save this woman's life and lose Lara.' Marcus was starting to understand. 'If I don't, you'll tell me where Lara is, but then you'll shoot the woman. In either case, I'm done for. I'm your true victim. The two choices are actually equivalent: you're trying to demonstrate that only by doing evil can we do good.'

343

'Good always has a price, Marcus. Evil comes free.'

Sandra was horrified. But she had no desire to be a simple spectator in this absurd situation. 'Let this bastard kill me,' she said. 'And then make him tell you where Lara is. She's pregnant.'

Jeremiah hit her with the grip of his gun.

'Don't touch her,' Marcus said, threateningly.

'Good, I like you that way. I want to see you react. Anger is the first step.'

Marcus hadn't known that Lara was pregnant. The revelation shook him.

Jeremiah noticed. 'Is it harder to see someone killed in front of your eyes, or to know that someone else is already dying far from here? The policewoman or Lara and the child she is carrying? You decide.'

Marcus had to gain time. It wasn't impossible that the police might arrive. What would happen then? Jeremiah had nothing to lose. 'If I let you shoot the policewoman, how do I know you'll then tell me where Lara is? The fact is, you could still kill both of them. Maybe you're hoping that, by doing that, you'll arouse my anger and force me to take revenge. Then you really will have won.'

Jeremiah winked at him. 'I did an excellent job with you, there's no denying it.'

Marcus didn't understand. 'What do you mean?'

'Think, Marcus. What led you to me?'

'The succinylcholine that Alberto Canestrari injected into himself: you got your idea from the last case.'

'Only from that? Are you sure?'

Marcus was forced to reflect.

'Come on, don't disappoint me. Think of the words I have on my chest.'

Kill me. What was he trying to tell him?

'I'll give you a little help: a while ago I decided to reveal the secrets of our archive to relatives and friends of the victims of crimes still officially unsolved but that I had solved. I practically handed them the results of the investigations on a plate. But then it occurred to me that, as I, too, had committed crimes, I had to grant the same chance to those I had made suffer. That was the reason for all that performance with the ambulance, the simulated heart attack. If instead of taking care of me the young doctor had let me die, I would have paid my debt. Instead of which Teresa's sister chose to let me live.'

It hadn't been a great choice, Sandra told herself. The evil Monica had avoided doing had found another way to manifest itself. That was why they were here, because Monica had been good. It was absurd.

'And yet it was so obvious that I'd arranged everything. I'd even written it on me to avoid there being any ambiguity . . . But no one knew how to read the words. What does that remind you of?'

Marcus made an effort to remember. 'The murder of Valeria Altieri. The word written in blood behind the bed. "Evil".'

'Good,' Jeremiah said, looking pleased. 'Everybody read it as "Evil", but it was actually "Live". They were looking for a sect, because of the triangular symbol traced in the victim's blood on the carpet, and nobody realised it was the base of a video camera. The answer is always in front of our eyes – *Kill me*. And nobody ever sees it. Nobody wants to see it.'

Marcus realised now what had inspired this absurd plan. 'The case of Federico Noni. Everybody saw a boy in a wheelchair, nobody could imagine he was his sister's killer – because he couldn't walk. It was the same with you: a man in a coma, apparently harmless. Only one policeman to guard you. After ruling out a heart attack, none of the doctors could figure out what it was you had. Instead of which you were under the effects of the succinylcholine, which would soon wear off.'

'It's pity that messes things up for us, Marcus. If Pietro Zini hadn't had pity on Federico Noni, he'd have caught him immediately. If this policewoman hadn't felt pity for me, she wouldn't have told me about the time she aborted her child. And now she's worried that Lara is pregnant.' He laughed derisively.

'You bastard. I didn't feel any pity for you.' In the position she was in, Sandra's back hurt. But she kept on calculating how to get out of this. She could take advantage of a moment when Jeremiah was distracted and try to throw herself on him. At that point, Marcus – that was the penitenziere's name, now she knew it – might be able to disarm him. Then they would beat the monster until he revealed to them where Lara was.

'I haven't learned anything from you,' Marcus replied.

'Subconsciously, you've absorbed all these lessons. That's how you got here. Now it's up to you to decide if you want to go further.' He looked at him solemnly. 'Kill me.'

'I'm not a killer.'

'Are you sure? To recognise evil, you have to have it inside you. You're exactly like me. So look inside yourself and you'll understand.' Jeremiah moved the barrel of his gun so that he had a better aim at Sandra's head, at the same time putting his other arm behind his back and assuming a martial pose. An executioner ready to strike. 'Now I'll count to three. You don't have much time.'

Marcus raised his gun and aimed at Jeremiah: he was a perfect target, from that distance he could easily hit him. But first he looked again at the woman: he realised she was going to try and free herself. He just had to wait for her to make a move, then he would shoot Jeremiah without killing him.

'One.'

Sandra didn't give him time to count: she leapt to her feet, knocking the gun out of Jeremiah's hand with her shoulder. But no sooner had she made the first move towards Marcus than she felt a spasm in her back. She thought she had been hit, but she still managed to reach Marcus and take cover behind him. That was when she realised she hadn't heard a shot. She immediately lifted her hand to her back and felt the object stuck between her ribs. She recognised it.

'My God.'

It was a syringe.

Jeremiah was roaring with laughter, rocking back and forth on the edge of the bed. 'Succinylcholine,' he said.

Marcus stared at the hand Jeremiah had abruptly taken from behind his back. He had even foreseen the policewoman's move.

'Incredible what you can find in a hospital, isn't it?'

He had prepared it after shooting the policeman guarding the door, that was why she had found him in front of the storage room. Sandra realised it too late. She felt first a numbness in her limbs, which quickly spread to her throat. She couldn't move her head and her legs yielded. She was on the ground. Her body was convulsing, without her being able to control it. She couldn't breathe. It felt as if there was no more air in the room. Just like in an aquarium, she thought, remembering the comparison she had made on first entering this place. But there was no water around her. It was quite simply that she was out of oxygen.

Marcus threw himself on the woman: she was flailing and turning cyanotic. He did not know how to help her.

Jeremiah pointed to the rubber tube next to the bed. 'To save her you have to put this in her throat. Or else give the alarm, but first you'd have to kill me, otherwise I won't let you.'

Marcus looked at the gun he had placed on the ground.

'She has four minutes, maybe five. After the first three, the brain damage will be irreversible. Remember, Marcus: on the border between good and evil there is a mirror. If you look into it, you will discover the truth. Because you, too—'

The gunshot interrupted the sentence. Jeremiah fell back with his arms open wide and his head thrown over the side of the bed.

After pressing the trigger, Marcus lost interest in him and the gun he was still clutching in his fist and concentrated instead on the woman. 'Please hold on.' He went to the door and pressed the lever to raise the fire alarm. It was the quickest way to get help.

Sandra didn't understand what was going on. She could feel herself losing consciousness. Her lungs were burning and she couldn't move, couldn't cry out. Everything was happening inside her.

Marcus knelt and took her hand. He felt powerless to help her in her silent battle.

'Out of my way!'

The commanding voice came from behind him. He did as he was told and saw a short young woman in a white coat grab Sandra by the arms and drag her to the nearest empty bed. He helped her by lifting Sandra's feet. They laid her down.

The young woman took a laryngoscope from an emergency trolley, put it into Sandra's throat, and calmly inserted a tube that she then connected to the respirator. With a stethoscope, she listened to her chest. 'Her heartbeat's getting back to normal,' she said, 'maybe we've been in time.' She turned towards the lifeless body of Jeremiah Smith and looked at the bullet hole on his temple, then at the scar on Marcus's temple, struck by the unusual similarity.

Only then did he recognise her. It was Monica, Teresa's sister. This time she had saved Sandra's life.

'Get out of here,' she said to him.

Marcus didn't immediately react.

'Get out,' she repeated. 'Nobody would understand why you shot him.'

Marcus still hesitated.

'Although I do,' she added.

He turned again to Sandra, who in the meantime was getting some colour back in her face. He even saw a gleam in her wide-open eyes. He agreed to go. He stroked her arm and walked away towards a service exit.

ONE YEAR EARLIER
PRYPIAT

The sun was setting over Chernobyl.

The nuclear plant, stretching placidly beside the river, was a smoking volcano. In reality, however spent and harmless it might appear, it was more alive and lethal than ever, and would continue to spread death and deformity for thousands of years to come.

From the road the hunter had a good view of the reactors, including number four, responsible for the greatest nuclear disaster in history, now wrapped in its fragile sarcophagus of lead and reinforced concrete.

The asphalt was full of holes and the suspension on his old Volvo groaned with every jolt. He continued across a vast area that was home to luxuriant woods. After the accident, because of the radioactive wind, the trees had changed colour. The people of the place, still unaware of what was really happening, had dubbed it the Red Forest.

The silent apocalypse had begun on 24 April 1986, at 1.23 in the morning.

At first the authorities had downplayed what had happened, trying naively to cover it all up. They were more worried about the news spreading than about the health of the population. The evacuation of the area did not begin until thirty-six hours after the incident.

The city of Prypiat was not far from the reactors. The hunter saw its spectral profile appear through the windscreen. Not a light, not a sign of life between the tall concrete buildings, which had been constructed at the same time as the plant. In the year it had been abandoned, it had had 47,000 inhabitants: a modern city with cafés, restaurants, cinemas, theatres, sports centres and two good hospitals. The living conditions had been better than in many other places in the country.

Now it was a grim black-and-white postcard.

A small fox crossed the street, and the hunter had to brake in order not to run it over. Nature had taken advantage of the absence of man, and many animal and vegetable species had reclaimed the habitat for themselves. Paradoxically, it had become a kind of paradise on earth. But no one could predict what would happen in the future, because of the long-term effects of radiation.

The hunter had a Geiger counter on the seat next to him. It continued to emit a rhythmical electrical sound, like a coded message from another dimension. He did not have much time. He should have bribed a Ukrainian official to obtain a pass to the exclusion zone, which extended for a distance of nineteen miles around the now disused plant. He had to take advantage of the dusk to complete his investigation. And it would soon be dark.

He started coming across abandoned military vehicles at the side of the road. There were hundreds of trucks, helicopters, tanks and other forms of transport that had been used by the army when it had intervened to contain the emergency. By the end of the operation the vehicles were so contaminated that they had simply been left here.

A rusty sign in Cyrillic lettering welcomed him to the city.

On the outskirts was an amusement park where the children had continued to play the day after the accident. It had been the first place to be hit by the radioactive cloud. There was the big wheel, now a skeleton rusted by acid rain.

A few concrete blocks had been placed in the middle of the road to prevent access to Prypiat. On the barbed wire hung danger signs. The hunter stopped the car, intending to continue on foot. He took a bag from the boot and swung it over his shoulder. Clutching the Geiger counter, he ventured into the ghost city.

His entry was greeted by the chirping of birds. The sound, along with that of his footsteps, echoed down the avenues lined with buildings. The raw daylight was fading fast, and it was getting colder. Every now and again he thought he heard voices echoing down the empty streets. Auditory mirages, or maybe old sounds imprisoned forever in a place where time no longer had any meaning.

Wolves wandered among the ruins. He could hear them, or sense their presence as grey patches. They were keeping their distance for now, but they were watching him.

He checked the map he had brought with him and then looked around. Each building was marked with a number painted in white on the facade. The one that interested him was Block 109.

Dima Karolyszin and his parents had once lived on the eleventh floor.

Hunters know that you have to start the investigation not with the last murder in a series, but the first. Because the murderer has not yet learned from experience and is much more likely to have made mistakes. The first victim is a kind of ground zero, the starting point for an unstoppable chain of destruction, and through him or her many things can be learned about a serial killer.

As far as the hunter knew, Dima had been the first subject whose identity the transformist had absorbed, when he was just eight years old, before he was taken to the orphanage in Kiev.

He had to take the stairs because there was no energy to work the lift. And yet, paradoxically, these places were saturated with energy in the form of radiation. The Geiger counter experienced a surge. The hunter knew that it was much more dangerous indoors than in the open air. Radioactivity clustered around objects.

As he climbed, he could see what remained of the deserted apartments. What had been spared by the scavengers gave a clear picture of the domestic scenes interrupted at the time of the evacuation. An abandoned meal. An unfinished chess game. Clothes left to dry over a heater. An unmade bed. The town was a huge collective memory where every person who had fled had left his or her own memories for safekeeping. The photograph albums, the most intimate and precious things, the family heirlooms: all waiting for a return that would never happen. Everything had been left hanging. Like an empty stage set at the end of a play, when the actors depart, revealing that it has all been make-believe. Like a trick of time. A sad allegory of life and death combined. Of what had been and would never be again.

According to the experts, it would be another hundred thousand years before human beings could safely set foot in Prypiat.

As soon as he entered the Karolyszins' apartment, the hunter noticed that it was almost intact. The narrow corridor led to three rooms, plus kitchen and bathroom. The wallpaper had peeled off in several places. Damp had gained the upper hand. Dust covered everything like a transparent curtain. The hunter started to walk through the rooms.

Konstantin and Anya's bedroom was perfectly neat and tidy. All their clothes were still in the wardrobe.

In Dima's little bedroom, there was a camp bed next to the main bed.

In the kitchen, the table was laid for four.

In the living room, there were empty vodka bottles. The hunter knew why. When the news of the accident had reached the town, the sanitary authorities spread the false information that alcohol would weaken the radiation. In reality, it was a surreptitious way of sapping the will of the population and preventing protests. On the table, once again, the hunter counted four glasses. The repetition of that number could mean only one thing.

The Karolyszins had had a guest.

The hunter looked at a framed photograph of the family that stood on a cabinet. A woman, a man and a child.

Their faces had been erased.

Turning back, he noticed that there were four pairs of shoes next to the entrance. A man's, a woman's and two children's.

He put together these details and deduced that the transformist had come to this apartment in the hours immediately following the accident at the plant. The Karolyszins, unaware of who he was, had given him hospitality. In that time of fear and agitation, they hadn't had the heart to hand over a lonely, frightened child to the authorities.

They could hardly have imagined what kind of monster they were welcoming into their home. So they had given him a hot meal and let him sleep in the same room as Dima. Then something must have happened. Maybe during the night. The Karolyszin family had vanished into thin air and the transformist had taken Dima's place.

What had become of the bodies? But, above all, who was the child? Where had he sprung from?

354

Darkness was already besieging the gates of the city. The hunter took his torch from his bag, intending to leave the building. He would come back the following day, at the same time. He wouldn't spend the night in this place. As he was getting ready to descend the stairs, another question struck him suddenly.

Why the Karolyszins?

He hadn't thought about it before. The transformist had chosen the family for a reason. It hadn't been chance.

Because he hadn't come a long way. He hadn't arrived from just anywhere, he must have been very close.

The hunter turned the beam of his torch towards the door of the apartment next to the Karolyszins'. It was closed.

A brass plate bore the name Anatoly Petrov.

He checked the time. Outside it was already dark and he would have to drive with his headlights off anyway in order not to be spotted by the Ukrainian guards who kept watch on the borders of the exclusion zone. So he might as well wait a while longer. The thought that he was close to an answer excited him, making him neglect the most basic precautions.

He had to know if his intuition concerning Anatoly Petrov was correct.

YESTERDAY

4.46 a.m.

The corpse was weeping.

This time he didn't switch on the light next to the bed. Nor did he pick up his felt-tip pen to add another detail on the wall of the attic room in the Via dei Serpenti. He lay there in silence, in the dark, trying to make sense of what he had seen in his dream.

He went back over the last clues he had brought with him from his nocturnal evocations of what had happened in the hotel room in Prague.

Broken window. Three shots. Left-handed.

By inverting them, he reached the solution to the mystery.

Jeremiah Smith's last words had been: 'On the border between good and evil there is a mirror. If you look into it, you will discover the truth.'

He had found the reason why he hated looking at himself in the mirror so much. One shot each, for him and Devok. But the killer wasn't left-handed. That was his own reflection. The first shot had shattered the mirror.

There was no third man. They were alone.

He had guessed it after what had happened in the intensive therapy department of the Gemelli, when he had fired without hesitation. But certainty had arrived only with the dream, making him revise the end of the scene. He still didn't know why he was in Prague, or why his master was there, or what they had talked about.

Marcus knew only that a few hours earlier he had killed Jeremiah Smith. But before him, he had done the same to Devok.

At dawn the rain had returned, taking over Rome and clearing night from the streets.

As he wandered through the alleyways of the Regola district,

Marcus took shelter under a portico and gazed up at the sky. The rain didn't look as if it would stop soon. He lifted the collar of his raincoat and continued on his way.

Reaching the Via Giulia, he entered the church. He had never been here before. Clemente had given him an appointment in the crypt. Descending the stone steps, he immediately realised the peculiarity of the place. It was an underground cemetery.

Before a Napoleonic decree had established the hygienic rule that the dead had to be buried far from the living, each church had its own graveyard. But the one where they were was different from the others. The fittings – candelabra, decorations, sculptures – were all made of human bones. A skeleton mounted in the wall greeted the faithful who dipped their fingers in a stoup. The bones were divided according to type and neatly grouped in the niches. There were thousands of them. The place was beyond macabre, it was grotesque.

Clemente was standing with his hands behind his back, bent over an inscription beneath a heap of skulls.

'Why here?'

Clemente turned and saw him. 'It seemed the best place after hearing the message you left me last night.'

Marcus gestured at the surroundings. 'Where are we?'

'Towards the end of the sixteenth century, the Confraternity of Prayer and Death began its pious work. Their aim was to give a dignified burial to the nameless corpses found in the streets of Rome or the countryside, or else fished out of the Tiber. Suicides, murder victims, or those who had simply died of poverty. There are approximately eight thousand bodies crammed in here.'

Clemente was too calm. In the message, Marcus had summarised what had happened the previous night, but his friend didn't seem at all perturbed by the outcome of the events. 'Why do I get the feeling you don't care what I have to tell you?'

'Because we've already learned everything.'

That condescending tone irritated him. 'Who? You say "we" but you won't tell me who you're referring to. Who's above you? I have a right to know.'

'You know I can't. But I'm very pleased with you.'

360

Marcus was increasingly frustrated. 'Pleased with what? I had to kill Jeremiah, Lara is done for, and last night, after a year's total amnesia, I recovered my first memory . . . I shot Devok.'

Clemente took his time. 'There's a prisoner on death row in a maximum security prison who committed a terrible crime and has been waiting to be executed for twenty years. Five years ago, he was diagnosed with brain cancer. When they removed it, he lost his memory. He had to learn everything again from the beginning. After the operation, he couldn't understand what he was doing in a cell, sentenced for a crime he didn't remember committing. Now he claims that he's a different person from the killer who murdered a number of victims. In fact he says he'd be incapable of taking a life. He's asked to be pardoned. If he isn't, he says, an innocent man will be executed. The psychiatrists say he's genuine, it isn't just a trick to avoid the death sentence. But that's not the real problem. If the person responsible for an individual's actions is the individual himself, wherein lies his guilt? Is it inherent in his body, in his soul or else in his identity?'

For Marcus everything was suddenly clear. 'You knew what I'd done in Prague.'

Clemente nodded. 'In killing Devok, you committed a mortal sin. But if you didn't remember it, you couldn't confess it. And if you didn't confess it, you couldn't be absolved. But by the same token, it was as if you hadn't committed it. That's why you were forgiven.'

'And that's why you've been keeping it hidden from me.'

'What is it the penitenzieri always say?'

Marcus thought again of the litany he had learned. 'There is a place in which the world of light meets the world of darkness. It is there that everything happens: in the land of shadows, where everything is vague, confused, undefined. We are the guards appointed to defend that border. But every now and again something manages to get through . . . My task is to chase it back into the darkness.'

'Always hovering dangerously over that line, some penitenzieri have taken a fatal step. They've been swallowed by the darkness, and have never returned.'

'Are you trying to tell me that the same thing that happened to Jeremiah had happened to me before I lost my memory?'

'Not to you. To Devok.'

Marcus didn't know what to say.

'He was the one who brought the gun into that hotel room. You just disarmed him and tried to defend yourself. There was a struggle and the gun went off.'

'How do you know what happened?' Marcus protested. 'You weren't there.'

'Before he went to Prague, Devok confessed. *Culpa gravis 785-34-15*: disobeying an order from the Pope and betraying the Church. That was when he revealed the existence of the clandestine order of penitenzieri. He'd probably already guessed that something was wrong: the archive had been violated, four girls had been kidnapped and murdered and the investigation was constantly being thrown off the scent. Father Devok started to harbour suspicions concerning his own men.'

'How many penitenzieri are there?'

Clemente sighed. 'We don't know. But we hope that a few of them will come out into the open sooner or later. In his confession, Devok wouldn't give any names. He said only, "I've made a mistake, I have to remedy it."'

'Why did he come to me?'

'We assume he wanted to kill all of the penitenzieri. Starting with you.'

Marcus was incredulous. 'Devok wanted to kill me?'

Clemente put a hand on his shoulder. 'I'm sorry. I was hoping you'd never find out.'

Marcus looked into the empty eyes of one of the many skulls preserved in the crypt. Who had that individual been? What was his name, what did he look like? Had anyone ever loved him? How had he died and why? Was he a good man or a bad man?

Some might have asked the same questions of his corpse if Devok had succeeded in killing him. Because, like all the penitenzieri, he had no identity.

I don't exist.

'Before dying, Jeremiah Smith said, "The more evil I did, the better I became at uncovering it." And I ask myself: Why is it I can't remember my mother's voice and yet I'm so good at uncovering evil? Why have I forgotten everything else, but not my talent? Are good and evil innate in each one of us, depending only on the path each person takes in his life?' Marcus looked up at his friend. 'Am I a good man or a bad man?'

'Now you know you committed a mortal sin in killing Devok and then Jeremiah. So you will have to make confession and submit to the judgement of the Tribunal of Souls. But I'm sure you will receive absolution, because in having to deal with evil we sometimes get our hands dirty.'

'And what about Lara? Jeremiah took the secret with him. What will happen to that poor girl?'

'Your task finishes here, Marcus.'

'She's pregnant.'

'We can't save her.'

'And her child won't even have a chance. No, I can't accept that.'

'Look at this place,' Clemente said, indicated their surroundings. 'The meaning of it is pity. Giving a Christian burial to an individual without a name, independently of what he was or what he did during his lifetime. I wanted to meet you here so that you could feel a little pity for yourself. Lara will die, but it won't be your fault. So stop torturing yourself. Absolution from the Tribunal of Souls will be useless if you haven't first absolved yourself.'

'So now I'm free? This isn't how I imagined it. It doesn't make me feel as good as I thought it would.'

'I still have an assignment for you.' Clemente smiled. 'Perhaps this will make things less burdensome for you.' He handed him a file from the archive.

Marcus took it and read on the cover: *c.g. 294-21-12.*

'You didn't save Lara. But you may still save *her*.'

9.02 a.m.

In the intensive care department, a surreal scene was taking place. The police and the forensics team were carrying out the initial investigations subsequent to the night's massacre. But everything was happening in the presence of the comatose patients, who could not be moved in such a short time. There was no risk of them interfering with the investigations, so they had been left there. The consequence was that the officers were moving quietly and talking under their breath, almost as if they were afraid of waking someone.

Watching her colleagues from a chair in the corridor, Sandra shook her head, wondering if it all appeared idiotic only to her. The doctors had insisted on keeping her under observation, but she had signed a form to discharge herself. She didn't feel at all well, but she wanted to return to Milan and get her life back. And try to start over.

Marcus, she said to herself, recalling the name of the penitenziere with the scar on his temple. She wished she could talk to him one more time, and try to understand. As she was choking, his grip on her had inspired her with the courage necessary to resist. She would have liked him to know that.

Jeremiah Smith had been taken away in a black body bag. As it had passed her, she had discovered that she did not feel anything. Last night, she had experienced what death felt like. That had been enough to free her of all the hate and resentment and desire for revenge. Because during those moments she had felt very close to David.

With her skill as a doctor, Monica had snatched her from certain death. Then she had put on a performance for the police, substituting herself for Marcus in the scene and assuming responsibility for shooting Jeremiah. Before they arrived, she had wiped Marcus's prints from the gun and put her own on it. It wasn't revenge, she emphasised, but self-defence. Everything suggested that they believed her.

Now, Sandra saw Monica coming towards her in the corridor after being questioned for the umpteenth time. But she didn't seem tired.

'So, how are you?' she asked, smiling cheerfully.

'Fine,' Sandra said, clearing her throat. Her voice was still hoarse from the breathing tube, and every muscle in her body hurt. But at least the horrible sensation of paralysis had passed. An anaesthetist had helped her to gradually put behind her the effects of the succinylcholine. It was like being resuscitated. 'Even slaps in the face teach you to grow, as your father says, if I'm not mistaken.'

They laughed. It had been pure chance that Monica had come back to the intensive care department the previous night. Sandra hadn't asked why, but Monica had told her that she didn't know what had driven her to return. 'Maybe it was because of the little chat we had earlier, I don't know.'

Sandra wasn't sure whether to thank Monica for that, or fate, or else someone up there who made sure every now and again that things worked out. Whether it was God or her husband didn't make much difference to her.

Monica bent towards Sandra and hugged her. There was no need for words. They stayed like that for a few seconds. Then the young doctor gave Sandra a kiss on the cheek and took her leave.

Distracted by watching Monica walk away, she had not noticed Superintendent Camusso approaching.

'She's a nice girl,' he said.

Sandra turned to look at him. He was dressed completely in blue: blue jacket, blue trousers, blue shirt, blue tie. She would have bet on it that even his socks were blue. The only exception was his white moccasins. If it hadn't been for his shoes and his hair, Camusso would have blended into the furniture and walls of the intensive care unit like a chameleon.

'I've been talking to your superior, Inspector De Michelis. He's coming from Milan to pick you up.'

'No, damn it. Why didn't you stop him? I was planning to leave tonight.'

'He told me an interesting story about you.'

Sandra started to fear the worst.

'Apparently you were right, Officer Vega. Congratulations.'

She was startled. 'Right about what?'

'The gas fire and the carbon monoxide. The husband who shoots his wife and son after the shower, and then goes back into the bathroom and faints, knocks his head and dies.'

The summary was perfect, but the outcome wasn't clear. 'Did the pathologist get to hear my theory?'

'He not only heard it, he agreed with it.'

Sandra couldn't believe it. This wouldn't make things any better. But the truth is always a consolation. Just as in the case of David, she thought. Now that she knew who had killed him, she felt free to let him go.

'All the departments in the hospital are monitored by security cameras, did you know that?'

The statement had come out of the blue, and a shudder went through Sandra. She hadn't thought of that. The version of events provided by Monica and corroborated by her was in danger. Marcus was in danger. 'Have you seen the tapes?'

Camusso gave a grimace. 'Apparently, the security cameras in intensive care were out of order because of the storms of the past few days. So there's no record of what happened here. A pity, don't you think?'

Sandra tried not to appear relieved.

But Camusso had something else to add. 'You did know the Gemelli hospital belongs to the Vatican, didn't you?'

It wasn't a chance statement, there was an insinuation in it, which Sandra ignored.

'Why are you telling me that?'

Camusso shrugged, gave her a sidelong look, but decided not to go further into the matter. 'Oh, just curiosity.'

Before he could go on, Sandra rose from her chair. 'Could you ask someone to take me back to my hotel?'

'I'll take you. I don't have anything else to do here.'

Sandra hid her disappointment behind a false smile. 'All right, but there's somewhere I'd like to go first.'

Camusso had an old Lancia Fulvia, which he kept in perfect condition. Getting in the car, Sandra had the impression she was going back in time. The interior smelled as if it had just come from the showroom. The rain was still falling steadily, but the bodywork seemed incredibly clean.

Camusso drove her to the address she had given him. On the way, they listened to a radio station broadcasting hits of the sixties. They drove down the Via Veneto and Sandra felt as if she was back in the time of the Dolce Vita.

This anachronistic tour ended outside the building that housed the Interpol guest apartment.

As she climbed the stairs, Sandra was hoping with all her heart that she would meet Schalber. She was far from sure she would find him here, but she had to try. She had a thousand things to tell him, and above all she was expecting him to tell her something. For example, that he was pleased she had survived, even though it had been stupid on her part to cover her tracks: if he had followed her to the Gemelli the previous evening, things might have been very different. When you came down to it, Schalber had only been trying to protect her.

But what she would have liked to hear him say more than anything else was that it would be nice to see each other again in the future. They had made love, and she had liked it. She didn't want to lose him. She might not want to admit it yet, but she was falling in love with him.

Reaching the landing, she found the door open. She didn't hesitate: filled with hope, she walked in. Hearing noises coming from the kitchen, she went straight to it. But when she got there, she saw another man, wearing a very smart blue suit.

All she could say to him was 'Hello.'

He looked at her in surprise. 'Haven't you brought your husband?'

Sandra didn't understand, but hastened to clear up any misunderstanding. 'Actually, I was looking for Thomas Schalber.'

The man thought this over. 'Maybe he was a previous occupant.'

'I think he's a colleague of yours. Don't you know him?'

'As far as I'm aware, the only agency handling the sale is ours. And there's nobody of that name working for us.'

Sandra was starting to understand, even though it wasn't at all clear to her. 'You're from an estate agency?'

'Didn't you see our sign on the front door?' the man said in an affected tone. 'The apartment is for sale.'

She didn't know whether to be more upset or surprised. 'How long has it been on the market?'

The man seemed puzzled by the question. 'Nobody's lived here for more than six months.'

She didn't know what to say. No explanation that came to mind seemed especially convincing.

The man approached her. 'I'm expecting some potential buyers,' he said affably. 'But if you'd like to have a look around in the meantime . . .'

'No, thanks,' Sandra replied. 'I made a mistake, I'm sorry.' She turned to go.

'If the furniture's not to your taste, you're not obliged to take it. We can deduct it from the price.'

She ran back down the stairs, so quickly that by the time she got to the ground floor she felt dizzy and had to lean against the wall. After a couple of minutes, she went out on the street and got back in Camusso's car.

'You look pale. Do you want me to take you back to the hospital?'

'I'm fine.' But it wasn't true. She was furious. Another deception of Schalber's. Was it possible that everything he'd told her was a lie? So what had that night they had spent together been all about?

'Who were you looking for in that building?' Camusso asked.

'A friend who works for Interpol. But he wasn't there and I don't know where he is.'

'I can find him for you, if you like. I know some people who work in the Rome office of Interpol. I can give them a call. It's no trouble.'

Sandra felt she had to see this through to the end. She couldn't go back to Milan with that question unresolved: she had to know if Schalber felt for her even a fraction of what she felt for him. 'Thanks, I'd really appreciate that.'

1.55 p.m.

Bruno Martini had gone to ground in one of the garages in the courtyard of the apartment block where he lived. He had turned it into a kind of laboratory. His pastime was small repairs. He repaired domestic appliances, but also dabbled in carpentry and mechanics. When Marcus saw him beneath the raised metal shutter, he was working on the engine of a Vespa.

Martini didn't notice him as he approached. The rain was coming down as vertically as a curtain, and he didn't see him until he was very close. On his knees next to the scooter, he looked up and recognised Marcus. 'What do you want with me now?'

He was a mountain of a man, with muscles strong enough to face the trials and tribulations of life, but his daughter's disappearance had left him feeling powerless. His quick temper was the one thing still protecting him from complete collapse. Marcus didn't blame him. 'Can we talk?'

Martini thought about it for a moment. 'Come inside. You're getting wet.' He got to his feet, wiping the palms of his hands on his grease-stained overalls. 'I talked to Camilla Rocca this morning,' he said. 'She was quite upset. Now she knows she'll never have justice.'

'That's not why I'm here. Unfortunately I can't do anything more for her.'

'Sometimes it's better not to know.'

He was surprised to hear Martini say this: a father who would do everything he could to find his daughter, who had bought a weapon illegally, turned himself into a lone avenger, stood up to the authorities. He wondered if he had done the right thing to come. 'What about you? Don't you still want to know the truth about what happened to Alice?'

'For three years I've been looking for her as if she was alive but mourning her as if she was dead.'

'That's no answer,' Marcus replied with equal sharpness.

'Do you know what it means not to be able to die?' Martini went on, lowering his eyes a little. 'It means continuing to live without any choice, like an immortal. But think about it, what kind of sentence is that? Well, I won't be able to die until I discover what happened to Alice. I have to stay here and suffer.'

'Why are you so hard on yourself?'

'Three years ago I was still a smoker.'

Marcus wasn't sure what that had to do with anything, but he let him continue.

'That day at the park, I'd walked away to smoke a cigarette when Alice disappeared. Her mother was also there, but I was supposed to be the one watching her. I'm her father, it was my job. Instead I got distracted.'

For Marcus, that answer was sufficient. He put his hand in his pocket and took out the file that Clemente had given him.

c.g. 294-21-12.

He opened it and took out a sheet of paper. 'What I'm about to tell you has one condition attached to it: you mustn't ask me how I found out and you mustn't ever say that you heard it from me. Agreed?'

Martini looked at him, puzzled. 'All right.' There was a new note deep in his voice. It was hope.

'I warn you that what I'm going to tell you won't be pleasant. Do you feel ready?'

'Yes,' Martini said in a thin voice.

Marcus tried to be delicate. 'Three years ago, Alice was kidnapped by a man and taken abroad.'

'How can that be?'

'He's a psychopath: he thinks his dead wife has been reincarnated in your daughter. That's why he took her.'

'So . . . ' He couldn't believe it.

'Yes, she's still alive.'

Martini's eyes filled with tears: the human mountain was on the verge of collapse.

Marcus held out the sheet of paper he had in his hand. 'Here is everything you need to trace her. But you mustn't do it alone, promise me.'

'I promise.'

'At the bottom of the page there's the telephone number of a specialist in tracing missing persons, especially children. Get in touch with her. She's an excellent police officer, so I'm told. Her name is Mila Vasquez.'

370

Martini took the sheet of paper and stared at it, without knowing what to say.

'I have to go now.'

'Wait.'

Marcus stopped, but Martini couldn't speak. Silent sobs shook his chest. Marcus knew what was going through his mind. Martini wasn't only thinking about Alice. For the first time, he was envisaging the possibility of reuniting his family. His wife, who had left him because of the way he had reacted to the disappearance, might return to him, along with his other child. And they would love each other again as they once had.

'I don't want Camilla Rocca to know,' Martini said. 'At least, not yet. It would be terrible for her to know that there's a hope for Alice, while her son Filippo will never come back again.'

'I have no intention of telling her. Still, she has her own family.'

Martini lifted his head and looked at him in surprise. 'What family? Her husband left her two years ago, he started a new life with another woman, they even have a child. That's what brought the two of us together.'

Marcus remembered the note he had seen in Camilla's house, stuck to the fridge with a magnet in the shape of a crab.

I'll see you in ten days. I love you.

God alone knew how long it had been there. But there was something else that disturbed him, even though he didn't know what it was. 'I have to go,' he said to Martini. And before the man could thank him, he turned and plunged once again through the curtain of rain.

The rain had slowed the traffic, and it took him nearly two hours to get to Ostia. The bus dropped him at a roundabout on the seafront, and from there he continued on foot.

Camilla Rocca's car wasn't parked on the little path, but Marcus stood for a while in the rain looking at the house, to make sure there was no one in it. Then he walked to the entrance and before long was again inside the house.

Nothing had changed since his visit the day before. The

furnishings in nautical style, the sand crunching under his shoes. The washing machine in the kitchen, though, had not been turned off properly and was dripping. The sound of it mingled with the rain pouring outside.

He went straight to the bedroom. There on the pillows were the two pairs of pyjamas. He hadn't been mistaken, he remembered it well. One was a woman's, the other a man's. The knick-knacks and other objects were as neatly arranged as ever. The first time he had been here, he had thought that this tidiness was a refuge from anxiety, from the chaos generated by the disappearance of a child. Everything had been in its rightful place, everything had been perfect. Anomalies, he thought, reminding himself what he should have looked for.

The smiling photograph of Filippo watched him from the chest of drawers, and Marcus felt as if he was being led. On the bedside table, on the side of the bed where Camilla slept, was the baby monitor with which the woman should have been listening to her new child sleeping. And that made him think again of the room next door.

He crossed the threshold of what had once been Filippo's bedroom, now divided into two equal parts. The one that interested him was occupied by a changing table, a mountain of toys and a cot.

Where's the child I ought to be seeing? What's behind all this show? He remembered Bruno Martini's words: Her husband left her two years ago, he has a new life now, with another woman, they even have a child.

Camilla had been forced to suffer a further blow. The man she had chosen to love had abandoned her. But his betrayal didn't lie in the fact that there was another woman, but in the fact that this woman had given him a child. A replacement for Filippo.

The worst thing isn't the loss of a child, he thought. It's the fact that life goes on regardless. And Camilla Rocca hadn't wanted to stop being a mother.

As soon as he realised the truth, Marcus noticed the anomaly. This time, it wasn't a presence. Rather, it was something that wasn't there.

Next to the cot, the other baby monitor was missing.

If the receiver was in Camilla's room, where was the transmitter?

Marcus went back to the first bedroom and sat down on the double bed, next to the bedside table. He reached out a hand to the baby monitor and switched it on.

Constant, uninterrupted surface noise, like the incomprehensible voice of darkness. Marcus put his ear closer, trying to perceive something. Nothing. He raised the volume to maximum. The noise invaded the room. He sat there waiting, on the alert. The seconds passed as he probed the depths of that sea of whispers, in search of a slight variation, a different colour.

Then he heard it, deep in the grey dust emitted by the loud-speaker: another sound. A rhythmical sound. It wasn't artificial, it was alive. Breathing.

Marcus grabbed the baby monitor and, holding it in his hands, started walking around the house in search of the origin of the signal. It couldn't be far, he told himself. These devices don't have a very long range. So where is it?

He opened all the doors, checked all the rooms. Reaching the back door, he looked out through the mosquito screen and saw the blurred image of an overgrown garden and a tool shed.

He went outside and for the first time noticed that the neigh-bours' houses were not especially near and that the property was surrounded by tall pines that acted as a screen. The place was ideal. He walked along the gravel path towards the shed. His steps sank into the wet ground, the rain beat down without respite. He was walking against the wind, feeling as though dark forces were trying to persuade him to give up. But at last he reached his goal. There was a heavy padlock on the shed door.

Marcus looked around and immediately found what he needed: a small iron pole stuck in the ground that served as the base for a sprinkler. He put down the baby monitor, grabbed the pole with both hands, and tugged at it until he managed to get it out of the ground. Then he turned back to the padlock and started hitting it as hard as he could. At least, the steel ring snapped and the door opened a few inches. Marcus flung it wide open.

The murky daylight invaded the small space, revealing a carpet of refuse and a small electric heater. The second baby monitor stood next to a mattress thrown on the ground with a heap of rags on it – a heap that moved.

'Lara . . . ' he called, and waited for a long time for an answer that did not come. 'Lara?' he repeated, more loudly.

'Yes,' came an incredulous voice.

Marcus rushed to her. She was huddled beneath filthy blankets. She was exhausted, dirty, but still alive. 'It's all right, I'm here for you.'

'Help me, please,' she said, weeping, without realising that he was already helping her.

She kept repeating the same words even when Marcus took her in his arms and led her out into the rain and along the gravel path and through the back door of the little house. Here, Marcus stopped.

Camilla Rocca was standing completely still in the corridor, soaked to the skin. She was holding a bunch of keys and some shopping bags. 'He took her for me. He said I could keep his child . . . '

Marcus realised she was referring to Jeremiah Smith.

She looked at him and then at Lara. '*She* didn't want it.'

Evil generates evil, had been Jeremiah's words. Camilla had received a bad deal from life. But it was what she had suffered that had made her become what she was now. She had accepted a gift from a monster. Marcus realised how she had managed to deceive him. She had created a parallel world, which for her was real. She was sincere, she wasn't playing a part.

He resumed walking and went past her with Lara in his arms. Ignoring her, he took the car keys from her hands.

Camilla stood watching them, then collapsed on the floor. She was talking to herself in a thin voice, constantly repeating the same words. '*She* didn't want it . . . '

10.56 p.m.

Inspector De Michelis was feeding coins into a coffee machine. Sandra was hypnotised by the care with which he carried out this

374

operation. She had never imagined she would be back in the Gemelli hospital so soon.

Camusso's call had come one hour earlier, as she was getting ready to pack her bags, leave the hotel and get in a train that would take her back to Milan together with her superior, who had come to fetch her. At first, she had assumed the superintendent had news about Schalber, but after assuring her that Interpol were dealing with it, he had told her the latest development in the case of Jeremiah Smith. At that point, she and De Michelis had rushed to the hospital to see with their own eyes if it was true.

Lara was alive.

The circumstances were unclear. The architecture student had been found in a vehicle abandoned in the car park of a shopping centre on the outskirts of Rome. There had been an anonymous tip-off, in the form of a phone call. The information was still sketchy and was not filtering beyond the door of the emergency department, where Lara was currently being kept for tests.

What Sandra did know was that Superintendent Camusso and his men had made an arrest in Ostia, led there both by Lara's testimony and by the documents found in the car. She wondered exactly how Jeremiah Smith had been involved, but of one thing she was sure: Marcus had had something to with this happy outcome.

Yes, it was him, she kept telling herself. Lara was bound to mention a mysterious saviour with a scar on his temple. Would the police be able to trace him? She hoped not.

As soon as the news that Lara was free had got out, the media had besieged the hospital. Reporters, cameramen and photographers were lying in wait in the grounds. Lara's parents had not yet arrived – it would take them time to get to Rome from the south – but her friends had started coming to ask after her. Among them, Sandra recognised Christian Lorieri, the assistant lecturer in art history and the father of the child she was carrying. They exchanged a fleeting glance that was more eloquent than a thousand words. The fact that he was here meant their little chat at the university had borne fruit.

So far, there had been only one medical bulletin. It reported tersely that the student's clinical condition was good and that, despite the stress she had suffered, there had been no harm to her unborn child.

De Michelis approached Sandra, blowing into a plastic cup. 'Don't you think you have a bit of explaining to do?'

'You're right, but I warn you, you'll need more than one coffee.'

'Then we won't be able to leave before tomorrow morning. We're going to have to spend the night here.'

Sandra took his hand. 'I'd prefer to talk to you as a friend, not as a police officer. Is that all right with you?'

'What is it, don't you like policemen any more?' he said teasingly. But seeing that Sandra was serious, he changed his tone. 'I wasn't there for you when David died. The least I can do is listen to you now.'

For the next two hours, Sandra told him the whole story. She knew she could: he was a man whose moral integrity had always served as an example to her. De Michelis let her speak, interrupting her only to clarify a few points. When she had finished, she felt much lighter.

'Penitenzieri, you say?'

'Yes,' she confirmed. 'Have you really never heard of them?'

De Michelis shrugged. 'I've seen so much in this job that nothing surprises me any more. It sometimes happens that there are cases that get solved through a tip-off or by chance, without any explanation. But I've never linked it to people investigating in parallel with the police. I'm a believer, you know. It's nice to think there's something irrational and yet beautiful that I can trust when I can no longer stand the ugliness I see every day.'

De Michelis stroked her arm, just as Marcus had done before disappearing from the recovery room and her life. Over the inspector's shoulder, Sandra noticed two men in jackets and ties addressing an officer, who then pointed in their direction. The two men approached.

'Are you Sandra Vega?' one of them asked.

'Yes, that's me.'

'Could we have a quick word?' the other man asked.

376

'Of course.'

They made it clear that the subject was confidential, and as they drew her aside, they showed her their badges. 'We're from Interpol.'

'What's going on?'

It was the older man who spoke. 'Superintendent Camusso called us this afternoon asking for information about one of our agents. He said he was calling on your behalf. The officer's name is Thomas Schalber. Can you confirm to us that you know him?'

'Yes.'

'When did you last see him?'

'Yesterday.'

The two men looked at each other. 'Are you sure?' the younger man asked.

Sandra was starting to lose patience. 'Of course I'm sure.'

'And is this the man you met?'

They showed her a badge with a photograph and Sandra leaned forward to get a better look at it. 'There's a definite resemblance, but I have no idea who this man is.'

The two men looked at one another again, and this time they looked nervous. 'Would you be ready to give a description of the person you saw to one of our identikit specialists?'

Sandra had had enough: she wanted to know what was going on. 'All right, boys. Which one of you is going to tell me what this is all about? Because there seems to be something I'm missing here.'

The younger man looked at his elder for approval. When he had obtained it, he said, 'The last time he was in contact with us, Thomas Schalber was working undercover on a case.'

'Why do you say "was"?'

'Because he then disappeared, and we haven't heard from him in more than a year.'

Stunned by this news, Sandra didn't know what to think. 'I'm sorry, if your agent is the person in the photograph and you don't know what's become of him, then who was the man I met?'

ONE YEAR EARLIER
PRYPIAT

The wolves were calling to each other in the deserted streets, howling their names at the dark sky. They were the masters of Prypiat now.

The hunter could hear them as he tried to break open the door of Anatoly Petrov's apartment on the eleventh floor of Block 109.

The wolves knew that the intruder had not left the city, and now they were looking for him.

He couldn't leave before sunrise. His hands were hurting with the cold and the lock was proving a tough proposition. But in the end he managed to open it.

The apartment was the same size as the one next to it. Nothing had been touched.

The windows had been sealed with rags and insulating tape to keep out draughts. Anatoly must have taken this precaution immediately after the nuclear incident, to stop radiation from getting in.

The hunter saw the tag with his photo on the uniform of the plant hanging just inside the door. He was about thirty-five years old. Smooth fair hair, with a fringe that covered his forehead. Glasses with heavy frames. Empty blue eyes. Thin lips surmounted by a light-coloured down. His job was 'turbine technician'.

The hunter looked around. The furnishings were modest. In the living room there was a flowered velvet sofa and a television set. In a corner stood two glass display cabinets, both empty. A bookcase covered part of one wall. The hunter went closer to read the titles of the volumes. There were texts on zoology, anthropology and many on ethnology. Among the authors represented were Charles Darwin, Konrad Lorenz, Desmond Morris and Richard Dawkins. Studies on animal learning processes, the environmental conditioning of species, the relationship between instinct and external stimuli. Not the usual reading matter of a turbine technician. On a lower shelf, a series of exercise books, about twenty of them, all numbered.

The hunter didn't know what to think. But the most important conclusion was that Anatoly Petrov had lived alone. There were no signs of the presence of a family. Or of a child.

He was overcome by a momentary sense of unease. Now he was forced to stay all night. He couldn't light a fire, because it would boost the effects of the radiation. He had no food with him, only water. He would have to find some blankets and a few tins. As he searched, he realised that there were no clothes in the bedroom wardrobe and that the shelves in the pantry had been emptied. Everything suggested that Anatoly had been farsighted enough to leave Prypiat immediately after the incident at the Chernobyl reactor, but before the mass evacuation. Unlike the others, he hadn't abandoned everything in a hurry. He had probably not believed the reassurances of the authorities who, in the immediate aftermath of the disaster, had kept telling the population to stay at home.

The hunter made himself an improvised bed in the living room, using the cushions from the sofa and a few quilts. He thought he would use a bit of the water he had with him to wash his face and hands and take away at least a little of the radioactive dust. He extracted the flask from the bag, and as he did so the stuffed rabbit that had once belonged to the false Dima fell out. He put it next to the Geiger counter and the torch, so that it could keep them company in this absurd situation. He smiled.

'Maybe you can give me a hand, old friend.'

The toy simply stared back at him with its one eye. The hunter felt stupid.

Nonchalantly, he turned to look at the row of exercise books in the bookcase. He took one out at random – number six – and took it with him to the bed, with the intention of leafing through it.

It had no title and was written by hand. The Cyrillic characters were in a precise, tidy handwriting. He read the first page. It was a diary.

14 February
I intend to repeat experiment number 68, but this time I shall change the method of approach. The objective is to demonstrate that environmental conditioning has an effect on behaviour by inverting the

dynamics of imprinting. For this purpose, I bought two white rabbits at the market today ...

The hunter abruptly raised his eyes and looked at the toy rabbit. It was a strange coincidence. And he had never cared for coincidences.

22 February
The two specimens have been raised separately and reached sufficient maturity. Today I shall set about changing the habits of one of the two ...

The hunter looked at the glass cases in the room. It was there that Anatoly Petrov had kept his animals. The living room was a kind of menagerie.

5 March
The lack of food and the use of electrodes have made one of the rabbits more aggressive. His tranquil temperament is gradually turning primitive and instinctual ...

The hunter didn't understand. What had Anatoly been trying to demonstrate? Why had he devoted himself with such single-mindedness to these activities?

12 March
I put the two specimens in a single cage. The induced hunger and aggressiveness have produced their results. One has attacked the other, wounding him fatally ...

Horrified, the hunter got up from his bed and went to take other exercise books from the bookcase. In some, there were photographs with captions. The rabbits had been forced to assume behaviour that was not in their nature. It was done by leaving them hungry or without water for some time, or else in darkness or in full light or provoking them with small electric shocks or giving them psychosis-inducing drugs. In the photographs, the expression in their eyes was a mixture of terror and madness. Every experiment ended in a cruel fashion, either with one of the specimens killing the other or Anatoly himself putting both of them down.

The hunter noticed that the last exercise book referred to others with higher numbers, which were not in the bookcase. Anatoly Petrov had probably taken them away with him, leaving behind those he considered less valuable.

There was a pencilled annotation on the last page that particularly struck him.

... All creatures in nature kill. Only man, however, does it for reasons other than necessity, sometimes out of pure sadism, which is the pleasure of inflicting suffering. Good and bad are not merely moral categories. In the past few years I have demonstrated that a homicidal rage can be instilled in any animal, erasing the inherited characteristics of its species. Why should man be any exception?

As he read these words, the hunter shuddered. Suddenly the toy rabbit's insistent gaze made him uncomfortable. He reached out a hand to move it and, as he did so, inadvertently knocked over the water flask, which, in falling, spilt a rivulet of water on the floor. When he went to pick it up, he noticed that some of the liquid had been absorbed by the skirting board beneath the bookcase. The hunter poured out some more water. That, too, disappeared.

He examined the wall, took note of the size of the room, and guessed that there was something behind the bookcase, perhaps an air space.

He also noticed that on the bricks in front of the bookcase there was a circular scratch. He bent down to get a closer look at it. Supporting himself on his hands, he blew along the groove to free it of the dust that had filled it over the years. When he had finished, he got to his feet and looked at it. It described a perfect arc of 180 degrees.

The bookcase was a door, and constant opening and closing had left that mark on the floor.

He grabbed one of the shelves and tried pulling it towards him to open the door. But it was too heavy. He decided to take out the books. It took him a few minutes to pile them on the ground. Then he tried again and started to feel the bookcase moving on its hinges. After a while, he managed to open it.

Behind it, there was a second small door, with two bolts to keep it shut.

In the centre was a spy hole, and next to it was a switch that, without any electric current, was no use at all. All the same, the hunter tried to peer inside, but without success. He decided to open that door too. It took him a while to get the bolts to move because the metal had rusted over time.

He finally succeeded, and found himself staring into a dark space. The stench forced him to retreat. Then, with one hand over his mouth, he picked up the torch and aimed it into the darkness.

The space measured about six square feet, the ceiling barely four feet high.

The inside of the door and the walls were lined with a soft material of a dark colour, the kind used for soundproofing. There was a lamp of low voltage, protected by a metal grate. In a corner, he could see two bowls. The surface of the walls was covered in scratches, as if an animal had been imprisoned here.

The beam of the torch fell on something shining at the far end of the cell. The hunter leaned forward, picked up a small object and examined it.

A blue plastic wristband.

No, whatever had been kept here was no animal, he thought with horror.

On it was carved in Cyrillic:

KIEV STATE HOSPITAL. MATERNITY WARD

The hunter stood up again, unable to remain in the room. On the verge of retching, he rushed into the corridor. In the darkness, he leaned on one of the walls, afraid he would faint. He tried to calm down and, finally, managed to catch his breath. In the meantime an explanation was taking shape in his mind. It disgusted him that there should be a lucid and rational motivation for all this. And yet he understood it.

Anatoly Petrov was not a scientist. He was a sadist, a psychopath. His experiments concealed an obsession. Like children who kill a lizard with a stone. What they are doing is no game. There is a strange curiosity in them that drives them to seek out violent death. They may not know it, but they are experiencing for the first time the pleasure of cruelty. They know they have taken the life of a useless creature, and that no one will reprimand them for it. But Anatoly Petrov must soon have tired of rabbits.

That was why he had stolen a baby.

He had brought him up in captivity, using him as a guinea pig. For years he had subjected him to every kind of test, in such a way as to condition his nature. He had provoked homicidal instincts in him. Are we born, or do we become, good or bad? That was the question he had been trying to answer.

The transformist was the result of an experiment.

When the Chernobyl reactor had blown up, Anatoly had left the city as soon as he could. He was a turbine technician, he knew how serious the situation was. But he couldn't take the child with him.

He may have thought of killing him. But then something must have made him change his plan. Probably the thought that his creature was ready to face the world. If he survived, that would be his true success. So he had decided to free his guinea pig, who had now become an eight-year-old child. The boy had wandered through the apartment, then had found refuge with the neighbours, who did not know who he was. Because there was one thing Anatoly Petrov hadn't thought of: he had forgotten to provide him with an identity. The transformist's mission to understand who he really was had begun with Dima and was still continuing.

The hunter again felt a sense of oppression. His prey had been deprived of any empathy, all his most elementary human emotions had been eradicated. His capacity for absorbing knowledge was extraordinary, but deep down, he was a blank page, an empty shell, a useless mirror. The one thing guiding him was instinct.

The prison behind the bookcase – which no one had ever known was there, in an apartment surrounded by others all identical, in a building full of people – had been his first nest.

As he thought about this, the hunter looked down. He had accustomed his sight to the gloom of the corridor and was now able to see the dark stains on the floor, next to the entrance.

This time too, there was blood on the ground. Little spots. The hunter bent down to touch them, as he had done at the orphanage in Kiev and in the apartment in Paris.

But this time the blood was fresh.

TODAY

As she finished packing her bags in her hotel room – something she hadn't managed to do the previous day – Sandra thought again about the evening she had spent with the man who had convinced her he was Thomas Schalber, in the apartment she had thought belonged to Interpol. The dinner he had cooked, the confidences they had exchanged. Including the photograph of the girl he had said was his daughter Maria, who he didn't see as often as he would have liked.

He had seemed so . . . genuine.

In the presence of the two real Interpol agents, she had asked herself who she had really met. But there was another question hovering in her head right now.

Who had she slept with that night?

It was an unpleasant sensation, not having an answer. The man had managed to insinuate himself into her life by playing various roles. At first, he had been only an irritating voice on the phone trying to convince her that she should doubt her own husband. Then he had played the part of the hero who had saved her life, removing her just in time from a sniper's line of fire. Then he had humoured her, trying to get round her in order to gain her trust. Then he had deceived her, getting hold of the photos from the Leica.

Jeremiah Smith had said that David had managed to find the penitenzieri's secret archive. That was why he had been forced to kill him.

Was the false Schalber also looking for the archive? Maybe he had had to give up when faced with that final dark photograph, which would probably have contained the solution if the image had come out.

At that point, as Sandra had feared, he had devoted his energies to tracking down Marcus, partly because the photograph that David had taken of the penitenziere was the only real lead he had.

But then he had reappeared in Santa Maria sopra Minerva, in

front of the chapel of St Raymond, just to provide her with an explanation of why he was acting the way he was, and then disappeared again. When you came down to it, there was no need for him to have done that.

So what had his purpose been?

The harder she tried to find a logical connection between these episodes, the more the significance of each single action escaped her. She did not know whether to consider him a friend or an enemy.

A good man or a bad man?

David, she told herself. Had he realised who he was dealing with? He had had his telephone number, he had even provided Sandra with the missing digits thanks to the photograph taken with the Leica in front of the bathroom mirror in this very hotel room. Her husband had not trusted him enough to hand over the clues, but all the same he had wanted her to meet him. Why?

As she mulled it over, other puzzling aspects emerged. She forgot about her packing for a moment and sat down on the bed to think. Where am I going wrong? She wanted to forget the whole story as quickly as possible. She already had plans for a new life, and forgetting was essential if she didn't want to jeopardise them. But she knew she wouldn't be able to live with these questions still unresolved. They might drive her mad.

David was the answer, she was sure of it. Why had her husband got involved with this story in the first place? He was a good photojournalist, but this whole thing was a long way from his usual concerns. He was Jewish and, unlike her, almost never talked about God. His grandfather was a Holocaust survivor, and David maintained that such horrors had been conceived not to destroy his people, but to make them lose their faith: once the Jews had proof that God did not exist, it would be easy to wipe them out.

The one time they had tackled the question of religion a little more seriously was not long after they got married. Sandra had been taking a shower when she discovered a little lump. David's reaction had been typically Jewish: he had made a joke of it.

She thought his attitude showed a certain weakness of character, assuming that the reason he ridiculed her health problems and turned them into a game was because he felt guilty at not being able to solve them. It was affectionate in its way, but no help at all. He had gone with her to do the tests, making fun of her all the time. Sandra had let him believe that he was relieving the tension with these jokes. In fact, she felt terrible and wanted him to stop. It may have been his way of dealing with things, but she wasn't sure she liked it. Sooner or later they would have to discuss it, and she sensed an argument looming.

During the week when they were waiting for the results of the tests, David had kept on with that irritating attitude. Sandra thought of confronting him with the question, but she was too scared to just blurt it out.

The night before they were due to receive the results, she had woken up and reached out her hand for David. But he was not there. She had got out of bed and noticed that there were no lights on in the apartment. As she was wondering where he was, she got to the doorway of the kitchen and saw him. He was sitting with his back to the door, bent over, rocking back and forth, incomprehensibly. He had not noticed her, or he would have stopped praying. She had gone back to bed and wept.

Fortunately, in the end the lump had turned out to be benign. But Sandra had needed to clarify things with David. They were bound to go through other difficult times during their marriage and they would need something more than irony to keep going. She told him about the night she had seen him praying and David, with a certain embarrassment, had been forced to admit how scared he had been at the thought of losing her. For himself he wasn't afraid of death, his work in the frontline led him automatically to downplay the very idea that he could die. But when it came to Sandra, he hadn't known what to do. The only thing that had come into his mind had been to appeal to a God he had always avoided.

'When you have no more resources to call on, all you have left is faith in a God you don't believe in.'

For Sandra it had been as good as a declaration of undying love. But now, in that hotel room, sitting on the bed next to a half-packed case, she wondered why on earth, if her husband had the feeling that he could die in Rome, the farewell message he had chosen to send her consisted of the clues to an investigation. Photographs, to be exact, because – thanks to the professions they were both involved in – that was their language. But why, for example, had he not made a video to tell her how important she was to him? He hadn't written her a letter, a note, anything. If he had loved her so much, why had his last thought not been for her?

Because David didn't want me to be tied to him in case he died, she told herself. And it was a revelation.

He gave me the rest of my life. The chance to fall in love again, to have a family, children. To lead a life that went beyond a widow's existence. Not in a few years' time but immediately.

She had to find a way to say goodbye to him. When she got back to Milan she would have to put away the memories, take his clothes out of the wardrobe, get rid of his smell – aniseed-flavoured cigarettes and out-of-date aftershave – from the apartment.

But she could start immediately. With David's last message, which had led her to Rome and which she still had on her mobile phone. First, though, she wanted to listen to it again. It would be the last time she heard her husband's voice.

'Hi, I called a couple of times but I always get the recorded message . . . I don't have much time, so I just want to make a list of what I miss . . . I miss your cold feet searching for me under the blankets when you come to bed. I miss you making me taste things from the fridge to make sure they haven't gone off. Or when you wake me up screaming at three in the morning because you've got a cramp. And I know you won't believe this, but I even miss you using my razor to shave your legs and then not telling me . . . Anyway, it's freezing cold here in Oslo and I can't wait to get back. I love you, Ginger!'

Unhesitatingly, Sandra pressed the *erase* key. 'I'll miss you, darling.' The tears rolled down her face. It was the first time in a long time that she hadn't called him Fred.

Then she gathered the copies of the photographs from the Leica: the originals were still in the possession of the fake Schalber. She put them in a little pile, putting the dark one at the top. She was ready to tear them up and forget, but she stopped.

Among David's photographs there wasn't one of the chapel of St Raymond, even though St Raymond had been a penitenziere. It was Schalber who had led her to the basilica by slipping that card under the door of her hotel room. Until now, Sandra had dismissed that detail. Why had he wanted to introduce her to that place with his deception?

The dark photograph.

The reason he believed there was an answer to the mystery of the penitenzieri's archive in that photograph was because the archive is hidden in that bare chapel, Sandra told herself. Except that Schalber was unable to locate it.

She looked at the photograph again. The darkness was not the result of a mistake, as she had always thought. David had deliberately wanted it to be dark.

When you have no more resources to call on, all you have left is faith in a God you don't believe in.

Before leaving for Milan, she had to go back to Santa Maria sopra Minerva.

David's last clue was a test of her faith.

ONE YEAR EARLIER
PRYPIAT

The hunter was not alone. There was someone else in the ghost city.

He's here.

The transformist had chosen the most inhospitable place on earth to hide. A place where nobody would ever think of looking for him.

He's come home.

The hunter could feel his presence. The spots of blood on the floor had not yet completely congealed.

He's close.

He had to think quickly. In the living room, next to the lamp, was the bag with the tranquilliser gun. But he didn't have time to get it.

He's been watching me.

All he wanted was to get out of Anatoly Petrov's apartment. His one hope of salvation was to get to the Volvo, which he had parked in front of the concrete blocks that had been placed in the middle of the road to stop vehicles entering the city. It was quite a distance. To hell with the wolves, he would make a run for it. There was no strategy involved. All he could do was run.

He rushed to the door and started tearing down the stairs. He was barely aware of them beneath him. In the darkness, he couldn't even see where he was putting his feet. If he fell, it would be the end. Instead of leading him to be cautious, the idea of being stuck here in this building with a broken leg, waiting for his enemy to appear, was making him take risks. Every now and again he jumped a few steps, narrowly avoiding heaps of refuse. He was panting and the sweat froze on his back. His steps echoed in the stairwell.

Eleven floors running hell for leather, and then the street.

Nothing but shadows around him. Buildings looking at him with a thousand empty eyes, cars like sarcophagi ready to welcome him, trees stretching out their thin wooden claws to grab him. The asphalt crumbled in contact with his shoes, as if the world was collapsing beneath him. He felt a sense of anguish growing in him. His lungs were starting to burn, and every breath was a spasm in his chest. So this was how it felt to run from someone who wants to hurt us.

The hunter had become the hunted.

Where are you? I know you're here and you're watching me. You're laughing at my desperation. And at the same time getting ready to show yourself.

He turned a corner on to a broad avenue. Suddenly he realised he couldn't remember the way he had come. He had lost his sense of direction. He stopped to think, bent double with the effort. Then he saw the rusty carcasses of the merry-go-rounds and realised that he was near the amusement park. The Volvo was less than a quarter of a mile away. He would make it.

I'll make it.

He put on speed, ignoring the pain and exhaustion, the cold and the fear. But out of the corner of his eye, he saw the first wolf. The animal had come up beside him and was running together with him. In a short while a second one emerged. And a third. They were escorting him, keeping at a distance. The hunter knew that if he slowed down, they would attack him.

So he kept going. *If only I'd had time to take the tranquilliser gun from the bag . . .*

He saw the Volvo, parked where he had left it. A small relief, even though he didn't know if it had been tampered with. If it had, that would be the final twist of fate. But he couldn't give up now. He still had a few yards to go when one of the wolves decided to try and attack. He gave it a kick and, although not hitting it very hard, persuaded it to keep its distance again.

The car was no mirage. It was real.

He started to think that, if he made it, many things would change. Suddenly he realised how much his own life meant to him. He wasn't afraid of death, just the thought of dying in this place, and in a way he couldn't even begin to imagine.

No, not like this, please.

When he reached the vehicle, he couldn't believe it. As he opened the door, he saw the wolves slow down. They had realised they wouldn't make it and were getting ready to withdraw into the shadows. He looked feverishly for the keys he had left in the dashboard. When he found them, he was afraid the car wouldn't start. But it did. He laughed, incredulous. He steered rapidly, putting the car in reverse. Everything was working perfectly. The adrenaline was still pumping but the signs of tiredness were starting to make themselves felt. Acid was rising in his chest and his joints hurt. Maybe he was starting to relax.

A last look in the rear-view mirror: his still-frightened eyes and the ghost city receding. And the shadow of a man emerging from the back seat.

But before the hunter could complete that thought, a painful darkness fell over him.

It was the sound of water that woke him. Little drops oozing from the rock. He could imagine the place even without opening his eyes. He didn't want to look. But in the end he did.

He was lying on a wooden table. The dim light came from three bulbs hanging from the ceiling. He could hear the buzz of the generator that kept them alive.

He couldn't move, he was tied up. He wasn't even going to try. He was fine like this.

Was he in a cave? No, in a basement. There was an all-pervading smell of mildew. But there was something else. A metallic odour. Zinc. And there was also the unmistakable miasma of death.

With difficulty, he turned his head to get a better view. He was in a crypt. The walls were a neatly arranged mosaic. It was beautiful and yet, at the same time, sinister.

They were bones.

Some piled one on top of the other, others slotted together. Femurs, ulnas, scapulas. Soldered to the zinc that lined the coffins to protect them from contamination.

This was the only kind of space the transformist could have used for his lair. He had been clever. In a place where every object was infected with radiation, the one thing not poisoned was the dead. He must have disinterred them from the cemetery and used them to construct a shelter.

He recognised three skulls blackened by time, watching him from the shadows. Two adults and a child. The real Dima and his parents, he thought.

The hunter heard the transformist approaching. He didn't need to turn. He knew.

He heard his calm, regular breathing, and felt his hand brushing the hair sticky with sweat from his forehead. It was like a caress. Then he walked around him until their eyes met. He was wearing military fatigues and a torn red high-necked pullover. His face was covered with a balaclava, from behind which only his inexpressive eyes and a few tufts of unkempt beard were visible.

The only emotion in those eyes was curiosity. He tilted his head, the way children do when they want to understand. There was a question in his gaze. Looking at him, the hunter realised there was no way out.

The transformist was unfamiliar with pity. Not because he was evil. But because nobody had ever taught him.

He was holding the toy rabbit and absent-mindedly stroking its little head. Then he walked away. The hunter followed him with his eyes. In a corner there was a bed made up of blankets and rags. He put the rabbit down on it, sat down cross-legged, and resumed staring at him.

The hunter would have liked to ask him so many things. He knew what his fate would be: he wouldn't get out of here alive. But what saddened him most was not knowing the answers. He had invested so much energy in this hunt, he ought to have answers. It was a matter of honour.

How did the metamorphosis happen? Why did the transformist feel the need to leave drops of his blood – a kind of signature – every time he stole someone's identity?

'Please, speak to me.'

'Please, speak to me,' the transformist echoed.

'Say something.'

'Say something.'

The hunter laughed. So did the transformist.

'Don't play with me.'

'Don't play with me.'

And then he understood. He wasn't playing. *He was practising.*

He saw the man stand up and simultaneously take something from the pocket of his fatigues. A long, shiny object. At first he did not realise what it was. As the man approached, he recognised the sharp blade.

The transformist placed the scalpel against his cheek and slowly traced the lines that he would soon go over more deeply. It was like being tickled. The feeling was both pleasant and chilling.

Nothing exists but hell, he thought. And it's here.

The transformist didn't want just to kill him. *Soon the hunted would become the hunter.*

But in the meantime, at least one question was answered. The transformist took off his balaclava, and for the first time the hunter saw his face. They had never been so close. He could say he had done it after all. He had achieved his aim.

But there was something on the transformist's face, something he didn't even seem to be aware of.

The hunter finally grasped the origin of what he had thought was a *signature*.

It wasn't a signature, it was a symptom of his weakness. The hunter realised that the man in front of him was not a monster but a human being. And like all human beings, the transformist had a distinguishing feature, a thing that made him unique, however good he was at hiding behind multiple identities.

The hunter would soon be dead, but at that moment he felt relieved.

His enemy could still be stopped.

NOW

Rain has descended on Rome like a black pall. Impossible to tell if it is day or night.

Sandra passes through the anonymous facade into the only Gothic church in Rome. With its luxurious marbles, its tapering vaults, its magnificent frescoes, Santa Maria sopra Minerva greets her. It is deserted.

The noise of her footsteps echoes in the right-hand nave. She proceeds towards the last altar. The smallest, the least graceful.

St Raymond of Penafort is waiting for her. Except that, previously, she did not know that. It is as if now she is presenting a case to Christ the judge between two angels.

The Tribunal of Souls.

In front of the fresco, the votive candles left by the faithful are still dripping wax on the floor. Unlike the other chapels in the church, only in this one – the poorest – is there such a profusion of candles. Obedient little flames that bow their heads in unison at each draught then stand up straight again.

On the other occasions she has been here, Sandra has wondered for what sins they have been lit. Now she has her answer. For everyone's sins.

She takes the last of the Leica photographs from her bag, and looks at it. The darkness of the image conceals a test of her faith. David's last clue is the most mysterious but also the most eloquent.

She should not look for the answer outside, but inside herself.

Over the past few months she has asked herself where David is now, what is the meaning of his death. Unable to answer this question, she has felt lost. She is a forensic photographer, she looks for death in the details, convinced that only through them can everything be explained.

I see things through my camera. I trust in details, because they tell me what happened. But for the penitenzieri there exists something beyond what we have in front of us. Something equally real, but that a camera cannot perceive. So I have to learn that sometimes it is necessary to give oneself up to the mystery. And accept that it is not granted to us to understand everything.

Faced with the great questions of human existence, the man of science frets, the man of faith stops. And right now, in this church, Sandra feels she has reached a borderline. It is not by chance that the penitenziere's words come back to her: 'There is a place where the world of light meets the world of darkness. It is there that everything happens: in the land of shadows, where everything is vague, confused, undefined.'

Marcus said it clearly. But Sandra has never understood it until now. The true danger lies not in the darkness, but in that intermediate state, where the light becomes deceptive. Where good and bad are confused, and you can't tell one from the other.

Evil does not hide in the darkness. *It is in the shadows.*

It is there that it distorts things. There are no monsters, she reminds herself, only normal people who commit terrible crimes. So the secret, she thinks, is not to be afraid of the dark. Because deep inside it lie all the answers.

Holding the dark photograph in her hands, she bends over the votive candles and starts blowing them out, one by one. There are dozens of them and it takes a while. As she proceeds, the darkness rises like a tide. Around her, everything vanishes.

When she has finished, she takes a step back. She cannot see anything, she is afraid, but she tells herself again that all she needs to do is wait and, at last, she will know. Just like when she was a little girl, lying in bed before falling asleep, and the darkness seemed threatening to her, but as soon as her eyes got accustomed to it, everything magically reappeared – the small room with her games, her dolls – and she could sleep peacefully. Slowly Sandra's gaze adapts to the new conditions. The memory of light fades and suddenly she realises that she can again see something.

The figures around her begin to re-emerge. On the altarpiece, St Raymond reappears, radiant. Christ the judge and the two angels are clothed in a different, brilliant luminosity. On the rough plaster of the walls, made grey by soot, forms begin to reveal themselves: frescoes depicting scenes of devotion, repentance and forgiveness.

The miracle is happening in front of her eyes and Sandra is incredulous. The poorest of the chapels, the one devoid of marbles and friezes, has become the most beautiful.

A new light appears on the bare walls, forming turquoise inlays. Filaments climb over columns that seemed bare. The total effect is a blue glow, like the tranquil depths of the ocean. It is still dark, but a blinding dark.

Sandra smiles. *Phosphorescent paint.*

Yes, there is a rational explanation, but there is nothing rational about the step she has taken inside herself to discover all this. It is pure abandonment, an acceptance of her own limitations, a wonderful surrender to the unfathomable, the incomprehensible. It is faith.

This was David's last gift. His loving message to her. Accept my death, without asking yourself why this happened to us. That is the only way you will be able to be happy again.

Sandra looks up and thanks him. There is no archive here. The secret is all this beauty.

She hears footsteps behind her and turns.

'The discovery of phosphorescence dates from the seventeenth century,' Marcus says. 'We owe it to a shoemaker in Bologna who collected some stones, roasted them over coal and observed a strange phenomenon: after being exposed to daylight, they continued to emit light for several hours, even in the dark.' He indicates the chapel. 'What you see here was executed a few decades later, thanks to an anonymous artist who used the shoemaker's substance to paint this chapel. Think how astonished people must have been at the time. They'd never seen anything like it before. It's not as surprising today as it was then, because we know the reasons for the phenomenon. Anyway, each person can choose whether to see this as yet another of the oddities of Rome, or as a miracle of some kind.'

'I'd prefer to see it as a miracle, I really would,' Sandra admits, her voice tinged with sadness. 'But reason tells me it isn't. Just as it tells me that there's no God and that David isn't in a paradise where life goes on forever and is always happy. But I really wish I was wrong.'

Marcus was not fazed by this. 'I understand. The first time someone brought me here, he told me I could find the answer to the question I asked myself when, after my amnesia, it was revealed to me that I was a priest. That question was: if it's true that I'm a priest, then where is my faith?'

'And what was the answer?'

'That faith isn't simply a gift. You always have to look for it.' He lowers his eyes. 'I look for it in evil.'

'What a strange destiny unites us. You must deal with the gap in your memory, and I must deal with all too many memories of David. I'm forced to try and forget, while you try desperately to remember.' She pauses and looks at him. 'What now? Will you carry on?'

'I don't know yet. But if you're asking me if I'm afraid something will corrupt me one day, I can only say yes. At first I thought it was a curse, this ability to look at the world through the eyes of evil. But finding Lara has given my talent a meaning. Even though I don't remember who I was in the past, thanks to what I'm doing I finally know who I am.'

Sandra nods, but feels as if she is at fault. 'I have to tell you something.' She pauses for a long time. 'There's a man looking for you. I thought he wanted to find the archive, but after what I've seen here, I've realised he has a different aim.'

Marcus is surprised. 'Who is he?'

'I don't know. He lied to me. He passed himself off as an Interpol agent, but it wasn't true. I don't know who he really is, but I suspect he's very dangerous.'

'He won't find me.'

'Yes, he will. He has a photograph of you.'

Marcus reflects. 'Even if he finds me, what can he do to me?'

'He'll kill you.'

Sandra's certainty does not affect him. 'How can you say that?'

'Because, if he isn't a policeman and he doesn't want to arrest you, then that's his one aim.'

Marcus smiles. 'I've already died once. It doesn't frighten me any more.'

Sandra lets herself be persuaded by the priest's composure, it inspires trust in her. She still remembers the way he stroked her arm at the hospital, and how good it made her feel. 'I've committed a sin and I can't forgive myself.'

'There is forgiveness for everything, even for mortal sins. It's not enough to ask for it, though. You have to share the guilt with someone: letting it out is the first step to being free of it.'

Sandra bows her head, closes her eyes and starts to open her heart. She tells him about the abortion, the love she lost and has found again, the way she has been punishing herself. Everything emerges naturally, the words gush out from somewhere deep inside her. She imagined the feeling would be the same you feel when unburdening yourself of a weight. Instead, it is the opposite. The emptiness left inside her by that unborn child fills again. The anguish she has been feeling in those months heals. Something in her is changing, she is becoming a new person.

'I also have a grave sin on my conscience,' Marcus says when she has finished. 'Like you, I have taken lives. But is that enough to make us killers? Sometimes we kill because we have to, to protect someone or else out of fear. There should be a different measure by which to judge such cases.'

Sandra feels relieved by his words.

'In 1314, in the Ardèche, in the South of France, the plague was ravaging the population. Taking advantage of this, a band of brigands sowed terror in the area, sacking, raping and killing. People were scared, barely able to survive. So some priests from the mountains, with little experience of the world, joined together to confront the criminals. They took up arms and fought. In the end, they prevailed. Men of God who had spilled blood: who would ever forgive them? But when they returned to their churches, the population acclaimed them as saviours. Thanks to their protection, there were no more crimes in the Ardèche. People started calling those priests *the hunters of the dark.*' Marcus takes a candle, lights it with a match and hands it to

Sandra. 'So the judgement on our actions is not up to us. All we can do is ask for forgiveness.'

In her turn, Sandra takes a candle and lights it from his. Then together they start to light all the candles at the feet of Christ the judge. As the collective flame comes back to life, she feels liberated, just as the penitenziere predicted. The wax again starts dripping on the opaque marble floor. Sandra is calm, contented, ready to return home. The phosphorescent glow starts to fade. The luminous frescoes and brilliant friezes disappear. Slowly, the chapel becomes bare and nondescript again. As she lights the last candles, Sandra happens to looks down and notices that some of the drops on the floor are red.

They form a small ring of brown stains. But it isn't wax. It's blood.

She looks up at Marcus and sees that he has a nose bleed.

'Careful,' she says, because he hasn't noticed.

He lifts his hand to his face and then looks at his fingers. 'It happens every now and again. But then it passes. It always passes.'

Digging into her bag, Sandra takes out some paper handkerchiefs, to help him staunch the flow of blood. He accepts them.

'There are things about me I don't know,' he says, throwing his head back. 'Before, every time I discovered another one, I felt scared. Now I'm just surprised. Even these nose bleeds. I don't know where they come from, but they're part of me. And so I tell myself that maybe one day they, too, will help me remember who I was before.'

Sandra goes to Marcus and hugs him. 'Good luck,' she says.

'Goodbye,' he replies.

ONE YEAR EARLIER
PRAGUE

He had stayed in Prypiat another few months, to make sure nobody else came looking for him. The work he had carried out on his latest victim had been long and demanding. This one hadn't been like the others. They had told him everything after a few hours of torture. But it had taken several days to force this one to tell him everything about himself, so that he could learn to become him. Strangely, the most difficult thing had been to get him to reveal his own name.

The transformist looked at himself in the mirror. 'Marcus,' he said. He liked it.

He had arrived in Prague three days ago, and had taken a room in a hotel. The building was an old one, with a view of the black roofs of the city.

He had a lot of money with him, taken over the years from the men who had yielded their lives to him. He also had a Vatican City diplomatic passport, stolen from his latest victim, whose photograph he had replaced. The identity on the document was already false, because it didn't coincide with the one he had extorted. The explanation was simple.

The hunter didn't exist.

It was the ideal condition for the transformist. Becoming a man nobody knew made it virtually impossible for him to be tracked down. But he couldn't yet be sure. He had to wait, that was why he was here.

He was going over the notes he had taken in Prypiat – a potted biography of his new identity: only the essential information, because he had learned the rest by heart – when all at once the door opened.

In the doorway there stood a weary-looking, hollow-faced old man, dressed in dark clothes. He was holding a gun. But he didn't immediately open fire. He entered and closed the door behind him. He seemed calm and resolute.

'I've found you,' he said. 'I made a mistake and I've come to remedy it.'

The transformist said nothing. He wasn't fazed. Calmly he put down the sheets of paper he had been reading on a little table and assumed an impassive expression. He was not afraid – he didn't know what fear was, he'd never been taught – he was merely curious. Why did this old man have tears in his eyes?

'I asked my most able pupil to hunt you down. But if you're here, that means Marcus is dead. And it's my fault.'

The old man was aiming the gun directly at him. The transformist had never found himself so close to death. He had always struggled to survive his own nature. Now he had no desire to be killed. 'Wait,' he said. 'You can't do that. It isn't right, Devok.'

The old man froze, a look of astonishment on his face. It wasn't the words that had stopped him dead, or the fact that he knew his name, it was the sound with which the words had been uttered.

The transformist had spoken in Marcus's voice.

Now the old man was disorientated. 'Who are you?' he asked, fear in his eyes now.

'What do you mean, who am I? Don't you recognise me?' He said it almost imploringly. Because the transformist's weapon – the only one he needed, the most effective – was illusion.

Something incomprehensible was happening, right here in front of the old man's eyes. He was witnessing a kind of transformation. 'It isn't true. You aren't him.' Although he knew with certainty that he was right, he hesitated for some reason. It was the affection he felt for his pupil that made him pause. That was why he no longer had the strength he needed to pull the trigger.

'You were my teacher, my mentor. Everything I know, I owe to you. And now you want to kill me?' As he spoke, he was getting ever closer to the old man, step by step.

'I don't know you.'

'There is a place where the world of light meets the world of darkness,' he recited from memory. 'It is there that everything happens: in the land of shadows, where everything is vague, confused, undefined. We are the guards appointed to defend that border. But every now and again something manages to get through ... My task is to chase it back into the darkness.'

The old man shivered, he was yielding. The transformist was close to him, close enough to grab the gun from his hand, when he saw the first drop fall on the carpet. He realised his nose was bleeding. Nosebleeds were the one thing about himself he couldn't change. The only original element, the rest was borrowed. His true identity, buried for decades, was contained in that one distinguishing feature.

The illusion shattered and the old man realised the deception. 'Damn you.'

The transformist threw himself on the hand clutching the gun, and grabbed it just in time. The old man fell to the floor. The transformist had him in his sights.

Lying on the carpet, the old man started laughing, wiping his bloodstained palm on his shirt. The transformist's face was covered in blood.

'Why are you laughing? Aren't you scared?'

'Before I came here, I confessed my sins. I'm free and ready to die. And besides, it amuses me that you think you only have to kill me and you'll solve all your problems. Actually, they're just beginning.'

The transformist scented a trap, he wouldn't fall into it. 'Maybe it's better to keep silent, don't you think? I don't like last words. They're usually quite undignified. All the men I've killed tarnished their deaths with insipid, trivial phrases. They asked for pity, they begged me. Without knowing that for me this was the confirmation that they had nothing else to tell me.'

The old man shook his head. 'Poor fool. A priest who's a lot better than me is hunting for you. He has the same talent as you: he can become whatever he wants. Except that he isn't a transformist and doesn't kill anyone. He's good at assuming the identities of people who've disappeared. Right now he's posing as an Interpol agent, which means he has access to police files. Soon he will track you down.'

'But you're going to tell me his name.'

The old man laughed again, coarsely. 'Even if you tortured me, it wouldn't get you anywhere. The penitenzieri don't have names. They don't exist, you ought to know that.'

While the transformist was trying to work out if he was bluffing, the old man took advantage of his distraction and somehow summoned up the strength to leap at him. He grabbed hold of the gun and pushed it downwards, revealing an unsuspected agility. The struggle began again. But this time the old man wouldn't let go.

A shot rang out, the bullet hit the mirror, and the transformist saw his own image shatter. He managed to direct the gun towards his adversary and pulled the trigger. The old man froze in dismay, his eyes and mouth open wide. The bullet had punctured his heart. But, instead of collapsing backwards, he fell forwards, hitting the ground together with his killer. The impact made the gun go off again. The transformist seemed to see the bullet pass like a fleeting shadow in front of his eyes, before lodging in his temple.

Lying on the carpet, waiting for the end to come, he looked at his own image reflected in the thousand fragments of the shattered mirror. All his identities were there, all the faces he had stolen. It was as if the wound in his temple had freed him from the prison of his mind.

They were looking at him. Moment by moment, he started to forget them.

By the time he died, he had completely forgotten who he was.

7.37 a.m.

The corpse opened his eyes.

Author's Note

This story has its origin in two unforgettable encounters.

The first of these was with an unusual priest, and took place in Rome late one afternoon in May. Father Jonathan had arranged to meet me in the Piazza delle Cinque Lune at dusk. Obviously, he was the one who fixed the time and place, and when I asked him to be a bit more specific about 'dusk', he calmly replied, 'Before sunset.' Not knowing how to respond, I decided to arrive well in advance.

He was already there.

Over the following two hours, Father Jonathan told me about the *Paenitentiaria*, the archive of sins and the role of the penitenzieri. As he spoke, it struck me as incredible that nobody had ever told this story before. Our walk through the back streets of Rome led us eventually to San Luigi dei Francesi, and to Caravaggio's *Martyrdom of St Matthew*, which is the first stage in the training of these priest-profilers.

In many cases, the priests collaborate with the police. In Italy, since 1999, there has been an anti-sect squad in which they work with the police to gain a better understanding of so-called Satanic crimes. Not because they are trying to reveal the existence of the devil, but because of the demonic significance that some criminals, especially murderers, attribute to their acts. Explaining this significance requires them to clarify the criminals' motives and to prepare a profile that may help the investigating team.

In the two months following our first meeting, Father Jonathan taught me many things about his unusual ministry and introduced me to a number of magical places in Rome, some of which took my breath away, and which are described in the novel. His range of knowledge was extensive, not only in the field of crime, but also in art, architecture, history, even the origin of phosphorescent paint.

As for questions of faith and religion, he good-naturedly tolerated my hesitations and dealt openly with my criticisms. At the end of it all, I realised that I had unwittingly been on a spiritual journey that helped me gain a better idea of the story I wanted to tell.

In modern society, spirituality is often seen as a bit of a joke, considered as something fed to the ignorant masses, or that has given rise to all kinds of 'new age' practices. Individuals have lost the elementary distinction between good and evil. The result has been to hand God over to the fundamentalists and extremists on the one hand, or the humorists on the other (because fanatical atheists are not so different from religious fanatics).

All this has produced an inability to look inside ourselves, beyond the categories of ethics and morality – not to mention the totally arbitrary category of the 'politically correct' – to find the essential dichotomy that allows us to judge human actions.

Good and *evil*, *yin* and *yang*.

One day, Jonathan told me that I was ready to tell my story, he hoped I would 'always be in the light', and then said goodbye, promising that we would meet again. That was the last I saw of him. I have looked for him in vain, and I hope that this novel will lead to us meeting again soon. Even though part of me suspects that will not happen, because everything we had to say to each other has already been said.

The second encounter was with N.N., who lived at the turn of the twentieth century.

The first (and so far only) transformist serial killer, and one of the most interesting cases in the history of criminology.

N.N. represents not the initials of his name but an abbreviation of the Latin expression *Nomen Nescio*, the term habitually used for unidentified individuals (the equivalent of John Doe in the United States).

In 1916, the body of a man of about thirty-five was found on a beach in Ostend, Belgium. The cause of death was drowning. His clothes and the papers he had on him indicated that he was a clerk from Liverpool who had vanished into thin air two years earlier. When the authorities showed the body to his relatives, who had come specially from England, they did not recognise him, insisting that this was a case of mistaken identity.

Photographs produced by these relatives, however, confirmed that there was a remarkable physical resemblance between N.N. and the English clerk. But that was not the only similarity. The two also shared a liking for puddings and for prostitutes with red hair. Both took medication for a liver ailment and, most important of all, both had a slight limp in the right leg (in the case of the drowned man, the pathologist inferred this from the wear and tear on the sole of his shoe and from the hard skin on the side of his right foot, a sign that the weight of his body had been concentrated there).

In addition to the evidence of these similarities, when the police inspected N.N's last known address they came across various documents and objects belonging to individuals from a number of European countries. Subsequent investigation revealed that they had all disappeared suddenly and without a trace. Not only that, but these disappearances could be put in chronological order according to the age of the victims, which rose constantly.

Hence the deduction that N.N. had chosen them with the purpose of taking their place.

No bodies were ever recovered, but it was assumed that N.N. had killed these men before appropriating their identities.

Due to the lack of supporting scientific evidence – a result of the backwardness of investigative techniques at the time – the case was forgotten, only to come back to public attention in the 1930s, when Courbon and Fail published their first psychiatric studies on Fregoli syndrome – named after the famous Italian quick-change artist – and articles began appearing on the neurological disorder known as Capgras syndrome. In both these syndromes, the phenomena observed were the reverse of the case of N.N.: those affected by them were convinced they saw a transformation in others. But their description opened the floodgates to a series of scientific investigations that led to the identification of other syndromes, such as the chameleon syndrome, which is very close in nature to the Belgian case (and which inspired Woody Allen's brilliant film *Zelig*).

The case of N.N. is the starting point for a new branch of criminology, forensic neuroscience, which studies crime from a genetic or physiological viewpoint. These techniques have allowed us to understand some crimes in a different way. One example is the reduction in sentence granted to a murderer with problems in the frontal lobes and a genetic map that indicated a predisposition to violence. Another is the demonstration that a man who stabbed his fiancée to death had been affected by a vitamin B12 deficiency as a result of the vegan diet he had been following for twenty-five years.

N.N.'s talents have remained unique. The only similar case known so far is that of 'the girl in the mirror', which I have recounted in this novel. The young Mexican woman really existed, even though, unlike N.N., she never killed anybody. For obvious reasons, I have changed her name, calling her Angelina.

N.N. is buried in a small cemetery by the sea. On his gravestone, the epitaph reads: *Body of an unidentified drowned man. Ostend –* *1916.*

Donato Carrisi

Acknowledgements

Stefano Mauri, my editor. For the passion he puts into his work and the friendship he bestows on me.

Along with him, I thank everyone at Longanesi, as well as my foreign publishers. For the time and energy they invest in making sure that my stories reach their destination.

Luigi, Daniela and Ginevra Bernabò. For their advice, care and affection. It's great to be part of your team.

Fabrizio Cocco – the man who knows the secrets of (my) stories – for his calm dedication and for being so *noir*.

Giuseppe Strazzeri, for the fire and vision he brings to this publishing adventure.

Valentina Fortichiari, for her drive and affection (I don't know what I would do without them).

Elena Pavanetto, for her smiling ideas.

Cristina Foschini, for her luminous presence.

The booksellers, for the task they take on every time they entrust a book to a reader. For the magical work they do in the world.

This story also owes a lot to the involuntary – and often unconscious – contributions of a great many people. I mention them in no particular order.

Stefano and Tommaso, because they're here now. Clara and Gaia, for the joy they give me. Vito Lo Re, for his incredible music and for finding Barbara. Ottavio Martucci, for his healthy cynicism. Giovanni 'Nanni' Serio, because he is Schalber! Valentina, who makes me feel part of the family. Francesco 'Ciccio' Ponzone, a great man. Flavio, a wicked man with a tender heart. Marta, who never spares herself. Antonio Padovano, for his lessons on the enjoyment of life. Aunt Franca, because she's always there. Maria 'Ià' for a wonderful afternoon at the Quirinale. Michele and Barbara, Angela and Pino, Tiziana, Rolando, Donato and Daniela, Azzurra. Elisabetta, because there is a lot of her in this story.

Chiara, who fills me with pride. My parents, to them I owe the best of myself.

Leonardo Palmisano, one of my heroes. I'll never talk of you in the past tense and I'll never forget you.

Achille Manzotti, who in 1999 gave me my first start in this strange profession by asking me to write the story of a priest named Don Marco. The choice of the name Marcus for the main character is a tribute to this great producer's genius, madness and, above all, instinct about screenwriters.